# "UNTIE ME. WE HAVE NO TIME TO LOSE."

"I fear I cannot." Rachel gulped, an uncertain smile on her beautiful lips. "B-B-Because I have abducted you."

For a moment Jerome could only stare at her, too dumbfounded to speak. Then he yelped, "You have *what?* Why would you do that?"

A glowing blush rose in her cheeks. "I want to marry you."

His heart gave the most inexplicable little leap of joy, then sanity returned. "What a unique way you have of proposing," Jerome snapped. "But you are mad to think I will accept your offer."

# Praise for Marlene Suson's previous romance *DEVIL'S ANGEL*

# MIDNIGHT BRIDE

## MARLENE SUSON

AVON BOOKS  NEW YORK

MIDNIGHT BRIDE is an original publication of Avon Books. This work has never before appeared in book form. This work is a novel. Any similarity to actual persons or events is purely coincidental.

AVON BOOKS
A division of
The Hearst Corporation
1350 Avenue of the Americas
New York, New York 10019

Copyright © 1995 by Joan Sweeney
Excerpt from *Midnight Lord* copyright © 1995 by Joan Sweeney
Inside cover author photo by Debbi De Mont
Published by arrangement with the author
Library of Congress Catalog Card Number: 94-96390
ISBN: 0-380-77851-3

First Avon Books Printing: April 1995

AVON TRADEMARK REG. U.S. PAT. OFF. AND IN OTHER COUNTRIES, MARCA REGISTRADA, HECHO EN U.S.A.

Printed in the U.S.A.

RA 10  9  8  7  6  5  4  3  2  1

To my mother,
Jean E.M. Sweeney,
who has inspired me in so many ways.
With love

# Chapter 1

*England, 1740*

"**W**arn yer master that Gentleman Jack's operating in the neighborhood," the garrulous owner of the posting house said, mistaking the tall, muscular man on a chestnut horse for a groom.

"Where?" Jerome asked eagerly. He wanted nothing more than to be accosted by that notorious highwayman.

It was the only reason he had made this god-awful journey to Yorkshire.

"Held up Lord Creevy in broad daylight yesterday on the Wingate Hall road, no more 'an half a league from here. Done it in the birch wood afore you get to the River Wyn."

Jerome's excitement rose at how close he was to the highwayman he had traveled to find. Now if only he could lure his quarry into a meeting.

"Relieved m'lord o' a fat bag o' gold coins, he did."

Jerome smothered a smile. He could think of no more deserving candidate for highway robbery than the greedy, irascible Creevy who hated to part with a groat. The old muckworm must have been apoplectic.

Gentleman Jack would have loved it. Jerome would have, too. Perhaps highway robbery had something to recommend it after all.

Jerome glanced at a freshly painted sign hanging over the posting house entrance. Large black letters proclaimed "The White Swan." A second line in much smaller letters read "Thomas Acker, Owner."

The posting house's hostlers were quickly and efficiently changing the horses on Jerome's traveling coach for the final leg of his journey. Its ebony finish, usually polished to a high gleam, was hidden beneath a thick coating of mud. This was the first day of the entire miserable trip that it had not rained hard, turning the execrable roads into quagmires.

Leather curtains were pulled across the equipage's mud-spattered windows, hiding its interior.

Mr. Acker looked enviously at the big chestnut stallion that Jerome was riding. "Never seen a better looking horse. Wouldn't mind working as a groom meself if me could ride a prime bit o' blood like that. Me'd say yer master, from the looks o' his carriage and horses, would be a fat one for Gentleman Jack's plucking. Who is he?"

"The Duke of Westleigh."

Clearly awed, Mr. Acker said, "Me's heard he's as haughty as they come." He nodded at the coach's drawn leather curtains. "That why he don't show his face? Thinks himself too good for the likes o' us to see him?"

Taken back, Jerome protested, "Not at all! He's—er, sleeping."

"How long you been the duke's groom?"

Jerome was tempted to answer, "Since I began talking to you," but instead he said, "For awhile."

Beside him, a strangled sound escaped from Ferris, who *was* the duke's groom. He was riding a younger, smaller copy of Jerome's chestnut.

The hostlers had finished changing the coach's horses. Jerome and Ferris galloped out of the posting house yard ahead of the coach and quickly pulled away from it.

A grinning Ferris inquired, "How do you like being a duke's groom?"

Jerome, looking down at his clothes, chuckled. He had shed aristocratic attire in favor of more utilitarian garments. An old leather vest protected him from the wind. Both his worn buckskin riding breeches and scuffed boots, down at the heels, were now liberally splattered with mud. There had been no point in ruining good clothes in the muck. Only his shirt of finest lawn hidden under the vest betrayed him as anything other than a groom.

When Jerome reached the River Wyn, he would stop and bathe in it, then don the clean clothes that his valet, currently his traveling coach's sole occupant, had laid out for him. He would arrive at Wingate Hall in apparel befitting a duke.

Although Jerome cared nothing for fashion, his father had been a stickler about dress. He had instilled in his son from an early age that when the Duke of Westleigh appeared publicly, his attire must always reinforce his ducal consequence.

"If I dress like a groom, I should expect to be mistaken for one," he observed to Ferris. "I doubt that Mr. Acker would have believed the truth."

"He'd have sooner believed you were Gentleman Jack!" Ferris's grin widened. "And 'tis more than your clothes. No 'haughty as they come' duke would be hobnobbing with his groom as you are."

But, to Jerome, Ferris was much more than a groom. They had been unlikely childhood friends who had forged a bond between them that had withstood the strains of time and vastly different social standing. Ferris was one of the very few people with whom the duke could relax and be himself.

And Jerome treasured the rare moments such as this when he could put aside his aristocratic raiment and demeanor and be the man he might have been had he not been born to the Duke of Westleigh's responsibilities.

He grinned at the thought of how shocked his peers would be to see him now, at ease in casual clothes and without the aloof facade that was his armor against the toadeaters, the encroaching social climbers, the boring fribbles, and the beautiful wantons eager to cultivate his notice.

The road cut through a high rolling moor, covered with heather and bracken. The sun, unseen during days of drenching rain, had finally made an appearance, shining down, hot and drying, on the treeless moor. The heather was not yet in flower, but an occasional gorse contributed a splash of golden color.

Jerome glanced over his shoulder. His coach was no longer in sight behind him. Even though the sun was out, the road was still little better than a muddy swamp, and it was slow going for the equipage.

A blue hare dashed across the road in front of their horses. Ferris's startled mount reared.

"Thunder's as skittish as they come," the groom muttered as he brought his unruly mount under control.

The sun beat down on the muddy road, unsheltered by a single tree, and Jerome welcomed the sight of a green birch wood ahead not only for the coolness it offered but also because it must be where Gentleman Jack had robbed Lord Creevy the previous day.

When Jerome and Ferris entered the woods, they slowed their mounts to a walk. If Gentleman Jack was about, Jerome wanted to give him plenty of time to see them.

As they rounded a sharp curve deep among the birches, a gruff voice suddenly growled, "Reach for the sky or ye'll be afeeling the bite o' me barking irons."

A large black horse blocked the road. Its rider, a big man dressed all in black and wearing a black mask and a black hat pulled low over his forehead, had a pistol in each hand aimed at Jerome and Ferris.

*Gentleman Jack.*

Jerome, breathing a deep sigh of relief, made no effort to comply with the highwayman's order. Instead, he said with a grin, "Your barking irons? Now really, Morgan."

"Oh hell! Not *you!*" Although the mask hid the bandit's expression, the disgruntlement in his voice was unmistakable.

"Don't sound so happy to see me, Gentleman Jack," the duke said placidly. "And do, please, lower your—er, barking irons."

The highwayman obediently shoved the pistols into his belt. He wore no coat, and his black shirt was open at the neck. "I thought you were that bastard Birkhall. He is expected at his estate north of here today, and this is the route he always takes to it."

Jerome secretly hoped that Gentleman Jack would succeed in giving that evil reprobate Lord Birkhall something to think about besides his depraved amusements.

"Why the hell are you here?" the outlaw asked.

"To talk to you. Why else would I make a tedious, uncomfortable journey to this godforsaken end of the earth? You know how much I dislike the north."

"This is neither the time nor the place to talk," Gentleman Jack said, his voice and diction having undergone a remarkable change. "Too many people travel this road. We are very near Wingate Hall, the Earl of Arlington's country house."

"Yes, I know. It is where I will be staying."

The highwayman's eyes behind his black mask were suddenly alight with curiosity. "Don't tell me the gorgeous Lady Rachel has caught your eye?"

Jerome stared at him blankly. "Who is she?"

"Arlington's sister."

"I did not know he had a sister."

"Then I do not understand why you are going to Wingate Hall. I recollect you disliked Arlington."

That was true. Jerome had no use for irresponsible

young rakes like Arlington who cared only for their own pleasure. "Surely you must know that Arlington is not there. He vanished without a trace a year ago while returning to England from a trip to the Continent."

"I know that, but if you did not like him, you will like what is at the hall now a hell of a lot less," Gentleman Jack said bluntly. "It astonishes me that Arlington was such a fool as to place his Uncle Alfred in charge of his estate. Say what you will about the young earl, I never thought him stupid until he did that."

"So his uncle's making a mull of the estate, is he?"

"Not him. That awful wife of his is running it."

Jerome's mouth tightened in distaste at the mention of Alfred Wingate's wife, the beautiful, faithless Sophia. She was all that he disliked in a woman. It had been clear to everyone but that old dolt Alfred, thirty years her senior, that she had married him only for the connection to the prestigious Wingate family.

The highwayman said mockingly, "I am surprised you would stay under the same roof with Sophia, knowing how you feel about women like her. She is certain to pursue you."

Sophia already was. That was why she had invited him to Wingate Hall. Jerome said dryly, "I made the sacrifice only because it masks my real reason for coming here. Which is to talk to you, Morgan."

"I do not need to ask about what," the highwayman said with an unhappy sigh, "but why did you pick this moment to come?"

"The Crown is about to offer a thousand pound reward for your capture."

The highwayman uttered a pungent expletive.

"I see you comprehend what that means. Every greedy thieftaker in the kingdom will be after you now."

Excited voices sounded in the distance beyond the wood.

The highwayman started. "I cannot tarry here. That could be men looking for me. You have delivered your warning, and I thank you. You can go back home now."

"No, I will not leave Wingate Hall until we talk further, Morgan. So if you want to be rid of me ... "

"As stubborn and implacable as ever," the bandit grumbled. "Very well. I promise I will meet you tomorrow at eleven a.m. at the Wingate ruins. The stable hands can give you directions."

The duke eyed him skeptically. "You guarantee you will be there?"

"I already promised you that I would. Damn it, Jerome, have I ever broken my word to you?"

# Chapter 2

**"W**hat?" Lady Rachel Wingate asked incredulously, certain that she could not have heard Sophia, her aunt by marriage, correctly.

The two women faced each other over a French tulipwood writing table in the book-lined library of Wingate Hall.

"Is your hearing defective?" demanded Sophia, a flamehaired beauty only eight years older than Rachel, who was twenty. Or was it seven years older now? Sophia seemed to grow younger with each birthday. "I said that Lord Felix has asked and received our permission to marry you. We are delighted by his suit—"

"Well, I am not delighted!" Rachel cried, appalled and furious at the thought of being wed to that enormously rich, enormously foolish fop. "I am horrified."

Sophia's brown eyes gleamed with malicious delight at Rachel's anger and dismay. For some inexplicable reason, Sophia had taken an immediate dislike to Rachel. She no longer took any pains to hide it except when guests were present.

Rachel had been about to go riding when she had been ordered to appear before her aunt and uncle in the library, and she carried her kid riding gloves in her right hand. Now she slapped them against her other hand to emphasize her words. "I will *not* marry Lord Felix!"

"You will do as you are told," Sophia snapped.

"Not by you!" And not when it would consign her to marriage to a man who revolted her. Rachel whirled on her white-haired uncle who was huddled in the corner of a green brocade settee.

"Uncle Alfred, you cannot want me to marry Lord Felix, whom I despise and cannot respect."

Sophia gave her husband no chance to reply. "It is precisely what he wants. It is your duty to your family and to yourself to make this brilliant marriage."

"I asked Uncle Alfred," Rachel said coolly, staring at her uncle. "He is my guardian."

Her uncle seemed to recede farther into the couch, looking miserable and refusing to meet her eye. He mumbled unhappily, "Sophia knows best."

Rachel knew that it would be useless to plead further with him. He would never dare go against the wishes of his termagant of a wife.

But Sophia would not get her way this time. Rachel would never bow to her will when it meant a lifetime of unhappiness for herself. She would find a way to outwit her aunt by marriage.

With steel in her voice, Rachel promised, "Upon my oath, I will never, never, *never,* marry Lord Felix. You cannot force the vows from my lips. I would sooner marry a stable hand."

With that, she turned on her heel with a swish of her full violet riding skirt and several petticoats and left the library.

As Rachel went out the side door where her mount was waiting, she glanced toward the terrace just as Sophia stepped out on it.

A short, thin gentleman in an intricately embroidered red silk coat minced across the slate stones on red, high-heeled shoes to greet Rachel's aunt. It was Lord Felix, resplendent in a heavily powdered tie wig with diamonds winking at his neck and lace cascading from his wrists and neck.

Rachel's lips tightened in disgust. She did not care what they did to her, she thought wildly. They could lock her in a dungeon, grind her on the rack (not that Wingate Hall had either), but she would not marry him.

Still seething, she claimed her mount and rode toward the river. Rachel had heard that it was near to bursting its banks from all the rain the past se'enight, and she wanted to see it.

Staccato yelps rang out behind her. She turned to see her low-slung terrier, Maxi, running as fast as his stubby legs would carry him. She slowed her mare to a walk until the dog caught up with them.

When she topped a hill and saw the river ahead, a gasp escaped her. A week of hard, relentless rain had swollen the usually placid ribbon to a raging torrent that gnawed at its steep banks and threatened to overflow them. Rachel was awed by this violent display of nature's power.

She was not the only one who had come to watch the river. Toby Paxton, an awkward youth with a mane of straw-colored hair, was standing with Fanny Stoddard by the old wooden bridge.

Fanny, a blond, almond-eyed beauty, was betrothed to the elder of Rachel's brothers, Stephen, the missing Earl of Arlington. Her other brother, George, was with the British Army in the English colony of New York.

Rachel dismounted and joined the pair. Maxi trotted along at her heels, his button eyes searching eagerly for a hairy rodent to attack.

Fanny, seeing Rachel's expression, observed, "You look furious. What is wrong?"

"Lord Felix has offered for me, and Uncle Alfred and Aunt Sophia say I must accept."

"But, of course, you must. He is a marquess's son," Fanny said, betraying what was most important to her in a husband.

Although Rachel had tried hard, she had not been

able to truly like her brother's choice of a bride. She wondered again why Fanny had suddenly descended, unannounced and uninvited, upon Wingate Hall for a visit. Fanny made no secret of her distaste for country life. In that, she and Stephen were well matched. He, too, much preferred London to Yorkshire.

Fanny said, "Even *you* would not dare turn down a *marquess's* son, Rachel."

"I do not care if he is the *king's* son and the crown prince in the bargain. I cannot tolerate him."

"You are a fool," Fanny cried. "Only think, you will have everything you want if you marry Lord Felix. Indeed, the best of everything. It is well known that he settles for nothing less than the best."

*Or at least the most ostentatious*, Rachel thought in disgust, from the huge diamonds he wore on his fingers to the six caparisoned white horses that drew his gilt carriage. Nor did she flatter herself that Lord Felix cared for her. She knew better than that. She would merely be another pretty ornament to adorn his consequence. Rachel dreamed of marrying a man who would love and cherish her as her father had her mother, a man whom she could love in return.

Fanny's eyes narrowed. "You are so used to having every eligible male in the shire fall at your feet that you think you are too good for any man."

"That is not true!" Rachel cried, much distressed that Fanny could think such a thing of her. It was true that she had attracted many smitten swains, but she had done nothing to try to do so. In fact, she was more embarrassed than pleased by her numerous suitors.

"If it is not true, then tell me who you want to marry," Fanny challenged.

That stopped Rachel, and she stared down into the river's boiling waters. Although she would rather marry almost anyone more than Felix, there was no one that she truly *wanted* to marry.

Not a single one of her many suitors made her heart flutter the way Papa had made Mama's. Since Mama had told her about that, Rachel had been determined to find a husband who had the same effect on her heart. Now she offered up a silent prayer that she would meet him very quickly.

Young Toby asked eagerly, "Did you hear that Gentleman Jack robbed Lord Creevy in full daylight yesterday in that very wood?" He nodded toward the birch forest across the river.

"It is an outrage!" Fanny cried furiously. "When will they find and hang that outlaw?"

*Never*, Rachel hoped, but she kept that thought to herself. During her frequent visits to the poor and sick in the neighborhood, she had perceived how much good the highwayman did. Like Robin Hood, he robbed the rich to help those who desperately needed it, and she applauded him for doing so. What he did might be against man's law, but she was certain it complied with God's to help the poor and unfortunate.

Maxi whimpered to be picked up, and Rachel obliged, lifting the silver-haired terrier into her arms.

Fanny asked, "When does the Duke of Westleigh arrive at Wingate Hall?"

Rachel was surprised that Fanny knew about the duke's impending visit. "Either today or tomorrow. Why?"

"Because I am anxious to meet him." Fanny's pouting face was suddenly alive with excitement. "I have heard that he is sinfully handsome. It is a great social coup to have him visit Wingate Hall."

"So I gather," Rachel said dryly. "Aunt Sophia has been preening herself insufferably since he accepted her invitation."

Rachel had been astonished that the duke had done so, for she knew her missing brother Stephen hated him, and she had gathered that the duke reciprocated Stephen's enmity.

"Sophia has good reason to preen," Fanny said. "Everyone knows Westleigh never accepts invitations to country houses. It is said he considers them all so inferior to his own Royal Elms."

"Stephen does not like the duke," Rachel told Fanny. "He says Westleigh is infuriatingly haughty and treated him with freezing condescension."

" 'Tis a duke's right," Fanny retorted, obviously unmoved by her missing betrothed's opinion.

"The duke clearly does not think much of our stable either. He wrote he would bring two of his own mounts for riding and their groom for us to house." Rachel was still indignant over this implied—and undeserved—insult to the quality of Wingate Hall's horses.

"By Jove, he must be bringing Lightning," cried young Toby, who was horsemad. "I heard he prefers him to any other mount and often brings him when he travels. 'Tis said Lightning is the premier stallion in the kingdom."

Suddenly Maxi began barking furiously and struggling to escape Rachel's arms. As she put the little terrier down, she looked across the river. Emerging from the birch wood were two of the finest chestnut horses she had ever seen.

Toby exclaimed in awe, "What a pair of prime 'uns? I'll wager the big stallion on the left is Lightning. It must be Westleigh's grooms arriving with his horses."

So, Rachel thought irritably, the arrogant duke had brought *two* grooms instead of one to be housed.

As Jerome and Ferris left the trees behind and emerged into the full sunlight, it blinded the duke, and he was suddenly too warm in his leather vest. He removed it and lay it across Lightning's back.

As his eyes became accustomed to the bright sunshine, he saw directly ahead of him a short, rickety wooden bridge. Jerome slowed Lightning to a walk, and Ferris followed his lead. The span would be barely wide enough for Jerome's coach, and he hoped that the flimsy structure would not collapse under the equipage's weight.

Then he saw the stream, its waters a crazy, rain-swollen cataract tearing with furious force at the banks. He heard Ferris's gasp.

Even before Jerome turned to see his groom staring whitefaced at the raging river he knew what was wrong. At age six, Ferris had fallen into a stream and had come within a hairsbreadth of drowning before he had been saved. Since then Ferris, so brave in every other respect, had been terrified of water. He had flatly refused all of Jerome's offers to teach him to swim. He would not go near water if he could avoid it.

"Come on, the bridge is short; we will be across in half a minute," Jerome said encouragingly.

As their mounts clattered onto the flimsy wooden structure, he advised, "Look beyond the bridge, not down at the water, and it will be easier for you."

Ferris forced his gaze forward. Suddenly, his eyes widened, his jaw dropped, and his hold on the reins slackened. "My God, have you ever seen anything as beautiful?" he muttered. All thought of the wild water beneath him seemed to have vanished.

Jerome's attention had been focused on Ferris, but now he jerked his gaze away to see what was so compelling that his friend had forgotten his terror of the roiling water.

It did not take Jerome more than a second to identify which of the two elegantly dressed young women standing with a gangling youth had such an effect on Ferris. One, a pouty-faced blonde, was a beauty, but the second was the most ravishing creature Jerome had ever beheld.

His own jaw dropped as he stared at this vision. Helen of Troy would have been jealous of that exquisite face, set with huge eyes, a perfect little nose, and a full cherry-red mouth that begged to be kissed. Her hair, as black and shining as a raven's wing, contrasted vividly with her fine, alabaster skin.

Her slender body was equally enticing in a violet riding habit. Its fitted jacket, trimmed in silver, was molded to her full breasts and to a waist so tiny Jerome could have spanned it with his hands. The habit's skirt was full, puffed out by layers of voluminous petticoats.

His breath caught. Much as he despised and distrusted beautiful women, it was all he could do to tear his eyes away from her. Ferris had not yet managed to do so but was still staring slack-jawed, the reins hanging loose in his hand.

Out of the corner of his eye, Jerome caught a glimpse of a silver terrier rushing forward from beside the beauty's violet skirt. The dog danced in front of the approaching horses, barking furiously.

Ferris's skittish chestnut, no longer held in check by a tight rein, erupted in rearing, whirling, bucking fury.

The groom, caught unaware, was hurled from the saddle into the tumultuous river.

"For God's sakes, Ferris!" Jerome cried in horror.

The colt, freed of his rider, raced from the bridge past the beauty and her companion, but Jerome paid no heed to the valuable runaway. His only thought as he vaulted from his horse was for Ferris.

"Help, help me," the groom shouted frantically.

"I'm coming, Ferris!" Jerome cried, yanking off his boots with two quick, vicious tugs.

Ferris's scream of terror as he sank beneath the surface into the swirling maelstrom was like a lance through Jerome's heart.

He looked down in dismay at the tumbling river beneath him. Strong a swimmer as he was, he was not certain that even he could conquer those fierce waters, but he had to try. Jerome would not let his friend drown.

The current carried Ferris beneath the bridge, and he disappeared from sight.

Jerome ran to the downstream side of the narrow span and dived into the tumultuous river. He surfaced very near to Ferris.

With powerful strokes, he closed the distance between them and managed to grab a piece of his coarse, homespun shirt.

The panicked groom was flailing about so frantically that he pulled Jerome beneath the water with him.

When Jerome resurfaced, he yelled, "Stop struggling!" He prayed that Ferris could hear this command above the roar of the water. "Relax and I will carry you to shore."

Apparently, the groom heard for he stopped fighting him.

Jerome managed to hook his arm beneath Ferris's and held him so that his head was above the frothy surface. The groom was choking and coughing and sneezing water.

Stroking one-armed and kicking with all the strength he possessed, Jerome fought his way across the powerful current that was pulling him relentlessly downstream. He prayed that his strength would last until he could reach the bank.

# Chapter 3

**R**achel watched with her heart in her throat as the rescuer, encumbered by his human burden, battled against the fierce current of the river trying to reach the bank. He was visibly tiring, and she doubted that he would make it.

If only she had a rope to throw to the two grooms, she and Toby could help pull them to shore, but she did not.

She looked around frantically for something else to use but saw nothing. In desperation, she thought of stringing together the long underpetticoats that puffed out her riding skirt. Although Rachel knew that no well-bred young lady would shed her petticoats in public, no matter what the reason, saving a human life—perhaps two of them—was far more important to her. She had to do everything she could to save the men, or she would not be able to live with herself.

She stepped back from her two companions who were staring transfixed at the life-and-death struggle in the water. Making certain that neither of them was looking in her direction, she hastily pulled off her three white underpetticoats.

Working feverishly, Rachel tied them together into a makeshift rope, then knotted a rock in one end. She cried, "Toby, come with me."

He followed her as she raced along the bank. When she was opposite the men in the water, she swung the petticoat rope in a circle over her head to give it momentum. Shouting at the men in the water, hoping that they could hear her above the crashing river, she flung it out over the foaming torrent.

As its knotted end containing the rock landed in the water, the groom who could not swim—the one the other groom had called Ferris—grabbed it. The petticoats grew taut so suddenly that Rachel was nearly yanked forward on her face.

"Help me, Toby," she cried as she struggled to retain her balance. He grabbed the petticoat just above her hands. She prayed that the cloth would not tear.

Ferris was clinging to the other end of the makeshift rope with both hands.

Together, Rachel and Toby strained, moving hand over hand, laboriously pulling the men to shore.

The rescuer, seeing what they were about, released his hold on the man he had saved. With his weight gone, Rachel and Toby were able to reel Ferris more quickly to the bank.

When he reached it, he staggered up under his own power. He was still wheezing and sneezing water, but he was clearly in good condition. Once he had put several feet between the torrent and himself, he fell to his knees at the base of a slender willow and kissed the earth.

Rachel looked back at the man who was still in the water. Seeing that he was almost to shore and would make it without help, she ran to the man on his knees. Dropping her soaked petticoats, she sank down beside him.

Ferris's teeth were chattering and he was shivering violently, but he was no longer coughing out water.

She hastily began to unbutton the jacket of her riding habit. "Let me give you my jacket to warm you." But even as she offered, she looked dubiously at his wide shoulders and thick body, "I am not certain, though, that you will fit into it."

"No, ma'am, I would not." Ferris wrapped his

arms tightly around his body. " 'Tis very kind of you to offer, but I do not need it. I'll be all right."

Picking up her wet, bedraggled petticoats, she scrambled to her feet and turned back to the river and the other groom.

She was awed that he had dared to dive into the raging river to try to save his companion, knowing that it would most likely mean death for himself, too. It was the bravest, most unselfish act she had ever seen.

As he emerged from the water, her eyes widened. His face was strong with a broad forehead, aristocratic nose, prominent cheekbones, a mouth that looked as though it did not smile often, and a jutting, determined jaw. Rivulets of water ran from blond hair that sprang into dripping curls around that arresting face.

Her drenched petticoats fell unnoticed from her suddenly nerveless fingers. When she had seen the groom on horseback, she had not noticed how tall or how handsome he was. The thin material of his soaked shirt was plastered against him, revealing the powerful muscles of his arms, shoulders, and chest. The garment was only half buttoned and wet swirls of golden hair decorated his chest. Rachel realized to her shock that his soaked clothing was almost as revealing as if he were naked.

Modesty required that she look away, but her gaze seemed beyond her control as it moved down that marvelous body to the sodden breeches molded to slim hips. Rachel drew in her breath and held it. He was a work of art! Something the great Michelangelo would have been proud to have sculpted.

Why he was so splendid he should be the Duke of Westleigh instead of his groom!

Rachel could not tear her fascinated gaze from his powerful body, all rippling muscle and sinew. A strange heat curled within her. She belatedly realized that this man was not merely making her heart flutter.

He was making it turn somersaults.

"Like what you see?" an icily sarcastic voice demanded.

Her gaze snapped upward, and she met blue eyes that radiated cold fury.

"I am not some damn stud on the auction block for milady's perusal!"

Fanny, standing beside Rachel, gasped in shock. "How dare you, a lowly groom, speak to the Lady Rachel Wingate, the Earl of Arlington's sister, in such a rude, vulgar fashion!"

He gave Fanny a look so scathing that it elicited another gasp from her. "How dare *Lady* Rachel look me over in such a rude, vulgar fashion," he demanded.

He was right, Rachel thought guiltily. She had been unwittingly staring at him in a most bold and improper manner. She felt her cheeks bloom hotly with embarrassment.

To hide her discomfort, she bent down to pick up Maxi who had scampered up to her. She lifted him and rubbed her burning cheek against his silver coat.

The handsome groom's expression became even more forbidding. "Is that your damned dog?"

She nodded.

"Then teach him not to run at spirited, skittish horses. He nearly cost Ferris his life!"

The angry groom not only looked as though he ought to be the Duke of Westleigh, he acted as though he was.

His blue eyes seemed to turn to the gray shade of the sea on a stormy winter day, and he said harshly, "But no doubt the life of a *lowly* groom means less than nothing to you."

"That is not true!" Rachel cried, stung by his sarcasm. She would never have forgiven herself if Ferris had drowned. "I am very, very sorry!"

"And you, boy, are insufferably insolent," Fanny said in her most supercilious tone.

"Please, Fanny," Rachel began, but the girl would not be silenced.

"You may rest assured that I shall complain to your master about your appalling speech and conduct toward Lady Rachel."

Fanny's threat did not seem to frighten him in the least. He gave her an odd, utterly unrepentant look that made him seen even more handsome to Rachel. "You do that," he said carelessly.

His rich, vibrant voice sent a tiny quaver of delight through Rachel. He was by far the most intriguing man she had ever seen, even if he was a groom.

"He has every right to be angry, Fanny," Rachel said. "Only his courageous risking of his own life averted tragedy. Maxi nearly cost his companion his life."

The stormy eyes snapped back to examine Rachel with something like surprise. Then he subjected her to the same kind of perusal, as leisurely as it was audacious and insulting, that she had given him.

Men might have studied her so boldly when her attention was elsewhere and she was unaware of it, but no man—and especially not a servant—had ever dared to do so to her face as he was doing now.

His daring examination kindled such a delicious, insidious warmth within her, however, that she could not be outraged as she ought to be. Deliberately echoing his earlier complaint, she said tartly, "I am not a brood mare on the auction block for your perusal."

He gave her a wicked grin that made her breath catch. "Tit for tat, my dear."

Rachel could feel her cheeks grow hot at his discourteous, insultingly familiar address. "You are impudent!"

"He is worse than that," Fanny cried. "His behavior is shocking."

The other groom, who was half a head shorter, had quietly gone to collect the big chestnut stallion and now led him up to his companion.

As the tall groom took the reins, Toby, staring at the horse in awe, asked, "Is he the Duke of Westleigh's Lightning?"

"Aye," the tall groom replied.

"By Jove, I knew it had to be," Toby exclaimed. "He's as prime as people say."

Yes, the stallion was, Rachel thought, forgiving the duke for bringing his own mounts. Even she would readily agree that no horse in Wingate Hall's stables could match Lightning.

The impertinent groom gave Toby a friendly smile that made Rachel's pulse race. "Thank you for your help in pulling Ferris from the river. I am not certain we would have made it otherwise. That was quick thinking on your part."

"Do not thank me, thank Lady Rachel. It was her quick thinking—and her petticoats that she sacrificed." Toby looked down at the wet, knotted cloth lying muddied and forgotten by Rachel's skirt. "I fear they are ruined now."

The groom's smile faded, and a shocked gasp escaped Fanny.

"Rachel, how could you?" she demanded.

"I could not let a man drown."

The groom looked at Rachel skeptically, as though he could not credit what she had just said. Water was no longer dripping from him, but his wet clothes were still pasted to his body in a way that fed the odd, aching heat within Rachel, and she could not seem to stop herself from staring at him.

Damn her, Jerome thought as he felt his body's response. Those big, violet eyes of hers were watching him as though she wanted to devour him. There was only so much provocation a man could take, even one with his iron discipline.

His wet, tight leather riding breeches seemed to be shrinking by the second while a part of his anatomy they covered was swelling. He hastily stepped around Lightning so that the big chestnut's body would conceal his arousal. Jerome could not believe that the chit had reduced him to such a state.

Nor could he believe that she had been so quick to react to the dire plight of two men she believed were grooms and to sacrifice her petticoats to help them. Yet the proof of her action lay in the wet, dirty heap of cloth beside her and in the way the voluminous skirt of her violet riding habit was no longer puffed out as it had been. Instead, it clung to her tantalizing hips and thighs in a way that sent a new bolt of desire coursing through him. Morgan had understated the truth when he had said Lady Rachel was gorgeous.

"So you are the Duke of Westleigh's grooms," the pouty-faced Fanny said. "Neither your manners nor your dress do him any credit. Why are you not in his livery?"

Jerome turned on her, welcoming the opportunity to vent some of his aching frustration. "In this muck?" he inquired scornfully. "Why ruin good livery? It would not have been recognizable by the time we got to Wingate Hall."

"You will address me with respect," Fanny cried indignantly. "I will have you know I am Miss Stoddard, Lord Stoddard's daughter and the Earl of Arlington's betrothed."

"No wonder the earl vanished," Jerome retorted. "If I were betrothed to you, I would, too."

"You ... you ..." Fanny sputtered. She was so angry that it was a full minute before she could get out a coherent sentence. "I forbid you ever to speak to me again!" She paused, then inquired with slow, precise enunciation as though he were a half-wit who could not understand if she spoke at a normal pace, "Do ... you ... understand?"

Jerome knew Fanny's kind all too well. If she had known who he really was, she would have been fawning over him in a disgusting manner. He raked her with a look of withering contempt, then turned to Arlington's sister.

"*Lady* Rachel, please tell Miss Stoddard I am delighted to give her my oath never to address her again."

"You obnoxious lout," Fanny screeched. "I shall see that the Duke of Westleigh sacks you immediately."

Jerome could not help grinning at that. "Lady Rachel, tell Miss Stoddard that she may try, but she is in for a surprise."

"I pray it will be she who is surprised and not you," Rachel said softly, her expression troubled.

He was startled by her clear concern for a humble groom. "Why would you care?"

"You deserve better after the brave way you risked your life to save your companion." Lady Rachel's voice was as sweet as warm honey, enveloping him in sensual pleasure that brought instant response from his beleaguered body.

Then she smiled at him, her eyes glowing with approval, and two marvelous dimples appeared at the corners of her delectable mouth. It took Jerome's breath away. She was the most sublime creature he had ever seen. Hellsfire, if she did not stop smiling at him like that, he was going to have to dive back into the damned river.

Flinging himself on Lightning, he hastily draped his leather vest across the saddle to hide the embarrassingly obvious effect she was having on him.

Ferris had gone to retrieve Thunder. The colt was placidly nibbling on the grass halfway up the slope from the bridge, and Jerome nudged his mount forward to join him.

After Ferris remounted, the two men cantered in

silence for a minute. Then the groom remarked, "You were rather rough on Lady Rachel."

Jerome, fighting hard to extinguish the flames of desire she had kindled in him, did not want to be reminded of her. "I was rougher on Fanny."

"She deserved it. Lady Rachel did not," Ferris said with the frankness of an old and trusted friend.

Jerome could not argue. He had been positively churlish to Rachel when he had seen her studying him with brazen admiration. He had felt like a damned footman being judged by a wanton mistress of the house.

He was used to squelching such female presumption with his freezing manner. But frigid hauteur was damned hard to affect when one was dressed in groom's garb and dripping wet in the bargain.

He said gruffly, "You saw the bold way she looked me over when I came out of the water."

"Aye." Ferris grinned. "I'd have been most pleased to have her do that to me."

The two riders topped the hill rising from the river and passed out of sight of Lady Rachel and her companions. They had ruined Jerome's plan to bathe in the river and change clothes. He would wait now until he ordered a hot bath at Wingate Hall before he'd struggle to get out of his wet garments.

Ferris observed, "The more beautiful a woman, the more disdainful and distrustful you are of her."

"With good reason!"

"Aye, but I think you are doing this one an injustice. If Lady Rachel had not thought to knot her petticoats into a rope and throw it to me, we might both be dead."

That was true, but Jerome hated to admit anything that would soften his opinion of such an exquisite creature.

"Did you know that after they pulled me out of the water, she offered me her jacket to warm myself?" Ferris asked. "I don't know many ladies who would have been as willing to sacrifice their fine garments as she was."

Nor did Jerome.

"Most ladies would have been like Fanny," Ferris continued. "That one would sooner have let me drown than have a *lowly* groom touch one of her precious petticoats."

Jerome wondered cynically how many men had seen Lady Rachel without her petticoats. Quite a number if she could so quickly shed them publicly as she had. No girl with any claim to propriety would have done so. Nor would an innocent miss have given him the shameless inspection she had. His blood ran hot at the memory.

"She's another damned faithless beauty," he growled aloud, determined to believe it in the hope it would squelch the desire he felt for her.

To his disgust, it did not.

"The word beauty does not begin to do Lady Rachel justice," Ferris said. "She is the most stunning creature I have ever seen."

Yes, she was, *damn her!*

Ferris said softly, "I know you are convinced all beautiful women are treacherous, but I think Lady Rachel is different."

"Not bloody likely," the duke snapped, still furious at the way his traitorous body had responded to her. It must have been because she took him by surprise.

It would not happen again.

# Chapter 4

**R**achel, carrying a small leather case, sneaked through the side door of Wingate Hall and ran up the back stairs. When she rushed into her bed-chamber, she found Eleanor Paxton, her best friend and Toby's sister, waiting in a chintz-covered chair by a window overlooking Wingate Hall's maze.

As Rachel closed the door, Eleanor asked, "Where have you been?"

"Treating one of our tenants' children who is very ill with an ague." Rachel set the leather case containing her herbal remedies on the walnut chest of drawers. She had learned the secrets of herbal healing from her late mother. So efficacious were her remedies that she was often called when illness struck.

"His father stopped me as I was returning from the river and begged me to help the poor little thing."

"Why did you not tell someone? No one knew where you were."

"Aunt Sophia forbade me to treat sick tenants so I am forced to sneak away to do so."

"Forbade you!" Eleanor's voice quavered with indignation. "How could she? They obviously depend on your healing skill."

"As if Sophia would care about that! She says a lady does not demean herself by tending to the ills of the lower orders."

"But you and your mother before you have been

doing that for years," Eleanor cried. "What will they do without you?"

And what would Rachel do without them? She loved treating them. It made her life so much more satisfying than empty days devoted to needlepoint and gossip.

"How is the sick child now?" Eleanor asked.

"I was able to bring down his fever." Rachel hastily stripped off the jacket of her violet riding habit, then stepped out of its skirt, revealing her white shift beneath. When she had learned how sick the child was, she had not taken the time to replace the petticoats that she had ruined earlier. She had stopped at Wingate Hall only long enough to get her case of remedies before setting out for the tenant's cottage.

"I admire your courage," Eleanor said. "I could not expose myself to disease to help people who are not even my family."

But to Rachel, the tenants she helped were all part of Wingate Hall's family and, as such, their well-being was the responsibility of the lord and lady of the manor. It had been the philosophy her parents had believed and practiced.

She fumbled with the buttons of her violet habit-shirt. "Why is it I am all fingers when I try to hurry? I dare not be late for dinner or Aunt Sophia will want to know why."

"Tell her you were waiting for me," Eleanor said. "Besides we will be downstairs before Fanny. The way she is fussing over her toilet she will be another hour yet. One would think she was going to the king's ball tonight."

"Why the fuss?" Rachel shed her blouse and hurried to the small washstand. She would have loved a hot bath, but there was no time. Instead she poured water from the pitcher into the basin.

"Fanny intends to become the Duchess of Westleigh."

Rachel was so shocked that her voice came out in a squeak. "But she is betrothed to my brother!"

"She does not think Stephen will return," Eleanor said gently. "It has been a year since he disappeared."

"I know, but I cannot give up hope that he is still alive." A lump rose in Rachel's throat. She loved her charming brother dearly, even though his negligent, irresponsible ways sometimes exasperated her.

"Did you wonder why Fanny suddenly paid this surprise visit to Wingate Hall when she dislikes Yorkshire?"

"Yes, and Aunt Sophia was livid when Fanny turned up here, uninvited and unexpected. Fanny told her she came because she missed Stephen so, and she felt closer to him here."

"She came because she heard that Westleigh would be here," Eleanor said. "She has set her cap for him."

"How can she do that to poor Stephen?" Rachel demanded, much distressed by Fanny's fickleness. She pulled out a hooped underpetticoat from her clothes press. As she donned it she said, "I am certain that my brother is alive and will return some day."

"Fanny does not share your conviction, and she is determined to snare another impressive title as quickly as possible." Eleanor, mimicking Fanny's wispy voice, quoted, " 'Westleigh's is one of the oldest and most illustrious dukedoms in the kingdom.' "

"You sound just like her," Rachel said, extracting a mustard-colored overgown and brown underdress from the clothes press.

"Fanny is a fool to think that she can snare Westleigh. Every beautiful woman in London has tried to do so, and he has ignored them all. 'Tis said he is so haughty that he does not think any woman worthy of him."

"He sounds as arrogant and condescending as Stephen said he was." Rachel pulled on the brown underdress. "I own I do not look forward to meeting him. Has no woman ever caught his fancy?"

"He was betrothed once, years ago, to Cleopatra Macklin who was said to be the greatest beauty of the age, but he jilted her."

"Jilted her?" Rachel echoed, shocked. "But a gentleman does not—"

Eleanor said dryly, "Westleigh is not a gentleman, he is a *duke*."

Rachel had finished dressing. Her mustard overdress, a short silk sacque, fell in voluminous pleats from a round neck to her hips. The floor-length undergown was also heavily pleated.

"Do you truly intend to wear *that* to dinner?" Eleanor asked. "I swear it is the most unflattering gown you have ever owned."

"That is why I chose it," Rachel confessed. "I want to look as ugly as I can to Lord Felix."

Eleanor burst out laughing. "You could not look ugly no matter how hard you tried."

"I must find a way to discourage Felix's suit." The thought of the mincing fop made Rachel cringe. "I will not marry him."

Eleanor sobered. "You will have no choice if your guardian agrees to it," she warned. "Half the wives in London society would not be married to their husbands if they had their choice. A girl must accept the husband her family chooses for her."

"I would rather die than marry Lord Felix!" Rachel cried passionately. She began brushing her long, ebony hair vigorously in her frustration. "Oh, Eleanor, what am I to do? Is there no way that I can escape him?"

"One. Find another man to marry who rivals Felix in wealth and social status. Then your aunt cannot object to your marrying him instead of Felix."

"But hardly any men surpass ... " Rachel's voice faded away in despair.

"I know," Eleanor said grimly. "The Duke of

Westleigh is one of the few. Perhaps you should try to fix his interest."

Rachel was appalled. She wanted nothing to do with a man so arrogant that even her heedless brother Stephen was affronted, a man who thought no woman good enough for him and cared so little for others that he would jilt his betrothed.

Her animosity did not extend, though, to the haughty duke's groom. Try as she might, Rachel had not been able to banish that maddening man from her mind all afternoon. Thinking about him now brought a rosy heat to her cheeks. "I pray Fanny does not carry out her threat to have Westleigh's groom dismissed."

"That is exactly what she intends to do. She means to make a great issue of his behavior when she is introduced to the duke." Once again, Eleanor mimicked Fanny's voice. " 'A man of Westleigh's consequence cannot permit such a groom to remain in his employ. I shall insist that the duke discharge the insolent, rude oaf without a character.' "

Rachel gasped in dismay. "But without that, he will never obtain another position."

"That is what Fanny wants. She says it will teach him the folly of being rude to his betters."

"He was no ruder than Fanny was!" Nor was he an oaf. His speech had been more grammatical and well-modulated than that of some gentlemen Rachel knew. But she could not deny that he had been impertinent. Her cheeks warmed again as she remembered the way he had looked at her.

To think that only moments before Rachel had seen him, she had despaired that any man could make her heart flutter. Her prayer to meet one who did had been answered with astonishing promptitude but with a singularly inappropriate marital prospect for the Earl of Arlington's sister.

Rachel sighed. Why did he have to be a groom? Fate could be tantalizingly perverse at times. Groom or not, he was vastly superior to Lord Felix, the Marquess of Caldham's son.

*I would sooner marry a stable hand.*

Her lips twisted in a wry smile as she recalled her angry statement to Sophia. What a firestorm of shock and outrage Rachel would unleash were she to announce she preferred a groom to a marquess's son. She would be considered ready for Bedlam.

But the groom's courage and willingness to risk his own life to save his companion meant far more to Rachel than his station in life.

Although he had been disconcertingly blunt for a servant, she admired a man who did not fear to say what he thought. But he would pay dearly for it if Fanny persuaded the duke to discharge him without a character reference.

Absently, Rachel pulled a fan from her chest of drawers.

She would not, could not, let Fanny destroy him like that, especially after he had been so courageous in rescuing his companion.

Eleanor exclaimed, "Oh, dear, I forgot my fan. I must run back to my room for it. I will be right back."

Rachel nodded absently, her mind still preoccupied with the problem of how to save the groom from Fanny's vengeance.

The Duke of Westleigh must be made to understand how brave his groom had been. Rachel must talk to his grace before Fanny could spill her venom in his ear. Once they were in the drawing room, though, Rachel might not have that opportunity. She should try to see him now before he went down to dinner.

Wasting no time in contemplating her action, Rachel impulsively hurried to the apartment that had been assigned to the duke and knocked on the door before she lost her courage.

A tall, angular man in a fashionably cut black coat

over white waistcoat and black breeches opened the door. His clothes were impeccable, though surprisingly plain and somber for a man of the duke's rank. Rachel wondered whether he was in mourning.

She looked at his long, thin face, and her heart sank at its supercilious expression. He had the look of a man whose heart, if he even had one, had shriveled long ago. No wonder Stephen hated him.

He raised one haughty eyebrow in silent inquiry.

"Your Grace, I have come—"

"I am not his grace," he interjected coldly. "I am his valet."

Rachel's cheeks flamed with embarrassment. Sweet heaven, if his valet was as overbearing as this, her courage faltered at what the duke himself must be like.

She wanted to turn and flee. Then she thought of what would happen to the poor groom after Fanny had poisoned the duke's mind against him. Rachel held her ground. The groom had been brave and so would she.

"Please, I must see the duke."

She was shocked at the contempt for her that curled the valet's lips. Rachel had no idea what she had done to deserve it.

"That is impossible. His Grace—"

"Let her in, Peters; then leave us," a resonant voice within the room ordered. It sounded vaguely familiar but Rachel was too embarrassed by the realization that Westleigh must have overheard her mistake his valet for him to refine upon it. A man of the duke's arrogance would consider it an unforgivable insult.

Peters looked startled by the duke's order, but he stepped aside to allow her to enter, then went out the door, shutting it behind him and leaving her alone with the duke. She was thankful that he had sent the valet away. With Peters's censorious gaze upon her, she would have found it very difficult to plead the groom's cause.

The duke was standing near the heavily carved tester bed with its curtains of scarlet brocade. After her faux pas in mistaking his valet for him, Rachel was too mortified to raise her eyes to his face.

He moved toward her, but her flustered gaze remained fixed on his muscular torso. His handsome coat of midnight blue was perfectly tailored to his broad shoulders and chest. To her surprise, the same odd sensation she had felt when she had first seen his groom twisted within her.

"Your Grace," she began, still unable to look at his face and so nervous now that she could hardly get the words out, "I have come to tell you how brave—"

"I know why you have come," he interrupted, his voice coldly cynical now. "You want to stake your claim ahead of Sophia."

Rachel had no idea what he was talking about, and her head snapped up in startlement.

For an instant she did not recognize him with his blond hair neatly brushed back and tied at the neck instead of curling around his face in wet, unruly curls. Then she stared into those unforgettable blue eyes, as icy now as they had been when she had first looked into them by the river.

Her jaw dropped in shock. "You!"

"Surprised are we?"

"Dear God, what are *you* doing here?" Her heart was suddenly pounding.

"Since you seem to mistake my servants for me and vice versa, let me introduce myself. I am the Duke of Westleigh."

She stared at him in disbelief. "Then who was the man you saved this afternoon?"

"My groom, Ferris."

"You cannot be the duke," she said with conviction.

"Why not? Your logic escapes me."

"Because you were so brave."

His mouth twitched in amusement. "Can a duke not be brave?"

"Yes, but from what I have heard of Westleigh," she blurted, "he would never risk his own life to save a groom—or anyone else."

"Then you will have to revise your erroneous opinion of me, will you not?" His sensuous lips curled in a humorless smile. "And now let us get down to your real reason for coming here."

He pulled her roughly into his arms. His mouth came down on hers in a hard, ruthless kiss.

Rachel was frozen by shock. Before she could recover from her paralysis, his lips gentled on hers, caressing them sweetly, warmly, sending shivers of pleasure through her. Her shock melted in the slow heat enveloping her.

She had never known that a kiss could be so exciting.

Not that she had ever been kissed like this. Although three of her besotted suitors had attempted to steal them from her, only Sir Waldo Fletcher had managed to touch even one corner of her mouth with his lips. And then Rachel had felt nothing but revulsion and outrage.

Now, however, disconcerting, wondrous sensations were exploding within her.

Her legs seemed to turn to mush. As if sensing her sudden weakness, his arms tightened around her, supporting her.

His tongue touched her lips, brushing them as lightly as a butterfly's wing, tasting her as though she were a particularly enticing sweet. His warm breath teased her face.

It was quite wonderful.

She kissed him back. She could not help herself. Emulating his example, she opened her mouth and touched his lips lightly with her own tongue.

He groaned and lifted his head slightly so that there was a scant half-inch of space between their lips. His voice was rich and husky. "I knew that you were bold, but I did not credit how truly brazen you are, my dear."

His words bewildered Rachel. She did not know what he was talking about, but before she could ask, his lips returned to hers as his hand came up to cup the soft weight of her breast.

His thumb rubbed its crest through the mustard silk pleats of her gown. The pleasure that rippled through her was so delicious that, despite her shock, she was helpless to protest his audacity.

Then his tongue invaded her mouth, exploring and tantalizing it with a rhythm that stoked a yearning, as intense as it was mysterious, deep within her. She scarcely noticed that his hands slipped down to the hem of her short overgown.

She clung to him, lost in the sweet storm that was swirling within her.

Eleanor's suggestion echoed in Rachel's bemused mind: "Perhaps you should try to fix Westleigh's interest."

She had indignantly rejected the idea then, but suddenly it seemed like wonderful advice. No man had ever made her feel as he did.

Her breath caught as she felt the warmth of his hand on her breast again. She reveled in the pleasure his touch gave her. Belatedly, she realized, though, that there was no silk buffer between her and his caressing fingers.

Startled, she wrenched her head back, breaking the contact between their mouths, and looked down. His hand had stolen up beneath the pleats of her pleated mustard sacque to claim the prize hidden beneath.

Rachel was startled out of her sensual torpor. "No," she protested, trying to push him away.

For a moment, she did not think he meant to let her go. But then, after a visible shudder, he released her abruptly.

"Damn you!" he growled, looking incensed as his hand dropped away from her gown.

"Why are you angry at me?" she asked, baffled by his sudden change toward her from tender to furious. "It is—"

"For God's sake, spare me any feigned outrage," he growled scornfully.

She blinked in puzzlement. "But you were—" Her voice faded away in embarrassment.

"And it was you who invited me to." His eyes were as hard as winter ice. "You were so eager to capture a duke, you invaded my bedroom before we were even introduced."

The contempt and disgust in his voice flayed Rachel like a whip's lash. "I do not care that you are a duke! Indeed, I liked you better when I thought you a groom!"

"Did you now?" he retorted with shriveling sarcasm. "So you are one of those ladies who has a taste for tumbling with the lower orders?"

Deeply insulted, she cried, "I tumble with no one!"

"Then why did you come to my bedchamber?"

"Certainly not to be tumbled!" she cried in indignation. "How could you think that I came here for that?"

"Well, what the devil was I to think? That is the only reason a lady seeks to be alone with a man in the sanctuary of his bedchamber."

Rachel was aghast. "Is that true?" She remembered the contempt on his valet's face. "I did not know," she gasped, mortified to the tips of her toes. "No one told me."

Jerome could not doubt that Rachel was telling the truth. Not even the very best of actresses could feign such dismay and embarrassment. Her face was as scarlet as the brocade bed curtains.

Hell, she was a damned innocent.

After the bold perusal she had given him at the

river and the brazen way she had come to his room, who would have guessed it?

Certainly he had not.

Especially after the way she had kissed him. His blood heated at the memory.

Then he recalled how she had frozen with shock when he had first placed his mouth on hers. He had intended to give her a punishing kiss, but her stunned reaction had prompted him to gentle it and to coax a response from her.

And he had succeeded in spades. Her rigidity and resistance had melted away and then she had returned his kiss with such sweet, untutored passion that it had taken his breath away.

A fresh wave of desire washed through him, and he ached to take her in his arms again.

When she had knocked on his door, Jerome had thought it was Sophia again. The vixen had already been to his room twice since his arrival, but Peters had turned her away both times. Jerome thought Sophia had returned for a third run at him. He had been astonished to see Rachel instead.

He had been a fool to allow Peters to let her in, but his body had been aching for relief since he had met her at the river. Thinking her shamelessly offering it to him, he had seen no reason to resist.

He inquired dryly, "Since you did not come to me for the obvious reason, why are you here?"

Her face was still the color of the bed hangings. "I wanted to help your—I mean, you."

"I was not aware that I required any assistance."

"But I thought you did."

She looked utterly flustered—and disconcertingly delectable. If Jerome thought he had been aching for relief before she had come to his room, it was nothing to the way he felt now. "Why would you think I needed help?"

"Fanny means to insist to the duke that he turn you out without a character." Her voice rose in indignation. "I was afraid that Fanny might succeed if he were not aware of what truly happened at the river and how brave you were." Admiration turned to chagrin in her voice. "Only you are the duke! But I did not know that."

Another wave of hot scarlet flooded her beautiful face. "I feel like such a fool. You must think me an idiot!"

He thought her the loveliest female he had ever seen with her guileless violet eyes and burning cheeks.

But his deep distrust of such beauty, instilled in him by hard, painful experience, made it difficult for him to believe her. He doubted she was capable of giving even a passing thought to a servant's fate. "I am astonished that you would care what happened to a groom—especially one you do not even know."

"I would have done it for any person who was as brave as you were today." Rachel's eyes were suddenly alight with admiration.

Jerome found himself basking in their glow. God, but he wanted her. He hoped to hell that she continued to keep her gaze fixed on his face. If the lovely innocent looked down his body, she was in for a shock.

He cast a quick, rueful glance at his bulging breeches. How the hell was he supposed to assume his haughty ducal facade and go down to dinner in his present state of splendid and clearly visible arousal?

Jerome studied the dazzling beauty before him. Her long ebony hair had not been dressed in one of those elaborate styles he abhorred, but cascaded in lovely, casual waves about her shoulders. He was torn between flaming desire and a nagging incredulity that Lady Rachel could be as innocent and forthright as she seemed.

Yet if she were intent on seduction, she surely would have worn something other than the god-awful gown that so successfully hid the tempting curves of her beautiful body. Its ugly mustard color must be the one shade in the palette that could dim the lustre of a complexion as soft and velvety as white rose petals.

She looked old enough to have had two or three seasons in London. Yet, if she had, he was certain he would have heard of her. Even in that sophisticated city, such rare beauty would not go unheralded.

"How old are you Rachel?"

"Twenty."

"Have you been to London?"

"I have never been outside Yorkshire."

So that was why she was still such a delightful innocent. That would change, though, once she got to London. Then she would become as faithless and promiscuous as every other damned beauty.

Her poor husband's life would be hell, spent wondering who her lovers were.

He had narrowly escaped that fate once when he had been young and stupid. His father had warned him, but he had been too wildly in love with Cleo to heed him. Jerome had learned his lesson then. It had been a bitter one, paid for with scandal and his broken heart.

No, Jerome told himself savagely, much as he hungered for Rachel's lovely body, Emily Hextable was the perfect wife for him. Although he had never mentioned marriage to Emily, he felt committed to her. Both his father and hers had wanted the union. Jerome knew that Emily—and everyone else acquainted with them—expected him to offer for her.

She was what he wanted for his duchess: a woman who devoted herself to good works, not some selfish beauty who would think only of herself as Cleo had. Nor would he have to worry about plain, pious Emily cuckolding him or presenting him with an heir that was not of his making.

Yet, remembering the stunning moment when Rachel had returned his kiss with kindling passion, he was enveloped by a yearning for her as fierce as any he could remember.

Wingate Hall offered a temptation that he had not anticipated. Jerome was much shaken to discover that neither his rigid self-discipline nor his loathing for beautiful women was protection against Lady Rachel. He needed to get away from her as quickly as possible.

He hoped to hell that Morgan would keep their appointment tomorrow morning so that he could be gone from here by tomorrow night.

# Chapter 5

Sophia Wingate swooped down on Jerome as he stepped into the drawing room. She was an overripe beauty with a generously endowed body and a heart-shaped face that bespoke either her or her maid's skill with powder and paint. Her flamered hair was dressed in an elaborate style piled high on her head, and a black, crescent-shaped beauty patch decorated her cheek.

She smiled seductively at him. Sophia had a reputation for being eager to bed aristocratic men. The higher their title, the more eager she was. Which was no doubt why she was looking at Jerome now as though he were an especially coveted prize. She purred, "I am delighted I could lure you to North Yorkshire."

It galled Jerome to let her think he had come because of her, but since the real reason for his visit must remain secret, he did not correct her.

Her green satin overgown was cut so precariously low at the neck that it scarcely contained her ample breasts. It was not the sort of gown a lady usually wore to her own dinner table.

But then Jerome doubted that Sophia was a lady. No one in London had heard of her until she had married her elderly, socially prominent first husband, Sir John Creswell, who had died less than a year after the union. His widow did not mourn him long. She married Alfred Wingate four months later.

Jerome, curious about her origins, inquired politely, "Are you a native of Yorkshire, Mrs. Wingate?"

"No," she said, her voice suddenly sharp.

"Then where?" he pressed.

She hesitated, as though debating how to answer, then said, "Cornwall."

Jerome smiled at her choice, which was as remote as she could get from Yorkshire. He doubted she was telling the truth. He had an acute ear, and he could discern no trace of a Cornish accent in her speech.

"Where in Cornwall?"

"A—a remote village near Land's End."

"What is its name?"

She did not immediately answer him. Jerome was willing to wager that she was frantically searching her memory for the name of a Cornish village. Finally, she said, "West Curry."

His knowledge of Cornish geography was considerably better than hers. West Curry was not in southwest Cornwall near Land's End, but in the northeast. The truth about Sophia's origins might prove the most interesting thing about her.

Jerome looked around at the half dozen other persons in the room. Two middle-aged couples he did not know were conversing among themselves on the other side of the room.

Alfred Wingate, Sophia's husband, stood by the fireplace, talking to the thin youth with straw-colored hair who had helped pull Ferris from the river. Jerome was shocked at how much Alfred had aged since he had last seen him. His dark hair had turned white, and he seemed to have shrunk into a timid, stooped old man.

The drawing room door opened, and Jerome looked eagerly toward it, hoping to see Lady Rachel. Instead Lord Felix Overend, the Marquess of Caldham's son, swept in. Jerome's mouth tightened in distaste. Felix was both a fop and a fool, and Jerome had no patience with either.

He had thought himself inured to Felix's flamboyant dress, but the coxcomb had outdone himself tonight. His canary yellow satin coat, worn over breeches of the same color, was lavishly embroidered with silver and brilliants. Flemish lace cascaded from his wrists. His white waistcoat and his yellow high-heeled shoes were embroidered with bouquets of yellow roses, pansies, and jonquils.

Felix loved to ornament himself and everything that surrounded him. His horses and carriages must always be the most showy; his dress, the most ostentatious. He delighted in attracting attention and had not the wit to discern the difference between stares of admiration and those of affronted sensibility.

He approached Sophia and Jerome. Even in his high heels, Felix was several inches shorter than the duke. Jerome's nose twitched at the overpowering smell of musk. Felix must have bathed in the damned scent.

Jerome despised musk.

He felt the same way about Felix.

As Caldham's second son, Felix had no expectations from his father, but he had been the favorite of his maternal grandfather who had died when he was six and left him his vast fortune. Jerome doubted that grandpapa would have been so generous had he lived to see his favorite reach foolish manhood.

"Heard you were expected, Westleigh, but I did not credit it." Felix's voice was high pitched and querulous. "Too far north for his grace to come, I told myself." Diamonds winked from the gold buttons on his coat and the rings on his fingers, and from the buckles at the knees of his breeches and on his high-heeled yellow kid shoes.

More than a little revolted by this display, Jerome said dryly, "You are looking quite—er, sparkling tonight."

Sarcasm was lost on Felix. "Thank you, thank you." He proudly held up the arm of his canary yellow coat. "My tailor assures me this shade will be all the rage next season, now that I have taken it up." His eyes darted about the room, and he said to Sophia, "Your niece is not here, ma'am."

She swished her fan coquettishly. "Dear me, Lord Felix, you make me feel quite ancient when you call me ma'am like that. You should know that I am only six years older than my niece."

That would make Sophia twenty-six. Jerome no more believed she was that young than he believed she had been born in Cornwall. He pegged her to be at least thirty.

Felix asked proudly, "Have you heard about my new Sykes?"

Who had not? Felix collected whatever struck his fancy—paintings, porcelains, silver, buttons—and no price was too high if he wanted an object. Lately, he had wanted the watercolors of a second-rate painter, Augustus Sykes. When one had come up for sale a fortnight ago, Felix and Lord Bourn had engaged in spirited bidding for it that had all London talking.

"Anyone who is acquainted with me knows that if I want something, I will have it, and I wanted that Sykes," Felix said. "Bourn was a fool to think he could outbid me."

Everyone else thought Felix the fool, knowing that Bourn, a close friend of the painting's former owner, had been obligingly driving up the price far beyond what it was worth.

Jerome slipped away from Felix and Sophia and went over to her husband. After greeting Alfred, he asked whether there had been any word on his missing nephew.

"None." Alfred's voice sounded old and raspy. "Nothing since the letter we had from the captain of *The Betsy*, the boat that he had booked passage on from France to Dover. It said that Stephen failed to appear at the Calais dock at sailing time. The vessel postponed its departure until the next tide, then could wait for him no longer because the other passengers wanted to be underway."

"When was Arlington last seen?"

"When he left Paris two days before *The Betsy* was to sail. We fear he was waylaid on the road to Calais."

More likely he had been attacked by ruffians who frequented the docks in port towns and his body dumped in the Channel.

The drawing room door opened, and Lady Rachel entered the room, accompanied by a young woman Jerome had not met. He instantly forgot about Rachel's missing brother. Even in that ugly mustard gown, she was still the most beautiful woman he had ever seen. Even more beautiful than the accursed Cleo, and Jerome had never thought to see any woman who could surpass that faithless witch in loveliness.

Lord Felix immediately deserted Sophia and minced toward her niece. Jerome wondered what Rachel's reaction to Felix would be. His prestigious lineage and enormous wealth made him a prize marital catch. Many nubile young ladies would be delighted to wed him.

Rachel clearly was not one of them. The revulsion in her eyes when she saw Felix was unmistakable, and she made no effort to conceal it. Hastily, she tried to evade him by joining the two middle-aged couples to whom Jerome had yet to be introduced.

For some reason, Rachel's reaction to Felix pleased Jerome enormously. Nor could he seem to tear his gaze away from her.

"I did not know young virgins were to your taste, Your Grace," Sophia said waspishly.

Jerome had been so engrossed in watching her niece he had not noticed that Sophia had come up beside him. He could not resist retorting, "I doubt that you know my tastes at all."

"Do not become enamored with her," Sophia

warned. "Although it has not yet been announced, she is betrothed."

A vague pain struck Jerome like a sneak blow from behind. Why should he care? Then his anger swelled as he remembered how passionately Rachel had returned his kiss in his bedchamber even though she was betrothed to another. Another damned faithless female!

Across the room, Lord Felix finally managed to corner Rachel. Had any woman looked at Jerome as she did at Felix, he would have left her instantly, but the fop, clearly oblivious to her distaste, made an exaggerated bow to her.

Jerome asked, "Who is the lucky man to whom Lady Rachel is betrothed?"

"Lord Felix."

Jerome's mouth curled in disgust. So Rachel's loathing for Felix was not strong enough to offset her willingness to enter an advantageous marriage.

Rachel bit her lip in vexation as Felix planted himself in front of her. As he bowed, she noted that his spindly legs were considerably more shapely than they had been earlier that day. He must have supplemented them with leg pads beneath his white silk stockings.

Straightening, he caught her hand in his own, diamond rings sparkling at her from every finger, and brought it to his lips. She found his touch so repulsive that she had to restrain herself from snatching her hand away.

As he released it, he asked in his affected, high-pitched voice, "May I have the happiness of conversing with you, Lady Rachel?"

Much as she would like to say no, Rachel was too well-bred to be rude to an invited guest. Having been subjected on previous occasions to his enthusiasm for musk, she was thankful for the large hoop in her underpetticoat that kept him an arm's length away.

It was the reason she had worn it.

Felix, granted the happiness of conversing with her, could not seem to think of anything to say. They stood in awkward silence, the brightness of his canary-yellow coat making her mustard gown look even more dreary. To break the quiet, she remarked jocularly, "I fear that our colors clash."

He frowned. "Yes, they do."

He looked so distressed by this that she suggested, "Perhaps we should decamp to opposite sides of the room."

His frown deepened. "No need for that. Must tell you, though, that your gown is not at all the thing. You must allow me to guide you in selecting your clothes." His tone betrayed what a signal honor he thought he was conferring upon her. "You will be in the forefront of fashion, just as I am."

As if she would allow anyone who dressed as ridiculously as he did to choose her clothes! She could not resist subtly retaliating with a lie. "But I love this dress."

Felix's horrified expression spurred her to greater fabrications. "It is my very favorite gown. The style is so flattering. And the color is perfect for me, do you not agree?" Actually, Sophia had chosen the color, undoubtedly because she knew how dreadful it looked on Rachel.

"It is my unhappy duty to disabuse you of both notions. You must let my superior wisdom guide you in such matters. You know we often cannot see ourselves as clearly as others can."

Rachel smothered a smile. Felix himself was the perfect example of that truism. She said hopefully, "I fear I have given you a disgust of me."

"You could not do that."

Rachel struggled to hide her disappointment.

She glanced toward the Duke of Westleigh, and the tempo of her heart instantly increased. Aunt Sophia was introducing their other dinner guests, Eleanor

Paxton and her parents, and Squire Archer and his wife, to the duke. As he greeted them, Rachel observed none of the condescension her brother had denounced in his manner.

He looked elegant in his handsome coat of midnight blue. It lacked the showy embroidery and brilliants that Felix's canary-yellow satin sported, but the duke cut by far the most impressive figure in the room. He needed no padding to enhance his legs or anything else.

Rachel's face grew warm with embarrassment as she remembered their confrontation in his bedchamber. Any doubt that she had been wrong to have gone there had been dispelled when Eleanor, returning with her fan, had seen Rachel leave the duke's chamber.

"What were you doing?" her friend had demanded in a shocked voice. "No respectable young lady would ever dream of going to a man's bedchamber."

No wonder the duke had called her brazen.

But Rachel had not known it was improper. No one had thought to tell her. Since her mother had died seven years ago, there had been no one to instruct her on the niceties of proper conduct for a young lady. Her father had spoken of hiring a gentlewoman to do so prior to her London debut, but he had fallen terminally ill before he could execute this plan. Nor had Rachel ever gotten to London. She had remained in Yorkshire to run Wingate Hall.

Felix leaned over her hooped skirt in an attempt to recapture her attention and managed to get his face only a few inches from her own. She was assailed by the overwhelming odor of musk that enveloped him. Rachel could not tolerate the smell. It always made her sneeze.

It did so now, and she could not seem to stop.

"I"—sneeze—"I"—sneeze—"cannot"—sneeze—"musk"—sneeze.

Her eyes were watering, and the guests were turning to stare at her. She slid quickly away from Felix. "Please, you must excuse me."

She started toward Eleanor who had joined her brother Toby, but Westleigh suddenly stepped into her path. Her heart lurched. His face was unreadable, his lips unsmiling. The memory of their kiss kindled a delicious warmth in her, and she felt herself blushing. Her gaze shyly met his, but words eluded her tongue.

He said coldly, "I understand that felicitations are in order."

Rachel looked at him blankly. "For what?"

"Your betrothal to Lord Felix."

"I am not betrothed to him! Aunt Sophia must have told you that. She insists that I must marry him, but I will not! Nothing will induce me to do so."

Suddenly, the duke smiled at her, a devastating smile. Its warmth melted his icy hauteur, deepened the color of his eyes to a rich, cyan blue, and permeated his low, vibrant voice. "You surprise me again, Lady Rachel," he said cryptically.

Excitement curled within her, and she suddenly had difficulty catching her breath.

The door to the drawing room opened with a bang, drawing everyone's attention. Fanny Stoddard appeared in an elaborate gown of white-corded silk brocade with an intricate floral pattern in shades of blue, red, green, and brown.

The duke's eyes narrowed in dislike at the sight of Fanny. Then he deliberately turned his back on her.

Silence settled on the room just as Fanny inquired of the butler, "Where is the Duke of Westleigh?" In the sudden quiet, her voice carried farther than she intended.

"With Lady Rachel," the butler said.

Fanny opened her fan with a snap and swept up to them. Rachel greeted her, but the duke kept his back turned to her.

Undeterred, Fanny trilled, "Your Grace, it pains me

to have to inform you that you have the most shockingly insolent groom that I have ever met. I know once you hear of his conduct you will want to discharge him immediately."

Westleigh turned to face Fanny. He was every inch the duke now, and she did not immediately recognize him in his fine clothes with his hair dry and neatly combed. The look he gave her was cold enough to freeze the Thames. This was not a man to cross, Rachel thought.

He said, "Lady Rachel, please remind Miss Stoddard of the oath she required of me that I never speak to her again. Assure her that the Duke of Westleigh always keeps his word."

Fanny, belatedly recognizing him, gasped in shock. "This is a joke." Her voice rose hysterically. "You are not the duke. How dare you come into the drawing room? You are a groom!"

Aunt Sophia hurried up to them. "Have you taken leave of your senses, Fanny? Of course, he is the duke."

Fanny stared at Westleigh's implacable countenance for a long moment. Then her face crumpled along with her bright dream of becoming a duchess. Tears trickled down her cheeks as she turned and fled the room.

Watching Fanny's departure, Rachel would have felt sorrier for her had she not been bent upon destroying a man's livelihood merely because she felt he had not been deferential enough to her.

Aunt Sophia said, "Your Grace, I cannot conceive what possessed the silly chit. I fear she is a trifle unhinged." She glanced toward the pendulum clock. "One of our guests, Sir Waldo Fletcher, has not yet arrived."

Rachel stifled a groan of dismay at hearing that Fletcher was invited.

"We shall start without him," Sophia decreed. She

looked at the duke, clearly expecting him to take her in to dinner.

Instead, he turned and offered his arm to Rachel. Her heart skipped a beat as he asked in that rich, resonant voice of his, "May I escort you into the dining room, *Lady* Rachel?"

"Your Grace!" Aunt Sophia cried indignantly.

The duke raised a haughty eyebrow. "Yes, *Mrs.* Wingate?"

Rachel suppressed a smile at how subtly he had reminded Sophia that her niece, as the daughter of an earl, took precedence over her.

As Rachel accepted his arm, she could feel the hard muscle concealed beneath his perfectly cut sleeve. A light, spicy scent that she found extraordinarily pleasant clung to him. As he led her into the dining room, a strange warmth bloomed within her.

The duke took the chair beside her that Aunt Sophia had meant for Felix. Rachel bit back a smile of delight and relief when the displaced fop ended up at the opposite end of the table beside Sophia in the place that she had intended for Westleigh.

Sophia, clearly furious at having her seating arrangement so neatly frustrated by the duke, glared at him and her niece.

As the footmen served the turtle soup, Rachel was acutely conscious of Westleigh's presence beside her, of his broad shoulders nearly touching her own, and of the warmth and vitality that emanated from him.

She watched his well-shaped hand, blessedly devoid of ornamentation except for his signet ring, as he toyed with his wine glass. His fingers were long and tapered, and she watched them in fascination as they stroked the stem of the glass, gliding over the crystal. Rachel remembered the pleasure that had coursed through her when those fingers had touched her and his hand had cupped her breast. She felt hot color rise in her cheeks.

The footmen began clearing the soup dishes away

in preparation for serving the fish course. Fanny's seat across from Rachel remained empty. So did Sir Waldo's across from Sophia. He would surely come. As socially ambitious as he was, he would never forgo a chance to dine with the Duke of Westleigh.

Had Rachel or her father still presided over Wingate Hall, Fletcher would not have been invited. The late earl had despised the boastful bore, both for his obsequiousness toward his betters and his meanness toward his workers.

Much of his enormous wealth came from his coal mines where miners labored long hours in wretched, dangerous conditions for barely enough pay to feed their families while Sir Waldo decked himself in costly clothes and trappings.

But Aunt Sophia liked Sir Waldo, which did not surprise Rachel. The two were very much alike in their clutch-fisted treatment of those in their power.

After Rachel's father died, Fletcher had fancied himself a worthy suitor for her hand and had the audacity to forcibly grab her and try to kiss her against her will. She had been so infuriated that she had told him bluntly what she thought of him and of his treatment of his workers.

Her denunciation had been overheard by others, and he had hated her ever since.

Midway through the fish course, a turbot in wine sauce, Sir Waldo finally arrived. Short and rotund, he was dressed almost as ostentatiously as Lord Felix in green satin coat and breeches. He looked to be on the verge of nervous collapse. His moon-shaped face beneath his powdered, pigeon-winged wig was white as falling snow. He was wringing his hands and trembling as though he had been stricken with St. Vitas Dance.

"So sorry I am late," he told the room in general, then his gaze settled on Lord Felix. "My most sincere apologies to you, too, Your Grace," he said fawningly, apparently mistaking the young fop for

Westleigh. "But I could not help it. I was waylaid and robbed by that scourge of the road, Gentleman Jack."

To Rachel's surprise, the bored disinterest with which the duke had been watching the newcomer vanished instantly at the mention of the highwayman.

Her gaze dropped to Fletcher's finger where he usually wore an enormous ring set with an emerald the size of a quail's egg. The finger was bare. He always carried a large bag of gold and silver coin on his person. She suspected that was gone, too.

Good for Gentleman Jack. Rachel silently applauded the daring highwayman. He had an uncanny way of picking as his victims obnoxious souls like Sir Waldo and Lord Creevy who, in her opinion, heartily deserved to be robbed.

What pleased her even more was that the highwayman then gave much of what he took to those who had suffered the worst at his greedy victim's hands. Rachel was certain that Sir Waldo's abused, needy miners would soon be sharing the fruits of Gentleman Jack's escapade this night. From all she had heard, they desperately needed it.

Sophia gestured toward the empty place across from her. "Do sit down, Sir Waldo." She told one of the footmen hovering behind the chairs, "Pour him a glass of wine."

When Fletcher picked up the newly filled glass, his hand was shaking so badly that Rachel feared the wine would slosh over the rim. He put an end to this threat by draining it in two large gulps.

The footman poured more, the baronet drank it down, and the servant filled the glass a third time.

"Took my magnificent ring, he did," Sir Waldo complained. "And my bag of coin. Had a thousand pounds in it, it did."

Knowing how Sir Waldo loved to boast, Rachel

suspected that he had doubled the sum the bag had actually contained.

Sophia exclaimed, "Why can they not catch that scoundrel?"

Sir Waldo took another deep draught of wine before answering angrily. "Because the rabble of the countryside hide and protect him. They love him."

And deservedly so, Rachel thought.

Crops had been poor the past two years, leaving many hungry. They had food to eat now because of the highwayman's generosity. Once they could have counted upon Wingate Hall to assist them during difficult times, but not since Rachel's aunt had seized control of it.

Sophia said loudly, "The sooner they can hang that vicious, evil bandit the better!"

Rachel, who had seen what good Gentleman Jack had done for the area's least fortunate inhabitants, said, "I do not believe that he is either vicious or evil."

Westleigh's head swiveled around, and he studied her with acute interest. No doubt Rachel had scandalized him by defending the outlaw, but she did not care. What Gentleman Jack did might be wrong in the eyes of the law, but if it kept people from starving, she believed it was morally right.

"He is called 'Gentleman' because he always acts like one during his robberies," she pointed out. "The only hurt that he has inflicted upon his victims is to their pride and pockets."

Aunt Sophia cried, "What nonsense you prattle, girl. The man is terrorizing us upstanding citizens."

"Are you not terrorized, Lady Rachel?" Westleigh asked, mockery tingeing his voice.

Was his scorn directed at her for defending Gentleman Jack? Rachel looked at him defiantly. "No, I am not, Your Grace, and I hope that Gentleman Jack is never captured."

Sophia demanded loudly, "Have you taken leave of your senses, girl?"

"No, I have seen the good that Gentleman Jack does." Rachel turned back to the duke. For some reason she could not explain, it was important to her that he understand why she felt as she did. She did not expect that he would, but she had to try. "You see, Gentleman Jack is a modern-day Robin Hood who robs the rich to help the poor. The rabble, as Sir Waldo calls them, love the highwayman because he is the only one *now* who helps them when they are in dire need."

Aunt Sophia glared at Rachel. "I fear, Your Grace, that my niece doesn't know what she is talking about."

"I know precisely what I am talking about! Any one of the so-called rabble will tell you that Gentleman Jack is far more generous than some people sitting at this table." Rachel looked pointedly at Sophia, then at Sir Waldo, who was finishing off his fourth glass of wine.

He gave her a murderous look. His hand holding his glass no longer shook, and his normal florid color had returned to his face. Rachel remembered her father once dismissing him as a man who found his courage in a wine glass.

Fletcher said in a boastful, slightly slurred voice, "I'll tell you, Gentlemen Jack did not escape unscathed. Had a pistol hidden beneath my seat, and I managed to get off a shot at him as he fled. I know I wounded the miserable cur."

His statement brought snickers from Squire Archer, Mr. Paxton, and Toby, who knew as well as Rachel what a terrible shot Sir Waldo was. Rachel was not at all concerned that the braggart had hit Gentleman Jack.

Beside her, the duke, sounding strangely alarmed, demanded, "Are you certain you hit him?"

Sir Waldo gave Westleigh a dismissive glance.

"Of course, I hit him, you young idiot," he said in a tone laced with condenscension, "I am an excellent shot."

Rachel could feel the sudden frost radiating from the duke. He said acidly, "I am Your Grace to you."

Sir Waldo visibly wilted at discovering the guest he had just called a young idiot was the duke he had so desperately wanted to impress and cultivate. He stammered profuse apologies.

Westleigh gave him a look of such icy hauteur and contempt that the baronet's voice faded away in mid-sentence, and he looked as though he wished he himself could do the same. His expression of dismay and chagrin was so comical that Rachel could not entirely bottle up the silent laughter that shook her and a strangled giggle escaped.

The duke whirled and glared at her with a furious hostility that baffled her. His eyes were as stormy as the sky before a rain. In a voice so low that only Rachel could hear it, he said icily, "What do you find so hilarious about a man, even a highwayman, being shot?"

She was aghast at his misinterpretation of her amusement. She whispered so only he could hear, "Sweet heaven, I was laughing because that odious Fletcher desperately wanted to impress the Duke of Westleigh and instead he insulted you. I do not for a moment think he wounded Gentleman Jack. Why the braggart is the worst shot in Yorkshire."

"Are you certain of that?" Westleigh inquired with an odd urgency in his voice.

"Yes, Sir Waldo has been known to miss the broad side of a barn when he aimed at it."

Her reassurance brought a look of intense relief to the duke's face. Even as she gave it, though, an icy finger of doubt suddenly touched her.

What if she were wrong? What if Sir Waldo had managed to shoot Gentleman Jack?

# Chapter 6

**J**erome drew his wool riding coat more tightly around him, glad for its warmth. The weather had changed during the night. A storm had moved through, bringing rain, and now a raw wind was blowing out of the north.

He had awakened early from dreams haunted by a pair of sparkling violet eyes and a dimpled smile that would drive a sane man crazy. To wipe it from his mind, he had taken to the saddle for an early-morning ride.

But even after an exhilarating gallop, Rachel still haunted him. Jerome had intended to ignore her last night. When he had not been able to do so, he had tried to tell himself it was because he wanted to annoy Sophia and escape her company; but he knew that for the canard it was. He wanted to be with Rachel.

He could not help smiling even now as he remembered her passionate response to his kiss in his bedchamber and the startled, innocent wonder her face had betrayed. God, but it was a sweet memory.

The sky was clearing, its blanket of gray clouds giving way to scattered white puffs. Jerome glanced back toward Wingate Hall. A lone female was riding toward it across the moor.

Jerome recognized Lady Rachel, apparently on her way home. He was surprised that she would be out riding so early instead of still abed. With no conscious thought of what he was doing, he turned Lightning in her direction.

As he reached her, she pivoted her face toward him. She was the loveliest thing Jerome had seen in all his twenty-nine years. Desire, sudden and unwelcome, coursed through him.

Although she slowed her mount to a walk as he rode up, she did not seem pleased to see him. Instead she looked rather like a little girl caught doing something naughty. He reined Lightning in alongside her mare, and the two horses moved forward at a sedate walk.

Jerome noted the leather case that she carried. He could think of only one reason why a woman would be carrying a case at this early hour, but surely she could not be returning from an assignation. She was an innocent, was she not?

He could not keep the suspicion from his voice. "You are up very early. Where have you been?"

Rachel's gaze skittered away from his and dropped to her case. "Nowhere," she said, a faint blush rising on her cheeks, accentuating the pale delicacy of her alabaster skin.

"Where is nowhere?" Even he was startled by the belligerence of his tone.

Her gaze still avoided his. "I—I was enjoying a morning ride."

She was a terrible liar. What the hell was she hiding? Had it been a tryst after all? Had a beautiful woman once again duped him into thinking her an innocent?

Jerome was furious. By God, he would learn why she was hiding the truth from him.

Rachel wondered at the sudden flash of anger she saw in the duke's fascinating eyes, as they seemed to change from rich blue to stormy gray in an instant. She hated lying to him, but she dared not tell him that she had gone to check on the condition of a tenant's ill child. She could not chance his informing Sophia that she had been defying her aunt's explicit order.

Furthermore, Rachel liked the duke so much that she did not think she could bear it if he mocked her concern for the people of Wingate Hall as her brother Stephen's male friends had done.

"I am surprised, my lady, that you would go riding without a groom."

There was an innuendo in the duke's voice that Rachel did not understand. Puzzled, she said, "You are more in need of a groom than I, Your Grace, for you do not know the countryside and I know every inch of it. I have been riding it alone for years."

The duke touched the leather case containing her herbal remedies. "What is in that?"

He raised his gaze to hers, and she was nonplussed by the anger and suspicion in his eyes. "N—nothing."

"If that is so, why are you bothering to carry it?"

Rachel could feel the color in her cheeks deepening. For a moment, the only sound was the clopping of their horses' hooves on the road. Then she said nervously, "Foolish of me, is it not?"

Again that puzzling anger flared in his eyes. "Tell me what is in it," he ordered.

Why on earth were the case's contents so important to him? "What it contains is none of your concern," she retorted sharply. "I fear Stephen was right. You are insufferably overbearing."

"Is that what he said about me?" The duke clearly did not care in the slightest what her missing brother thought of him.

That piqued Rachel into saying, "Yes, he did not like you."

"Nor I him."

She stiffened angrily but then reminded herself that the duke was merely being as bluntly honest with her as she had been with him. "Why did you not like Stephen?"

"Your brother cared far more about the cut of his coat than the cut of his fields. I have no patience with heedless, careless aristocrats like him who live only for their own pleasure and ignore the duties that rank and a great estate carry with them."

Rachel's head snapped around, and she stared at the duke. Much as she loved Stephen, she had to admit sadly that the duke had summed him up all too accurately.

Apparently misinterpreting the reason for her surprise, he asked, "Did you not see your brother for what he was?"

"Aye." Rachel swallowed hard. Careless Stephen might be, but he was at heart a good man. She was convinced of that. "I—I wish you could have known my brother when we were children."

She blinked back tears at the memory of the wonderful, charming Stephen of her childhood. A little sister could not have asked for a more protective or better-hearted brother, and Rachel had adored him. "After he went away to school, Stephen changed, and he changed even more when he began living in London. He fell in with the wrong companions who encouraged his irresponsibility."

Papa had particularly blamed Anthony Denton, a sophisticated rake a few years older than Stephen, for leading him astray. That was one of the reasons Rachel had never liked Denton, even though he was always most charming to her.

The duke said in a softer tone, "To give Stephen his due, he was a charming, intelligent man."

"Aye, he *is*."

Rachel looked around at the duke. He was so handsome with that jutting, determined jaw and his blond hair ruffled by the wind that Rachel's pulse accelerated. The odd sensations that had plagued her yesterday returned now stronger than ever.

"Your brother's intelligence and charm were part of my problem with him," he said with a frown.

"Arlington had the potential to be so much more than he was. It was his wasted ability that irritated me the most."

It was what had most irritated Rachel, too. She had not given up hope, though, that in time Stephen would mature and become more responsible. She stared up at a merlin circling in the clearing sky, searching for prey, and confessed. "I love my brother dearly, but I am sorry to say that you are right about him." She dropped her gaze from the merlin to her companion. "I confess I am startled, though, that you do not share his faults. All his men friends were worse than he."

The duke looked at her as though she surprised him. "Unlike them, I appreciate both my great good fortune in having been born rich and titled and the responsibilities it carries with it. I once tried to talk some sense into your brother, but he took great umbrage at my presumption and I think hated me for it."

Rachel wondered whether that was the reason for Stephen's animosity toward him. She studied the man riding beside her with growing appreciation. Never would she have dreamed that she and the "haughty, condescending" duke would think so much alike. He was the kind of man she had longed to meet.

Her heart soared like the merlin above them at this realization, and she suddenly was eager to confide in him. "Papa often tried to instill a sense of duty in Stephen, too, but with no more success. The country bored Stephen. He loved what Papa called 'the frivolous life' in London." Rachel could not disguise the troubled note that crept into her voice. "Papa feared that Stephen took after our grandfather."

"I collect your father did not intend that as a compliment," the duke said dryly.

"No, Papa's father was a wastrel and a rake who cared nothing for his lands or his family. He left Papa to run the estate from the time he was very young. Not that Papa minded, but he never forgave his father for the way he treated my grandmother. He lived openly with his mistresses in London while exiling his wife and children to Wingate Hall."

The duke made a disgusted face. "I cannot conceive how a man could act like that toward his family."

Nor could Rachel. What had angered Papa most was the lodge that her grandfather had built on the estate to house his current convenient on the rare occasions when he came to Yorkshire. That had humiliated Rachel's grandmother—and left her granddaughter with a determination never to marry a man like her grandfather. She gave the duke a worried glance. "Are you a rake?"

He looked amused. "If I were, I would not answer that question honestly. Rakes are notorious for lying to lovely young ladies."

Rachel frowned. "Does that mean you are one?"

His deep, rich laughter sent a shiver of pleasure through her.

"No, I am not, and I am telling you the truth." It was Jerome's brother who was the rake of the family. Not that Jerome had been a monk. He had had a few discreet liaisons, but he was no womanizer. And he had his principles. He never slept with another man's wife. He wanted nothing to do with a woman who would cuckold her husband. Nor had he ever taken an innocent's virtue.

The approving smile his answer brought to Rachel's delectable mouth made Jerome's breath catch. He remembered their kiss, and a hot wave of desire surged through him. He longed to sweep her off her sidesaddle and into his arms. Then his gaze fell again on the case she carried, and his eyes narrowed. "Why are you so secretive about what is in your case?"

"You must vow not to tell anyone, especially Aunt Sophia. Will you promise?"

Rachel's question only added to his puzzlement and curiosity about its contents. When he assured her that he would keep her secret, she said, "It contains my herbal remedies. I have been to check on one of our tenants' children who is sick with the ague."

Jerome could not have been more surprised if she had confessed the case held the crown jewels that she had stolen. His lurid imaginings about her case were so far from the truth that he felt as though he owed her an apology. He knew that he was gaping at her, but he could not help it. It confounded him that a woman as exquisite as Lady Rachel was so willing to help others.

She shifted nervously in her saddle under his silent stare. "You promised you would not tell Aunt Sophia," she reminded him.

"I keep my word, but why do you not want her to know?"

"She has forbidden me to treat the tenants as I used to do."

"Hellsfire, why? She should be grateful that you would do so."

"She says that no lady would lower herself like that. She called me a disgrace to the Wingate name."

"Sophia is the disgrace," Jerome snapped.

Rachel's expression mirrored surprise and intense relief at his reaction. "You mean I have not shocked you?"

Actually, she had, but not in the way she meant. He could scarcely believe that such a beauty would be willing to expose herself to disease to help the ill. His estimation of her rose sharply. "How did you learn about herbal healing?"

"From my mother who was taught it by an old woman in the fen country where she was born. I have all Mama's recipes. The one for reducing fever is particularly effective."

Rachel's remarkable violet eyes mirrored her enthusiasm for her work. Hellsfire, but she was more temptation than Jerome could withstand. It was a good thing he would be leaving Wingate Hall after he saw Morgan. Jerome started as he recalled his scheduled meeting with the highwayman. Rachel had so bewitched him that he had forgotten all about it. He said abruptly, "I am going to ride some more."

As he turned Lightning away from Wingate Hall, she asked, "Would you like company?"

"No!" It came out more emphatically than he had intended. The truth was he did want her company—much too much. "I prefer to ride alone," he lied.

Her bright smile faded, and Jerome knew that his sharp answer had hurt her feelings, but he could hardly take her along to meet the highwayman.

Jerome walked among the thick weeds and tumbled stones of the Wingate ruins as he waited for Morgan to appear. He stifled the impulse to check his pocket watch again, reminding himself that he had done so no more than five minutes earlier. The time then had been twenty-seven past noon.

Gentleman Jack had not wanted this meeting, but he had promised that he would be here an hour and a half ago. As he had pointed out, he had never broken his word to Jerome. So why had he not come?

Jerome forced himself to sit down on a large stone to wait. He was within the crumpled remains of what had once been the walls of a large medieval abbey. Beyond them, behind a pile of fallen stones, Lightning munched placidly on the wild grass.

His ride across the Wingate estate to the ruins had been instructive. He had passed fields that were no longer tended as they should have been and cottages that were falling into disrepair. Their occupants had watched him with sullen faces. A careful landlord himself, Jerome recognized the signs of festering discontent when he saw them. Had it been his land, he would have learned the reasons for it and remedied them.

He could see why Morgan had picked this ruin for their meeting. Located in a remote section of the estate, it was surrounded by woods that screened it from view if someone happened to pass by. He suspected that Gentleman Jack had used this site before for rendezvous.

Jerome's mouth curled ruefully. Morgan was such a paradox. Although he had embraced a dishonorable occupation, he had done so for an honorable reason. Incensed by the mistreatment and exploitation of the poor and downtrodden, Morgan had taken it upon himself to right some of society's legal wrongs in his own unorthodox way.

That was why he picked as his victims rich, stonehearted men like Lord Creevy or Sir Waldo Fletcher who were notorious for their heartless treatment of those within their power. Then the highwayman would distribute his booty among those who had suffered most at his quarry's hands.

Morgan called it justice.

The law called it criminal.

Morgan called it a more equitable distribution of wealth.

The law called it a hanging offense.

And Jerome had no intention of seeing his beloved younger brother, Lord Morgan Parnell, dangling dead at the end of a rope.

He had to persuade Morgan to give up his criminal career.

It would not be easy, though. Being a highwayman did more than assuage his brother's sense of justice. It appeased the danger-loving Morgan's thirst for adventure.

Jerome envied the freedom his brother had to slake that particular thirst. Although the Parnell brothers were thought to be very different, they were actually much alike. Only Jerome—molded by his rigid father's training and the responsibilities of an ancient, honored title and great estates—had ruthlessly stifled the wilder impulses that his brother indulged.

That was why Jerome had enjoyed abandoning his ducal facade for a short time yesterday, wearing old clothes and riding with Ferris. The owner of the posting house, ignorant of his true identity, had not hesitated to talk to him. Had he realized Jerome was the duke, he would have been stilted and distant and kept his observations to himself.

Jerome most envied Morgan for the easy, instant rapport he had with people from all walks of life. Although Jerome wanted to keep some people at a distance, there were others with whom he longed to have frank conversations, but he had not his brother's knack of putting them at ease and getting them to open up to him.

Where the hell was Morgan? Jerome jumped up from the stone and began pacing again. He was growing increasingly alarmed.

He anxiously recalled Sir Waldo Fletcher's claim the previous night that he had shot Morgan. Fletcher's marksmanship had been held in such contempt by Rachel and the others at the table that Jerome's fears had been quieted.

But what if they had been wrong? What if Morgan had been wounded? Perhaps even killed?

Jerome heard a horse galloping behind him. Whirling, he expected to see Gentleman Jack, but it was Ferris riding toward him on Thunder.

Jerome stepped out from the ruins to greet him.

"You have been gone for hours, and I was worried," Ferris explained as he dismounted.

"Morgan has not come yet. Did you learn anything of interest last night?" Jerome had sent Ferris to a popular tavern to see what gossip he could pick up. He was invaluable to Jerome as his eyes and ears among the lower orders.

"The neighborhood is not a happy place since Arlington vanished, and Alfred or, more accurately,

Sophia Wingate took control," Ferris reported. "Everyone is praying that the young earl will reappear soon."

"They must have seen a side of Arlington that was not apparent to me," Jerome said wryly.

"They say the devil himself would be better than Sophia Wingate. Besides they hope Arlington would do what he did before: let Lady Rachel run the estate."

"She ran it?" Jerome's voice echoed his incredulity.

"From all reports she did an excellent job of it."

"I cannot believe that!" A mature woman might be able to manage the estate, but Rachel was far too young and beautiful to handle such responsibility.

Or was she? He remembered how her face glowed as she talked of her herbal healing.

Ferris said quietly, " 'Tis hard to say who is more loved hereabouts—Lady Rachel or Gentleman Jack. The people are deeply concerned for her. They're afraid someone means her harm."

"*What!*" Jerome's tone betrayed his shock.

"Two months ago a shot narrowly missed her as she was walking in the woods. It was blamed on a poacher who mistook her for game yet was never caught, but people have their doubts. For one thing, she was wearing a bright yellow gown at the time. It would have been hard to mistake her for game."

Jerome did not question why he should feel so sick in the pit of his stomach at the thought of Rachel dead. "Have there been any other incidents since then?"

"No, and Lady Rachel herself dismissed it as an accident, but the people are still fearful for her."

"Is there anyone they suspect?"

"One of her rejected suitors."

"Undoubtedly she has many," Jerome said, inexplicably irritated by that thought.

"Dozens, but the most likely suspect is Sir Waldo Fletcher. She never liked him, and when he tried to force his attentions on her, she rebuffed him with a scathing indictment of his character that was overheard by several people. He has never forgiven her for that humiliation, though he royally deserved it."

Jerome remembered the hating look Fletcher had given Rachel the previous night. He had wondered at the time what she had done to inspire such enmity.

Ferris said, "Shortly after that, the shot was fired at her. Fletcher was hunting in the same woods at the time, but he insisted he was nowhere near her and denied knowing anything about it."

Jerome frowned. When he had met Fletcher last night, he had pegged him as a cowardly blowhard—just the type who would skulk about, furtively seeking revenge. But against a defenseless woman, for God's sake! "I heard that Fletcher is a notoriously poor shot."

"Which may be why he missed Lady Rachel."

"I hope to God he also missed Morgan," Jerome said fervently. "Fletcher claims he shot Gentleman Jack last night."

Ferris paled. "Can that be why Morgan is not here?" he asked, putting into words Jerome's own fear. "It is not at all like him to be so late."

No, it was not. Whatever Morgan's other faults, he was always punctual. What if he were lying somewhere, wounded and helpless?

If he were still alive.

A shudder ran through Jerome. His brother could not be dead. They were so close and attuned to each other that he was certain he would have sensed Morgan's loss.

Nevertheless, Jerome's fear for his brother's well-being was escalating. "Ferris, were you by chance able to learn anything about where Gentleman Jack hides out?"

"Not even a hint, but knowing how much Morgan loves his comforts, I wager it is not some abandoned tenant's hovel."

# Chapter 7

When Jerome reached Wingate Hall, the first person he saw was Eleanor Paxton. He felt a pang of disappointment that Rachel was not with her.

As though Eleanor's penetrating gray eyes read his mind, she said in a conspiratorial tone, "Lady Rachel is in the maze."

He meant to tell Eleanor that he did not care in the slightest where Rachel was. It was what he was telling himself.

Instead he found himself asking curtly, "Entertaining a favorite suitor?" Where had that querulous note in his voice come from?

Eleanor laughed. "No, hiding from a most unfavorite one. Lord Felix is terrified of labyrinths and will not set foot in one. The maze is the only place that Rachel can be assured he will not follow her."

Jerome would not follow her there either. He had no intention of going near Lady Rachel.

No intention at all, he told himself firmly.

None whatsoever.

As Rachel sat on a bench deep in the maze with Maxi, her little silver terrier, dozing at her feet, she was thinking about the Duke of Westleigh. The more she learned about the duke, the more he fascinated her. Rachel had dreamed of meeting a man like him, but she had not dreamed that he would also raise such strange, delicious yearnings within her.

He was so different from Stephen's heedless, titled friends. She had once overheard them mocking Papa as a fool for his devotion to his land and his people and for his fidelity to his wife when he could have many women. To his credit, Stephen had defended his father to his friends, who had then mocked him, too.

"Woolgathering, Lady Rachel?"

Her heart leaped at the duke's resonant voice, and she could feel the color rushing to her cheeks as she looked up at him. "I came here because it is so quiet," she said weakly.

The duke's arrival awakened Maxi who, embracing his duty as Rachel's defender, made a protective stand in front of her, barking loudly at the intruder.

Jerome quirked an amused, questioning eyebrow, and looked pointedly down at the little terrier.

"Well, it *was* quiet," Rachel said defensively.

The duke flashed her that wicked grin of his, the one that deepened the color of his amused eyes to a rich blue and set her heart racing. "Very secluded, too. Avoiding Lord Felix again, are we?"

"Is it so obvious?" she blurted in surprise.

"Probably to everyone but him. I doubt that anything could dent his conviction of his own superiority."

Maxi, having failed to frighten his ducal adversary into retreat, attacked his ankles, nipping at his riding boots and growling furiously.

His mistress, remembering how angry the terrier's behavior had made the duke yesterday at the river, feared an explosion. To her surprise, however, he bent down to ruffle Maxi's fluffy, silver topnotch and scratch his ears.

Watching those long tapering fingers skillfully reduce Maxi to quiet, docile happiness, Rachel felt a bit envious of her terrier.

Straightening, the duke asked, "May I join you?"

Rachel could not hide her delight. "Yes, if you wish."

She moved to make room for him on the narrow bench, and he sat down. His thigh brushed against hers, sending a little thrill through her.

Maxi, clearly displeased that he no longer had the duke's attention, attempted to regain it by jumping up and planting his muddy paws on his grace's immaculate buff breeches.

Rachel, cringing at the dirty imprints the terrier left, expected an angry reprimand from the duke. Instead, he compounded the damage by lifting Maxi on his lap and giving the elated animal the ministration he wanted.

Rachel was bemused—and charmed—by this unexpected benign side of the duke. Smiling, she remarked, "You have made a slave for life."

He laughed, then his humor faded, and he said, "I was told that you managed Wingate Hall for a time for your brother."

"Yes, and before that for my father when he was too sick to do so any longer."

The duke looked so incredulous that Rachel said, "You are surprised that my father would have placed his estate in a mere girl's hands. But you see, I was the only one of his children who shared his interest in agriculture and in administering the estate properly."

She proudly remembered how Stephen, when he had not wanted to abandon the excitement of London for the quiet of the country, had asked her to continue to run it after their father's death. "You do a far better job of managing it than I would do," her brother had told her with one of his charming, ingratiating smiles. "I am the first to admit that. Everyone will be happier with you in charge."

Including Rachel. She had loved running the estate, and she had appreciated her brother's confidence in her. Few men would have allowed a female such authority.

She absently watched the duke's long, lean fingers toying with Maxi. "Papa often said he wished that I had been his first-born son, for I would run the estate better than either of my brothers."

"How long were you in charge of it?"

Her gaze met his. "Three years. Papa was ill for a year. After he died, I continued running it for Stephen until he vanished."

"Is that why you did not have a London season— you were too busy here with the estate?" Jerome felt his anger rising on Rachel's behalf. She should have had a London season. It was her due. Her damned irresponsible brother should have insisted upon it instead of pushing his burden onto her shoulders.

"Yes, but I did not mind," she said cheerfully. "I do not think that I should like London."

"Why not?" Jerome was not fond of it either, but he had never before met a beautiful woman who did not yearn for its exciting social life.

"From what I hear, it is endless social calls and parties."

"But that is what women love about it."

"Why? I think it sounds dreadfully boring and useless."

"It is." Jerome was amazed that he and this exquisite creature were in perfect agreement. "That is why I spend as little time in London as I can."

Rachel looked surprised. Then she bestowed on him a dimpled smile so full of admiration that he felt as though he had been crowned the king of the universe.

"I cannot understand why my brother and his friends loved it so."

"Nor I," Jerome said. "Why are you no longer running his estate?"

Rachel's smile vanished. "Stephen left behind instructions in case anything happened to him that

Uncle Alfred was to act as my guardian until I am twenty-five and to run the estate until Stephen's heir, my other brother, could return to England to claim it."

Jerome frowned. "Stephen must have been displeased with your management of the estate to do that."

"But he was not!" Rachel cried in agitation.

"Why else would he not have continued to leave you in charge?"

"But Stephen never once voiced a single complaint to me. Indeed, he always praised me for how well I did and said he did not know what he would do without me."

Jerome's frown deepened. He remembered what Ferris said about Rachel having done an excellent job of running the estate. Why then had her brother taken it away from her? "What reason did Stephen give you for wanting Alfred in charge should something happen to him?"

Rachel's chin trembled. "None! That was what hurt me the most. He never once mentioned to me that he was leaving such instructions. No doubt he never expected anything to happen to him, but he might at least have told me what he intended if it did."

It sounded exactly like the feckless, irresponsible earl not to have said anything, Jerome thought. Still, it was monstrous of him to reward his sister's work on his behalf in such a heartless fashion.

Jerome found himself wanting to comfort her. "Perhaps Stephen acted as he did because he felt it would be too much of a burden to impose on a young sister who should be marrying and beginning her own family."

"But to place Uncle Alfred, of all people, in charge!" Her lovely face grew even more troubled. "Stephen thought Alfred a fool."

So did Jerome. "Is your uncle now proving that assessment correct?"

"It is Aunt Sophia who controls everything. My uncle dares not oppose her in anything, and it is terrible what she is doing. Crops have been poor the past two years, and many people are hungry. Yet she cares for naught except extracting more rent than the tenants can pay."

Jerome had forgotten about Maxi on his lap, and the dog barked to regain his attention. He absently resumed petting the little terrier.

"I was giving them food," Rachel confided, "but Sophia put a stop to that. She even forbade me to give away Wingate Hall's leftovers, although they go to waste otherwise. It is unconscionable of her!"

Rachel looked at Jerome defiantly, her violet eyes bright with indignation. Did she expect him to defend Sophia? As though he would defend the indefensible. What a poor opinion she must hold of him.

His own of her, however, continued to rise. Her kindness and concern for others both pleased and surprised him. Until now, he had never met a beautiful woman who had challenged his bitter assumption, bred of heartbreak and disillusionment, that she was also selfish and devious, manipulative and faithless.

But Rachel had spirit and courage. She did not hesitate to speak up for what she believed was right. She had been so concerned for his "groom" that she had come to his bedchamber to plead on his behalf. Rachel had a caring heart, a very rare thing for a woman of her exquisite beauty.

She was turning out to be vastly different from Jerome's first impression of her. And from every other beautiful woman he had ever known.

Or was she merely more clever? His distrust of lovely women was so profound that he could not help fearing it might all be an ingenious act to bait the trap for him.

Rachel said, "If it were not for Gentleman Jack,

some people would have starved. Thank God, he turned up when he did."

Jerome had been so fascinated by Rachel that he had forgotten for a few minutes his fear for his brother, but now, at her mention of him, his concern returned stronger than ever. He also remembered the attempt on Rachel's life. "I understand that you may be in some danger, that someone fired a shot at you recently."

"Oh that," she said in a dismissive tone. "It was an accident. I am certain of it. There are hungry people in the neighborhood who have been driven to poaching to feed their children. I cannot blame them."

Nor could Jerome, but he did not so easily accept that the shot had been accidental. "How can you be certain that is what it was?"

She smiled serenely. "Who would want to kill me? And why?"

Jerome remembered what Ferris had said about everyone loving Rachel—except Fletcher. "Perhaps it was a rejected suitor like Sir Waldo."

Rachel grimaced. "He is an odious creature to be sure, but I cannot believe that he would try to kill me." Her lips curled in a waggish grin. "But if he is, he is such a dreadful shot that he would never be able to hit me."

Jerome hoped to hell she was right about Fletcher's accuracy. "What if Sir Waldo is a better shot than you think? What if he actually wounded Gentleman Jack last night—do you think the people he has helped would return the kindness? Would they aid him or would they turn him in for a reward?"

"They would help him, I am sure of it." She studied Jerome with a baffled expression. "You sound as though you truly care what happens to Gentleman Jack. I cannot imagine why you would."

He thought of sharing with her his apprehension for his brother, then caught himself. To confide in her about Morgan would be madness. It could cost his brother his life. No female, especially not one as beautiful as she, could be trusted to keep such a dangerous secret.

Lady Rachel had bewitched him into momentarily forgetting that. Damn, but the woman was dangerous. He had been determined not to come into the maze. Yet he had not been able to stay away from her.

And now he would not be able to escape her and Yorkshire today as he had planned. He could not possibly leave until he knew for certain that his brother was all right. If he was not careful, he could lose his heart to the ravishing Lady Rachel. And he knew too well the pain and disillusionment that would bring him.

He abruptly deposited Maxi, who had dozed off on his lap, on the ground and stood up. For the remainder of his stay at Wingate Hall, he must force himself to keep his distance from the enticing Rachel, even if it meant enduring her aunt's company instead.

He despised Sophia but, unlike her niece, she was no temptation at all.

After dinner that evening, a devastated Rachel hurried up the stairs to her bedchamber. She had eagerly looked forward to the duke's company, but instead of taking her into the dining room as he had the previous night, he ignored her and took the seat Sophia had assigned him next to her. When the company gathered in the drawing room after dinner, Rachel seemed to be invisible to him.

She was stunned and hurt by this sudden, inexplicable change in his behavior toward her. Worse, it left her with no protection against Lord Felix's fatuous attentions. Unable to bear the fop another moment, Rachel excused herself after a quarter hour in the drawing room, murmuring that she did not feel well, and fled to her room.

She had been there no more than three minutes when Eleanor appeared, concern for her friend stamped on her face. "Are you sick?"

Rachel smiled wanly. "Only of Lord Felix's company. He attaches himself to me like a leech, and nothing I say discourages him."

"He is so full of his own consequence that he cannot imagine any woman is not ecstatic to have his attention."

Rachel sighed. If only the duke would show her a fraction of the interest that Felix did. No other man had ever excited her as Westleigh did, and he was good and honorable in the bargain. She was surprised and delighted by how similar their thinking was.

He was precisely the kind of man she dreamed of marrying. An odd heat flared within her at the thought. When Eleanor had first suggested that Rachel should try to fix his interest to defeat Lord Felix's suit, she had been appalled, but now she wanted to do so.

Except that Rachel did not have the faintest notion how to go about it. She had never been to London nor exposed to sophisticated society. She asked Eleanor, who had both these advantages, "How do I go about fixing a man's interest?"

Eleanor looked confounded, then burst out laughing. "You are asking *me* how to do that when every eligible man in the shire has fallen in love with *you*."

"But I never tried to make them do so," Rachel protested. "I mean it just happened, and I wish it had not." The thought of being kissed by any of them as the duke had kissed her made her shudder in revulsion. The memory of his kiss, however, triggered a very different kind of trembling in her.

Eleanor grinned. "I collect your quarry is Westleigh. You cannot make a more prestigious marriage. Your Aunt Sophia can have no objection to your marrying him instead of Lord Felix. And Westleigh was most attentive to you last night."

"But tonight he acted as though I did not exist."

"I noticed," Eleanor admitted. "He is infamous in London for just that sort of behavior—dancing attention on a lovely lady one night and ignoring her the next. You have picked a most elusive man. Every beauty in London will tell you that."

"What must I do to win him?"

Eleanor shook her head. "I wish I could help you, but no woman alive has found the answer to that question."

"If Stephen does not return, the duke is my only hope of escaping marriage to Felix. Oh, Eleanor, I am certain that my brother is still alive, but where can he be?"

If only Rachel would hear from Anthony Denton. Stephen's friend had promised her that he would hire an investigator to find out what had happened to her brother and, if the man learned anything, Tony would come instantly to tell her. Every time Rachel heard a horse ride up, she looked out, hoping that it was Tony with word of Stephen.

Eleanor said, "Speaking of your brother, his loving betrothed departed quickly enough today once she realized she had not a prayer of becoming Westleigh's duchess."

"I am glad she is gone." It was rare for Rachel to dislike anyone, but she did Fanny. The girl could think of nothing but pedigrees and parties, and her eagerness to abandon her betrothal to poor Stephen if she could snare the duke had shocked Rachel. Her brother deserved better than that.

A quiet scratching sounded at the door. It was a chambermaid. "Cook asks ye come to the kitchen at once," she whispered to Rachel, glancing nervously up and down the hall to make certain that she was not observed.

Rachel knew what the summons meant. Since

Aunt Sophia's ban on her treating the sick, requests for her assistance were being funneled through Cook, who risked the loss of her position to deliver them.

Rachel slipped down the backstairs. Cook, an ample, gray-haired woman, was waiting for her at the foot of the staircase with a Wingate Hall tenant, Sam Prentice, a burly, bushy-haired man in his early thirties.

There was a frantic look in his steel-gray eyes as he told Rachel, " 'Tis me little Sammy. Me fears him'll not last the night if ye don't help him, m'lady."

"I shall come as soon as I change into riding clothes and get my case. While I am doing that, have Benjy, the stablehand, saddle my mare." Benjy was utterly faithful to Rachel and could be counted on not to tell anyone of her departure.

She turned and ran back upstairs. When she came down again a scant ten minutes later, she had on the nondescript brown riding habit she had worn that morning and was carrying her leather case.

Prentice was waiting near the stable with her mare and his horse. Once they were mounted, he led the way at a sedate walk until they were out of earshot of the house. Then he urged his horse to a gallop and Rachel did the same.

They did not slow until he left the road for an overgrown path so narrow that they could not ride abreast, and Sam went first. It twisted through a beech wood in a remote section of the Wingate estate.

Rachel wondered at the peculiar route they were taking, and she felt a prickling of alarm. No faint-heart was Rachel, though, and she tried to quiet her unease by telling herself that Sam must have picked a shortcut that would get them to his son's bedside more quickly.

They came to a building so well-concealed by the trees surrounding it that they were almost to its door before Rachel saw it. Sam stopped abruptly in front of her and was off his horse in an instant. This was

# Chapter 8

◦◦◦

"**N**ay, m'lady, but I beg ye to help the poor creature inside for ne'er was one o' God's creations more deserving o' help."

Sam Prentice looked at Rachel with such an abject, pleading expression that her alarm faded. He was a good man, and Rachel trusted him.

Puzzled she followed him into the lodge. It was, she belatedly realized, the place that her grandfather had built for his mistresses.

Her father had ordered it boarded up after her grandfather's death years ago. Rachel had thought no one had been inside it since then, but it was clearly being lived in now. But by whom?

It was the first time that she had been inside the lodge, and she looked around curiously. To her left off the entry was a handsomely furnished drawing room and to her right a kitchen with a trestle table in the center.

The rear of the house was devoted to a large bedroom that boasted a big tester bed with ornately carved walnut posts, a sitting area with a comfortable settee and chairs, and a sizable walnut cupboard in one corner.

A stone fireplace along the far wall had a small blaze burning in it. A large kettle of water was suspended over the flames. That pleased Rachel immensely. Her mother, contrary to prevailing opinion, had been a devout believer in cleanliness and had attributed her success in healing as much to her insistence upon it as to the remedies she concocted from her herb garden.

After Mama died and Rachel succeeded to her healing work, she took to instructing all those she helped to put a kettle of water on to heat before they set out to get her so that it would be ready when she came. By now, it was rare for her to arrive without hot water waiting for her, as it was here.

The glow of a triple-branched candelabra on a bedside table illuminated the outline of a form beneath the covers. She hurried to the bed, curious to see her mysterious patient.

He was a man, full grown and startlingly handsome despite a nasty bruise on his temple. His rich, russet-colored hair was damp and curling about his face, which had a disturbing pallor. His eyes were closed, and she could not tell whether he was unconscious or merely asleep.

Rachel noticed a pile of discarded clothing, caked with mud and blood, near the bed. "What happened?" she asked tersely.

" 'Tis his leg m'lady," Sam said.

She flipped the covers off him. He was a big, impressively muscular man, and he wore no clothes but a pair of breeches. The garment's left leg had been cut off, revealing a raw, ugly wound on his thigh.

"Why he's been shot!" she exclaimed.

Memories of Sir Waldo's braggadocio the previous night about hitting Gentleman Jack swirled through Rachel's mind. She remembered assuring the duke that Fletcher could not hit the broad side of a barn, but now she had the proof before her that the duke's puzzling concern for the highwayman had been merited.

"What happened?" Rachel asked Sam. Although she was certain she knew, she wanted to hear what he would tell her. "Who is he?"

"Me cousin from the other side o' York coming t'

see me. Him was walking through the woods when someone musta took him for a deer."

Rachel said sharply, "Do not lie to me, Sam. He is Gentleman Jack."

Sam looked crestfallen. He opened his mouth as though to deny the identification, hesitated for an instant, then said in a defiant tone, "He be as good a man as e'er there lived, m'lady. Please, ye must help him."

"Of course I shall, Sam."

The highwayman moaned, and she touched his forehead. He was burning with fever.

She bent over him to examine his wound. Blood had clotted and dried about it. Worse, dirt had gotten into it, and it had not been properly cleaned. It should have been attended to hours ago. Had it been treated then, it would not have been that serious, but she did not like the look of it now.

Nor did she like the look of him, what with his raging fever and the pallor that indicated he had lost considerable blood.

"It doesn't look good," she told Sam frankly. "You should have come for me last night instead of tonight."

"Me didn't know he'd been shot then," Sam said grimly. "Me and me brother found him this morning in the woods."

"Not until then!" Rachel exclaimed, remembering the storm that had moved through the previous night. She was horrified at how long the highwayman must have lain wounded and helpless on the cold, muddy ground as the rain beat down on him. No wonder he was so sick. It would be a miracle if he were not stricken with an inflammation of the lungs.

"His horse ran away. Tried t' crawl here, he did, but didn't get far afore he passed out. Still out cold when we found him."

Rachel examined the swollen bruise on the highwayman's temple, then checked the rest of his body for other injuries, but found none. The ball might have chipped a bone in his thigh, but nothing had been broken. "Why did you not come for me earlier in the day, Sam?"

"Him was conscious then and wouldn't hear o' it."

"Is there any clean linen?"

"In the cupboard in the corner."

Rachel went to it and found a man's clothing arranged in neat stacks. She pulled out two cravats of finest lawn and several linen handkerchiefs. From their quality, Rachel suspected that Gentleman Jack's nickname was more accurate than people suspected.

As she opened her leather case beside the bed, Gentleman Jack was suddenly racked with shuddering chills. Another bad sign.

Rachel went to the fireplace to ladle hot water into a basin from the kettle and set about cleaning the highwayman's angry, festering wound. Then she made a poultice to draw the inflammation and pus from it.

He moaned frequently as she worked on him but, to her relief, did not regain consciousness. He was much easier to deal with this way.

With Sam's help, she forced her herbal concoctions down the highwayman's throat to fight the inflammation and lower his fever.

When she had done all she could for the moment, she pulled a chair over to the bed and sat down beside him, resigning herself to a long, anxious night.

Sam said, "Me best get ye home now, m'lady."

"No, I cannot leave him yet. He will require careful nursing if he is to make it through the night." Rachel prayed that her absence from Wingate Hall would not be discovered. She would be taking a terrible chance by remaining here. She shuddered at the thought of Sophia's rage. Even worse, if Rachel were found with the highwayman, it would go very badly for her with the authorities. She knew that she should go home rather than chance it, but she could not abandon the wounded man.

Sam did not argue with her but said simply, "Me'll be sleeping in the hall by the door. If ye need anything, m'lady, call."

After Sam withdrew, Rachel studied the highwayman's face in the light from the candelabra. Something about his jutting jaw and the curve of his cheek and lashes reminded her of the Duke of Westleigh.

Sweet heaven, had she become so fascinated by the duke that she was starting to see him in other men, too? But no other man, including this highwayman, had ever generated the odd, fluttery yearning deep within her that the duke did.

If only she could inspire the same reaction in him that he did in her, she thought unhappily, her feelings lacerated by his indifference to her tonight.

Looking around the large, comfortably furnished bedroom, Rachel wondered how long Gentleman Jack had been using the lodge.

Her grandfather had clearly spared no expense in furnishing his love nest. It infuriated her to think of the way her grandfather had humiliated her grandmother, openly keeping his mistresses here.

Rachel wanted a husband like her father who would be faithful to her. She feared, however, that such a man was rarer than she liked to believe. She had seen enough of Stephen's male friends to know that they, married or not, thought it their birthright to bed as many females as they could.

As the hours crept by, Gentleman Jack, tormented by delirium and nightmares bred of fever, tossed about on the bed, moaning and rambling incoherently.

With Sam's help, she poured more of her fever remedy down him. Then, holding his hand, she talked to him in low soothing tones, and that seemed to quiet him a little.

Through the night, she bathed him repeatedly with lavender water and gave him more fever medicine.

Then shortly after six, as Rachel's hope for him was fading, his fever broke. Smothering a cry of joy, Rachel offered up a silent prayer of thanks for his deliverance.

Once again, her fever remedy had worked. She did not know why it did, only that it did. It was a concoction that her mother had learned from the old healer in the fen country, a wizened crone whom many had called a witch. But Mama had not. She had known the woman's real worth.

Gentleman Jack fell into his first restful sleep, and Rachel prayed that the worst was over. To do her best to assure that it was, she gave Sam a supply of her remedies with precise, detailed instructions on how and when to administer them to the highwayman.

Before leaving, she examined the highwayman's wound one final time. Her poultices had done their job in drawing out the poison, and it looked much better than it had the night before.

As she redressed it, Gentleman Jack's eyes, sunken and dull, fluttered opened.

It was a moment before they focused, but when they did, he gaped at her. His face was haggard from fever and pain, his chin covered with a reddish stubble, his russet hair boyishly tousled.

"Good God," he exclaimed weakly, "can it be that I have died and gone to heaven?"

"Why would you think that?" Rachel asked.

"Only an angel could be so beautiful."

She smiled. "Thank you for the compliment, but I must inform you that you are still alive and very much earthbound."

"I should have known." He grinned at her.

"Why is that?" Rachel asked. His condition did not dilute his charm. Yet she felt none of the strange excitement that plagued her in the duke's presence.

"If I were dead, heaven would never allow me in." His voice was deep and cultured with no trace of a Yorkshire accent.

It bolstered Rachel's conviction that Jack was a gentleman in more than nickname.

"M'lady, is he awake?" Sam asked, coming to her side.

"M'lady," the highwayman echoed in alarm. "Who the hell is she, Sam?"

"Lady Rachel."

*"Arlington's sister?"*

"Aye," Sam admitted.

Gentleman Jack muttered a furious expletive under his breath. "And you brought her here! Are you out of your bloody mind? I forbade you to do so. Now, you will hang with me, you damned fool!"

"Me couldn't leave ye t' die after all ye done for us."

"Better to let me die than for both of us to dance upon nothing."

"Neither of you will, as you so charmingly phrase it, dance upon nothing if I can help it," Rachel interjected briskly. "I assure you I did not spend the night trying to save your life so that you might hang. Your secret is safe with me."

Gentleman Jack looked thunderstruck. "You have been here all night?"

"She never left yer side," Sam assured him. "Weren't for her, we'd be puttin' ye t' bed with a shovel."

"Hell and damnation," the highwayman exploded at Rachel, "why did you stay the night here? What if you are discovered? Why did you risk so much for me?"

"Because I am as grateful to you as Sam is for all

your help to people who are in desperate need. I am mortified at how many of them are Wingate Hall tenants. It would not have been thus in my father's day."

"Nor when ye was managing the estate," Sam said loyally.

"Your wound is looking much better," Rachel told Gentleman Jack. "Did Sir Waldo Fletcher shoot you?"

"Aye."

"I own I am most surprised. I had not thought him able to hit an elephant at ten paces."

"Especially not if the elephant were facing him," the highwayman said contemptuously. "You should have seen the coward grovel in terror before me. Then when I rode away from him, he tried to shoot me in the back. He managed only to hit a tree, but the ball ricocheted off of it and, in the most damnable bit of luck, hit me. My horse reared, I fell off and struck my head. Fortunately, Fletcher's coach had already careened away in the dark, or I would likely be in a gaol instead of here."

As Rachel picked up her leather case to leave, he said, "You look exhausted. Will you go straight home to bed?"

"Yes." But Rachel knew that it would be an hour or two before she would unwind enough to go to sleep. She would pass the time writing her brother George yet another letter pleading with him to return from his Army post in Colonial America and take charge of Wingate Hall.

As she turned to leave, Gentleman Jack grabbed her hand and gallantly kissed it. "I have heard much praise of both your beauty and your kindness, Lady Rachel, but none of it has done you justice."

"Why thank you," she said, a little disconcerted by his praise and by the unwanted, flustering thought that she wished it were Westleigh instead of this highwayman who gazed at her with such admiration.

Gentleman Jack tightened his grip on her hand. "Should you ever need assistance, my lady, I swear to you that I will do whatever you ask of me."

# Chapter 9

When Jerome strode into the breakfast parlor, a small, cheerful room beside an herb garden, Alfred and Sophia Wingate and Mr. and Mrs. Paxton were eating at the round table. Jerome was disappointed to discover Rachel was not there. His reaction made no sense since he was determined to avoid her.

His mouth tightened at the memory of her hurt expression when he had ignored her the previous night. She had not been the only one suffering, however. Jerome had underestimated how much he enjoyed her company. It had been a test of his willpower to stay away from her. He was not at all certain he would have succeeded had she not excused herself shortly after dinner and gone up to her bedchamber.

Jerome made his way to the sideboard where an array of breakfast dishes had been laid out. Behind him, Sophia and the Paxtons were gossiping about King George II. He half listened to them as he helped himself to the various dishes.

"Whatever you say about this king, he is better than his father," Mr. Paxton argued.

"Anything would be better than him," Sophia said scornfully. "I remember when the first George arrived from Hanover with his two fat German mistresses. How disappointed everyone was. It was a sad day for the English monarchy."

Jerome's eyes narrowed. Sophia had a remarkable memory indeed, for if she were the age she claimed to be—twenty-six—she would have scarcely been born at the time. He was increasingly interested in discovering the truth about Sophia Wingate's background.

He sat down as far from her as he could. As he ate, his mind was preoccupied with his brother. After Ferris had learned the exact location where Gentleman Jack had robbed Fletcher, he and Jerome had ridden there.

What they had found in the crushed underbrush near the road had chilled Jerome to the marrow. The soggy ground showed silent evidence of a man having crawled a fair distance through it. At that point, they found fresh footprints of two other men who apparently had lifted the fallen man and carried him to the road. The scene left Jerome with little doubt that his brother had indeed been wounded. But how badly, he could not tell.

Jerome and Ferris had scoured the surrounding area, looking for an abandoned structure where Morgan's benefactors might have taken him, but everything in the vicinity was occupied. Someone had to be sheltering him.

*Or they had already buried him.*

But Jerome was certain this was not the case. Ferris had gone back to the tavern last night. Had the popular highwayman been killed, his death would surely have been on every tongue. It was clear everyone thought him alive.

The Paxtons left the breakfast parlor after bidding Jerome farewell. They and their children, Eleanor and Toby, were leaving that morning. Alfred Wingate accompanied them from the room, but his wife remained behind with Jerome. He had no desire to be alone with Sophia, and he decided he would cut short his breakfast.

"Aunt Sophia, has the post been here this morning?"

Jerome rose automatically at the sound of Rachel's voice from the doorway. He was shocked by the sight of her exhausted face with heavy black half moons beneath eyes that had lost their sparkle. She looked as though she must have been very ill during the night.

"No," Sophia answered. "The post is late this morning."

"I have a letter for it when it comes." Rachel handed the missive to her aunt.

Jerome was so concerned for Rachel that he forgot all about ignoring her. "Are you still ill?"

She avoided his gaze. "I did not sleep well."

Her aunt glanced at the addressee on Rachel's letter. "Another missive to George. You inundate him with them."

*Who the hell was George?* Jerome wondered, suddenly and inexplicably furious that Rachel should be writing him—and frequently, too.

Sophia turned to Jerome. "I handle all the incoming and outgoing mail at Wingate Hall. If you have anything you wish to post while you are here, you may give it to me."

"I doubt that I will."

The butler Kerlan appeared to tell Sophia that the post had come. "Is there anything for it?"

"Yes," she said, rising from her chair and following Kerlan from the room with her niece's letter in her hand.

Jerome went over to Rachel. "You look terrible. You would be better served getting your sleep instead of staying up all night writing letters to your admirer."

She looked baffled. "Admirer?"

"George."

"He is my brother."

Jerome's irritation vanished. "Why are you inundating him with letters?"

Her tired eyes met Jerome's frankly. "I want him to come home and remove Wingate Hall from Aunt Sophia's control."

"Where is he now?"

"He is an army captain, stationed in the American colonies. I have written him repeatedly since Stephen's disappearance, telling him what Sophia is doing and begging him to come home and take control of the estate, but he refuses to do so."

Rachel sounded so unhappy that Jerome had to smother an impulse to take her in his arms and comfort her. "What reason does he give you for not returning?"

"He would have to resign his commission, and he will not do that," Rachel explained with a sigh.

"Is he that fond of the military?"

"Unfortunately, yes. Papa was opposed to an army career for him, but George would hear of nothing else. Papa finally gave in."

"Have you told him what Sophia is doing?"

"Repeatedly."

Jerome cursed both brothers for leaving their sister and Wingate Hall in such unhappy circumstances. He had not known George, but he suspected that the younger brother must be as irresponsible as the missing Stephen or he would long since have come home.

When Jerome gave voice to this opinion, however, Rachel protested, "He is not at all like Stephen! The problem is that he is certain, as I am, that Stephen is alive."

"Why do you think that? Because his body has never been found?"

"No, it is just that I have an intense feeling that he is alive. I cannot explain it, but I am convinced that he is."

Jerome was about to rebuke her for clinging to her

futile hope when he realized that he had the same feeling about his own brother.

"George wrote me that he is convinced Stephen will turn up soon, perhaps even before George could reach England and then he would have made the trip and resigned his commission in vain."

Jerome frowned. "Surely, George could get a leave without resigning his commission."

"That is what I thought, too, but he says he cannot." She paused, then exclaimed in agitation, "Since Stephen disappeared, George's letters are so unlike him that he does not even sound like the same person. He seems to have changed so much since he went to the colonies that I am almost as worried about him as I am about Stephen."

The following day, as Rachel changed the dressing on Gentleman Jack's wound, she noted aloud, "It is beginning to heal."

She was alone in the lodge with the highwayman. Sam was outside gathering firewood.

The poultices she had applied had drawn the infection from the wound, and she was encouraged by the way it looked. He was still a little feverish, though, and that worried her.

As she rebandaged his thigh with another fine handkerchief from those she had found in the cupboard, she noticed that it was embroidered with the tiny letters, "MP." Either the highwayman had stolen the handkerchiefs or his name was not Jack. She suspected it was the latter, but she knew she would be wasting her breath to ask him his real name.

After she finished dressing his wound, she went into the kitchen and returned with a bowl of thick soup that Sam's wife had sent.

As he took it, he asked, "Is something troubling you?"

Something was: the Duke of Westleigh's baffling, hurtful behavior toward her. During their conversation yesterday about George, he had seemed so concerned, but after that he had again ignored her.

It was very clear that he was deliberately avoiding her, but she did not understand why. For the first time in her life, she cared about a man and, perversely, he did not reciprocate.

She wished that Gentleman Jack would not study her so closely with his penetrating blue eyes. The gleam of male interest in them was unmistakable. If only the duke would look at her like that, Rachel thought wistfully, rather than this highwayman who held no romantic attraction for her.

"Why have you not married, Lady Rachel?" he asked bluntly. "Surely it has not been for lack of suitors."

"No," she admitted, "but none of them caused my heart to flutter."

"Not a single man has done that?"

Since the duke's arrival at Wingate Hall, this was no longer true. Incorrigibly honest, she answered, "Only one, but he is not a suitor. Indeed, he does not even seem to like me."

"Why ever not?" Gentleman Jack asked.

"I wish I knew." Rachel's brow furrowed as she recalled her first meeting with the duke. "Perhaps it is because when we met, he complained that I looked him over like a stud at auction."

"He complained! I would have been pleased. It must be more than that." The highwayman took a spoonful of soup. "Did you do anything else that made him angry?"

"I invaded his bedchamber."

Gentleman Jack choked on his soup. "That made him *angry*?"

"He called me brazen."

The highwayman frowned. "Then what did he do?"

"He kissed me." She could feel herself glowing at the memory of that thrilling moment.

"I see you liked it," Gentleman Jack said dryly.

"Oh, yes, it was quite wonderful. I never dreamed I could feel the way he made me feel."

He studied her thoughtfully. "Perhaps he had that effect only because you have never been properly kissed before."

Rachel was shocked. "I cannot believe that."

"But how do you know? Shall we do a test that will tell you for certain?"

"There is such a thing? What do I do?"

"Nothing. I merely kiss you properly and—"

"But I do not want you to kiss me!" Rachel protested. Indeed she did not. She never wanted any man but the duke to kiss her.

"It is the only way to know for certain," Gentleman Jack insisted. He set his bowl of soup on the table beside the bed and pulled her down beside him.

She started to protest, but then curiosity got the better of her. What if he was right? What if it was the kiss, and not the man that had affected her.

So she let the highwayman kiss her.

He did seem very accomplished at it, but excitement did not curl within Rachel the way it had when the duke had kissed her. Nor had she any desire to kiss Gentleman Jack back.

When the highwayman's tongue sought entry, she found herself instinctively clamping her mouth shut against it instead of welcoming it as she had the duke's. For a moment they were at an impasse. Then she pushed him away.

With her usual candor, she informed him, "I am certain now—it was the man."

She wondered why he looked so disappointed and chagrined. It had only been a test, after all.

"Who is the blockhead?" he demanded irritably.

She colored crimson. "Oh, I could not tell you that."

He shrugged and reached for his bowl of soup, which he ate in silence while he studied her with unnerving intensity. He had the graceful, tapering hands of a gentleman, she noted, certain that he was one.

When he had finished his soup, he set the bowl aside. "I understand the Duke of Westleigh has condescended to visit Wingate Hall."

Rachel felt herself blush again. Then a worrisome thought struck her, and she blurted, "Sweet heaven, I hope you do not mean to rob him?"

"Why not? Do you not think him as deserving as Lord Creevy or Sir Waldo Fletcher?"

"Oh, no, the duke is not at all like those two."

"Is he not?" Gentleman Jack was watching her intently. "But it is said that he is the coldest and haughtiest of men."

"Yes, that is what my brother Stephen said about him, but the duke is not like that at all," she cried, rushing to his defense. "He is a man who hides his real self from the rest of the world behind his reserve and hauteur."

"So you do not find the duke cold and condescending?"

"No."

"Even though he does not like you?"

She shot him a startled look.

The highwayman said gently, "I guessed."

"I do not understand him," she burst out. "After he kissed me, he acted like he wanted to do so again, but now he avoids me."

To Rachel's astonishment and indignation, a wide grin suddenly embraced the highwayman's face. "I do not see why that should give you so much joy!"

"Because it is an excellent sign, my innocent," Gentleman Jack said gleefully. "No, do not ask me to explain for I cannot. Now you must go or you will be late for dinner."

Rachel had forgotten the time. She gathered up her leather case and headed for the door. As she opened it, he called to her with a devilish gleam in his eye,

"Tell Sam that I must see him. I have an important errand for him."

Ferris handed a folded sheet of paper to Jerome. "A man sneaked into the stable a few minutes ago and gave me this. I knew you would want to see it immediately."

A brief message was scribbled on the outside of the sheet: "Ferris, for J."

Jerome instantly recognized the sprawling, untidy handwriting, and relief flooded through him. Morgan was still alive and well enough to write. Jerome had been growing increasingly frantic about his brother.

Hastily unfolding the sheet, Jerome read aloud the cryptic message it contained: "Could not meet you because I was wounded in the leg. Nothing serious, but will be several days before I can use it. And I must see you. Most urgent. Wait for me at Wingate Hall. I will come as soon as I can. Burn this. M."

Jerome offered up a silent prayer of thanks that his brother had not been badly wounded.

Then he knit his brow in puzzlement as he reread the message. Morgan had been reluctant to meet him earlier, yet now he was saying that it was urgent he do so. Jerome did not think it could be to discuss his wound. Something else must have happened.

"What will you do now?" Ferris asked.

Jerome grimaced. "What can I do except wait here until Morgan comes?"

That meant Jerome would be stuck at Wingate Hall with the irresistible Lady Rachel for God knew how many days.

He stifled a groan. Morgan could not have the smallest inkling of what torment he was inflicting on his older brother.

# Chapter 10

**S**ince receiving Morgan's message two days ago, Jerome had been doing his damnedest to stay away from the tempting Rachel. She was so exquisite that any eligible man she wanted would be delighted to offer for her.

Except Jerome.

No matter how much he wanted her—and it shocked him how much he did—he would never marry such a breathtaking beauty. He was not that great a fool. Although Rachel might be innocent now, once she got to London, every rake there would be in hot pursuit of her. Once she met sophisticated, irresistible libertines like Anthony Denton she would become as wanton as her aunt.

And Jerome would be damned if he would spend his life defending his honor with his wife's lovers.

No, Emily Hextable was the wife for him. And he was, after all, committed to her even though he had not said so to her in words.

He must continue to ignore Rachel until he left Wingate Hall.

But it was one of the hardest things he'd ever done. At dinner, his ears strained to hear what Rachel said at the other end of the table. After dinner, he forced himself to take a seat across the drawing room from her, but he could not keep his eyes off her.

He had to get away from Wingate Hall. As soon as he saw Morgan, he would go home to Royal Elms

and ask Emily for her hand, as he should have done
months ago.

That thought brought an unconscious frown to his
brow. The prospect of Emily as his wife suddenly
seemed as unappetizing as subsisting on gruel when
he might have enjoyed a feast. Yet, he was committed
to her in spirit if not in fact, and the Duke of
Westleigh never backed away from his commitments.

Jerome sought refuge in the rose garden. A high
hedge encircled it, hiding its occupants from the
view of anyone in the house. As he stepped into it,
he was startled to discover Lord Felix, resplendent in
purple satin coat and breeches and an extravagantly
plumed hat of the same color, pacing among the
bushes, practicing a speech. The fop was, he explained to Jerome, rehearsing the offer he intended to
make that very night to Lady Rachel for her hand in
marriage.

Her revulsion for Felix was so obvious that Jerome
was astonished the fool would consider doing so.
Nor did Lord Felix look to Jerome like a man whose
heart, if indeed he had one beneath all that lace and
satin and embroidery, was engaged.

The duke asked bluntly, "Why are you offering for
her?"

Felix looked at him as though he were daft. "Your
Grace has but to look at her. There is no more beautiful woman. I defy you to name one."

Jerome could not.

"I have her aunt and uncle's blessings," Felix confided. "Asking her is a mere formality."

Jerome doubted Rachel would regard it in that
light.

"Want to do it right though," Felix said. "That is
why I wrote out my offer and memorized it. My
tongue tends to mix things up when I am nervous."

"If your offer to her is a mere formality, why
should you be nervous?"

"Can't help but be. Never proposed to a woman

before. Never met one beautiful enough to make me want to. Let me rehearse it for you, and you can tell me what you think."

Jerome steeled himself for a long and flowery declaration.

With a great flourish, Felix swept his plumed hat from his head and, bringing it against his chest, made an extravagant bow, then intoned, "Will you do me the honor of becoming my wife? You—you—" He stumbled and looked hastily down at the sheet in his hand to prompt himself, then continued, "You will make me the happiest of men."

He looked expectantly at Jerome.

"Is that all?"

"Yes, is it not eloquent?"

"Original, too," Jerome said dryly.

A worried frown creased Felix's forehead. "Perhaps I should make it a question: 'Will you make me the happiest of men?' 'Tis the sort of thing a woman remembers all her life. You know what foolish, romantic creatures they are. One wants to say just the right thing."

Felix looked down at his pristine silk stockings, and his frown deepened. "I know I should get down on bent knee to propose, but I cannot tolerate smudging my stockings. Surely Lady Rachel would not expect that of me."

"What if she refuses your offer?"

"Refuse me?" Clearly the possibility had never occurred to Lord Felix. "Ridiculous. Lady Rachel is no fool." His voice rose indignantly. "She will be overjoyed by an offer from me. How can you think she would refuse me? She is very intelligent for a woman."

Jerome forebore telling him that was precisely why he thought she would.

Rachel stared with affronted eyes at Lord Felix when he presented himself to her before dinner. His purple satin coat was extravagantly decorated with gold embroidery and braid, and he reeked of musk. She feared she would soon suffer the overpowering urge to sneeze.

Fortunately, Aunt Sophia came up at that moment and greeted Felix. Rachel slipped away to join her Uncle Alfred, who was talking to the duke and Squire Archer's wife who had been invited to dinner.

Uncle Alfred asked, "Did you hear that Lucinda Quincy was married today?"

Rachel was very fond of Lucinda, a sweet, shy heiress of sixteen who lived with her guardian a league to the west of Wingate Hall, and she exclaimed in surprise, "Married to whom? She was not even betrothed."

"Phillip Rutledge."

Rachel was so shocked that she cried, "Surely not! Lucinda despises Rutledge!" Her voice, raised in distress, drew her aunt's frowning attention and she came over to them.

"Lucinda would never marry him," Rachel protested. "The slimy toad is naught but a ne'er-do-well fortune hunter."

Aunt Sophia said coldly, "Then the silly chit should not have spent the night with him. Once an unwed girl has done so, she must marry the man or she is ruined."

"I cannot believe that Lucinda would have gone anywhere with Rutledge," Rachel cried. "Why, she cannot abide him."

"She did not go with him willingly," Mrs. Archer said. "He abducted her by force and took her to an inn so that she would have to marry him. He knew full well that she would never wed him otherwise."

"The circumstances are immaterial," Sophia said coldly. "All that matters is she spent the night with him and so had to marry him."

Incensed at the injustice of that, Rachel cried, "Lucinda is the one who was wronged! Why should she have had to marry Rutledge when he forced her to go with him against her will? Why was *she* punished for what *he* did to her? It is grossly unfair!"

Beside her, the duke said softly, "Yes, it is, but unfortunately, Lady Rachel, life is rarely fair."

Her heart skipped at his closeness. "Has life been unfair to you, Your Grace?" she inquired archly.

His mouth quirked wryly. "No, it has been more than fair to me, but few are as lucky as I am."

Rachel was impressed by his acceptance of his place in life as the stroke of good fortune it was, not merely his entitlement. But before she could pursue the conversation, he turned away. The more she discovered about the duke, the more enamored of him she became. If only he could reciprocate her affection.

As the Wingates and their guests went into the drawing room after dinner, the duke slipped away.

"Rachel, dear girl," Aunt Sophia said, "Lord Felix is a great admirer of harpsichord music."

Rachel had learned to be on her guard whenever Sophia called her dear girl in that sugary tone.

"Pray take him into the music room and demonstrate our harpsichord's fine tone to him."

Rachel would rather walk over hot coals barefoot than be alone with Felix, but she knew that it was hopeless to protest against something that Sophia wanted.

As Rachel led Felix from the drawing room, she was perplexed to see him put on his wide-brimmed, extravagantly plumed hat, and she explained, "We do not go outside, my lord; the music room is but a few steps down the hall."

It was his turn to look perplexed. "Did not think we did."

Maxi trotted into the music room behind them. Rachel went directly to the harpsichord. She was lifting the cover over the keyboard when behind her, Lord Felix cried, "Lady Rachel."

Alarmed by his strangled tone, she let the cover drop and whirled around. "What is it?"

He had come up very close to her, trapping her against the harpsichord bench. He reeked of musk, and it had its inevitable effect on her. Fighting to keep from sneezing, she leaned backward as far as she could over the instrument.

Lord Felix opened and closed his mouth several times with no sound issuing from it. He had the unnerved look of a man who was frantically trying to remember what he intended to say.

Finally, it seemed to come to him. With an extravagant flourish, he swept his plumed chapeau from his head. Unfortunately, he was standing so close to her that its plume struck her in the face. She stepped back, trying to avoid it, and tripped over the bench behind her. Unable to recover her balance, she sat down hard upon it.

Lord Felix, oblivious to what he had done, made her a low bow, straightened, and announced in dramatic, if somewhat rattled, accents, "I will do you the honor of making you my wife."

Rachel stared up at him in kindling outrage.

"I will make you the happiest of women," he concluded, then muttered under his breath, "There, by God, I have said it all."

Revolted, Rachel choked back her yearning to tell him that, to the contrary, he would make her the most miserable of women. She realized with a sinking heart that the battle lines would be drawn now between her and Sophia. But no matter what her aunt did, Rachel would not marry this insufferable fop. She said with icy politeness. "It is an honor, my lord, that I refuse."

He was paying her no heed. Just as the insufferable prig would pay her and her wishes no heed once they were married! Instead he leaned down so that his face was no more than three inches from hers. "We shall be married in London, in St. Paul's Cathedral."

The smell of musk was too much for Rachel's affronted senses. The sneeze she had been trying to suppress exploded.

Insensible to her discomfort, he continued, "Ours will be the wedding of the decade, perhaps of the century."

Rachel could not stop sneezing.

Maxi, displaying more perspicacity than Lord Felix, recognized he was annoying his mistress. The terrier launched himself with a fierce growl at Lord Felix, attacking his ankle.

His lordship, more surprised than hurt by the terrier's nipping, reeled back from Rachel. With his unencumbered foot, he aimed a brutal kick at the fluffy little silver dog. Maxi yelped in pain as he was propelled across the room by the force of the impact.

Felix yelled, "I'll kill you, you miserable beast."

Maxi scuttled out of the room, whimpering.

Rachel, appalled and sickened by Felix's vicious, unwarranted treatment of her dog, jumped up from the bench, torn between wanting to follow Maxi to ascertain that he was all right and wanting to rip the enormous plume from Felix's hat and throttle him with it.

She opted to go after her terrier, but Felix grabbed her arms in a surprisingly strong grip.

"How could you kick a poor little dog like that?" she demanded in revulsion and disgust.

"Poor little dog!" he squeaked. "That vicious beast attacked me."

"You are the beast!" Rachel jerked free of his grasp. In a voice seething with anger and loathing, she said, "I would never marry you. *Never*. Nothing on earth will ever force me to marry you, Lord Felix. I trust I make myself clear."

She brushed past him and ran into the hall. Maxi had vanished. Listening, she heard quiet whimpering and a deep, soothing human voice coming from a small anteroom across from the music room.

Rushing into it, she stopped abruptly at the sight of Maxi in the duke's arms.

"What's the matter, little fella?" he inquired. His voice, as soft as velvet, sent a tremor of pleasure through Rachel. His long, lean hand stroked the injured dog comfortingly.

The terrier whimpered again, and Jerome continued to soothe him with gentle murmurs and skillful fingers.

"Is Maxi all right?" Rachel asked.

"What happened to him?"

"Lord Felix kicked him across the room."

The duke looked appalled. "Bastard! Why?" He sat down and, holding the dog on his lap, began to examine him gently with his hands.

"Maxi was trying to protect me from Felix's unwanted attentions."

The duke touched a spot over the terrier's ribs. Maxi yelped in pain.

"Sorry, little fella," he said as his hands concentrated on that area. "I have to do this."

Rachel watched his graceful fingers gently probe Maxi. How different he was from Lord Felix. Behind his ducal hauteur was a kind, gentle man, and he did not shirk his responsibilities. He believed, as she did, that his inheritance brought with it duty as well as privilege. He was not spoiled and weak like Felix or feckless like her brother Stephen.

And he was the most exciting man she had ever met. No other man had ever had the effect on her that he did, turning her to pudding.

He finished his careful examination of Maxi and looked up at Rachel. "He appears to be suffering nothing more than bruised ribs."

"Thank God," she said, gathering her terrier up in her arms.

"Am I to understand that Lord Felix has just made you a most flattering offer?"

"Flattering? Flattering!" Rachel's cheeks reddened with anger. "Do you know what he said to me?"

Amusement gleamed in the duke's cyan eyes. "He asked you to do him the honor of becoming his wife."

"He asked me nothing! He *told* me, 'I will do you the honor of making you my wife.' It is not funny!" she cried indignantly. "How can you laugh?"

"I am persuaded his tongue got a little twisted."

"It was what he thought in his heart," Rachel cried, unmollified. "The insufferable coxcomb."

"Only think," the duke said gravely, although his lips were twitching, "you may have broken his heart with your rejection."

"His pride perhaps, but not his heart. I do not flatter myself that Felix has the smallest affection for me. I know better than that. There is no room in his heart for anyone but himself. I am merely another ornament to adorn his consequence."

Jerome regarded her quizzically. "You do not think he entertains a great passion for you?"

"His only great passion is for collecting things," Rachel said with asperity. "I am another pretty object for him to acquire like his watercolors and his sculptures and his porcelain vases. I would merely be one more of his possessions."

The sudden admiration for her in the duke's eyes was unmistakable. And something else was there, something deep and warm that made her blood race.

He bent toward her slowly, almost as though he were being drawn to her by a power beyond his will to resist. He was going to kiss her. Maxi was still in her arms, and she wished she had had the foresight to put him down. Jerome's mouth descended purposefully toward hers. She yearned for his lips on hers. Her heart was thudding like a wild thing.

In a moment of shattering insight, Rachel realized that she had fallen in love with him.

She remembered once asking her mother how she would know if she met a man with whom she could find the kind of deep and satisfying love that her parents had. Mama had said that she would know when it happened. Rachel had been skeptical, but now she saw that Mama had been right.

And the duke was that man.

When his lips were a scant inch from hers, he froze. To Rachel's startled dismay, his brilliant blue eyes turned hard and gray. He stepped hastily back. Mumbling something about getting back to the drawing room, he left her.

Sadly, Rachel watched his retreat. Foolish man. Could he not see that they belonged together?

No, he could not! Mama had warned her that oft times even the most astute of men could be quite stupid when it came to recognizing what would make them happy, and they had to be nudged down the right path. Mama confessed that she had to do that even with Papa, wise as he was.

Except Rachel did not have the foggiest notion of how she was to do that with the duke.

Eleanor's warning echoed in her memory: *You have picked a most elusive quarry. Every beauty in London will tell you that.*

If only Mama were here to advise her. Rachel cursed herself for not having had the foresight to ask Mama what she had done to persuade Papa to wed her.

Rachel had to find a way to get the duke to marry her. Not only was he her one hope of escaping Felix, but Jerome was her destiny. She was not going to let it pass her by, no matter what she had to do.

# Chapter 11

〜〜ↄↄ〜〜

U nable to sleep, his thoughts haunted by a pair of brilliant violet eyes, Jerome slipped down the stairs of the darkened house, intent on finding a book to read in the library.

He thought of what Rachel had said about Felix regarding her as another pretty object for his collection. She had the right of it, Jerome thought admiringly. It surprised him how wise beyond her years she was in judging people. Those violet eyes saw so much.

He smiled at the memory of how lovely she had looked as she had sputtered out her indignation over Felix's botched offer.

He had been unable to resist her beguiling mouth. As he had leaned forward to kiss her, breathing deeply of her scent of lavender and roses, he had been struck by the thought that no woman since Cleo had had such an effect on him.

*Cleo*. He had frozen at the memory of that perfidious bitch.

It had brought him to his senses. Much as Jerome wanted Lady Rachel, he would not make her his wife. Bedazzled as he was, he had not taken entire leave of his sanity.

So the only way he could have her was as his mistress. And that was out of the question. Not even a duke could make the innocent daughter of an earl his convenient without bringing down the wrath of society upon him. Once she was married, though, the strictures would no longer apply, and she would be fair game.

He should hope that she married Lord Felix, but the thought filled him with disgust.

Given Felix's character, Jerome feared that Rachel's rebuff of him would only make him more determined to have her. The spoiled fop had never in his life been denied anything he wanted. If he was refused something, he merely upped the price he would pay for it until he got it.

Jerome moved silently down the hall, dimly lit by flickering candles in wall sconces.

As he passed a slightly opened door, he heard Lord Felix's querulous voice complaining. "She refused me. *Me!*" His tone turned accusatory. "You told me that I should have her. You will not get a penny of the sum I promised you until she is my wife."

Jerome stopped dead in his tracks, so shocked by this disclosure that any scruples he might have about eavesdropping evaporated. He moved as close as he could to the crack in the door without being seen from within.

"I must have her," Felix said, sounding so like a whining child that Jerome grit his teeth. "I have my heart set upon her. She is by far the most beautiful woman I have ever seen. No other woman will do for me. Lord Felix Overend does not settle for second best."

"You will not have to." It was Sophia Wingate speaking. "If you want her badly enough, you shall have her."

"She said nothing on earth could force her to marry me."

"I can." Sophia uttered those two words with such chilling certainty that Jerome felt the hair on the back of his neck rise.

"However," Sophia continued, her voice hardening, "after you have made such a mull of it, it will not be easy for me to persuade her. She is furious that you kicked her dog."

"Ugly beast," Felix complained. "I hate dogs. I tell you she will not have him or any other after we are married. I forbid it."

"Well, don't tell her that until after you have exchanged your vows!" Sophia warned. "You are causing me a great deal of trouble that I did not bargain on when I agreed to our arrangement. I shall require additional compensation for it."

"How much more?"

"Twice the amount we agreed upon, the entire sum to be paid on your wedding day. You are still getting a bargain, my lord."

Felix, whom Jerome knew was used to paying outrageous prices for whatever he desired, did not quibble. "You will have it."

Revolted, Jerome thought of telling Alfred Wingate about his wife's agreement to sell his niece to Felix, but he would be wasting his breath. Jerome had seen enough of Alfred since he had been at Wingate Hall to know that sorry excuse for a man would not dare oppose his wife in anything.

Silently Jerome went back up the stairs to his bedchamber. With a disgusted curl of his lip and a furious glint in his eyes, he sat down at the writing table there to pen a letter.

The next morning, Jerome strode down to the stables and handed his sealed, franked letter to Ferris. "Take this into the village, and post it at once."

His groom glanced down at the letter directed to Captain George Wingate with the British Army in the American colony of New York. He gave Jerome an inquiring look.

"Sophia Wingate handles all the mail that goes in and out of Wingate Hall. I have no desire to explain to her why I am writing her nephew."

Nor would George be pleased by the message

when he received it. Jerome had outlined in blunt language what Sophia was doing to Wingate Hall and to Rachel. He had added a scathing indictment of George's dilatoriness and irresponsibility, then demanded that he return home to take control of Wingate Hall before Sophia destroyed it and his sister.

After Ferris rode off, Jerome strode back toward the house. His letter should bring the heedless Wingate back to England posthaste.

But it would take anywhere from one to three months for it to reach America and a like length of time for George to sail back to England. Jerome hoped that Rachel would be able to stave Felix off for that long. If she could not, what, if anything, could Jerome do to help her? He was sickened by the thought of her being forced to marry that disgusting little fop.

Late that afternoon, Jerome stood at the window of his bedchamber, looking out at a sky that was growing increasingly ominous. A storm was brewing. He glanced down at the maze beneath his window, and a bright splash of yellow against the green drew his attention.

Lady Rachel was crouched down beside one of the tall boxwood hedges that formed the interior of the labyrinth. What the devil could she be doing?

Jerome's curiosity got the best of him. He hurried downstairs and out to the maze. When he came up behind her, she was still crouched beside the hedge.

"What have you there?"

Rachel started at the sound of his voice and turned her head toward him, her violet eyes wide and her lovely mouth half-open. She looked so irresistibly kissable that he was hard-pressed not to take her into his arms and do just that.

"You frightened me," she complained. "I was

afraid you might be Sophia. I do not want her to see these."

He looked down and saw that she was playing with two tiny calico kittens.

"I hid them here because Sophia would order them killed if she knew about them. She considers cats and dogs a nuisance." Rachel stroked one of the little balls of fur gently. "Their mama has disappeared."

Jerome noticed the saucer of milk beneath the hedge. "And you have been feeding them."

"Yes," she admitted.

Smiling, he knelt down beside her and picked up one of the little puffs of fur, holding it in one hand as he caressed it with the other. It mewled, then curled up in his hand, contented with his stroking.

Jerome glanced up at Rachel. Her extravagantly thick lashes, black and curling, shadowed her violet eyes and, as she watched him with the kitten, a delighted smile tugged at her delectable mouth, revealing her dimples.

God, but she took his breath away.

Rachel asked, "Are they not the sweetest little things?"

"Yes," Jerome agreed. *Almost as sweet as you.* He remembered her passionate response to his kiss and the startled, innocent wonder her face had betrayed.

Rachel dipped her index finger into the bowl of milk and held it out to the kitten still on the ground. It began licking the tip of Rachel's finger.

It made Jerome think of other parts of Rachel that he would like to be licking, and his body hardened with desire.

He wanted her, ached for her.

He could not resist her.

Jerome's defenses against her had been under assault for days. Now they crumbled all together. He could no longer fight his overwhelming attraction to her.

No longer wanted to.

Rachel was the woman he yearned for, not Emily Hextable. Shocked by the strength of this feeling, he tried to remind himself that although he had never formally offered for Emily, it was expected, especially by her, that he would.

Hastily, he laid the kitten on the ground and got to his feet before he succumbed to his longing to kiss Rachel's lovely mouth.

Startled by his sudden movement, Rachel started to rise, too. He automatically gave her his hand to help her up. As she stood, she took a step forward to balance herself, tripped on her hem, and stumbled. He caught her in his arms.

The press of her soft, curvaceous body against him was more provocation than his own could withstand. So was that lovely, smiling mouth only inches from his own.

She smelled of lavender and roses, and she felt so good in his arms that he could not force himself to release her. The urge to taste her lips again was so strong that it swept away on its tide both his good sense and years of iron, self-imposed discipline.

He bent his head and kissed her, caressing her face with his fingertips as tenderly as he caressed her lips with his mouth. It was a long, slow kiss as he skillfully coaxed from her the same passionate response that she had given him the first time they kissed.

With a low moan that sent fire coursing through his blood, she clung hard to him as she unconsciously parted her lips for him and returned his kiss.

His tongue began a quick, tantalizing dance, and she moaned again. His fingers buried themselves in the luxurious silk of her hair. His mouth grew more insistent, and her own answered in kind. Hot and hungry.

His passion ignited, and it was all he could do to keep from lying her back down and making love to her. If he did not stop now, he soon would not be able to.

He forced himself to pull away from her. It was one of the most difficult things he had ever done.

She stared at him, her eyes dazed with passion, her cherry lips still slightly parted. "You ... you make me feel so strange," she murmured.

He turned away from her to hide the effect her innocent confession had on him.

Jerome had tried to tell himself that Emily, to whom he felt committed, was the best wife he could hope to have, one who would always be faithful to him. But he realized with searing pain that he would never want her the way that he wanted Rachel.

He no longer trusted himself to be alone with her in this far-too-private spot. "Come," he said gruffly, "we must get back."

As they strode along the path that led to the house, a tall, strikingly handsome man came toward them. Jerome recognized Anthony Denton with a rush of dislike and dismay. What was the bastard doing here?

Whenever Denton looked at a beautiful woman, his bedroom eyes were full of tantalizing promise. His multitude of conquests among the fair sex had long ago won him the nickname, the prince of rakes. It was said he could charm even the primmest and most virtuous of ladies into his bed.

Jerome's face hardened into a bitter scowl. Certainly Denton had no difficulty coaxing Cleo into it.

Rachel had not yet noticed Denton, but at that moment he called to her.

Jerome had never seen such a look of jubilation and happiness as crossed Rachel's face when she recognized Denton. She ran down the path toward the newcomer, crying elatedly, "Tony, Tony!"

For a moment Jerome was incredulous. It was as though he were reliving again that awful moment of a decade ago.

The man was the same, the woman was different. But Rachel was even more beautiful than Cleo. At least she was not in bed with Denton as Cleo had been. But, damn it, if Rachel's ecstatic greeting to him was any indication, she would be within a few hours.

The pain in Jerome's heart was almost unbearable and so was his mortification. He had been fooled into thinking that Rachel was different. But now he knew the truth. She was like every other damned, faithless beauty, and she could not resist Denton's polished, lying tongue.

Thank God, Jerome had discovered it in time.

He did not trust himself to greet Denton civilly. To avoid smashing his fist into the reprobate's handsome face, Jerome turned away and headed for the stables.

As Rachel ran toward Denton, she had only one thought in her mind. Her brother Stephen. Tony, his dear friend, had promised her that he would try to find her brother and that he would come to tell her the moment he had any word that the missing earl might still be alive.

Certain that was why he was here now, she took Tony's outstretched hands in her own. "Where is Stephen?"

For an instant, Tony looked confused. "I have no idea, my lovely. Why would you think I do?"

Rachel, her bright hopes dashed, said brokenly, "I thought that was why you came. You promised me you would try to find him and would tell me the moment you had any word."

For the briefest of instants, Tony looked discomforted, then he said hastily, "Ah yes, I did. Unfortunately, I have been able to learn nothing more about him."

Because he had not tried, Rachel thought. How like him to have promised her to hire someone to search for Stephen and then not given it another thought.

She had seen enough of Denton that she should have known better than to believe anything he said. Empty promises fell from Tony's lips like raindrops in a spring shower. And he had been one of Stephen's friends that she had overheard ridiculing her father for his fidelity to his wife when he could have had many women.

She asked curtly, "Why are you here then?"

He gave her a charming smile. "I was passing through the neighborhood. Your brother always insisted that I stop to see him when I was in the north."

"But you know he is missing." Rachel could not imagine why Denton would want to stop when Stephen was not here.

Tony said casually, "I hear Wingate Hall has another visitor, the Duke of Westleigh."

"Yes." Rachel had momentarily forgotten him and everything else in her burst of happiness at the thought that Stephen had been found. She looked around for the duke, but he had vanished. She frowned, wondering where he had gone.

"Why is Westleigh here?" Denton asked. "No, let me guess. Aunt Sophia invited him. Is she having success with him?"

Rachel looked at him blankly. "What do you mean?"

He laughed. "What a delightful innocent you are. Is it too much to hope that you would dislike Westleigh as much as Stephen does?"

"What a peculiar thing to say." The way Denton was looking at her, as though she were some tempting dessert, made Rachel uncomfortable. "Why would you hope that?"

"You are asking me a question, instead of answering mine," Tony pointed out.

"The duke is very different from what Stephen said." Rachel did not like the way Tony's suddenly narrowed eyes were studying her so assessingly. "I must get back to the house."

Tony protested, "No, don't leave."

But Rachel was already hastening up the path away from him.

In the drawing room after dinner, Jerome was cynically amused by the stratagems of various members of the company. Sophia tried to pair off Felix and Rachel but was circumvented by her niece. Both Tony and Felix vied for Rachel's attention, but she seemed to want only Jerome's.

Perhaps he had misjudged Rachel's feelings for Denton since she seemed to be ignoring him tonight. Jerome was entertained by the furious, jealous looks Denton was casting in his direction. At last, the rake was getting a tiny taste of the misery he had caused other men.

The butler Kerlan came up, his face grave, "Lady Rachel, may I speak to you for a moment."

She allowed him to lead her away from Jerome. The moment she was gone from his side, Denton strode up, his dark eyes full of malice and dislike. "I see, Westleigh, that we are once again after the same fair prize."

Jerome could not resist retorting, "And this one clearly favors me." He ignored the flash of anger in Denton's eyes and continued smoothly, "However, Sophia Wingate no doubt will be delighted to entertain you."

Denton looked offended. "As though I would let her. Bloody hell, even I have my standards."

Jerome raised a skeptical eyebrow. "Do you indeed? What a surprise."

"Yes I do. What is the challenge, I ask you, of bedding a female who will lay anything in breeches? The bitch tried so damned hard to bed me, and I rebuffed her. Since then, she has done everything in her power to keep me away from her niece."

Denton always brought out the worst in Jerome, and he could not help observing sarcastically, "That must not be difficult since Lady Rachel clearly does not care for your company."

The jibe obviously infuriated Denton but, when he spoke, his voice was controlled. "You delude yourself, Westleigh. What she is doing tonight is all show."

"Show? To what end?"

"Rachel wants you as her husband; she wants me as her lover." Denton's mouth twisted in a malicious smile. "I assure you, Westleigh, you will be no more successful against me this time than you were the last. Rachel will marry you to become a duchess, but she shall be mine for as long as I want her."

Denton turned on his heel and stalked away before Jerome could smash his fist into the scoundrel's mocking face.

Tony went up to Rachel as she turned away from Kerlan. He led her to a quiet corner where they talked for a few minutes, nourishing the doubts that Denton had planted in Jerome's mind.

Then Rachel came over to Jerome to tell him good night.

"Retiring rather early, are you not?" Jerome asked suspiciously.

"I am tired."

"Before you leave, my dear, tell me one thing: Have you ever lost your heart to a man?"

His question caught her by surprise. Her eyes widened, and color flooded her face.

Her response betrayed that the answer was yes.

Jerome demanded brusquely, "Who is he?"

Rachel, usually so forthright, dropped her gaze and her color deepened. She stammered, "I shall not answer such an impertinent question."

"I see." Jerome was convinced that had he been the recipient of her love, she would not have passed up this opportunity to signal her interest in him. His mouth hardened. Denton was right. "Good night, Lady Rachel." He turned and walked away from her.

Rachel had been gone from the drawing room no more than two minutes when Lord Denton also begged to be excused.

"So early?" Jerome inquired.

"The company pales once Lady Rachel is gone."

That was quite true. Jerome, too, was anxious to escape, and he managed to do so only a minute after Denton.

Upstairs in his bedchamber, Jerome strode over to the windows. Seething gray clouds covered the sky, and in the distance lightning flashed, followed a minute later by the low rumble of thunder. The storm appeared to be moving toward Wingate Hall. It was not a night to be out.

That was why he was startled to see a figure come out of the side door and hurry down the path toward the stable. Jerome would have known that it was Anthony Denton even if he had not glanced back toward the house, revealing his face.

Where the hell was he going?

Jerome's mind was a seething cauldron of emotions and suspicions.

No more than two minutes later, his worst fears were confirmed when a second figure slipped out the door. This one, too, was distinctive. It was Lady Rachel, wrapped in a heavy cloak. He watched her disappear down the hill.

Jerome unconsciously gripped the heavy brocade draperies that framed the windows at the realization that she was sneaking out to meet Denton.

A few minutes later, a sheet of lightning illuminated in the distance two figures on horseback, one using a sidesaddle.

Jerome turned away from the window in disgust. Once again, his bitter distrust of beautiful women had been justified. It was said that no woman could resist Denton. Cleo had not been able to. Why had he thought Rachel would be any different?

Her flattering attention to Jerome tonight had been exactly what Tony had said, a charade designed to win an offer of marriage from Jerome. Like Cleo, Rachel wanted to be his duchess and Tony's lover.

Jerome felt as though a broadsword had been plunged into his heart and then brutally rotated.

# Chapter 12

**R**achel rose from Gentleman Jack's bedside, satisfied that he was in no danger.

Alarmed after the highwayman's chest had become congested and his fever had risen, Sam Prentice had come for her. But in the three hours since she had ridden with Sam to the lodge, Gentleman Jack's fever had dropped again, thanks to her remedy. The poultice that she had applied to his chest had loosened the congestion so that he was now coughing it up.

She had also checked his wound. It was clean and still healing nicely.

"Before I go, I will make you a brew to help you sleep," she said, going to her leather case for the ingredients.

As Rachel made the herb drink, she hoped her return to Wingate Hall would be easier than her leaving it had been. After Kerlan had come into the drawing room to tell her that Cook must see her, Rachel had the devil's own time getting away from Tony Denton.

Insisting that he had something of utmost importance to tell her, he dragged her off to a corner where he warned her against the Duke of Westleigh, particularly of his elusiveness and his wicked reputation for breaking the hearts of nubile young ladies who made the mistake of falling in love with him. Denton had cautioned her that not even betrothal meant anything to the duke, citing as proof his jilting of the incomparable Cleopatra Macklin.

How could Rachel hope to succeed with Jerome when so many others had failed? Small wonder then, when he had demanded to know whom she loved, she had been too distressed and embarrassed to confess to him that he was the one.

When she had finally escaped the house with her leather case hidden beneath the folds of her voluminous brown cloak, Sam told her that she narrowly missed Denton who had slipped down to the stables only a minute or two ahead of her. Rachel knew that Tony must be going to the comely maid at the White Swan Inn whom he visited whenever he came to Wingate Hall. Tony, she thought scornfully, was no better than her grandfather.

As Rachel carried the tisane in to Gentleman Jack, a flash of lightning illuminated the bedroom, accompanied by a crash of thunder so loud that she jumped and nearly spilled the drink.

"That bolt must have struck very nearby," Gentleman Jack observed.

It was followed by a second, then a third, fourth, and fifth, all attended by the roar of thunder so violent that the cottage shook. Rain beat down in angry torrents on the roof.

Gentleman Jack said, "You cannot go home in this storm, Lady Rachel. Even if the rain stops, you must stay until it is light. The woods will be black as pitch with downed trees and other obstacles in your path that you will not be able to see in the dark."

He was right, but Rachel hesitated.

Gentleman Jack said, "I swear to you that you will take no harm of me this night or any other."

"Oh, I do not fear you, only what would happen should it be discovered that we spent the night together." She was thinking of poor Lucinda Quincy's unhappy fate.

That teasing gleam that reminded her of Jerome

danced in Gentleman Jack's eyes. "Then I would have to marry you."

"But I do not want to marry you!"

"What a pity," he said ruefully. "I rather think I should like marrying you. So you still prefer the Duke of Westleigh."

"Yes," she admitted.

"Lucky man!"

Jerome watched from his bedroom window as the first gray light of an overcast dawn crept over the land. Between the violent storm during the night and his rage at Rachel's wanton perfidy, he had no sleep, and he was exhausted.

A movement on the path that led past the maze to the stable caught his eye. It was Rachel in a brown cloak, sneaking back to Wingate Hall. Fury, as violent as any of the lightning bolts that had shattered the night's quiet, ripped through Jerome.

The damned little witch was as wanton as every other beauty he had ever known. If he had needed proof of that, she had just given it to him, skulking up the path, her beautiful ebony hair tumbling tangled and uncombed about her. She looked as though she had arisen from Anthony Denton's bed no more than a few moments before.

The thought of Denton making love to her made Jerome grind his teeth together in rage. Once again, the bastard had taken the woman Jerome wanted.

As he watched, Rachel slipped in the side door, never suspecting that he was watching her. He cursed her viciously. Then he cursed himself for even though he knew what she was, what she had done, even knew that she had slept with Denton, Jerome still wanted Rachel.

Wanted her more than he had ever wanted Cleo.

*Damn it to hell*, Rachel had bewitched him. He had to get away from her and Wingate Hall. He would go straight home to Royal Elms and offer for Emily Hextable.

Except that would require him to leave Yorkshire without accomplishing what he had come for: convincing his brother to give up his career as a highwayman. Jerome could not leave without doing that. But neither would he stay at Wingate Hall.

He would have to tell the Wingates that he was leaving Yorkshire, but he would go only as far as the White Swan where he would stay until he could talk to Morgan.

With that plan in mind, he lay down on his bed.

When Jerome awoke, it was, to his shock, nearly three in the afternoon. "Why did you not awaken me?" he demanded of his valet.

"Because Your Grace once informed me that the day I dared to do so would be the day my employment was terminated."

Jerome gave Peters an abashed grin. "Yes, I recall that but, hellsfire, I have slept most of the day away."

Too much of it, in fact, to announce now that he intended to leave Yorkshire that day. Although it would not take him long to reach the White Swan, he wanted everyone at Wingate Hall to think he was going to Royal Elms. No one would depart on such a long journey so late in the day. He would have to postpone his departure until tomorrow.

After he had bathed, shaved, and dressed, he went in search of Sophia to tell her that he would be leaving in the morning.

Kerlan thought that she was in the morning room but, when Jerome went there, he found Lady Rachel, looking particularly lovely in a pink silk gown, which emphasized the pale loveliness of her flawless complexion.

He thought that he had steeled his heart against her but when she saw him, her smile, punctuated with those charming dimples, was so brilliant that he felt his resolve melting.

And that infuriated him. Why, the damned wanton had spent the night in another man's bed, and now she was smiling at him as though he were the love of her life.

He asked coolly, "Where is Denton?"

Her beautiful eyes widened in surprise. "I have no idea." She sounded as though she did not care either. Had she found her night of lovemaking disappointing?

"Your Grace, Kerlan said you were looking for me." Sophia swept into the room.

"Yes, I wanted to tell you I am leaving in the morning."

Jerome's announcement seemed to have the same effect on both aunt and niece. They looked shocked and dismayed. Both exclaimed simultaneously, "Why?"

"A pressing matter at Royal Elms requires my return."

Sophia batted her eyes seductively at him and cooed, "What could be that pressing, Your Grace?"

Some devil within him prompted Jerome to reply, "The final details of my betrothal to Miss Emily Hextable." He wanted to see Rachel's reaction, but it was Sophia who blurted in accents found in London's slums rather than its fashionable drawing rooms, "Who 'n 'ell is 'er?

Jerome was so nonplussed that he could only stare at Sophia, certain that she had just betrayed her real origins—and how low they were.

Recovering himself, he glanced toward Rachel. She looked so pale and shaken that Jerome marveled she could have cared *that* much about becoming a duchess.

She said in a frayed voice. "You have my felicitations, Your Grace."

Then she ran from the room.

* * *

Rachel, frantic with shock and despair, galloped recklessly toward the lodge where Gentleman Jack was hiding.

As she rode, she wondered how Jerome could kiss her so tenderly one day, then announce the next that he was offering for another female. And men thought women were fickle!

Rachel plunged into the woods surrounding Gentleman Jack's hideaway, oblivious to the twigs and brush that caught at her hair and clothes as she rode between the trees.

She could not let Jerome leave. She loved him too much. She might be naive, but she sensed that what they had together was very special and not to be lightly tossed aside.

If he was not wise enough to see that, she was, and she could not allow him to ride out of her life. If he did, not only would she lose the man she loved, but she would be forced to marry Felix, and she would rather be dead than do that. She had to get Jerome to marry her.

And she had conceived a wild plan to force him to do so.

It was a brazen stratagem. She would be the first to admit it. But, with Gentleman Jack's help, it would work. She intended to collect on the highwayman's promise to help her.

She halted her mare in front of his lodge and ran inside. The highwayman was sitting up in bed reading.

When he saw her face, he shut his book with a snap. "Hell and damnation, what is it?"

For an instant her courage failed her. What if he laughed at her plan? Or reneged on his earlier promise and refused to help her? Without him, her cause was hopeless.

She forced herself to speak. "You . . . you swore to

me that you would help me if I needed it. I hope you meant that, because I need it now desperately."

"Certainly I meant it." He smiled at Rachel. "You have only to tell me what it is. What do you wish me to do for you?"

"Help me abduct the Duke of Westleigh."

# Chapter 13

**T**he highwayman stared with slack-jawed incredulity at his distraught visitor. Surely, Rachel had not just asked him to help abduct his own brother!

"I fear I misheard you. I thought you said you wanted to abduct the Duke of Westleigh?"

"Yes, I do."

"Hell and damnation, why?"

Her guileless eyes met his without faltering. "Because I want him to marry me."

"You and a thousand other women," Morgan muttered under his breath, thinking of all the females who had vied in vain to be Jerome's duchess. "How will abducting the duke induce him to marry you"—he paused, then scowled—"unless I am also expected to torture him into doing so."

And knowing his stubborn brother, even that would not work.

Lady Rachel looked horrified. "Oh, no, I could not bear to have him hurt! I only want to spend the night with him."

"Lucky him. But that will not induce him to marry you."

"Do you not see, he will have no choice if I abduct him? That is what Phillip Rutledge did to poor Lucinda Quincy. She despised him. But after he made her spend the night with him, she was forced to marry him even though he was the last man on earth she wanted to wed. So you see, if I abduct the duke, he will have to marry me."

Instead of pointing out the fallacy in her reasoning, Morgan asked, "Why do you want to marry him—because he is a duke and rich besides?"

"Sweet heaven, no!" she exclaimed, clearly shocked that he could think that. "I do not care in the least about his title or money."

"Then why?"

"I love him. I think that we are meant for each other."

Morgan thought so, too, but abducting Jerome was not the way to convince his brother of that.

"What makes you think that Jer—the duke must be forced to marry you? In time, perhaps, he might make you an offer."

"Yesterday I thought that he would. I mean the way he kissed me . . . " Her eyes grew dreamy.

Jerome was a damned fool. If this divine creature had wanted Morgan, he would have been on bent knee immediately.

"But today he acted as though he hated me, and he is leaving Yorkshire tomorrow."

Morgan knew how determined Jerome was to talk him into abandoning his career as a highwayman. The fact that he would quit Yorkshire before doing so told his brother that Rachel was proving more temptation than Jerome could resist. Morgan could understand that. A man would have to be blind, deaf, and a eunuch not to want Rachel. She was the most exquisite creature he had ever beheld.

He asked, "What reason does the duke give for leaving?"

"He is going home to announce his betrothal to Emily Hextable."

*"Emily Hextable!"*

Rachel's eyes widened in surprise. "Do you know her?"

"Unfortunately, yes." And Morgan would be

damned if he would have that humorless, Friday-faced bitch as his sister-in-law. He had long ago dubbed her Saint Emily for her sanctimonious, self-righteousness. It boggled Morgan how Jerome could consider marrying her when he could have a gem like Lady Rachel.

Yet Morgan knew why Jerome would pick Emily over Rachel. He would assume that because of Rachel's great beauty, she must be another selfish, ambitious wanton like Cleopatra Macklin. Damn that woman for what she had done to his brother!

Jerome wanted a woman of unimpeachable propriety and virtue, who would never succumb to the passions of illicit affairs.

Nor was Emily likely to succumb to a husband's passion either, Morgan thought grimly. Jerome deserved better than that.

Morgan knew that his brother, who shared his own concern for the poor and unfortunate, wanted a wife who felt as they did and thought he had found her in Emily. She would be the first to assure him that he had for she talked endlessly about all the good works she did.

But, in reality, she parceled out her charity in the smallest dabs possible. Lady Rachel did far more good than Emily, and she did it out of compassion. Emily, smugly confident of her own moral superiority, preached at great length to the recipients of her dubious generosity and expected them to be grateful for even the smallest dole. She had no idea how despised she was by the recipients.

Nor did Jerome, who was isolated by his title and his responsibilities. He had not his brother's—or Lady Rachel's—ability to be at home with all manner of people.

Jerome needed a woman who could break down his icy reserve and teach him to enjoy life. Yes, Lady Rachel was just the lively, fun-loving, yet kind and generous wife that his self-controlled brother needed.

Morgan thought grimly of what Emily's reaction would have been had she been asked to aid a highwayman as Rachel had. She would have summoned the sheriff and had him hanged.

Furthermore, Emily would make Jerome miserable. If he could not see that, Morgan could. And he was not going to let that happen. He loved his brother too much. Jerome needed Rachel more than he realized.

Morgan knew his stubborn brother too well to think for an instant that merely abducting him would get him to marry Rachel. But if it were done just right, Jerome might be brought around. Morgan had an idea of how to accomplish that. It would be an audacious gamble, and he was not at all certain it would succeed, but it was Rachel's only hope.

And Jerome's.

"Very well, I will help you," Morgan said, "but only on the condition that you promise to do exactly as I tell you."

Rachel gave him a radiant smile. "I promise."

"Then here is what you must do."

# Chapter 14

**P**eters was busily packing for the early-morning departure from Wingate Hall. Jerome escaped the bustle in his bedchamber, taking with him a copy of one of his favorite books, *My Philosophy* by the Earl of Ashcott, and sought refuge in the quiet of Wingate Hall's library.

He had scarcely settled in a comfortable chair there and opened his book when Rachel came in.

"Kerlan told me I would find you here."

Jerome looked up, and his breath caught at the sight of her. She had on the same riding habit that she had been wearing when he first saw her—the violet that matched her eyes and displayed her full bosom and tiny waist to perfection. He felt his own body tighten. She was the most beautiful thing he had ever seen. Even knowing what she was, he still wanted her. Damn her!

She shut the door behind her and came toward him, holding out a folded sheet of paper to him. "I was asked to deliver this to you."

He closed his book, set it down on the table beside the chair, and rose, taking the paper from her. He saw that his name had been written on it in Morgan's hand. His head snapped up. "Where did you get this?"

"From the man who wrote it."

"Do you know who he is?" Jerome asked tersely,

135

hoping against hope that Morgan had not been such a fool as to tell Rachel his real identity.

"Aye."

"And who is that?"

"Read it and find out."

He unfolded the paper and quickly read the note in his brother's unmistakable handwriting.

> *Dear Jerome:*
>
> *Must see you immediately. Most urgent. Lady Rachel will bring you to me. It is important that you not tell Ferris or anyone else where you are going.*
>
>             *M.*

Jerome looked at her with narrowed, suspicious eyes. "Tell me who gave you this."

She blinked in surprise. "Is it not signed?"

"By an initial. What name did he give you?"

"Gentleman Jack."

"How did you come upon him?"

"I was called to treat his wound."

Alarm hoarsened Jerome's voice. "How bad was it?"

She was clearly startled by his anxiety. "Not bad. He was wounded in the thigh. It did no permanent damage, and it is healing well."

"Why does Gentleman Jack want me to come to him?"

"You must ask him that." She gave him an enigmatic smile. "I told him you were leaving on the morrow, and he said he must see you before you go."

It seemed to Jerome that they had been traveling in circles for a bloody hour. First, they had ridden south, crossing the River Wyn at the bridge where Jerome had rescued Ferris, then through the birch woods on the other side.

Halfway to the White Swan Inn, they had turned

west for a half mile, then north again, doubling back across the river at a narrow bridge farther downstream.

When Jerome demanded to know where Rachel thought she was going, she told him that she was following Gentleman Jack's instructions to take a circuitous route to his hideaway.

She had refused to answer Jerome's other questions, saying Gentleman Jack would do so after they reached their destination.

They entered another woods, this one densely studded with oak, sycamore, and English elm. Jerome, riding Lightning, followed Rachel's mare down a narrow trail, scarcely wide enough for a single horse.

They emerged into a clearing, and he saw in front of him a substantial lodge of gray slate.

They dismounted and went to the door. Rachel walked in without knocking. Jerome followed her, eager to see his brother. He stepped inside, calling loudly for Gentleman Jack.

There was no answer. A quick glance at the handsomely furnished drawing room to the left and the kitchen to the right told him both rooms were empty. He went down the narrow hall to a door at the end and found himself in a large bedroom.

Neither Morgan nor anyone else was there.

"Hellsfire, where is he?" Jerome demanded. He noticed a note on the bedside table, one of its corners tucked beneath a bottle of brandy. A lone glass had been placed beside the bottle. The note was addressed to him.

Jerome snatched it up and scanned his brother's familiar handwriting.

*Dear Jerome:*
*If you arrive before I return, make yourself at home. A little matter arose that I must deal with. I*

*will be back as quickly as I can. Help yourself to my*
*very excellent French brandy while you wait.*

*M.*

Jerome sank down on the bed and slammed his fist
down so hard on the table's surface that the brandy
bottle danced unsteadily on it. Damn it, now he must
wait still longer for his meeting with his brother.
Even worse, that waiting must be alone in Rachel's
company in this isolated lodge.

She had followed him into the bedroom, and he
looked at her enchanting face above her equally enchanting figure and felt his body harden. His frown
turned to a scowl.

"What is it?" Rachel faltered.

He handed the note to her. "Read it for yourself."

She did, then looked up, her eyes alight with curiosity. "What does M. stand for?"

So Morgan had not divulged his real name to her.
Thank God for that. "It stands for Monsieur." Seeing
her incredulous look, he improvised, "I believe Gentleman Jack's father was French."

Jerome suppressed a smile at the thought of how
his—and Morgan's—father, who had been so exceedingly proud of his unsullied English lineage, must be
turning over in his grave at that lie.

"Perhaps Monsieur will not be long," Rachel said
consolingly. She smiled at Jerome, that dazzling, dimpled smile that sent another surge of desire through
him.

He swallowed hard and reached for the brandy
bottle. Hoping to hell that Morgan showed up very
soon, Jerome pulled the cork and poured a generous
amount of liquor into the glass.

When he asked Rachel if she would like some, she
made a face. "Nay, not that. Perhaps I shall make
myself a dish of tea in the kitchen."

He sipped the liquor and rolled it about in his

mouth before swallowing it. It was, as Morgan had promised, a very fine French brandy. His brother liked only the best.

Jerome followed Rachel into the kitchen. She removed her jacket, revealing the matching violet lawn habit-shirt that she wore beneath it. He watched her tantalizing body as she stretched to reach a teapot on the top shelf of the cupboard. Another bolt of desire coursed through him. He took a gulp of brandy. It was excellent except that it had a faint, odd aftertaste.

Rachel went to the fireplace where a kettle of water was boiling over the glowing red embers. She was standing sideways to Jerome as she bent over to ladle water into the teapot. Her generous breasts thrust against the fine lawn of her habit-shirt. He remembered what it had been like to hold that sweet weight in his hand.

Hastily, he took another, larger gulp of brandy.

She moved around the kitchen as gracefully as a swan gliding on a lake. Hellsfire, how much provocation was a man supposed to bear? Jerome prayed that Morgan would return soon. Very, very soon.

He looked about him curiously. This was no tenant's or woodcutter's home. It was too large and well-furnished for that.

Jerome yawned and took another swallow of brandy. He could hardly keep his eyes open. If Morgan did not show up soon, his brother was going to fall asleep.

"You look exhausted." Rachel gestured toward the bedroom. "You could take a nap on the bed while we wait."

It was a most appealing suggestion. And it would have the added advantage of keeping him in another room, away from Rachel.

He went into the big bedchamber, stripped off his riding coat, cravat and boots, sank down on the bed, and promptly fell asleep.

* * *

Jerome awoke slowly, his eyes so heavy he did not want to open them, his mind strangely lethargic and unwilling to accept consciousness. He forced his eyelids apart. Darkness had settled, and a candelabra burned beside his bed.

For a moment, he was at a loss to place his surroundings. He shook his head, trying to clear it of cobwebs. What was wrong with him?

Somewhere in the distance, he heard the low rumble of thunder. Slowly, it came to him where he was. Hellsfire, he must have slept for hours. Was Morgan here, waiting for him to awake?

Jerome tried to sit up and found his arms and legs could not obey the command of his brain. Puzzled, he attempted to bring his hands down from their awkward position stretched above his head. He felt the sting of rope biting into his wrists, preventing him from moving them. Jerome started to bend his knees and more rope scraped cruelly at his ankles.

That brought him to full wakefulness. By twisting and lifting his head, he confirmed his worst fear. His hands and his feet were bound to the bedposts.

Bloody hell, he was a prisoner!

But whose, and to what purpose?

He had come here at Morgan's bidding, but his brother would not have done this to him. Of that, he was certain.

And where was Rachel? Dear God, had she been seized, too, and ... He felt sick at the thought of what might have happened to her. It was enough to make him want to commit murder. He would find a way to free himself, and then he would kill whoever was responsible for this. Yes, by God, he would.

A shadow moved quietly, gracefully forward into the circle of light cast by the candelabra beside the bed.

It was Rachel, as beautiful as ever, but clearly nervous and frightened. He ran a quick eye over her.

Her raven hair was still neatly arranged. So were her clothes. She had not the terrified, disheveled look of a woman who had been forced against her will. He drew in a long breath of relief.

She bent over him, touching his cheek. Unwanted desire for her snaked through him.

"At last, you have awakened." Her warm honey voice caressed him with her concern. "I was becoming worried about you."

"What time is it?" he whispered.

"Nearly midnight."

Thunder rumbled again, still low, but not quite so far away this time.

"Who else is here?"

"No one," Rachel said. "We are alone."

"Then why the hell are you standing there?" he exploded. "Untie me. We have no time to lose."

Her lovely, expressive face tightened into unhappy lines. "I fear I cannot."

"Why not?"

She gulped. "Be—because I have abducted you."

For a moment Jerome could only stare at her, too dumbfounded to speak. She met his gaze timorously, an uncertain smile on her beautiful lips.

He yelped, "You have *what?* Why would you do that?"

A rosy blush rose in her cheeks. "I want to marry you."

His heart gave the most inexplicable little leap of joy, then his sanity returned. Surely, she must be hoaxing him, but her grave violet eyes told him she was not. He could not believe this was happening to him.

"What a unique way you have of proposing," Jerome snapped. "But you are mad to think I will accept your offer."

Rachel met his glare with a guileless gaze. "You will have no choice. Once we have spent the night together, you will be forced to do so just as poor

Lucinda Quincy was forced to wed that awful Phillip Rutledge after he abducted her."

"You are truly mad," Jerome said with strong conviction. "Now, damn it, untie me at once!"

"I am sorry, but I dare not do so."

Since his father's death when he was eighteen, Jerome had been the duke, always very much in control of every situation. Now suddenly he had none at all. Instead, he was lying here, the helpless prisoner of a beautiful, unscrupulous female who apparently would stop at nothing to achieve her ends.

Jerome experienced a flash of rage so brilliant and intense that it seemed to blind him for a second. Never, in his entire life, had he been as livid as he was now.

Suddenly the full significance of his situation struck him. They had been gone several hours. When both Rachel and he had been missing from dinner, a search would have been launched for them. They might be found at any moment.

He cringed at the thought of being discovered in this ignominious position, tied to a bed, after being abducted and taken prisoner, not by a gang of outlaws who had overpowered him, but by one demure young girl.

And he, damned fool that he was, had followed her blithely into her trap, like a lamb to slaughter.

What if they found him like this—trussed up on this bed like a damned chicken? A wave of the most intense mortification Jerome had ever experienced washed over him. He would be the laughing stock of England! He would never live it down.

It was humiliating beyond bearing that he, the twelfth duke of Westleigh, the scion of a long, distinguished line of brave men, had been reduced to this shameful, ludicrous state.

All the famous pride of the Parnells, generations of it, rose up in full fury. He would never forgive her! He would rather kill her than marry her!

Thunder boomed very close now, but Jerome scarcely noticed it in his rage. In that moment, he hated Rachel more than he had ever hated anyone. The damned devious witch! He had known better than to trust her, but fool that he was, he had let her worm her way through his guard.

But she was not just another scheming, faithless beauty. No, indeed! She was the *most* perfidious, devious, diabolical female that he had ever had the misfortune to meet!

Why, she made Cleo Macklin look like a damned saint in comparison.

In his shame, fury, and frustration, Jerome fought to escape his hemp shackles.

His frantic thrashing availed him nothing, however, for the ropes were tied far too tight. He succeeded only in abrading his wrists and ankles until they bled.

Rachel grabbed his wrists, trying to arrest his wild flailing. "Please, stop," she pleaded. She sounded on the edge of tears. "You are hurting yourself dreadfully."

It was nothing compared to the hurt she had inflicted on his pride. "Why am I so unfortunate as to be singled out for the dubious honor of being your husband?"

She flinched at his sarcasm. "I loathe Lord Felix and I cannot bear to marry him." Her eyes pleaded with him for understanding. "You are my only hope of escaping him."

"Then, my dear, you have no hope at all."

She looked as though he had taken a whip to her.

"Why not marry Felix? Most women would happily do so. He is very rich."

"As if I cared for that!" she cried scornfully. "Can you not understand? I do not want to be another ornament that he has collected. Even if he were not repulsive to me with his ridiculous ways, and his diamonds, and his musk, how do you think a man who would kick a little dog would treat his wife?"

Rachel had a point. Furious as he was at her, Jerome could not help feeling for her plight. "Then marry Tony Denton," he suggested.

"Aunt Sophia would never accept him as my husband in place of Lord Felix. Tony is not nearly rich enough."

"But were he, you would prefer him as your husband."

"No, I think Tony would make as bad a husband as Lord Felix. Although he can be pleasant and charming, he is not at all what I want in a husband. He is a rake who cares for naught but his own pleasures."

Her accurate assessment of Denton's character caught Jerome by surprise. For a moment, he was pleased that she saw the reprobate for what he was. Then Jerome remembered that, despite this, she had still slept with Tony. Like Cleo Macklin, Rachel was delighted to have Denton as her lover, but she preferred a rich duke, a faithful fool, for her husband.

It was fortunate Jerome's hands were tied or he might have strangled her. He closed his eyes to block out the sight of her and considered how he could best get her to untie him.

When he opened his eyes again, Rachel smiled shyly at him and moved a little away from the bed. She began removing the pins that anchored her hair atop her head.

He watched in fascination as her long, thick tresses tumbled down about her shoulders in rich, silken profusion. Jerome, stifling a groan, tried not to think of what it would be like to bury his hands and his face in that shining ebony cascade.

Rachel's fingers toyed with the top button of her violet habit-shirt. He wondered why she looked so uncertain. She was clearly wavering over something.

Finally, he saw her jaw tighten in grim determination, and she unbuttoned the top button. As her hand moved down to undo the second one, he noticed that it was trembling.

By the time she unfastened the third button, Jerome's mouth was dry. The cleavage of her beautiful breasts, firm and full, was revealed in the gap, and he felt his body's hot response.

"Damn you," he growled, "did you strip like this for Denton?"

Her fingers fell away from the buttons and her confused gaze met his. "What?"

"Did Denton put you up to this—and to abducting me?"

"Why would you think such a thing?"

"Because it is the sort of backhanded knavery that bastard would do with relish. It would please him immensely to succeed in trapping me into marriage with one of his mistresses."

"Mistress!" she cried, clearly staggered. "I am not his mistress!"

Jerome did not for one moment believe her. "How, then, did you pass the hours with Denton the night before last?" His voice was thick with derision. "Playing whist?"

"Sweet heaven, I was not with Tony that night!"

Jerome was so incensed that, forgetting his restraints, he tried to sit up only to be jerked painfully back by them. "Do not deny it, damn you! I saw you and him sneak out!"

"Not together!"

"No," he conceded, "but within three minutes of each other, and I saw you return after dawn the next morning. Or will you try to tell me you spent that night at Wingate Hall?"

"No, I did not," she admitted quietly, "but neither was I with Tony."

Jerome did not know whether to believe her or not.

"Then where the hell did you go—and where was Denton?"

"I suspect that he went to the pretty maid at the White Swan Inn that he favors whenever he is at Wingate Hall."

She said it with such unconcern that Jerome wondered whether she might possibly be the one woman in England who had been able to resist Denton's seductive advances.

She checked his wrist nearest her, then leaned across him to examine the other one. Her scent of lavender and roses wafted over him. Her breasts moved forward against the gap in her shirt, swaying enticingly only scant inches above his face.

He recalled how soft her breast had been in his hand. That memory had the opposite effect on his own anatomy. Beads of sweat formed on his forehead.

After what seemed like an eternity to him, she finished her examination of his wrists and sat up straight, looking at him with reproach, "Can you not see that your struggles are futile? You only hurt yourself."

Jerome fought to even out his choppy breathing. When he succeeded, he inquired, "If you were not with Tony that night, where were you?"

"Here with Gentleman Jack. He had suffered a relapse. Not a serious one, as it turned out, but I was caught by the storm, and it prevented me from returning until light. I had to sleep on the settee in the drawing room." A smile played on her lovely mouth. "I seem fated to spend stormy nights here."

Jerome had forgotten about the note from Morgan that had lured him into this trap. "What part did Gentleman Jack play in my abduction?"

"He wrote the note to give to you, and then he moved out of his hideaway here so that we could be alone." She gave him one of her irresistible, dimpled smiles. "I own I did not believe Gentleman Jack's note would bring you here, but it did. Why did you come?"

"Curiosity." Deducing that Morgan had not told her they were brothers, Jerome did not intend to inform her either. So long as Morgan was known only as Gentleman Jack, he would have no difficulty resuming his life as that personable and popular young rake, Lord Morgan Parnell, when he forsook his Robin Hood role. But if the highwayman's true identity was discovered, not even the Duke of Westleigh, with all his power, could save him. "How did you persuade Gentleman Jack to write that note?"

"He was so grateful for my treating him after he was shot that he promised me he would do any favor that I wanted of him. When I asked him to help me abduct you, he was very reluctant to do so, but he is a man of his word."

Yes, Morgan was that. Having given Rachel his oath, he would feel compelled to keep it even at his own brother's expense. "Did Gentleman Jack tell you to tie me to the bed like this?"

"No, he said that if you were not tied, you would overpower me and leave, but the bed was my idea. I thought you would be more comfortable."

*Comfortable!* Damn her, it was the most humiliating position in which he had ever found himself. His wounded pride festered, and his earlier rage, having receded, now washed back over him stronger than ever.

He must persuade her to untie him before they were found like this.

But not, damn it, at the price of marrying her.

"We have been gone for hours," he said. "Your relatives must be wondering what has happened to you."

"Oh, no, I left them a note that we had eloped."

Jerome swore under his breath. "Did you also tell them that you had abducted me?"

"No, only that we were going to be married."

"Like hell we are." Her certitude that he would wed her fired his rage like a torch set to gunpowder. No one had ever been able to force Jerome to do something he did not want to do. He would never permit her either to trick or shame him into marriage.

"You are dead wrong about that, my dear." His voice was frigid. "With this insane scheme, you have guaranteed exactly the opposite result from what you intended."

"What do you mean?" she faltered.

"I would not marry you if you were the last female in the universe. I would rather be drawn and quartered than do so."

# Chapter 15

**R**achel looked down at her captive, his handsome face set in hard lines of implacable hatred
and absolute rejection. Her heart seemed to sink to
her toes.

Gentleman Jack had warned her that Jerome might
react like this. She tried to remember what the highwayman had told her that she must do to make the
duke forget his anger at her, but she was so devastated by the hatred in his eyes that she could not
think.

"I am curious why you want to marry me so much
that you would pull this insane stunt." Jerome's
voice was like shards of ice. "Are you that determined to be a duchess?"

Rachel was insulted. "Sweet heaven, no! I care
naught for that!"

"I do not for a moment believe you. What other
reason can you have for being so resolute about marrying me?"

She wanted to tell him the truth, that she had
fallen in love with him, but Gentleman Jack had
warned her most emphatically that she must not confess that to the duke. To do so, he had insisted,
would deliver a mortal blow to her cause.

"He will not believe you," the highwayman had
told her. "He will think you a liar."

Swallowing the words of love she longed to say to
Jerome, Rachel belatedly recalled Gentleman Jack's

very explicit instructions on what she must do next. When he had given them to her, she had blushed crimson and said she did not think she could possibly follow them.

Now, she *knew* she could not possibly follow them when Jerome was so furious at her. Her courage faltered, but then she remembered the highwayman's stern warning: *You must do exactly as I tell you. It is your only hope of getting him to marry you.*

Gritting her teeth, Rachel forced herself to unbutton Jerome's shirt. He started at her touch, then grew rigid beneath her hand.

As she undid the final button, he demanded in an oddly hoarse voice, "What the hell do you think you're doing?"

" 'Tis not obvious?" she asked in surprise. "I am undressing you."

He swore at her. So much for Gentleman Jack's insistence that a man loved to be undressed by a woman.

Nervously, she forced herself to focus on Jerome's body. She pulled his shirt aside and found herself staring in helpless admiration at his golden chest, strong and muscled and lightly decorated with swirls of blond hair, a little darker than that on his head. Her breath caught, and she yearned to touch him, to feel the contrasting textures.

She sat down on the bed beside him and lay her hand on his chest, her pale extremity a sharp contrast against his golden skin. She ran her fingers over him, marveling at his strength and warmth.

He seemed to cease breathing for a moment.

She loved the feel of him. His skin beneath her hand was strangely exciting, and she could not resist trailing her fingers down to the waist of his breeches and his flat belly.

He audibly sucked in his breath.

Her fingers moved upward again and lightly, innocently circled one of his nipples.

He moaned. His breathing became quicker and shallower.

She looked quickly up to his face. His eyes were closed, and his jaw was clenched as though he were in pain.

Alarmed, she asked, "Did I hurt you?"

His eyes opened, and he glared at her. "As if you did not know what you are doing to me, damn you!"

Rachel blinked at him in perplexity, but his eyes had closed again.

Her hands were shaking with nervousness and her face was red with embarrassment as she tried to undo the first button of his breeches, the one at his waist. When she succeeded in opening it, he groaned and jerked at his restraints.

"Merciful God, stop it," he ground out. "Do not touch another button!"

That frightened her. He sounded as though he were truly in pain. Was it that? Or could it be that he was shy about her seeing his body? If the latter were the case, she understood his feelings perfectly.

That was the reason she dreaded carrying out the next steps of Gentleman Jack's instructions. She had protested against them vehemently, but he had been adamant that she must undress in front of Jerome. The highwayman had told her flatly that if she did not promise him she would do so, he would not help her.

Swallowing hard, Rachel stood up. Her captive was watching her with the strangest expression. She forced herself to smile at him as Gentleman Jack had instructed her to do. But when she tried to unfasten the skirt of her riding habit, her fingers were trembling so, it took her more than a minute to manage it.

Letting it drop to the floor was one of the hardest things she had ever done. Taking her horse over a high fence was easy compared to this.

"Rachel, I will not marry you, no matter what you

do." Jerome said hoarsely, looking almost desperate as he stared fixedly at her face with hard, angry eyes.

That made it even harder to do what Gentleman Jack had told her she must do now. She hesitated and turned away. She could not do it. Then she remembered the highwayman's firm admonition that it was the only way she could hope to get Jerome to marry her. She had to continue, and she did, hoping that he did not notice how badly her hands were shaking as she turned back to him and finished unbuttoning her shirt.

Her face, flushed with embarrassment, felt as hot as a fire. It took every ounce of courage and determination she possessed to slip her shirt off and stand before him in her thin white chemise, delicately embroidered with tiny flowers.

Jerome's gaze flicked down to the garment's deep neck that was cut so low it barely hid her nipples. It froze there, and a choked sound escaped him. His eyes were no longer stormy with anger, but had deepened to a rich cyan blue.

His intense gaze remained fastened on her breasts. It seemed to penetrate the thin fabric of her chemise. She felt as though he were physically touching her. Her nipples hardened, peculiar shivers rocked her, and suddenly a hot flood of moisture welled between her legs. Rachel was shocked and utterly baffled by her body's reaction to him.

With clumsy, shaking fingers, she undid the top button of the chemise, but her fingers faltered beneath his hot gaze and her affronted modesty rebelled. She had exposed more of herself to his eyes than any man had ever seen. If he had thought her brazen for returning his kiss, what must he think of her now?

The thought shriveled her resolve. She had hoped that Jerome would want her, that he would discover that he cared about her as she cared about him, but it was clear that he did not.

And nothing would be worse than to be married to a man who did not want her. At least Lord Felix wanted her, although for the wrong reasons. Rachel could not force herself to follow the remainder of Gentleman Jack's instructions. She turned away from Jerome and tried to rebutton her chemise, but her hands were shaking so badly she could not manage it.

"Do you mean to stop now?" he asked in a strangled voice.

She nodded, keeping her face averted, so that he could not see the tears welling up in her eyes.

Cursing violently, Jerome pulled furiously, vainly, at the ropes around his wrists, gouging bloody furrows into them.

"Dear God, stop it," she cried, whirling around. Horrified by the bright red drops that were dripping from his wrists, she grabbed for them, trying to restrain him. But she could not reach the one on the far side of the bed.

Hardly realizing what she was doing so frantic was she to stop him from hurting himself, she clambered up on the bed, yanking the skirt of her shift out of the way, and straddled his upper chest. Leaning forward from this position, she managed to capture both his wrists and hold them down.

He went absolutely still. Indeed, he seemed to have stopped breathing.

"Are you all right?" she asked.

"Hell, no," he replied in an agonized voice.

"You have hurt your wrists terribly," Rachel said, fighting back tears at the sight of the raw, ugly wounds he had inflicted by fighting the ropes. "I have some salve that will ease the pain. I will get it for you if you will promise to stop these futile struggles."

"Yes, for God sakes, get it," Jerome croaked. Anything to get her off of him. She was sitting so far forward on his chest that he could actually smell the seductive perfume of her feminine essence, and it was driving him out of his mind. No man not already in the grave could possibly resist such temptation.

Angry as Jerome was at Rachel, her innocent efforts at seducing him had made him want her as he had never wanted a woman in all his twenty-nine years, and that made him all the more furious. Furious at her—but even more so at himself for his own weakness.

She scrambled off of him and ran to the cupboard in the corner, returning with a container of salve that she applied liberally to his wounded wrists. Rachel looked so distressed by them that he was afraid she was going to burst into tears. He was touched, in spite of himself, by her concern for him.

The pain in his wrists, however, was nothing compared to the one in his groin. His manhood was straining, aching and throbbing, against the confines of breeches that had become far too tight.

He had to have the little witch. Jerome was quite certain that he would die if he did not. He was so desperate for her now that he was willing to agree to anything, except marriage, to have her.

When she had finished ministering to his wrists, he asked in a voice that was as raw as they were, "Are you going to remove that damned shift?"

"I cannot do it." Her voice was suffused with mortification and defeat. "I had hoped . . . I would rather die than marry Lord Felix, but I cannot do this."

She turned her face away to hide her tears from Jerome, but he could see the wet track down her cheek as he watched her profile. Every other woman would have sought to use her tears as a weapon, but she tried to conceal them.

She reminded him of one of those forlorn kittens she was caring for beneath the hedge in the maze. Jerome forgot his lust and his anger at her in the involuntary swell of compassion that her drooping, humiliated figure generated in him. Had he not been bound he would have taken her in his arms and comforted her.

"Rachel," he said, his voice suddenly gentle, "I do not blame you for wanting to escape marriage to Lord Felix, and I will do anything I can to help you do so—except marry you myself."

Nothing on earth would persuade him to do that. He was not such a fool that he would spend his life wondering who had really fathered his purported children.

"You will?" she asked, turning to him, her violet eyes bright with tears. "Then would you ... do you think you could at least bring yourself ..."

He smiled encouragingly at her. "What are you trying to ask me?"

Her face was crimson. "Will—will you be so kind as to ruin me?"

Jerome sputtered at her choice of words. "It is hardly a kindness that I would be doing you," he exploded. "Do you know what will happen to you if I do? No other man will marry you."

"Including Lord Felix," she pointed out.

Jerome should take what was being offered to him. He was not a damned saint. Yet, his conscience troubled him, deflating the physical evidence of his desire for her. She was such an innocent that he wondered whether she even knew what she was asking him to do. "Look at me," he said sharply. "Do you know what 'ruining you' involves?"

She nodded, her eyes grave and certain. "Yes, you will tumble me."

"And if I do, you will be robbed of husband, children, everything that a woman yearns for. Think of what you will be giving up."

"Better that than being married to a man I despise and who will make me miserable."

Perhaps it was. And, when he thought about it, it did not much matter whether he tumbled her or not.

After the note she had left, she was effectively ruined no matter what he did. He would be assumed to have slept with her whether he did or not, and he would be roundly castigated for refusing to marry her.

He might as well deserve the censure that would be his.

And enjoy the pleasure of bedding her.

He was convinced now that it was the only way that he could cure his body's hunger for her.

She swallowed hard. "Please, will you ruin me?"

She was so earnest and anxious that he could not help smiling. "With pleasure. But if I am to do so, I must be untied. It will be impossible otherwise, unless you wish to ruin me."

She looked at him suspiciously. "Will you run away?"

He gave her a wicked grin. "And miss all the fun of—er, ruining you? Not likely."

"Oh," she exclaimed naively, "will you enjoy it?"

"I intend that we both will." Still he gave her a final chance to back out. "But I must be certain that you fully understand I will not marry you. Nothing will force me to do so."

"I do not want you to when you feel that way," she said proudly, and he knew that she was sincere. "I cannot think of anything worse than being married to a man who does not want me. Even marriage to Lord Felix would be preferable to that."

Rachel untied Jerome's wrists. With a sigh of relief, he brought his stiff arms down to his sides, rubbing and flexing them to chase the numbness from them.

She released his feet, then watched him with nervous eyes. Despite his promise, she was clearly afraid that he would bolt. "I am not going anywhere," he assured her.

He reached out to draw her down beside him on the bed, but she instinctively jumped back.

He gave her a teasing grin. "It will be quite impossible for me to ruin you if you insist upon keeping that much distance between us. Now, come here."

Still she hesitated.

He rolled off the bed and stepped toward her. "I give you my word, Rachel. I won't hurt you."

At least not physically. But she would pay a terrible price for this night. He knew that better than she. His earlier fury at her was forgotten. Her courage, her kindness, and her stubborn determination had touched him. He would make their costly night together as good as he possibly could for her.

Rachel let him draw her into his arms. As he held her tightly against him, breathing deeply of her lavender and roses scent, he could feel her body quivering and knew that she was still afraid. He wanted her trembling for him but not from fear.

He stroked her long, beautiful hair and murmured again, "You will enjoy this night. You have my word on that, too." He continued to hold her to him, caressing her hair, her face, and her back with his hands until he felt her fully relax against him.

Then he gently tilted her chin up, and his mouth descended on hers in a long, slow kiss that was at first tender and reassuring, then became coaxing and seductive as his tongue traced and teased her lips into opening for him, then explored her mouth.

His hands moved over the curves of her body, warm and soft through the thin cambric of her shift. His body was hardening again, hungry for her. Without breaking their kiss, he stepped back slightly so that she would not feel what was happening to him.

His hand came up to cup her breast, and his finger lightly circled its rosy tip, bringing it to instant attention. His lips dipped to her throat trailing kisses down it.

Rachel was adrift on an ocean of sensation so wonderful that she never wanted to come ashore again. Pleasure and an odd yearning licked through her like a newly set fire.

His fingers unfastened the remaining buttons of her chemise, freeing her breasts. Her cheeks flaming, she started to protest, but then Jerome's head dipped to one of the sensitive peaks, and he drew it into his mouth. She gasped at the delight radiating through her. He suckled her as a babe would its mother, and it was so exciting she buried her hands in his thick blond hair, holding him to her.

His hand, warm and gentle and unspeakably exciting against her bare skin, slid up beneath the skirt of her chemise, caressing her thighs and belly.

When he at last lifted his head and withdrew his hand, she was so lost in bliss that she hardly noticed what he was doing. She gave a little gasp as her chemise suddenly fell away from her and dropped to the floor.

No man had ever seen her naked before, and she instinctively tried to hide herself from Jerome's eyes by closing her arms around herself. But he would not let her. Instead he looped her arms over his neck and pulled her into his own.

She reveled in the warmth and texture of his skin pressed against her breasts, and she could feel the fierce beat of his heart, its accelerated pace matching her own.

"Do not hide yourself from me—you are the most gorgeous creature I have ever seen," he murmured against her ear, his voice hot and husky and enticing. "Let me look at you."

And she did, shyly thrilling to the appreciation, as loud as words, in his hot, cyan eyes.

Smiling, he asked, "Would you like to finish what you started earlier with my breeches and unbutton them, or shall I?"

Rachel looked down and gasped at the sight of the bulge in them. "Sweet heaven, what is wrong with you? Have you been bitten by a poisonous creature?"

His eyes alight with amusement, he said, "You are

the poisonous creature, my sweet temptation. It is the effect you have on me."

"What an unkind thing to say to me," she said indignantly, certain that there was no way she could be responsible for such an obviously painful condition. "You cannot blame that terrible swelling on me. I have not even touched you there."

"No, more's the pity," he said hoarsely.

"That swelling is not normal."

"Believe me," Jerome said grimly, "it is very normal when I am around you."

She looked at him, baffled. "I do not understand."

"I see that you do not, but you will soon."

Rachel was still worried for him. Such swelling must surely be dangerous, and she said, "I want to understand *now*."

"Patience, my sweet, and I will show you. Trust me, it will be better that way. First, though, you must get into bed."

"Are we going to tumble now?"

"Rachel, do you know what will happen when we tumble?"

"Yes. We will roll around on the bed in each other's arms." She thought it must be something like when she and her brother George had wrestled as children. She could never quite understand why people seemed to think it was so enjoyable, yet were so unwilling to talk about it.

Jerome's eyes were a brilliant, shimmering blue now. "What else happens?"

"Oh, is there more?"

A strangled groan escaped him, and he said, "Please, get into bed. And make some room for me."

She did as he bid her, sliding over toward the wall to give him space. When she turned back to look at him, he had shed his breeches and was already pulling the covers over both of them.

"Should we extinguish the candles?" she asked.

"No, I want to be able to see you while we—er, tumble."

That seemed sensible enough, and Rachel made no protest.

Then instead of grabbing her and rolling around the bed as she had expected him to do, he drew her against his side, cuddling her in the protection of his arm.

Then he kissed her, a long kiss, full of tenderness and passion, that left her breathless and clinging to him.

She smiled at him, saying shyly, "I like this much better than tumbling."

He looked amused. "Do you now?" His voice took on a rich, husky timbre. "Let me see what else you like."

His mouth, his tongue, and his hands began a new assault on her that left her gasping and writhing beneath his touch.

Then one long, lean finger suddenly slid into the dark triangle at the apex of her legs where the moisture she had felt earlier was now gushing like some previously unknown spring.

Mortified to have him discover this inexplicable phenomenon, she clamped her legs together and cried in alarm and embarrassment, "No!"

"You will like what I do, I promise you, Rachel."

"You do not understand," she cried, feeling her face flame. "The strangest thing has happened to me there. I am all ... all ..." She was too ashamed to finish.

"Wet," he finished for her. "And that delights me."

She looked at him with wide, shocked eyes. "Why?"

"Because it is your body's way of saying that you want me. It is quite as normal as my 'swelling' that you noticed earlier. That is how my body shows that it wants you. Now, my sweet temptation, let me feel the proof of your desire for me as you have seen the proof of mine for you."

Rachel thrilled at his words. *He desired her.* At last he must have realized how right they were together and had decided that he wanted to marry her.

Before she could say anything, however, his clever fingers took advantage of her momentary confusion to steal into the heart of that strange spring between her legs. Gently, he caressed a mysterious spot there that sent a lightning flash of pleasure through her, and all rational thought fled from her mind. As he teased and probed and tormented, the spring gushed again.

He whispered, "Your body is telling me that you are ready for me."

*Ready for him how?* she wondered, too bemused by the strange sensations rocking her to ask aloud. Her breath was coming in quick pants and a strange heat suffused her body.

As though reading her thoughts, he said gently, "I'll show you."

He raised and braced himself over her. She felt something hard begin to slide into the slick passage between her legs.

She did not know how or why, but some primordial intuition told her this would ease the wild ache within her and she quelled her instinctive reaction to try to close herself to him.

He pushed a little farther, stopped, then tried again, and halted against some internal barrier within her. His face was clenched with strain and sweat beaded on his forehead.

"I told you I would not hurt you tonight, my sweet temptation, but I am afraid we have reached the point where I must do so if I am to ruin you. It is the only way. But it is your choice. Do you want me to continue?"

"Yes," she gasped, awash in violent sensations.

"Are you certain?" he asked urgently. "We can stop now."

"I am certain."

"Thank God," he groaned and plunged deeply into her. Hot agony gripped her, wringing a cry of pain and protest from her.

Her eyes flew open and she stared up at his face. He looked as though he were hurting, too. "I am sorry, so sorry, my sweet, but there is no other way," he murmured soothingly, holding himself very still within her and bathing her face with light, consoling kisses.

Just as she thought her body had adjusted to his invasion, he began to move inside her, slowly at first then more quickly, renewing the pain. His breathing grew short and harsh.

She said in a tight voice, "I think we should stop now."

He groaned as though he were in as much pain as she was. "I am sorry, but it is too late to tell me that now."

Then, after a minute, she began to forget her discomfort in the building excitement within her. Suddenly she was moving in rhythm with him, and she felt herself soaring to the brink of some great precipice.

She looked at him and saw that he was watching her intently, strain etched on his face.

Suddenly her body seemed to explode with sensation. Intense spasms shook her, generating a pleasure she could never have imagined, and she cried out in wonder and delight.

Jerome stiffened, and to her amazement, his body, too, was rocked by repeated, convulsive tremors. With an exultant cry, he collapsed atop her, his breath coming in short, heavy pants. He held her tightly, their bodies still joined.

Rachel felt as though she were floating on a mystical pool of bliss and wonder and contentment.

Later, well after his breathing had returned to normal, he rolled on his side and, with a mischievous grin that set her pulse racing, inquired, "So, now that you have been tumbled, how do you like it?"

"That is tumbling?" she exclaimed. "It was not at all like I imagined it would be."

"Was it better or worse?"

"Oh, better," she cried. "Infinitely better."

He laughed and pulled her into his arms, holding her protectively against him.

She loved the feel of his body against hers, and she began to run her hands over it, exploring it as he had explored hers. She was so much in love with him that she could not help showering him with exuberant kisses.

"Careful or you shall have me so aroused I will have to tumble you again."

"Really," she cried, eager to experience that ecstacy once more. "You mean we can do it again?"

"Aye."

"Soon?" she asked hopefully.

"Considerably sooner, my sweet temptation, than I would have thought possible."

They had not closed the curtains in the bedchamber, and Jerome awoke to light pouring through the windows. He looked down at the beautiful woman asleep on the pillow beside him.

He had made love repeatedly to her during the long night, unable to get enough of her. And she had answered him with her own intense passion that was all the more exciting for being innocent and untutored.

Then he remembered how he had come to be in this bed, and his feelings of tenderness for her vanished. She had drugged and humiliated him, abducted him and enticed him until he was out of his mind with wanting her, and then she had begged him to ruin her.

Jerome doubted any man could have withstood such a seductive assault. Certainly, he had not. He had been so wild for her that he had managed to forget every principle he possessed.

He had never before taken a girl's innocence. He had only contempt for men who did so without marriage. Now he was one of that company. He was racked by disgust for himself and anger at the sleeping woman beside him who had driven him beyond sanity.

She had given her word last night that she would not insist Jerome had promised her marriage, but, of course, she would lie about it now and say that he had.

Well, he would be damned if he would let her trap him into marriage. Not even the ecstacy of their lovemaking would change his stubborn determination not to wed her. He would not reward her outrageous behavior by giving her what she wanted.

# Chapter 16

Rachel awoke, aglow with the memory of the wonderful night she had shared with Jerome. He had forgotten his anger at her for abducting him, and he had made such tender, passionate love to her that she knew he would want to marry her now.

Belatedly she realized that his warmth was no longer against her. With her eyes still closed, she reached out to touch him, hoping that he would gather her in his arms and hold her against the comforting warmth of his body.

But he was not there.

Her eyes flew open. The bed was empty, and she looked around the room. He stood by the window, dressed only in his breeches, staring grimly outside. Apparently sensing she had awakened, he turned toward her.

She smiled at him.

He did not return it. His face was grim, his hard jaw jutting stubbornly. "You must be very pleased with yourself this morning."

Rachel stared at him in dismay, a sudden icy numbness creeping through her. What had happened to the tender, caring lover of the night before?

He had vanished as though he had never existed. Her happiness burst like a shattering vase, leaving only painful shards of memory to cut at her.

"You had better get dressed." The coldness of his voice chilled Rachel. "In view of the note you left about our eloping, we could have visitors at any time."

He picked up his lawn shirt and put it on. As he was buttoning it, he glanced at her still lying in the bed, the covers pulled up about her chin.

"Get dressed, damn it, or do you want to be found as naked as the day you were born?" His gaze raked her scornfully. "Believe me, that is not necessary to assure your relatives that I have ruined you. All the proof required is on the sheets."

Rachel had no idea what he was talking about. He continued to watch her, and she could not bear the thought of exposing herself to his icy eyes. She said in a small, embarrassed voice, "Please turn your head, so I can get up."

His eyes narrowed angrily. "Such belated modesty, my dear. After last night, there is not an inch of you that I do not know intimately."

But last night had been different. Then he had been warm and tender and teasing. Now he was a contemptuous stranger, and it was beyond her command to subject herself to his cold, hating gaze. "Please," she said miserably, staring down at the covers.

He uttered a sharp expletive and stalked out of the room, saying as he went, "You have five minutes."

Hastily, she got out of bed and pulled on her discarded clothing as fast as she could. Remembering what he had said about proof of ruining her, she looked down at the sheet. It was badly rumpled and stained with a patch of blood.

When he came back in the room, she gestured toward the blotch. "Is that what you meant by proof of ruining me?"

"Aye. But you need not worry that I will attempt to deny what I have done." His eyes narrowed, and his voice took on a bitter edge. "I imagine it is too much to hope that you will be equally honest."

Once again, she had no idea what he was talking about. "What do you mean?"

"Will you admit to your relatives that I told you from the beginning that I would not marry you?

She fought back tears. "I . . . I hoped you had changed your mind."

"I am certain that you did, but our so-called elopement has served only to make me more certain than ever that I would never marry you."

Rachel felt as though he had slapped her hard across the face. She looked hastily away from him, not wanting him to see the sudden sheen that misted her eyes. She had gambled her future on winning him, and she had lost.

He said bitterly, "I told you that I would not marry you, but no doubt you will lie and say that I promised you that I would."

"No!" she cried, in a broken voice. "I will not!"

He shrugged on his riding coat. "Then we had better return to Wingate Hall and pay the piper."

She looked at him uneasily, remembering Gentleman Jack had admonished her that she must never tell anyone she had kidnapped the duke. "I . . . I will not lie, but I would prefer not to tell anyone that I abducted you."

He looked relieved. "I would prefer that, too. It will enhance neither of our reputations. I will go along with whatever story you wish to tell so long as you do not claim I offered to marry you. Nor can you mention Gentleman Jack. It would go hard with you if it is learned you have been consorting with an outlaw."

Rachel had not considered it before, but that was true.

He held out the coat of her violet riding habit for her to put on. "Come, let us be on our way."

"Will—will they not think it odd if we return so soon?"

"You can tell them that you had second thoughts when I continued to refuse to marry you."

She stared at Jerome's hard, unsmiling face and,

swallowing hard, asked, "Did our night together mean nothing to you?"

"Only that you are an excellent tumble. I liked it well enough to want you in my bed again," he said carelessly. "I will not marry you, but I might be persuaded to make you my mistress."

He might as well have stuck a bayonet through Rachel's heart. It was not enough that he did not want her, but he had to add to her shame by issuing that insulting proposition.

She managed to say with quiet dignity. "You have humiliated me, Your Grace."

"Then we are even," he snapped.

Jerome had thought Alfred would be the angriest of the Wingates over his niece's "elopement," but instead it was Sophia. Her ire, however, was not directed at Jerome. It was focused entirely on Rachel.

"How could you do this to us?" Sophia screamed. "You are a humiliation to the Wingate name! You have ruined yourself, and you have thrown away the opportunity of a lifetime to be Lord Felix's wife. He left a half-hour ago, saying he would not have you now."

Jerome's eyes narrowed. That meant Felix would not be paying Sophia the sum he had promised her. Was that why the greedy bitch was so enraged?

Rachel said defiantly, "I told you, Aunt Sophia, that I would never marry Felix."

Her Uncle Alfred broke in, "Did the duke promise you marriage, Rachel?"

Jerome held his breath. This was the moment when Rachel would reveal her true colors. Despite her protestations to him that she would not lie, he could not believe that she would do anything else.

"No, he did not." Her voice was firm, but Jerome saw the faint tremble of her chin that betrayed how hurt she was. "He was adamant that he would never do so."

Alfred asked her, "Did he steal your virtue?"

"No."

Jerome's eyes widened. Did she mean to deny that they had slept together in a desperate, vain attempt to save herself from ruin?

"Are you certain?"

"Very certain. He did not steal it. I gave it to him." Rachel held her head proudly, defiantly, but Jerome saw the two bright spots of shame in her cheeks. "Indeed, I begged him to take it."

That was more truth than even Jerome had wanted. What a courageous woman Rachel was. His admiration for her soared, but he would be damned if he would condemn himself to a marriage spent wondering who his wife's lovers were. And while his heart ached for her, his fierce pride rebelled at rewarding her crackbrained abduction of him by giving her what she wanted.

"You shameless slut!" Sophia screamed at Rachel.

The slur infuriated Jerome, especially coming from a wanton like Sophia. He glared at her. "There is only one slut in the Wingate family, and I am looking at her."

A shocked silence descended on the room. Then Sophia demanded, "What are we to do with her now that you've ruined her?"

Jerome stood up. "I will be happy to take her off your hands, but I will not marry her."

Rachel flushed and her eyes were suddenly violet fire. "I will never be your mistress."

Jerome would not let her know how much he wanted her. He would not give any woman that power over him. Instead he shrugged. "I am leaving in an hour. If you change your mind before then, let me know."

After a bath and shave, Jerome put on fresh riding clothes. His plan was to depart in his traveling coach. Once he was out of sight of Wingate Hall, he would mount Lightning and send his coach on to the White Swan while he and Ferris rode to the lodge in the hope Morgan would have returned to his hideaway. After what this journey to Yorkshire had cost Jerome, he was not going to leave without seeing his brother.

Nor, he realized with aching dismay, did he want to leave Rachel behind at Wingate Hall. But he knew now that she would not go with him unless he married her.

Jerome remembered that he had left his copy of Ashcott's *Philosophy* in Wingate Hall's library the previous evening, and he went downstairs to retrieve it. He found Sir Waldo Fletcher in the hall, hovering near a tray of food that had been left on a pier table there.

"What are you doing?" Jerome demanded.

"I am here to see Mrs. Wingate."

"I doubt that she is receiving visitors."

"So I was told, but I am certain she will want to see me."

Kerlan, the butler, came down the stairs. "Mrs. Wingate sends her apologies, but she is not well enough to see even you."

At that moment, a skinny, teen-aged chambermaid came rushing down the hall and handed Sir Waldo a cloth. He used it to wipe a minute spot of mud from his gleaming top boots, then handed it back to the girl without so much as a thank you, and departed.

Jerome went into the library to retrieve his book. As he came back into the hall with it in hand, Kerlan was demanding angrily, "Tillie, is this Lady Rachel's breakfast tray? You were told ten minutes ago to take it up to her."

"Me was on me way when the gent what was just here sent me to find a cloth t' clean him boots. Me told him me was taking the tray up t' her, but him insisted me get the cloth first."

"Take it up immediately," Kerlan ordered. "It is not

bad enough that Lady Rachel is locked in her room, must you starve her, too?"

"Locked in her room?" Jerome questioned.

The butler glowered at him. "Her aunt locked her there as punishment—for what you did to her." Kerlan rudely turned his back on the duke and stalked off. It was the first time in Jerome's life that a servant had treated him with anything but utmost deference. Yet he could not help but admire Kerlan for his loyalty to Rachel.

Jerome followed Tillie up the stairs. So he was to be made the villain of this piece. Well, perhaps he was at that. Now that Rachel had relieved him of all responsibility in the affair, he had never felt more like a cad in his life.

As the maid ahead of him reached the top of the stairs, Sophia called through the slightly opened door of her room. "Tillie, bring me up a pot of tea from the kitchen."

"Aye, ma'am, soon as me takes this tray to Lady—"

"Now, Tillie!" Sophia ordered sharply. "Put that tray down and do as I say at once."

"Aye, ma'am." Tillie set the tray on a narrow hall table flanked by two chairs and obediently went back downstairs.

Jerome went into his bedchamber. He had been there only a few minutes when he heard a scratching at his door that was almost drowned out by the chattering of a gaggle of maids in the hall.

He opened the door to a young footman. "Begging your pardon, Your Grace, but your groom says you must come to the stable at once. Says 'tis urgent."

Jerome was alarmed. It would have to be very urgent for Ferris to send him such a message.

# Chapter 17

Jerome snatched his coat from the chair where he had tossed it and shrugged into it. When he stepped into the hall, both the footman and the maids he had heard chattering had disappeared.

But Rachel's breakfast tray had not. It was still on the table where Tillie had left it. Damn it, Rachel would be lucky if she got it by dinnertime. Anxious as Jerome was to get to the stable to answer Ferris's urgent summons, she needed sustenance.

With a muttered curse, he picked up the tray, which held a covered plate, a cup, a pot of tea that was undoubtedly cold by now, and a small pitcher of milk. He carried it down the hall to Rachel's room.

The key had been left in the lock on the outside of the door. Juggling the tray with one hand, he unlocked it with the other, then knocked.

"Who is it?" called Rachel's warm, honeyed voice that he loved.

"Breakfast."

"Go away, Your Grace." Her voice turned cold. "I do not want to see you."

"Do you not?" He opened the door and went inside. "Too bad for both of us you did not feel that way last night."

Rachel jumped up from a small table by the window where she was sitting. Her rose silk dressing sacque gaped at its neck, giving him a brief, tantalizing peek at her breasts before she pulled it closed. "You cannot come in here. I am not dressed!"

"I saw you last night in considerably less than that," he reminded her, setting the tray down. "Here is your breakfast at last."

The dressing sacque skimmed the curves of her lovely body, sending a bolt of desire through him that was so intense he had to grit his teeth. He had thought that having Rachel would cure his lust for her, but now he was racked by intense longing to feel that delectable body against his own again.

And the thought of leaving Wingate Hall without her filled him with bleakness.

He tried to take her in his arms to persuade her to go with him, but she pushed him away. "Do not touch me!"

"Come with me, Rachel. I promise you will be happier living under my protection than here. I will take very good care of you, and you will want for nothing."

"Except your name!"

Her expression was so full of pain and disillusionment that Jerome involuntarily took a step back. No one had ever looked at him like that before, and he felt like a scoundrel.

Her lip curled scornfully. "I would not go with you now, even if you promised to marry me."

Jerome did not believe that. She would change her mind quick enough if he were to offer for her. His title held that kind of allure, he thought bitterly.

"I will not promise you that, Rachel, but neither do I want to leave you here. I do not trust your aunt." He would not put it past her to try to sell Rachel to Felix as his mistress. Jerome's hands clenched involuntarily into fists at the thought. "Let me take you away."

"Take me to what? Life as the mistress of a man who has only contempt for me?" She tilted her head and met his gaze with proud, flashing eyes. "Never!

I prefer to remain here. You did what I asked. You ruined me. I thank you. Now, please, *go away!*"

Jerome could not help admiring how stubborn and determined and brave she was. He thought of how soft and yielding she had been beneath him. And how passionate. He would do anything to help her—short of marrying her.

"Rachel, you do not know what it will be like for you here. You will be a social outcast."

"Better that than having to marry Lord Felix."

"Listen to me, Rachel. After last night, you may be with child." Certainly, Jerome had made no effort to prevent it. He had been too out of his mind with wanting her to think of anything else.

"Oh, do you think so?" she asked in surprise. Clearly that thought had not occurred to her. "But if I am, it is no concern of yours."

"Of course it is! It would be my child, too."

She looked at him curiously. "Would you care?"

"Certainly I would care." Jerome wished that he had more time to reason with her, but he had to answer Ferris's urgent summons to the stable. "I have something I must do. While I am gone, think about what I have said. I will stop back in a few minutes."

"Do not bother. I will never change my mind."

"Rachel, damn it, let me help you!"

"By making me your mistress?" The scorn in her voice flayed him. She thrust the small pitcher from her breakfast tray at him. "The only way you can help me is to take this milk down to the kittens in the maze."

*Hellsfire*, he thought in exasperation she was worrying about those kittens when she ought to be worrying about her future.

"The poor little creatures will be starved by now, and I am not allowed out of my room, so I cannot feed them."

Jerome could not help but be touched that despite the crisis in which Rachel's life was, she could still worry about the motherless kittens. He took the pitcher from her. He did not want the kittens to go hungry any more than she did. Besides the maze was on his way to the stable.

Jerome stepped into the maze, carrying the milk, and went directly to the spot where the kittens were hidden. They scampered up to him, meowing piteously. Their dish was empty, licked dry. As he poured the milk into it, the calico puffs began lapping eagerly even before he could finish.

He put the pitcher down near the bowl, thinking he would retrieve it on his way back to the house from the stable. The ground where he set it was uneven, and it tipped over, spilling the rest of the milk out of it before he could catch it.

He could not seem to do anything right today. With a muttered curse, he stood up and headed for the stable. Ferris met him halfway there.

"Morgan is waiting for you in the grove behind the stable," the groom said. "He says he must see you before you leave."

Jerome stalked toward the indicated spot, torn between anxiety to see his brother again and anger at him for helping Rachel abduct him.

Morgan was leaning against the trunk of a thick oak, watching a pair of brown chiffchaffs on the branch of a nearby tree so intently that he did not notice his brother's approach.

"Planning another abduction?" Jerome inquired dryly.

Morgan turned away from the birds and started toward Jerome, a wide grin on his face. He moved slowly with a pronounced limp that sent fear coiling through Jerome for the brother he loved.

"For God's sake, Morgan," he burst out, "give up this insanity before you are killed! Once that reward is posted for your capture, it will only be a matter of time before you are seized. And when you are, you will not escape the noose. You have robbed too many important men."

"None that did not deserve it."

"That may be true, but it only increases your peril. Even I will not be able to protect you."

Morgan flashed an impudent grin. "But only think of the legend I am creating. I understand at least a half-dozen ballads have been composed, lauding my deeds."

"Damn it, Morgan, I do not want a dead legend, I want a live brother."

"For all the trouble I have caused you, you should wash your hands of me. If you had a son of your own and I were not your heir, you would not have to worry about my fate."

That hurt Jerome as much as if Morgan had driven his fist into his gut. "Surely you cannot think *that* is why I am so concerned about you!"

The highwayman gave his brother a sheepish, affectionate smile. "No," he admitted.

"Quit this dangerous nonsense, and come home to Royal Elms."

Instead of responding to this plea, Morgan asked, "Did you enjoy last night? I hardly need ask after seeing the condition of my bed."

"Damn it, Morgan, how could you have helped Rachel?" Jerome demanded, his anger rising. "How could you have done that to me? My own brother for God's sake!"

Morgan grinned unrepentantly. "Somebody has to worry about the future of the dynasty. It is past time that you married and produced an heir."

"You cannot expect me to marry that female after what she did to me?"

"If I were you, I would jump at the chance."

"You are not me! And I am quite capable of picking my own bride."

Morgan raised a quizzical eyebrow. "Are you now, My Lord Duke? Then why are you not married?"

"You need not worry. I will offer for Emily Hextable as soon as I return to Royal Elms." Why did the thought of marrying Emily suddenly seem as grim as Judgment Day?

"You have been intending to offer for Saint Emily for years, but you never have. Why is that?"

The question stopped Jerome.

"I will tell you why," Morgan continued. "It is because you know in your heart that humorless, sanctimonious prune will bore you to death."

"I am committed to her," Jerome said doggedly, as much to convince himself as his brother.

"Why do you think that? Have you ever told Emily that you wished to marry her?"

Although Jerome had not, neither had he discouraged her hopes as he had other women's. "No, but it was what our father and hers expected. It is what *Emily* expects." That was why she had eschewed London society to remain close to Royal Elms when he was there. In truth, her assumption had irritated him, but he had not tried to correct it because he thought eventually he would offer for her. Except, as Morgan had pointed out, Jerome had been putting off doing so for years.

"Many women have marital dreams beyond their grasp," Morgan said. "I promise you, Jerome, that if you marry Emily, I will never come home to Royal Elms again. Hell and damnation, marry Rachel instead. *She* will not bore you."

*No, she would not*, Jerome thought. Shock, madden, enchant, cuckold, but never bore him.

"Rachel is the perfect wife for you."

"The perfect wife?" Jerome's voice rose in protest. "A woman who excites lust in every man that lays eyes on her."

"That is irrelevant in a wife."

"Not in *my* wife!"

"All that matters is whether she returns other men's admiration or cares only for her husband. A husband who ensures his wife loves him will have no worry about her faithfulness."

"A woman of Rachel's beauty would never be satisfied with one man," Jerome scoffed.

"You do her an injustice. She is not like Cleo Macklin or those other faithless lovelies of London society."

"The hell she isn't." Jerome's blood ran hot at the memory of Rachel's seductive behavior at the lodge. "You should have seen her tempt me last night."

"But I had to show her how to do it," Morgan said in amusement. "The innocent had not the least notion of how to go about it."

Jerome glared at his brother. "Damn it, you mean you taught her how to seduce me?"

"Yes, I did," admitted Morgan, clearly proud of his tutoring. "I knew it would do you a world of good. Let me tell you, had I not thought Rachel was the perfect woman for you, I would have been busy on my own behalf instead of yours. I hope to hell you appreciate the sacrifice I made for you. You ought to be thanking me."

"Thanking you for getting me into this damnable scandal? I could throttle you!"

"But you won't," said the unperturbed Morgan.

Jerome, trying to rein in his anger, glanced toward Wingate Hall. His traveling coach had pulled up and stopped before its front portico, awaiting his pleasure. "I notice you did not trust Rachel enough to tell her your real identity."

"I am quite happy for her to know who I am. She would not betray me. I would trust Rachel with my life. Indeed, she has already saved it. I would not be alive now if it were not for her."

Jerome frowned. "What are you saying?"

"After I was shot, Rachel risked her reputation, perhaps more, to nurse me through a crisis, just as she has helped dozens of others in the neighborhood with her herbal remedies. When the ill need her, she goes to them, no matter what their station in life. That is not the behavior of a selfish, heedless beauty."

No, it was not, Jerome thought. Was Morgan right? Was Rachel different from the other beauties he had known?

"If nothing else," his brother was saying, "you should be grateful to Rachel for saving my life."

Jerome, certain that Morgan was embellishing her role, glanced toward his coach. A quartet of footmen were loading his baggage into it under his valet's watchful eye.

Interpreting his brother's impatient look, Morgan demanded, "Are you going to ride off and leave her?"

Jerome did not want to do that, but he was not about to admit that to his brother. "I offered to make her my mistress, but she declined."

"Your mistress! Hell and damnation, Jerome, surely you did not insult her like that. She is the daughter and sister of earls!"

"I was adamant from the beginning that I would not marry her."

"Then why the hell did you steal her innocence. That is not like you, Jerome."

No, it was not at all like him, but he had wanted her to the point of madness. Hiding his own disgust with himself behind a casual tone, he said, "She begged me to ruin her, and I complied."

Morgan looked at him as though he were seeing him for the first time. "I never suspected you could be such a heartless, uncaring bastard."

Jerome was stung by his brother's contemptuous assessment. "What the hell did you expect after what she did to me?"

"What I expected was, that having ruined her, your code of honor would require you to marry her."

"That's why, damn you, you taught her how to seduce me! Well, your devious plot failed."

"You cannot go off and leave Rachel here!" Urgency rang in Morgan's voice. "Someone is trying to kill her."

Fear clutched at Jerome, but he told himself that Morgan was not above using exaggeration to bring him around to marrying her. "Are you referring to the incident when she was accidentally shot at *two months ago*? That hardly means someone is trying to kill her now."

"Few believe that shot was accidental."

"Rachel does. Do you think Sir Waldo Fletcher wants to kill her?"

"Perhaps. He was humiliated by her vocal rejection of his suit, but I do not believe it is him."

"Whom do you suspect?"

"Her brother George," Morgan said.

"Are you mad? He is not even in England. He is with the army in the American colonies."

"Shortly before that shot was fired, a stranger came to the tavern near here. He was looking for a Wingate Hall servant or tenant that he could bribe into helping arrange an 'accident' for Lady Rachel."

"Hellsfire, do you think he found one?"

Morgan shrugged. "People here love Rachel. He barely escaped the ale house without being tarred and feathered. Still, in a household that size, there could be one person unscrupulous, greedy, or desperate enough to be bought. He was not seen again, but the next day the shot was fired at her. I doubt that could have been a coincidence."

Jerome doubted it, too. "But why do you suspect Rachel's brother?"

"The scoundrel said he worked for a man across the sea."

"And George is across the sea! But why would he want to harm his sister?"

"Think about it, Jerome. Does it not seem strange that first Arlington mysteriously disappears and now someone is trying to harm his sister who stands to inherit Wingate Hall."

"Not if George is alive. He is Stephen's heir."

"To his title, but Wingate Hall is not entailed. Everyone thinks the estate will go to George, but that is not necessarily so."

Jerome frowned. "Explain what you mean by 'not necessarily so.'"

"The vicar—who is a surprisingly radical thinker—and I have become unlikely friends. One night when he was foxed, he let it slip that he had witnessed a secret agreement between George and his father, who opposed his son's military career. The old earl agreed to buy George a captain's commission in return for a certain concession on his son's part."

"What was the concession?"

"That if Stephen should die without issue and George inherited the title, he must either resign his commission or forfeit Wingate Hall to his sister."

Jerome remembered what Rachel had said about her father's wish that she had been his first born son because of her dedication to the estate and its people.

Morgan said, "Apparently the old earl was determined to prevent an absentee master from letting Wingate Hall deteriorate."

"And George agreed to that?"

"Not willingly. The vicar said that George was clearly furious about having to sign the agreement, but it was the only way he could get his father to buy him the commission he wanted."

Jerome said hoarsely, "But if Rachel were dead . . ."

"Brother George would inherit everything without having to give up the army. If you are going to benefit from the death of a young and healthy woman, would it not be better for her to die while you were still across the sea?"

Could that be why George has ignored all Rachel's pleas to return? Jerome remembered the scathing letter he had written George for his negligence. No doubt it would afford the bastard great amusement.

"If you do not take Rachel away from Wingate

Hall now, *you may never have another chance.* She may be dead."

The thought wrenched Jerome's heart, but he could not believe that she was in such dire danger as Morgan intimated. "I will be happy to take her away from here."

"But not as your wife?"

"No."

"Hell and damnation, if you do not wed her, then I will."

Rage ripped through Jerome with the force of a lightning flash. His hands involuntarily clenched into fists, and he realized with profound shock that although he did not want to marry Rachel, neither could he stand the thought of another man doing so.

Jerome eyed his brother suspiciously. Surely Morgan, the rake of the family, could not be serious about wedding her. It was simply another ploy to get his brother to do so. Well, it would not work. "It is past time I left. My coach is waiting for me."

"Will you leave without Rachel?"

"Yes."

Morgan pressed his mouth into a tight, thin line. "You are so anxious for me to give up my career as a highwayman. Well, I will make you a bargain. Marry Rachel, and I swear to you that Gentleman Jack will immediately vanish from the face of the earth."

"So if I am to save you from the gallows, I must consign myself to a life of misery."

"You damned fool, Jerome! I recognize, as you do not, that Rachel is the perfect wife for you. She is everything you want in a wife. All I want is for you to be happy. With Rachel, you will be."

"Like hell I will. A beauty like her will never be satisfied with only one man. I will not spend my life wondering who has fathered my purported children." Jerome whirled and headed toward his coach.

Morgan called after him. "That damned Cleo

ruined you! Rachel is nothing like that heartless, faithless wanton, who had a soul as black as pitch. Rachel is as beautiful within as she is without. Hell and damnation, why can you not see that?"

Jerome kept walking. He turned into the maze to retrieve the milk pitcher. As he approached the kittens' hiding place, they did not rush out to greet him as they had before. Probably too busy still lapping the milk. Jerome knelt down and looked beneath the box hedge.

For a moment, he thought the kittens were napping. One was stretched out stiffly beside the bowl of milk. Then he saw that the other's head was lying in the bowl, having tipped it on edge so that the milk had spilled out and soaked into the ground.

The kitten's eyes were open, its paws extended in an unnatural position. Jerome snatched up the tiny ball of fluff from the bowl, confirming his fear.

It was dead.

So was its companion.

Jerome stared down at the lifeless little bodies with disbelief. Slowly the full significance of what he was seeing penetrated his shocked mind. The milk that he had given the kittens must have been poisoned.

Milk intended for Rachel.

Waves of horror and acute nausea swept over him. *In a household that size, there could be one person unscrupulous, greedy, or desperate enough to be bought.*

All Jerome's anger at Rachel was forgotten, and a hundred images of her danced through his mind: Rachel staunchly defending Gentleman Jack; Rachel lovingly cuddling the kittens to her; Rachel innocently clambering over him on the bed in her desperate effort to stop himself from further damaging his wrists; Rachel driving him mad with her guileless, thrilling passion in bed last night.

Jerome recalled Sir Waldo Fletcher hovering over the tray.

But he was not the only one who'd had access to

Rachel's breakfast. It could have been someone in the kitchen, or any one of that covey of maids in the hall, or a passing footman, or the negligent Tillie.

If Jerome raised a hue and cry, he would merely warn the killer he must be more careful and cunning next time.

Jerome laid the dead kitten on the ground beside its sibling. Ironically, Rachel's concern for them had saved her own life. But whoever wanted her dead would try again.

And perhaps succeed. Then it could be Rachel lying dead, her beautiful limbs frozen as the kittens' were now. Jerome broke out in a cold sweat. He could not leave her at Wingate Hall to be murdered.

He straightened, his jaw unconsciously hardening in determination. Scarcely knowing what he was doing, he marched like an automaton into Wingate Hall and up the stairs to Rachel's room.

# Chapter 18

**R**achel, still in her silk dressing sacque, spun around as the door to her bedchamber crashed open.

Jerome stalked in, his face as hard and grim and determined as she had ever seen it.

"What are you doing here?" she sputtered. "I told you not to come back."

He did not answer her, did not say a word.

Instead he marched over to her clothes press and rummaged through the garments in it. His face was pale, his eyes had an odd, stunned expression, and his movements were choppy, lacking his usual grace. He looked like a man who had just received devastating news and was in shock.

He pulled out a forest green cloak and shoved it at her. "Put it on. You are coming with me."

Did he still think she would become his mistress? Well, he was wrong. She refused to take the garment from him. "I will go nowhere with you. I will never, never be your convenient!"

"Fine," he snapped, grabbing her arm in a far from gentle grip. "But you are still coming with me."

She gaped at him as he threw the cloak around her. He had a wild, desperate look about him that frightened her. Had he taken leave of his senses? "I will not leave Wingate Hall with any man but my husband."

His jaw jutted in grim, stubborn determination. "If that is what it takes, then I will marry you."

Rachel was so flabbergasted that she let him fasten the cloak on her without resistance. This was the very same man who had told her only hours ago that nothing would induce him to marry her.

Now he was saying he would. And looking as happy about it as a condemned man contemplating the hanging tree. "But you do not want to marry me."

"No," he agreed, "but I am going to do it. No doubt I will regret it all the rest of my days."

Hardly the sort of romantic proposal designed to fill its recipient with joy and eager acquiescence. It filled Rachel with fury. How could he barge in like this and not ask, but *tell* her that he was going to marry her? It was even more insulting than Lord Felix's offer had been!

"Well, I am not going to marry you!" she cried, revolted to the depths of her romantic soul. "I *know* that I would regret it all the rest of my days!"

"I wish to hell you had realized that before you abducted me last night," he ground out. "You were far too eager to marry me then."

But then she had thought that she was giving him the nudge he needed to realize that he cared about her, to appreciate that they belonged together. But now she was convinced that, marriage or not, he would always hate her for what she had done. The thought of marrying a man who felt that way filled her with despair, and she would not do it.

Suddenly Jerome swept her off her feet and into his arms. He carried her toward the door.

"What are you doing?" she demanded in alarm.

"Taking you with me."

"Put me down!" she hissed. She tried to struggle out of his arms as he carried her along the hall past gaping servants and down the wide staircase, but he was far too strong for her. He held her locked against his chest with arms that were like bands of steel.

At the bottom of the steps, Kerlan tried to step in front of him. "Your Grace! You cannot . . . " His voice trailed off as Jerome brushed past him toward the entrance.

"Kerlan, please inform Mr. and Mrs. Wingate that their niece is doing me the honor of becoming my wife."

Rachel squealed in outrage. "I told you that I would not marry you."

"I heard you," he said, carrying her through the front door.

Maxi dashed out of the house after them. Apparently under the misapprehension that this was a delightful new game, the little terrier barked at Jerome's heels as he carried Rachel down the stairs toward his waiting coach.

The duke's valet, coachman, and groom stood as stiff and still as if they had suddenly been turned to stone, staring in amazement at the scene unfolding before them.

"What are you doing?" Rachel sputtered.

The door to his coach stood open, and Jerome thrust her inside, none too gently. "This time, *I* am abducting *you*."

He told the coachman, "We are going to Parnlee, John."

"But, Your Grace," the startled coachman began, "we were going to Royal—"

"To Parnlee at once!" Jerome reiterated in a tone no servant would dare challenge. The coachman scrambled on to his box as the duke told his valet, still standing beside the coach, "Be so kind as to ride with John."

Peters climbed on the perch beside the coachman while Maxi danced around below the coach door, barking furiously.

With a muttered curse, Jerome jumped out,

grabbed the excited terrier, and set him down on the floor of the coach. Then he got in again, slamming the door after him. As he settled on the seat beside Rachel, he gave the signal to start.

The coachman's whip cracked, and the carriage leaped forward at unsettling speed. Maxi, suddenly uncertain about this grand new game, began to whine.

Jerome reached down, hauled the terrier onto his lap and began placating him with his skillful fingers. It did not take long. Maxi soon collapsed into a complacent silver ball.

Rachel glared mutinously at this man who had broken her heart by assuring her that she was not good enough to be his wife, only his mistress. And now he had the gall to tell her that he was going to marry her as though he were doing her some great favor. Well, he could keep his great favor.

With steel in her voice, she said, "I will never, never, *never* marry you."

Jerome ran his hand irately through his own thick blond hair. "Women," he snapped in exasperation. "Damn you all, if you are not the most perverse creatures. Have you forgotten that last night you abducted me to force me to marry you? Now that I say I will, you do not want it. Well, that's too damn bad. You no longer have any choice in the matter."

"Yes, I do," she contradicted hotly. "You cannot force the vows from my lips!"

"Why are you being so damned stubborn? It sure as hell isn't because you find me repulsive. Last night proved that."

Rachel could feel herself blushing crimson at the memory of her abandon in his arms.

His penetrating blue eyes beneath the thick, golden lashes apparently read her thoughts for he suddenly looked amused, and the grim lines of his face relaxed.

Mortified that her thoughts were so transparent,

Rachel swiveled her head away from him and stared out the window at the barren, treeless moor that was flashing past. Her mind was swirling with confusion and uncertainty. If only he would offer her some sign of affection. His earlier rejection of her still burned in her memory like a hot brand.

What had caused him to change his mind so abruptly about marrying her? Whatever it was, his hard face assured her that it had nothing to do with undying love on his part. And she could not bear to be shackled to a man who did not want her. Both her pride and her heart rebelled against that.

After a few minutes, Jerome remarked casually, "It is extremely boring landscape to be studying so closely."

He was right. She turned back toward him. His fingers were still gently soothing Maxi, who was a picture of sublime contentment on his lap. She remembered all too well what it had been like to enjoy the magical attention of those long, graceful hands. An insidious desire to have them pleasure her again undermined her resistance. "Where are you taking me?"

"To Parnlee, a hunting box of mine near York."

Why there, she wondered, instead of Royal Elms if he meant what he said about marrying her. Was he too ashamed of her to take her to his country seat? Swallowing her hurt, she warned, "My uncle will come after us." But she knew that was an empty threat.

"All your Uncle Alfred cares about is that I marry you, and I have agreed to do so."

"I told you that I would not—"

"I know you did," he interrupted, "and you are wasting your breath—not to mention becoming a shrew on the subject. So, pray, let us try another one."

Rachel sighed. "How long do you intend to stay at Parnlee?"

"For however long it takes me to bring you to your senses and get you to marry me."

"*That* would be taking leave of my senses!" she shot back. She would rather be a spinster the rest of her life than marry a man who could not even take the trouble to ask her. "I will never marry you."

He cocked an amused eyebrow. "Then we will have a very long stay at Parnlee."

But he did not sound the least bit worried. Handsome, arrogant man that he was, he was certain that once he got her there, he could charm her into anything he wanted.

That infuriated Rachel into saying, "I do not care what you do to me—lock me in a dungeon, grind me on a rack—"

"Oh," he interjected with an unprincipled, engaging grin that had an alarming effect on her heart, "I do not intend anything so unpleasant for you." He perused her, his eyes suddenly warm and brilliantly blue.

Rachel was certain that he was thinking about the amazing responses that he had coaxed from her the previous night with his expert lovemaking, and she felt herself blush again.

Maxi had fallen asleep in the duke's lap. Jerome, taking care not to awaken him, deposited him gently on the seat opposite them.

The coach rounded a curve rapidly, throwing Rachel against Jerome. He put his arm around her and held her against his hard body. A thrill rippled through her. She breathed deeply of his spicy scent and was ambushed by a longing to have him kiss her as he had last night. He did not do so, but after the road straightened again, he continued to hold her to him. There was something so comforting about the sheltering warmth of his body that she could not bring herself to pull away. They rode that way in silence for several minutes.

Finally, Jerome asked, "What was the lodge you

took me to last night? It was far too substantial to be a tenant's home."

"My father's father built it. Grandpapa had the lodge constructed to house his current convenient during those rare times when he was in Yorkshire."

"Did your father ever use it?"

"No! Papa had no need for it! He said that God had blessed him by giving him the only woman he ever wanted as his wife. He had the lodge boarded up."

Jerome's expression was suddenly cynical. "Was your mother as faithful to him as he was to her?"

"Of course she was!" Rachel cried, indignant that he could suggest Mama would have been anything else. "She adored Papa. They were very happy together."

"Then your father was truly a lucky man," Jerome said with obvious sincerity.

"They loved each other so much." Rachel's tone was wistful. "After Mama died, Papa was never quite the same. It was as though the light went out of his life."

"How old were you then?"

"Thirteen." It was still painful for Rachel to remember her mother's death, and she sought to change the subject. "After what you said to me earlier, I do not understand why you would decide to marry me now."

Jerome still had his arm around her, and she held her breath, waiting for his answer. She hoped that it was because he had come to the belated realization that he cared about her after all.

He sighed. "I am not certain I understand myself."

Rachel was so stung that she jerked away from him and scooted across the seat to the far corner. She eyed him balefully, and her pride prompted her to cry, "Obviously, you cannot think of a good reason why you should marry me. And I can think of *none* at all why I should agree to do so."

"Oh, I can think of several excellent reasons why *you* should, my dear."

It set Rachel's teeth on edge when he called her "my dear." Whenever he did, his sarcastic tone contained none of the affection the phrase implied.

He said, "One, you are ruined, and you will be a social pariah, without any hope of ever having a husband or family unless you marry me. Two, God knows what devious scheme your Aunt Sophia may devise for your future if you remain at Wingate Hall. Three, you will be my duchess with all the social status that situation carries with it."

"I have no interest in marrying a man for social status." Nor in marrying one who did not want her, not even when she loved him as much as she did Jerome.

"Then you should have married Tony Denton."

But she did not love Tony. Instead of telling Jerome that, however, she said, "Aunt Sophia would never have permitted it. Besides I think he would make a terrible husband."

"You think I will make a better one?"

She was certain that Jerome would, if only he could come to love her; but, if he could not, there would be no happiness for either of them.

"Answer me," he ordered.

Rachel turned her head away to hide from him the hot tears that stung her eyes.

"Look at me."

When she did not comply, he muttered a curse and moved across the seat to her. Determined fingers seized her chin and turned her face toward him. A handkerchief appeared in his other hand, and he gently wiped away her tears.

Then he gathered her back in his arms and held her silently, comfortingly. Rachel did not know what to make of this man with his mercurial twists. One moment he was infuriating, the next charming. He had been by turns grim, angry, amused, protective, cynical, teasing, brusque, and gentle. His constantly changing manner toward her did nothing to quiet her own pain and roiling confusion. At this rate she would soon be ready for Bedlam.

Both the afternoon and the coach grew progressively warmer. Maxi still slept on the seat opposite them. Jerome shed his riding coat.

After a time, he observed, "You are too hot in that cloak. Why do you not take it off?"

"I cannot with you sitting there."

He raised one golden eyebrow in challenge. "Why not?"

"I have no gown. I am in my dressing sacque."

"I have seen you with less on."

"That was different," she said in a strangled voice. Then she had thought that he cared about her. Now she knew better.

"Why was it different?" he asked, sounding amused.

No doubt he would laugh at her stupidity if she told him. Her chin raised defiantly. "Please, leave me alone."

Cursing under his breath, he signaled for the coach to stop. "As you wish," he said brusquely. "I will finish our journey on Lightning."

He was out of the coach before it had fully stopped. As he mounted his chestnut stallion, Rachel heard Ferris say, "I am astonished you would leave Morgan behind."

"When he hears the details of my departure from Wingate Hall," Jerome said sardonically, "be assured his curiosity will drive him posthaste to Parnlee after us."

Who was Morgan? Rachel wondered as she removed her cloak.

The coach clattered forward. She immediately missed Jerome's presence. She seemed to feel the bumps and jolts of the road more sharply without him. God help her, but she wanted this baffling, exasperating man.

As Jerome rode beside his coach, he thought about the exquisite creature whom he was going to make his duchess. He knew it was a terrible mistake to marry such a beauty. It would only bring him unhappiness—even heartbreak.

Yet he had no choice. He could not leave her at Wingate Hall for an unknown killer to claim her life.

His discovery of the dead kittens had so shocked and horrified him that he had scarcely known what he was doing when he had marched into Rachel's room and carried her down to his coach.

His mind had been fixated on the single thought that he must get her away from Wingate Hall. If he had to marry her to do it, then he would. He would do anything to save her, but he had no time to consider why he was acting so unlike himself.

He had seen the confusion he had caused Rachel mirrored in her eyes. Little did she know that he was even more confused by the contradictory emotions buffeting him. He was a man at war with himself.

He would be marrying a woman who would no doubt bring him misery, and he would be hurting another woman, Emily, who did not deserve such treatment. It was true that he had never made her a formal offer, but Emily had long expected he would. He did not delude himself into thinking that he loved her, but he felt guilty as hell. Emily was far too good a woman for him to hurt as he was being forced to do.

What a coil, Jerome thought with a weary sigh. There was no honorable way out of it for him. So he had to do what was most important.

And that was saving Rachel's life.

By marrying her, he would also be salvaging her reputation and quieting his own nagging conscience about having ruined her.

He also intended to hold Morgan to his promise to give up his highwayman career. So several goods would come out of his marrying her, but Jerome had to admit that more than altruism was involved in his decision to marry Rachel.

He could no longer deny to himself how much he wanted her. He had been shocked by the realization that he could not tolerate the thought of another man, even the brother he dearly loved, having her. He had thought bedding Rachel last night would cure him of his desire for her, but instead it had only intensified it.

After he'd suggested she remove her cloak, the thought of seeing her enticing body again in her dressing sacque had made him so hot and hungry that he had not dared remain alone in the closed coach with her. He had jumped at the excuse to escape.

He sighed. He might be able to hide the truth from Rachel, but he could no longer hide from himself that he had come to care for her far more than he should, fool that he was.

But he would not let himself fall in love with her. *The Duke of Westleigh must not be weak.* If he loved her, this breathtaking creature would break his heart as surely as the sun sets each night.

# Chapter 19

⌒◝◞◟⌒

**R**achel stirred groggily as strong arms lifted her from the coach seat where she was sleeping. The pleasant, spicy scent that enveloped her told her that she was in Jerome's arms. She forced open her sleep-weighted eyes and saw that it was dark.

They had stopped once earlier at a wayside inn for dinner. It had been dusk then. Since she had only her dressing sacque beneath her cloak, she could not go into a public place, and Ferris had brought her a tray of food.

Although she had been too proud to ask Jerome, Rachel had secretly hoped that he would join her and eat in the coach. Instead he had said brusquely, "You need not worry that I will spoil your dinner by subjecting you to my unwelcome presence."

Hurt by his curtness, she could not bring herself to tell him she would actually welcome his company. So, while the men ate in the inn, she had dined in lonely solitude, which further depressed her flagging spirits.

Within a few minutes of leaving the inn, the rocking and swaying of the coach had lulled her to sleep, and she had not awakened until Jerome had scooped her from the seat. It was so dark that she could make out no more than the outline of the structure to which he was carrying her.

He stepped into a small, dimly lit entry and strode

down the hall of what appeared to be a deserted cottage. She looked up at him questioningly.

"We are at Parnlee," he said as he carried her into a cozy bedroom.

She looked around the comfortably furnished room with undisguised curiosity. "So this is your love nest."

A muscle in his jaw quivered. "No, it is one of my hunting boxes."

"You have more than one?"

"Yes, but unlike your grandfather, I do not use them for assignations. You are the first woman I have ever brought here, or to any of them."

Rachel felt an odd burst of happiness at his words.

She had seen no servants, but the covers on the large tester bed had been neatly folded back as though in preparation for their arrival.

He laid her on the bed, removed the green cloak in which she was wrapped, and draped it over his arm. With the glimmer of a smile, he said, "Now, my lady, you are my prisoner."

She gulped, wondering if he meant to treat her as she had him. "Are you going to tie me to the bed?"

His face was unreadable. "Would you like that?"

"No," she cried in alarm. "No more than you did. Please, say you will not."

"I see no need to do so. You will not run away."

"You are very confident of that! Do you fancy yourself so irresistible that I could not possibly leave you?"

"I should be so fortunate! No, my confidence is based on a much more mundane reality."

"What is that?"

His hot gaze ran appreciatively down her body. "Your lack of clothes."

"Oh-h-h-h," she wailed as he turned and left the room, taking her cloak with him. She had forgotten that she had only her dressing sacque and her chemise.

She rose from the bed, removed the sacque, and slipped back beneath the covers in her chemise.

Staring up at the carved walnut canopy, she wondered whether Jerome would join her in it. Or would he ignore her as he had during the journey here? She thought of the previous night spent in his arms, and a little shiver of pleasure snaked through her.

But now Rachel was entirely in his power. That made her nervous and even a little frightened. Jerome had shown her so many different moods today that she no longer knew what to expect from him.

The door opened and Jerome came in. Her nervousness expanded like a thunderhead in the afternoon sky, and she rolled on her side so that her back was toward him. She heard him moving about, then the bed dipped beneath his weight.

Her apprehension got the better of her, and she tried to escape out the other side.

He grabbed her chemise and hauled her back, rolling her over to face him. "Where do you think you are going?" he demanded as he drew her against the warmth of his powerful body.

He was naked, she realized, and the heat of him through her shift made her pulse race.

"Let me go," she protested weakly.

"No. We must talk."

"Here?" To Rachel's embarrassment, her voice came out in a nervous squeak.

"Why not, we seem to communicate better here than anywhere else," he said wryly.

"What did you wish to talk about, Your Grace?" Rachel was proud of how coolly she managed to ask that. He would never guess that his naked closeness was turning her to quavering jelly.

"Us. After our scandalous departure from Wingate Hall, the sooner our wedding day the better."

"*That* day, Your Grace, will never come."

"Yes, it will," he contradicted calmly. "You *will* marry me, if it takes me a year to convince you."

His certainty irritated her, yet she was afraid that if she stayed in his arms he could convince her of anything. She pushed away from him and levered herself into a sitting position. Pulling the covers up about her neck, she retorted, "A lifetime will not be long enough for you to convince me!"

"Hellsfire, you are as stubborn as I am," he said ruefully. "God help our children. They will be mules."

*Our children.* The thought of having his children filled Rachel with such happiness and excitement that her eyes misted, and she looked away from him, unable to meet his gaze.

Jerome sat up, placed his fingers lightly beneath her chin, and turned her face back toward him. He smiled at her, his eyes bottomless blue pools. "You like the thought of our children, do you not?" His voice was like midnight velvet.

She did. Oh, yes, she did.

He bent his head and kissed her lips, gently at first, then with a hot passion that fired her own.

Hard as she tried to resist the persistent seduction of his mouth, she could not. Soon she was kissing him as hungrily as he was her.

His arms went round her, holding her tightly against his warm, naked skin. She could feel his heart beating at a suddenly accelerated tempo against her breast. It pleased her to know she could have that effect on him.

When at last he lifted his lips, he continued to hold her in the circle of his arms. "Now, my sweet temptation"—his voice was a warm, gentle caress against her cheek—"instead of cutting up at me, explain why you are suddenly so adverse to marrying me."

She threw her head back defiantly and glared at

him. "You made it very clear that you do not want me. After insisting you would never marry me, suddenly you told me that you were going to marry me. *Told me!* You did not even deign to ask me. You are worse than Lord Felix."

"No, I am not," he protested with an irresistible smile. "I never wear musk. Or diamonds. And I sure as hell am not marrying you to ornament my consequence."

"You are not marrying me at all!"

Jerome gave her an amused, quizzical look. "Am I not?"

Rachel was awash in confusion. This morning he had been adamant that he would never wed her. Now he was just as adamant that he would and the sooner the better. "Why are you suddenly so eager to marry me?"

He hesitated, watching her through assessing eyes, as though he were weighing various answers, trying to decide which would be most effective with her.

And, she thought bitterly, the only one that she wanted to hear—that he loved her—would never even occur to him.

"My conscience would not permit me to leave you behind to face an uncertain future." His fingertips brushed her cheek lightly. "I have never evaded my responsibilities. And I am responsible for ruining you."

Rachel's heart and her pride revolted at the idea of any man—even Jerome—marrying her because it was his duty. The last thing she wanted was to have him regard her as yet another of his onerous responsibilities. Did he not care at all for her? In a strained voice, she pointed out, "But I begged you to ruin me."

"True, but I did not have to comply." Jerome glanced downward and his gaze froze.

She had let the covers fall down around her waist.

The low neck of her thin chemise revealed more than it concealed of her breasts. Beneath his hot, sensual stare, their rosy tips tightened as though he were stroking them.

When he finally looked up and his eyes met hers again, the passion in his glittering gaze stoked an answering hunger in herself.

Flustered, she jerked the bedclothes up about her chin.

He grinned. "What a shame to hide that lovely view from me." His nimble fingers slid beneath the covers and began to unbutton her chemise.

She tried to push his hands away but failed. "No-o-o-o," What began as her protest stretched into a stammer of pleasure as his palm slipped beneath the thin cloth to capture her breast and gently massage it.

His mouth found hers, and he kissed her with a fervor that melted what was left of her resistance. His hand left her breast to push her chemise from her shoulders. The thin cloth fell away, leaving her naked to the waist.

Suddenly, he broke their kiss. With one quick, fluid move he had her on her back again. Then he took her mouth, his tongue wooing her with a wildly erotic dance. Desire bloomed within her like flowers in the spring sunshine. His hands caressed her body in a way that made her moan.

He lifted his head from her mouth and looked down at her. There was no mistaking the appreciation in his glittering cyan eyes.

"God, but you are the most beautiful creature I have ever seen," he murmured. "Say you will marry me."

"No-o-o-o-o."

Once more her protest faded into a moan as he put his mouth to her neck and sucked lightly along its sensitive cord. As his head moved leisurely lower, he said, "Please, marry me."

She did not answer him, and his mouth closed over the crest of her breast. His fingertips drew lazy, maddening circles on her belly. She arched beneath him in pleasure.

"Marry me," he murmured, as he lifted his head to turn his attention to her other breast.

He licked its aureole as though it were ambrosia while his hand explored her body, sending waves of heat and desire through her. Her breath came in gasps.

As his mouth moved lower, he urged, "Marry me."

He blazed a trail of hot kisses down her body that sent quivers of pleasure through her.

"Marry me," he urged as his tongue teased her, and his fingers skillfully explored her feminine core, drenched with her body's plea for him.

Rachel was writhing now in pleasure and in need. She wanted—nay, she ached for his body to free her from the desperate hunger that gnawed at her. But he showed no inclination to sate it.

Instead he seemed bent on driving her out of her mind with his erotic assault.

And he was succeeding.

His tongue teased her ear. "Marry me."

"No," she gasped.

At last, she begged, "Please, no more."

"Marry me."

"No!" She moaned as his mouth and his hands resumed persuading her.

"Marry me," he demanded.

Finally, she could bear his sweet torment of her no longer.

"Marry me," he whispered.

"Yes ... yes." The words were torn from her in a groan.

But they did not satisfy him. "Give me your oath, my sweet temptation, that you will marry me. Swear to me."

Her body yearned wildly for his and the ecstacy she knew it would bring her.

"I . . . swear . . . please."

He took her then, sweeping them to a climax so intense and stunning that Rachel was not certain she would ever be able to move again.

Afterward she lay blissful and content in his arms. Surely a man who made such tender, passionate love to her must care for her. She clung to that hope and to him.

The minutes passed as they lay entwined, their bodies in soothing, silent communication.

Finally Jerome said, "I am sorry, my sweet, but we must get up."

"Why?" Rachel asked in dismay, unwilling to have this serene spell between them broken.

"Now that we have enjoyed the pleasures of a wedding night, it is time we make it that legally. York is less than an hour away. We will be married at the Minster tonight."

"But it must be nearly midnight."

"Only half-past ten." Jerome rose from the bed and went to the door.

"You are mad," Rachel exclaimed. "You cannot walk into the cathedral and demand that they marry us in the middle of the night."

He looked amused. "Can I not?"

"Why tonight? Are you afraid that I will renege on my vow to marry you."

"I am trying to hold the scandal to a minimum. If we are married before midnight, I will be able to say with all honesty that I did not take your innocence until our wedding day." Jerome grinned, a boyish, irresistible grin that set Rachel's heart dancing. "I will not mention that the events were a little out of order."

He left the bedchamber but returned a minute later carrying a pink gown that he handed to Rachel. "Try this on. I think it will fit you tolerably well."

It was a simple, unstylish one-piece cotton gown with no frills or decoration, but it gave Rachel something other than her dressing sacque to wear.

As she put it on, Jerome quickly dressed. The gown fit her surprisingly well.

"Where did you get it?" Rachel asked.

"Bought it from a maid at the inn where we stopped to dine last evening. She looked to be about your size."

Although Rachel was pleased that he had thought to do so, she felt a flash of pique that he had been looking so closely at another woman.

"It is not elegant, but it was the best I could manage under the circumstances." Jerome took Rachel's arm and led her into the hall. "We will leave as soon as Morgan arrives."

"Who is Morgan?"

Maxi, barking furiously, dashed out of the drawing room where he had been ensconced to greet his mistress, and Rachel bent to pet him.

Jerome cocked his head at the sound of a horse galloping up outside. "Most likely that is Morgan now."

When the door to the lodge was flung open a moment later, Gentleman Jack strode inside.

"Sweet heaven," Rachel exclaimed in shock at the sight of the highwayman. "What are *you* doing here!"

She glanced toward Jerome and saw that he clearly did not share her surprise. Instead he said affably, "You are rather later than I expected you to be."

The highwayman gave him a sour look. "Yes, you knew after your dramatic departure from Wingate Hall, my curiosity would not allow me to stay away." Gentleman Jack turned to Rachel and bowed. "Is he going to do right by you, my lady?"

Confused by his question, she asked, "What do you mean?"

Before the highwayman could answer, Jerome said, "You are just in time to accompany us, Morgan."

"Morgan?" Rachel echoed in surprise.

Gentleman Jack smiled at her. "You have not been properly introduced to me, my lady." He looked expectantly at Jerome.

"Rachel, this is my brother, Lord Morgan Parnell."

"Your . . . but he is Gentle—"

Jerome cut her off. "Gentleman Jack no longer exists. He has vanished from the face of the earth. Is that not true, Morgan?"

The highwayman studied his brother intently for a moment, then said with a shrug, "If you say so. I collect you agree to my terms for giving up my criminal career."

Rachel was eager to hear Jerome's answer, but instead he asked blandly, "Will you witness Rachel's and my wedding tonight?"

Morgan grinned. "With pleasure, but before we leave, I beg a moment in private with you, Jerome."

The brothers stepped outside into a misty darkness.

Morgan said, "For a man who abhors scandal as much as you do, Jerome, you certainly are creating a good deal of it lately. Tales of your dramatic departure from Wingate Hall spread through the neighborhood like wildfire. What on earth possessed you? One moment you tell me you are not going to marry Rachel, and the next you march into Wingate Hall and carry her off."

Jerome gave Morgan a sardonic grin. "I would do anything to get you to end your career as a highwayman. You promised to quit your criminal activities if I married her, and I intend to hold you to it."

"I will keep my word, never fear."

Profound relief enveloped Jerome. At least his brother, the one person he loved more than any other, would be safe now.

Morgan studied Jerome with penetrating eyes. "There is more to this than you are telling me. It is too unlike you to act so precipitously. I want the truth. What happened?"

"You were right about someone trying to kill Rachel." Jerome told Morgan about the kittens and the poisoned milk meant for her.

"Hell and damnation, who do you think was responsible?" Morgan exploded.

"So many people had access to the milk before the tray was delivered to her that it is impossible to answer that. It could have been Fletcher or it could have been any one of a dozen servants—especially if your theory about her brother George is correct."

Morgan uttered a barnyard expletive.

"I was so shocked and sickened when I saw the dead kittens and realized the implication that I hardly knew what I was doing," Jerome confessed. "I only knew that I had to get Rachel away from Wingate Hall immediately."

Morgan studied his brother thoughtfully for a long minute, then asked, "Have you told her?"

"That someone is trying to kill her? No, all that will do is terrify her. And upset her terribly. She loved those poor kittens. I do not want her to know."

Morgan's face furrowed. "Do you think she will be safe at Royal Elms?"

His brother's troubled question had not occurred to Jerome, and he paled at the thought that the man who wanted her dead might try again at her husband's estate.

If Sir Waldo Fletcher was the scoundrel, Jerome did not think he would do so. Bedfordshire, where Royal Elms was located, was a long way from Yorkshire. And Fletcher was too much of a coward to run the great risk to his own life entailed in killing a duchess.

Morgan said, "If her brother George is behind the

attempts, and I think he is, then his hired assassin is almost certain to try again."

Jerome agreed with Morgan that George was the most likely villain. Stephen's disappearance and the attempts on Rachel's life must be connected. George was the only one who would benefit from their deaths. Rachel would be devastated if she learned of his and Morgan's suspicions about her younger brother. Jerome strongly doubted that she would even believe them.

His jaw clenched in determination. "I must take care to ensure that she will be safe."

"Aye, you must. I am very fond of Rachel."

"How fond?" Jerome blurted, singed by a sudden flash of jealousy. What the hell was the matter with him? There was no one in the world that he trusted as much as his brother.

"Jealous, are we?" Morgan chuckled. "You should not be. I told you I think that she is the perfect wife for you, and I, too, am willing to make sacrifices for my favorite brother. Now, if you will trust me alone with my future sister-in-law, I would like a private moment with her."

Rachel cast a quizzical eye as Morgan came into the drawing room where she was sitting with Maxi dozing on her lap. "Why did you help me abduct your own brother?"

"I promised you that I would do anything you asked, and I keep my word, no matter what. Besides I am delighted to have you as my sister-in-law. I think you are the perfect wife for my brother."

"I wish he thought so." A lump that felt as large as a hen's egg swelled in Rachel's throat. "He does not want to marry me, you know, even though he is doing so."

Morgan sat in a chair opposite her. "What do you want, Rachel?"

She stared unhappily down at her hands resting on

Maxi's silver coat. "Not a man who does not want me."

"But Jerome does! Believe me, I know my brother better than anyone. It is just that he cannot let himself admit yet how much he does care for you."

Rachel wondered if she dared accept this small shred of hope. "Why can he not admit it?"

"Because you are so ravishing. My brother cannot trust beautiful women, and for several good reasons. The first and most important of them was named Cleopatra Macklin."

Rachel remembered what Eleanor Paxton had told her. "But he jilted her!"

"When Jerome was eighteen, he fell wildly in love with her. Cleo was his first love. He worshiped her and was determined to marry her despite the furious opposition of our father."

"Why did your papa oppose it?" Rachel asked.

"He saw Cleo for what she was, an ambitious, scheming, wanton. Unfortunately, my father had not the smallest notion of how to go about persuading a stubborn son to change his mind. He was as stiff-necked, imperious an old martinet as ever lived."

"How can you talk of your father that way?" Rachel demanded, much shocked.

"Because it is the truth. Instead of using even a modicum of tact with Jerome to discourage the alliance, he ridiculed him as grossly stupid for not seeing her as a conniving, faithless female. Unfortunately, for once in his life, Father was right."

"What happened?" Rachel asked. Maxi turned his head to nuzzle her arm, and she absently began petting him.

"There is no one more stubborn than Jerome when he is determined about something. He defied Father and announced to the world that he and Cleo were betrothed. A few weeks later, my brother discovered her in bed with Anthony Denton."

"Tony!" Suddenly Rachel understood why Jerome had been so angry when he had thought she had sneaked away to spend the night with Denton.

Morgan's eyes narrowed. "Do you know him?"

"Yes, he was one of my brother Stephen's closest friends. The night I was trapped at your hideaway by the storm, Jerome thought I was with Tony."

Morgan groaned. "Denton is at Wingate Hall?"

Rachel nodded, still absently petting Maxi.

Morgan studied her assessingly. "What do you think of Tony?"

"Oh, he is very charming and handsome, but I confess I do not like him. He was, I think, a very poor influence on Stephen. Why are you grinning?"

"I am impressed by your astuteness in seeing Tony for what he is. Few women do."

Rachel wished Jerome thought as highly of her as his brother did. "What happened after Jerome found Tony and Cleo together?"

Morgan's face tightened into grim lines. "Her infidelity shattered my brother's heart. She was determined to be a duchess and utterly shameless about it. She refused to end their betrothal, thinking she could force him to marry her. As you know, a gentleman does not jilt a lady, but Jerome did so, although he did not let the world know that he, not she, was actually the injured party."

Rachel smiled at this new insight into Jerome. As was often the case, the truth was very different from what the world believed.

"After that, my father mocked Jerome incessantly for what a 'stupid fool' he had been to let Cleo hoodwink him. Father also reiterated over and over how a beautiful woman could not be trusted nor faithful to one man. Jerome's subsequent experiences with other beauties served to strengthen the distrust my father worked so hard to instill in him."

"Why did your father do that?"

"He was determined that Jerome marry the daughter of his old crony and neighbor, Lord Hextable. Nobody would call Emily even pretty."

Rachel caught the hostility in his voice. "You do not like her, do you?"

"No. Unfortunately, Emily is very careful to conceal her real nature from Jerome, and he has never seen her as she really is. You will make Jerome a far better wife than she. He is overburdened with responsibilities, and he needs a woman who will help him as you helped your father and brother at Wingate Hall."

"You seem to know a great deal about me," Rachel observed.

"I could not have spent the past few months in your neighborhood without hearing at great length about the beautiful Lady Rachel. You are much loved in North Yorkshire."

She felt herself blushing at his approving words and smile.

"Jerome takes his responsibilities very seriously. He thinks it is his duty to shoulder them all himself." There was a harsh, sardonic twist to Morgan's voice. "Our father drubbed that into him."

"You did not care much for your father, did you?"

"He was a hard man to feel affection for. He could show his love only by finding fault. He did not know how to praise, only to criticize."

Rachel shuddered. How dreadful life with such a man must have been. After her loving, kind father who had encouraged her in whatever she wanted to do, such a parent was almost beyond Rachel's comprehension. She had not known how lucky she had been. "What was your mother like?"

"A charming butterfly of a woman, much younger

than Father, and very unhappy with him. After I was born and she had done her duty by providing an heir and a spare, she escaped Royal Elms as often as she could and took me with her."

Maxi cocked a sleepy head toward Morgan's voice, then jumped off Rachel's lap and trotted over to sniff the newcomer's boots.

Morgan said, "Jerome was not so lucky. Father would not permit Mother to take his heir with her. He wanted to come with us so badly, but he had to remain with our father while she and I spent wonderful months at her brother's estate. It was like being freed from a prison."

Rachel thought of what it must have been like for the unhappy little boy left behind with that rigid, critical parent, and her heart went out to him.

"Jerome's childhood was miserable. My father devoted himself to training him to his own exacting standards. A crown prince has an easier time of it. You have no idea how often I have thanked God that I was born the second son. Nothing was worth what my brother went through."

Maxi put his front paws on Morgan's knees, earning only an absentminded pat. "Not only did I escape to my uncle's, but when I was at Royal Elms, I had Jerome to protect me from Father's ire. He even took the blame for things I did to save me. It was Jerome who gave me the love that my father never did. If ever a man deserved happiness it is my brother, and I think you are exactly the woman he needs to find it."

"If only he agreed," Rachel said wistfully.

"Listen to me, Rachel, I meant it when I told you that Jerome cares for you very much, but he cannot admit that yet, not even to himself. In time, though, he will come to do so."

"But what if you are wrong?" A sharp pain gripped Rachel in the vicinity of her heart.

"You can bring him round."

She did not share Morgan's optimism. "How?"

"Just be yourself. Eventually, Jerome will discover that he needs you far more than he yet realizes."

*But what if he does not?*

she did not share Morgan's opinion that Jerome was just the vessel. Eventually, Jerome would discover that he needed you far more than you would realize
but...

# Chapter 20

**B**y the time their coach pulled away from the
York Minster, Rachel concluded that virtually
nothing was impossible for the Duke of Westleigh.

Take their marriage, for example. Although it was
nearly midnight when they arrived at the Minster, its
officials were happy to comply with the duke's surprise wish to be married there at once and obligingly
provided him with the license that made the immediate nuptials, outside canonical hours, possible. The
brief ceremony was concluded at the stroke of midnight and duly recorded in the register.

If the Minster's ecclesiastics found either the
duke's sudden rush to embrace matrimony or his
bride's plain, unstylish gown odd, they kept their
thoughts to themselves until after the departure of
the unusual wedding party, which consisted of the
duke's brother and groom and the bride's dog.

Rachel and her new husband were sharing the carriage with Maxi, who promptly fell asleep on the seat
opposite them. Morgan and Ferris rode beside the
coach on horseback.

As they left York behind, Jerome said, "We will
spend the night at Parnlee and leave for Royal Elms
in the morning."

Rachel, remembering their earlier interlude there,
felt a sudden heat twist within her. She studied her
husband's chiseled profile with its determined jaw,
aristocratic nose, and thick sweep of golden lashes.

She could not deny that, want to or not, she had fallen hopelessly in love with this complex man. And now, for better or for worse, he was her husband. For the better, she hoped, a little shiver coursing through her.

Neither of them spoke for a few minutes. The silence was broken only by the rattling of the speeding coach and the song of a night bird.

Jerome said, "I must get you a wedding gift. What would you like, jewels?"

They did not interest her. Instead she decided to ask him for something she truly wanted. "The only gift I wish is some word on my brother Stephen's fate."

"Are you serious?" Incredulity permeated Jerome's voice.

"Very serious. If you can learn what happened to Stephen, it will make me far happier than jewels."

He shrugged. "I will see what I can do, but I fear it is not likely to be good news."

She flinched at his bluntness and could not keep tears for Stephen from misting her eyes.

Jerome hastened to say in a lighter tone, "Then again, perhaps Stephen is hiding until his witch of a betrothed chooses another husband."

"I confess I cannot understand why my brother wanted to marry Fanny. It was not as though he seemed ... "

She broke off, looking embarrassed, and Jerome finished the sentence for her. "To be in love with her? Undoubtedly, he was not. I fancy her great attraction for Stephen was her father's power."

"What?" Rachel gasped.

"Her father, Lord Stoddard, is one of the most powerful men in English politics," Jerome said cynically. "A connection to Stoddard would be most advantageous for any man—even an earl."

The earl's sister was truly shocked. She had not

thought her brother would choose a wife for such a reason.

Her reaction clearly surprised Jerome. "Don't tell me you are so naive that you believed your brother would have married for love? Men of your brother's position rarely do."

Or of Jerome's, she thought sadly. "My father did. And he and Mama were very happy together." It had been the kind of happiness that Rachel had dreamed of having in her own marriage, but would she find it with Jerome?

She remembered what Morgan had said about his brother's inability to trust beautiful women after his unhappy experiences with them. She sought to reassure her husband that she was nothing like the women he had known. "I will do everything in my power to be a good wife to you," she promised.

"Will you?"

Jerome's skeptical tone wounded her.

He studied her through narrowed eyes. "What is your definition of a good wife, my dear? Does it include being faithful to me?"

He might as well have struck her. Hurt and anger flared within her. "If you must ask that, why on earth did you change your mind about marrying me, then seduce me into agreeing?"

"You evade answering my question by asking one of your own," he pointed out.

"I will be faithful to you! How could you think that I would not be?"

"Beautiful women never are."

"This one will be!"

"I know your kind."

"You clearly do not know *me* or what my kind is at all!" Somehow Rachel would have to make him see that she was different.

Rachel and Jerome reached Royal Elms two nights later. At her insistence, they had made that part of the journey on horseback, leaving Peters and Maxi to ride in the duke's coach. She loved to ride, and she had not wanted to spend interminable days cooped up in a closed coach while it bounced across wretched, bone-wrenching roads when she could be on horseback. Jerome had clearly been astonished by her request but agreed to it with obvious relief at being spared the trip by coach.

Morgan had left the newlyweds at Parnlee to go to Wingate Hall. He had volunteered to inform Alfred Wingate that his niece and the duke were properly wed. Morgan had assured Jerome that no one at Wingate Hall would recognize him as the highwayman who had lately plagued the area.

He was also commissioned to bring what he could carry of Rachel's clothes on horseback to Royal Elms and to see that the rest of her personal belongings at Wingate Hall were packed up and dispatched to her.

"You must bring my leather case with you," Rachel had told her new brother-in-law as they parted. "Please, do not leave that. And ask Benjy, the stable hand, to care for the pair of kittens I have hidden in the maze."

"And do not forget your promise to me, Morgan," Jerome had interjected. "Gentleman Jack no longer exists."

It was late when the duke arrived at Royal Elms with his bride. Rachel's first impression of her new home in the light of a slender crescent moon was of a massive stone palace. Twin cupolas flanked the great pediment of its central block and long, rusticated pavilions extended on each side.

"It is very . . . grand," Rachel managed, awed by its size.

"Yes," Jerome said wryly. "My father did not think the original Tudor house grandiose enough for the Duke of Westleigh, and he had part of it knocked down, then rebuilt it on a larger scale. It was he who added the pavilions."

Tired as she was, Rachel noticed the subtle change in Jerome as they dismounted and approached the door to the great house. She could almost feel the ducal hauteur and reserve dropping into place like a sharply honed portcullis.

Jerome had sent no word ahead of either his marriage or of their arrival. As a result, their only welcoming committee was a startled, sleepy footman.

Rachel was so tired after two days in the saddle that her first impressions of her new home were confined to its great marble hall, soaring two stories high, its wide marble staircase, and her husband's bedchamber where she fell asleep the instant her head touched the pillow.

When she awoke the next morning in the massive bed covered in crimson and yellow velvet, Jerome was already up and dressed. Heat curled within her at the sight of his tall, muscular body displayed to perfection in a superbly tailored forest green riding coat and fawn breeches.

She wished that he would come back to bed and make love to her, but he seemed to have no such inclination. Swallowing her disappointment, she asked, "Will you take me on a tour of my new home this morning?"

"I cannot. I am afraid that you must remain in this room today on the pretext that you are too exhausted from our arduous journey to leave it."

"Why on earth must I do that?"

He came over to the bed and sat down beside her. There was no mistaking the appreciation in his eyes as he looked at his wife, and it generated a little shiver of warmth in her.

"As soon as you emerge, custom requires that I introduce you to all the servants. Although you look lovely in anything, that maid's simple gown is hardly suitable attire for your debut as my duchess."

Jerome was right. The servants would be better dressed than she was, and they would be shocked.

He gently pushed a wayward lock of hair away from her face. "I am buying time until Morgan can get here with some of your own clothes. I ordered a hot bath and a breakfast tray sent up for you, and I instructed the housekeeper, Mrs. Needham, that you are not to be disturbed for any reason." His expression became troubled. "I hope that you can get along with her. She is an excellent housekeeper, but in the past year, she has become dour and contrary."

Jerome, to Rachel's disappointment, rose from the bed and went over to his chest of drawers where he picked up his leather riding gloves. "Now I must be on my way."

"To where?" It was unfashionably early to go calling.

"To see Emily Hextable."

Jealousy ate at Rachel. "Why? Are you that anxious to see the woman I prevented you from marrying?"

His face tightened, and his demeanor turned cool. "I owe Emily the courtesy of telling her about my marriage before she hears about it from someone else."

Jerome returned an hour later, grim and silent. From his expression, the meeting with Emily had been unpleasant, but he refused to tell Rachel about it. When she tried to press him, he said curtly, "It is between Emily and me." He paused, then added in a guilty tone, "She is a fine woman, and it pains me to have hurt her. She devotes herself to good works. I hope you will see fit to follow her example."

Rachel winced. When her husband measured her against Emily, the paragon of virtue, she fell short in his eyes.

She did not see Jerome again until dinner was brought to their bedchamber. Although he joined her there for the meal, she wondered why he bothered. He was so preoccupied that her attempts at conversation floundered. Was he thinking about Emily?

Finally, Rachel demanded in exasperation, "Will you please tell me what is wrong?"

His head snapped up, and he looked contrite. "I am sorry that I am such poor company tonight. A multitude of problems has arisen in my absence." He gave her a rueful smile. "I fear I could not have picked a worse moment to go off to Yorkshire."

"Then why did you go?"

"To save my brother. A huge reward is about to be offered for Gentleman Jack's capture. It will draw every greedy thieftaker in the kingdom. When I heard of it, I had no choice but to drop everything and go to Yorkshire to try again to persuade him to give up his life as a highwayman."

"And you succeeded this time." Rachel wished that he would tell her what arguments he had used to convince Morgan, but he did not. "What problems arose in your absence?"

"I will not bore you." Jerome ran his hand distractedly through his hair. Rachel noted the weariness of his eyes and the fine lines of fatigue around his mouth.

She lay her small, fair hand on his larger one. "I shall not be bored. You forget that I have much experience dealing with estate problems. Furthermore, you are my husband, and I care about whatever troubles you." She squeezed his hand. "Please, Jerome."

He studied her with the oddest expression, as though he wanted to believe her but did not quite dare to do so. Then, he said, "I have widespread business interests, and several of them require crucial decisions. Royal Elms's steward was taken seriously ill the day I left, and much on the estate that should have been done has not been. In addition, my purchase of another estate adjacent to mine, Stanmore Acres, became final while I was gone. Now I am faced with the task of trying to restore it to some semblance of prosperity."

"If it is in such a bad way, why did you buy it?"

Jerome picked up his wine glass, and his long, lean fingers toyed with its stem. As Rachel watched, an insidious desire to have them toying with something else crept over her.

"Stanmore Acres used to be a fine property when Lord Stanton owned it, but after his death it went to his cousin, a lazy wastrel, who bled it and its people unconscionably to finance his insatiable hunger for gaming."

"But why did you buy it?" Rachel persisted.

He hesitated, then said bluntly, "I could not tolerate what was happening to it and its people."

A wave of appreciation for this complicated man she had married washed over Rachel. "What can I do to help you?"

Her question seemed to astonish him. "Nothing, my dear, but I appreciate your asking."

*Jerome takes his responsibilities very seriously and thinks it is his duty to shoulder them all himself.*

Morgan arrived later that night with Rachel's leather case and a few of her clothes from Wingate Hall. He reported that he had overseen the packing of her remaining belongings and had hired a fast post chaise to transport them to her as quickly as possible. He estimated that she would have them in three to four days.

Rachel asked, "Did you remember to tell Benjy about the kittens?"

For an instant, Morgan had a peculiar look on his face that Rachel could not decipher. "Aye, I did."

Soon after this exchange, Rachel retired to her chamber. Unpacking her case, she was startled to discover the one nightgown that Morgan had chosen to bring with him was a confection of billowing pink silk and lace.

But when she donned it to go to bed, she was thrilled by Jerome's expression when he saw her. His weariness seemed to vanish and the sudden hunger in his eyes as he crossed the room to her was unmistakable.

He took her in his arms, and as his lips moved toward hers, he whispered, "God help me, you would defeat any man's effort to resist you."

# Chapter 21

The following morning Rachel put on one of her gowns from Wingate Hall, a lace-trimmed overgown of flowered yellow silk that emphasized her tiny waist. Her cream petticoat was decorated with tiers of Mechlin lace.

The gleam in Jerome's eye told her he liked her choice, but when he spoke it was in a tone of unhappy resignation. "We must go down and be done with it as quickly as possible."

"Be done with what?" Rachel asked.

"Your introduction to the servants." Jerome looked as though he were about to take a dose of bitter medicine.

Rachel struggled to conceal her hurt. Why did he dread introducing her to the servants? Was he ashamed of her?

That thought did nothing for her peace of mind as she descended the broad staircase to the great marble hall.

The servants were waiting there to meet their new mistress. She was astonished to see what an army of them there was. They rather looked like soldiers, too, standing stiffly at attention, their faces grave and uneasy.

They were clearly fearful of what she would be like, and Rachel could not blame them for their apprehension. A new mistress could bring great change, for better or for worse, to Royal Elms and to

222

their lives. She forgot her own nervousness in her eagerness to reassure them.

The servants were lined up in order of their hierarchy within the household with the butler and the housekeeper, who was as dour as Jerome had warned, at the head.

As her husband introduced her to the servants one by one, Rachel managed a friendly comment or a question for each of them to put them at ease.

She wished that she could do the same for Jerome. He obviously hated this ceremony. His ducal demeanor that held everyone at a distance was firmly in place, and she suspected that he was not even aware of it.

Or of the effect it had on his servants. They all clearly respected him, but they were nervous and uncertain in his presence.

One of the last servants in the line was a young girl who hung her head so low that her chin rested on her chest. Even when she was introduced to Rachel, she did not raise her head but only mumbled a couple of inaudible syllables.

At first, Rachel thought the girl, a scullery maid named Jane, was afflicted by abnormal shyness, then she realized that the problem was more serious than that.

Rachel put her fingertips beneath the maid's chin and gently tipped her face up. It was covered with an ugly, blistered rash.

The girl gasped and flinched away, clearly humiliated. She hid her face behind her hands.

"It is nothing to be ashamed of, Jane," Rachel assured her. "It looks to be Saint Anthony's fire."

"That's what Cook thought," Jane said mournfully.

Rachel was glad that Morgan had brought her leather case. "I have an excellent remedy for it. I will get it for you."

"For me," the girl stammered, "but me's a scullery maid."

"But that is an indispensable position," Rachel assured her. "We could not get along without clean dishes on which to eat."

A shy, pleased smile tugged at Jane's mouth.

After Rachel had met everyone, Jerome guided her toward the drawing room. One of the platoon of footmen jumped to open its door for them.

Rachel smiled at him, "Thank you, Paul."

As the door closed behind them, Rachel turned to Jerome. He was staring at her. "What is it?"

"I am amazed that having just been introduced to scores of servants, you could manage to remember Paul's name."

"And I was astounded by the number of servants you employ. Surely you do not need so many, even for a house of this great size."

"No," Jerome admitted with an embarrassed little shrug. "But the past two years have been hard ones in Bedfordshire, too. Many people need work, and I can afford to employ them."

"How very kind of you!" The more Rachel discovered about him, the more convinced she was that she had married exactly the kind of husband that she had wanted. If only, she thought sadly, he could feel the same way about her as his wife.

"Thank God that introduction scene is over. I suspect the servants hate it as much as I do, but it is a tradition." Jerome smiled approvingly at her. The pride in his eyes made Rachel's heart sing. "I was impressed by how you managed to say something to each servant in that endless line. I have not that talent. I wish I did."

"Perhaps if you did not hate it so much, the servants would enjoy it more."

"What?" he asked blankly.

"I think because you are uncomfortable and reserved they may be, too," she said with a gentle smile. "Now, I must go deal with Jane's rash."

Rachel went upstairs and came down carrying a

bottle and a feather from her leather case. When she asked Jerome the way to the kitchen, he took her there, to the consternation of the cook and the shock of her gaping minions who had never before been visited by the duke.

"Sit down there," Rachel directed Jane, gesturing at the bench beside a long trestle table in the center of the kitchen.

When the maid complied, Rachel shook the bottle in her hand, uncapped it, and dipped the feather into it. "Now, this is how you apply it." She anointed the girl's face lightly with the aromatic liquid. "You must take care to avoid your eyes."

As Rachel worked, she was aware of Jerome's penetrating eyes upon her, an odd light in them. She wondered whether he was displeased because she was ministering to a servant.

"You must do this frequently," Rachel instructed, corking the bottle, then handing it to Jane. "Initially, it will seem to make your face redder, but you should be well in two or three days."

When the duke and duchess had emerged abovestairs, Rachel asked, "Are you annoyed that I treated a servant?"

"No! Frankly, I was astonished that you had the inclination to do so, but I was far from annoyed. Why would you think that?"

"Aunt Sophia was nearly apoplectic the first time she caught me treating a servant. She said it was disgraceful."

"She is the disgrace!" Jerome snapped.

They had reached his bedchamber, and he pulled Rachel inside. "As it happens, my lady healer, I, too, am suffering from a malady—one that I know you can cure."

"What is it?" she asked, instantly anxious for him. "How can you be so certain that I can?"

"Because you have done so before." He gave her a

wicked, sexy grin that turned her blood to liquid fire. "I have this dreadful swelling. 'Tis most painful."

She could feel her face growing hot as she grasped his meaning. "But it is the middle of the day," she protested.

"You would not want me to suffer unnecessarily, would you?"

Jerome studied Rachel's lovely, sleeping face on the pillow beside him. Her lustrous hair spilled about her in ebony waves, and her intoxicating scent of lavender and roses enveloped him.

His wife was full of surprises. Who would have thought such a beauty would show the genuine interest in the servants that she had or would be willing to help that poor scullery maid.

Her pluck had surprised him, too. She had endured the arduous trip on horseback to Royal Elms without complaint.

But what surprised Jerome most of all about his new wife was his own response to her.

He could not believe that he had been so wild for her that he had not been able to wait another moment to make love to her. To do so, he had ignored all the crises and other urgent matters that had accrued in his absence and required his immediate attention.

It unnerved him the way she could make him forget himself, his duties, everything but her.

It had been the same at Wingate Hall after he had seen the dead kittens. The memory sent a shudder through him. He hoped to God he would be able to keep her safe from whoever wanted her dead.

To do so, he would have to play the stern husband and insist that she go nowhere unless she were accompanied by himself, Ferris, or Morgan. His independent, free-spirited wife, he thought ruefully, would not like this curb at all.

Jerome hoped that the wedding present she

wanted would be more to her liking. He had dispatched Morgan to London that morning to hire Neville Griffin to learn what he could about Stephen's disappearance. It would not be easy after all these months, but if anyone could solve the mystery, it was Griffin. He had once directed the Crown's network of spies. Now he was in business for himself, employing several of his former agents.

For Rachel's sake, Jerome hoped that Griffin's findings would be happy, but he feared that Stephen must be dead by now or there would have been some word from him. If Griffin found evidence linking George to his brother's death, Jerome's "present" to Rachel would devastate her.

He had given Griffin a second assignment: to discover Sophia Wingate's background before her marriage to her first husband, Sir John Creswell. She had piqued Jerome's curiosity. Since he was hiring Griffin, he might as well assuage his own concerns, too.

A little sigh escaped Rachel's sleeping lips. A sharp wave of desire swept over Jerome, and he fought down the urge to awaken her and make love to her again. Taking her only seemed to make him want her more fiercely.

What the hell was happening to him? It was totally out of character for him to act as irresponsibly as he had today. But then, much of what he had done involving Rachel had been out of character.

It told him how much he was coming to care for her.

And that was a mistake.

A fatal mistake. Hellsfire, how could he be so stupid?

If he did not take care, he would pay for this mistake as he had paid for loving Cleo—with a broken heart. He could not stand going through that despair and disillusionment again.

Nor the aching loneliness and gnawing sense of betrayal that followed.

Cleo had been the second lovely woman to break his heart. He remembered the first, remembered all those times as a small boy he had stood on the front steps of Royal Elms, begging his mother to take him with her as she and Morgan, the two people he had loved most in the world, had left for another long visit to her brother.

But her impatient answer had always been the same. "No, Jerome, do not plague me like this. You must stay with your father."

And he had watched with tears in his eyes as the coach pulled away, then gone with dragging steps back into the big house that was suddenly so lonely.

There his austere father had angrily chastised him for the weakness that his tears betrayed: "The future Duke of Westleigh cannot be weak like other men, Jerome. You disappoint me terribly."

It was during one of his mother's and brother's long absences that the four-year-old Jerome had met Ferris, the son of the estate's master of the horse. The two boys had become fast friends. Ferris had been one of the few bright spots in Jerome's bleak, lonely childhood.

Rachel's vivacity and beauty reminded him a little of his mother. And in time, like his mother, would she, too, desert him? Or betray him as Cleo had?

Jerome tried to tell himself that Rachel was different, but he had been so certain that Cleo was, too.

He would not make that mistake again.

It hurt too much.

Forcing himself to get up and away from the temptation in his bed, he dressed and left his chamber.

In the hall he met Mrs. Needham.

"I have had the duchess's bedchamber cleaned and prepared for her grace," the dour housekeeper said.

Jerome had given no thought to the other bedchamber in the suite. He wanted to keep his wife beside him in his own bed. How quickly he had grown accustomed to the warmth and comfort of having her there.

"Had I had advance warning of her arrival, it would have been ready for her when she came," Mrs. Needham complained. "Shall I have her moved into it now?"

Jerome did not want that. He loved holding Rachel in his arms during the night.

Hellsfire, he was beginning to act like a besotted fool over her. His father's repeated admonition echoed in his memory. *The Duke of Westleigh cannot be weak like other men.*

He had to curb his hunger and growing affection for Rachel.

His mouth hardened in determination. "Yes, after she awakens."

Jerome had to distance himself from her.

He had become very good at that.

Rachel stepped into the hall in her violet riding habit. She had put it on in the hope that she could persuade Jerome to give her a tour of Royal Elms.

She had been disappointed when she had awakened from her nap to find him gone from their bed, but her mood brightened at the memory of how passionately he had made love to her—and in the middle of the day. Surely Morgan was right. Jerome did care for her.

Mrs. Needham, moving slowly and stiffly, came toward her. Rachel smiled at her, but it brought no answering response to the sour woman's mouth. "If Your Grace is going riding now, I will have the maids move your things into the duchess's bedchamber."

"*What?*" Rachel had assumed that she would continue to share Jerome's bedchamber as her mama had shared her papa's.

"His grace told me to move you after you awakened."

Rachel was shocked that her husband would have

given such an instruction to the housekeeper. Had he suddenly decided that he did not want his wife with him? Struggling to hide her dismay, she asked, "Where is my husband?"

"In the estate office."

Rachel found him there at a large walnut desk, frowning over a ledger, one of several open on the desk before him. His golden hair was badly mussed, as though he had been running his fingers through it.

He looked up at her entrance. Something leaped in his eyes at the sight of her, but it did not erase his forbidding frown. Before she could speak, he said, "If you are going riding, Ferris will accompany you."

Rachel struggled to conceal her disappointment that Jerome showed no interest in going with her.

"You are to go nowhere on Royal Elms," he went on, "unless Ferris, Morgan, or I are with you."

"Why?" she demanded, bridling at this restriction on her freedom.

"Because as my duchess, it is unseemly for you to go about alone as you used to do at Wingate Hall. Your consequence requires an escort."

"I do not give a fig about my consequence, and I am not—"

"Well, I do! You are *my* duchess."

Rachel stared at him in dismay. What had happened to the ardent lover of two hours earlier? She tried to disarm him with a smile. "I was hoping that I could persuade you to show me some of Royal Elms."

For a fleeting instant, his face betrayed how much that idea appealed to him, but then it tightened into determined lines. "I have not the time. I must deal with urgent problems."

"I see," Rachel said stiffly. "Mrs. Needham said you told her to move me out of your bedchamber."

"Yes," he said blandly. "I knew you would be more comfortable in your own room."

The sudden pain in Rachel's heart was so sharp

that she nearly gasped. It was followed by anger equally as sharp. "As you definitely will be!" She whirled and stomped out the door, slamming it hard behind her.

What in the world was wrong with the man? First, he refused to marry her, then he carried her off and seduced her into doing so. This afternoon he could not wait to make love to her. Now, he was shutting her out of his bed.

And Rachel was furious about it.

She marched up to her new bedchamber. While it was a lovely room, done in rich blue silk with delicate, feminine furnishings, it lacked the one thing she most wanted—her husband.

Rachel noted that it had a connecting door to his bedchamber and that the key to the lock was on *his* side of the door. Angrily, she yanked it out and put it on her side.

And maybe, just maybe, she would lock it against him, and let him see how it felt to be shut out.

When Rachel went up to her bedchamber that night, she walked to the connecting door and resolutely turned the key in the lock.

After she had left the estate office that afternoon, she had not seen Jerome again until dinner in the great, gilt-encrusted state dining room that could easily accommodate fifty.

The meal was a silent, strained affair, eaten at a long table under the watchful eyes—and listening ears—of the phalanx of footmen who were serving them.

Rachel was still angry and hurt that her husband had moved her out of his bedchamber, but he did not appear to notice her pique, and she could not give voice to it in front of all those servants.

Afterward he went immediately to his estate office. As she undressed for bed, she listened for the sound of his steps in the hall, but she had been in bed for nearly an hour when she finally heard them.

He went into his room, and she waited apprehensively for him to discover that her door was barred to him. She was certain that he would be furious when he discovered it.

Well, so was she!

The minutes ticked slowly by until an hour had slipped away. Rachel, curled up beneath the covers, strained in the darkness to hear any sound in the other room, but there was only quiet.

Finally, she had to concede to herself that he had gone to sleep in his own bed and had no intention of trying to join her tonight. Rachel blinked back tears of pain and defeat. She had counted on his wanting her as much tonight as she wanted him.

How could she teach her infuriating husband a lesson by barring him from her bedchamber if he would not even put himself in a position to learn it?

# Chapter 22

❦

The post chaise that Morgan had hired to bring the rest of Rachel's belongings from Wingate Hall to Royal Elms arrived three days later, only two hours after the duke's coach with Peters and Maxi pulled up.

At the sight of his mistress, the little terrier raced up the steps, barking furiously, and hurled himself at her. She gathered him into her arms, hugging him to her, delighted to have something that lavished affection upon her at Royal Elms.

After the trunks from Wingate Hall arrived, Rachel supervised the unpacking. Time was hanging heavily on her hands.

Since the afternoon her husband had pulled her into his bedroom at midday and made passionate, exhilarating love to her, she had not seen him except at dinner in the state dining room, which she had already come to hate. The oppressive formality of the huge room and the half dozen hovering footmen made the private, intimate conversation she wanted to have with Jerome impossible.

He seemed determined to avoid her at all other times, excusing himself after dinner to return to the estate office.

The cold reserve that he used to keep the world at a distance was now being employed against his wife with the same effect. He was deliberately isolating

233

himself from her, and Rachel did not understand what she had done to cause him to do so.

Her initial anger at him for having moved her out of his bedchamber had given way to dismay and pain as she realized that he seemed to be ousting her from his life as well as from his bed. She no longer locked the door between their bedchambers. What was the point? Besides, by now, she would welcome a nocturnal visit from him.

Rachel had clung to Morgan's assurance that his brother cared about her. But it was becoming harder for her to believe that. She wished that Morgan would come back from London where he had gone on business for Jerome. Rachel desperately wanted to talk to her brother-in-law. She had no one in whom she could confide, and she felt so lonely and isolated.

These feelings were exacerbated by her new home. Built on a grand scale and furnished with ornate splendor, it left Rachel, used as she was to the informal comfort of Wingate Hall, overwhelmed and ill at ease.

At least, she decided with characteristic resolution, she could do something about that. After all, whether Jerome liked it or not, she was the mistress of Royal Elms now. She would strive to make this awesome house more comfortable and less intimidating.

After her trunks were unpacked, Rachel changed into a riding habit and went out on horseback, accompanied by Ferris who was her faithful shadow wherever she went. She enjoyed his company and had learned a great deal from him. He and her husband had been unlikely friends since early childhood. Jerome had even insisted that Ferris be given lessons with him. Jerome's father had been horrified, "but no one can be more stubborn than your husband when he sets his mind to something," Ferris had told her.

As Rachel and Ferris rode today, she felt him studying her. Finally, he said, his voice full of sympathy, "You must be patient with the duke. He may seem remote at times, but no man is more loyal and caring to those he loves."

If only he could love her, Rachel thought, a lump rising in her throat.

"Why," Ferris was saying, "when he heard of the reward about to be offered for Gentleman Jack's capture, he dropped everything and went immediately to Yorkshire. There was nothing the duke would not have done to get Lord Morgan to end his career as a highwayman."

"How did my husband convince his brother to do so?"

Ferris shrugged. "I do not know that—only that he succeeded."

That night as Jerome escorted Rachel from the dining room after another strained, stilted dinner, she asked, "Why did you send Morgan to London?"

"To hire an investigator to try to learn what happened to Stephen."

"You did?" Rachel had thought her husband had forgotten about the "wedding gift" she had requested. That he remembered lifted her spirits. She turned to him with excited, shining eyes. "Why did you not tell me before?"

Jerome stared at her with the oddest expression. It sent heat twisting through her body. For a moment, she thought he meant to kiss her.

Then he frowned, and the strange spell was broken. "I was waiting until I heard whether the man thinks he can discover anything. You must excuse me, my dear, but I have more work to do tonight in the estate office."

Rachel hated it when he called her "my dear," in that cool tone. She wanted to engage him in conversation, to make him respond to her! She would not let him dismiss her so easily. In a low voice, she asked, "How did you convince your brother to give up his life of crime?"

A sardonic smile tugged at one corner of his mouth. "I married you."

"*What?*"

"Morgan promised that if I married you, he would do so."

Rachel could only stare at Jerome in shock. *There is nothing the duke would not have done to get Lord Morgan to end his career as a highwayman.*

Now she knew the real reason for Jerome's sudden change of heart about marrying her. She had been clinging to the forlorn hope that it had been because Jerome had realized he cared for her.

But now she knew the bitter truth.

He had married her because he loved his brother.

She felt as though her heart had been pulverized. Turning away from him, she said coldly, "I am happy to learn our marriage had some benefit for you. Good night."

She went up to her bedchamber where she spent a sleepless night trying to come to terms with the reality of her marriage.

She had been living in a fool's paradise, clutching at Morgan's assurance that his brother cared about her. She had told herself that in time, when Jerome learned that she was not fickle and perfidious like Cleo Macklin had been, his budding love for her would bloom and flourish.

Now it all seemed so hopeless.

And she had no one to blame but herself. She had abducted him to get him to marry her. Now they were both trapped. The lonely years stretched ahead of her, endless and bleak. Burning tears spilled down her cheeks.

Rachel got up from her solitary bed and went to the window. The first light of dawn was turning the world from black to a gray that matched her despairing mood.

Maxi trotted in from his bed in her dressing room and came to her side. She bent and gathered him up in her arms, resting her cheek on his soft, silver coat. What was she to do now?

Rachel looked out across the park of Royal Elms, carefully landscaped to offer lovely prospects and vistas. With her tears still flowing, she thought of her paternal grandmother. Rachel could feel sorry for herself as she was doing now, or she could do what her grandmother had done when she had discovered that her husband preferred other women to her.

Grandmama had put her pain and humiliation aside and set out to make the lives of others happier. Her granddaughter would follow her example. Rachel would keep so busy at Royal Elms that she would have no time to weep and mope over a husband who did not want her.

Maxi lifted his head and licked at her tears. She squeezed him to her and looked at the rolling green hills. All the land as far as her eye could see belonged to Royal Elms. Jerome might not have wanted her, but he had made her his wife and the estate's mistress.

And Rachel was determined to be the best one that Royal Elms had ever had. She would make the house a more relaxed and pleasant place to live. She would learn as much about the people of Royal Elms and their lives as she had known about those at Wingate Hall. And she would have her healing work. She would start an herb garden and seek out other herbal sources here for her remedies.

Perhaps Jerome would never love her, but at the very least she intended to win his respect.

In time, perhaps she could win more.

The next day, Rachel launched her campaign to make Royal Elms a home she could enjoy. She began with the food that, though excellently prepared, was bland and unimaginative.

Armed with her mother's recipe book, which had been included among Rachel's belongings sent from Wingate Hall, she diplomatically told the cook that she had a yearning for some of the food she had been used to at home and asked her to make some of the recipes.

The woman accepted the book eagerly, confiding, "There was not much the old duke liked, and so the menu was very restricted. Your husband gave no indication he wished it changed, and I was afraid to do so."

As the cook left, Mrs. Needham came into the room. Studying her stiff, aching movements and swollen joints that bespoke rheumatism, Rachel wondered whether her sour disposition stemmed from her being constantly in pain.

"Do you take anything for your rheumatism, Mrs. Needham?"

The housekeeper looked startled that Rachel should have noticed. "Nothing that has worked."

"I make an excellent bolus. Perhaps it would help you."

Hope flared in the woman's dull eyes. "Perhaps it would. The scullery maid's face is nearly healed. All the servants are talking about how well your treatment worked."

After Rachel gave Mrs. Needham the medication, she questioned her about Royal Elms when she had first come to work there, back when Jerome's grandfather had been duke.

Among the things Rachel learned was the house had once had a small family dining parlor, but Jerome's father had refused to use it, insisting that nothing less than a formal dining room befitted his lofty status in life. The parlor had been turned into another sitting room, and its original furnishings relegated to the attic.

An inspection of the room with its oriel overlooking a meandering woodland walk lined with irises and lily of the valley convinced Rachel that it should be restored to its original use. She decided against telling Jerome what she intended, fearing he would object. Instead she would surprise him.

When Rachel discovered a guitar in a corner of the room, she inquired whose instrument it was.

"Why the duke's," Mrs. Needham replied. "Not that he has used it for a long time, but he used to like to sit in the oriel and play it."

Rachel, accompanied by Maxi, went up to the attic, a treasure trove of retired furnishings and outmoded clothing. Eventually, she located the furniture and table linen that had been in the dining parlor.

Then she rummaged through the trunks of clothing. From one, she pulled out a voluminous black cloak and a heavily veiled black hat. It would have been perfect for one of the theatricals that had been staged at Wingate Hall before her mother's death. Rachel took them down to her room, certain that she would find some use for them.

Two nights later, Rachel was suffering through what she hoped would be her last dinner for a long time in the state dining room. Her project to recreate a more intimate dining parlor was nearly completed, and she hoped to introduce Jerome to it tomorrow night. If only he would be as happy with it when he saw it as she was.

Her husband seemed more preoccupied than usual tonight.

And grumpier. What on earth was wrong with him? None of her attempts to converse with him prospered, and by the time dessert was served, she gave up trying.

As Paul, one of the footmen, was spooning strawberry sauce over a custard he had just served the duke, he dropped a spoonful of it on the snowy white cloth.

"Must you make such a mess," Jerome snapped at him.

Rachel had not heard her husband speak like that to a servant before. Apparently, from the shocked, stricken expressions of the footmen, they had not either. Paul looked as though he wanted to burst into tears as he stammered his apologies.

Feeling sorry for him, Rachel said soothingly, "It is all right, Paul. It was an accident, and we all have them. Do not worry about it."

He flashed her a grateful look.

Rachel waited until she and her husband left the dining room to tell Jerome, "You should not have snapped at Paul like that."

He glared at her. "You think I do not know that?" Self-disgust permeated his voice. He turned away from her. "I must get back to work now."

Rachel yearned to help him as she had helped her father with Wingate Hall, but Jerome had rejected her offers to do so. He seemed intent on shutting her out of his life.

Before she got into bed that night, she went to the connecting door and turned the key. Not that Jerome would discover the door was locked against him, but in her anger at him, it made her feel better to know she had done so.

Jerome lay awake in his big bed, lusting for his wife in the room next to his. He had been avoiding her in his determination to protect his heart from the inevitable disillusionment and pain that such a beautiful woman would cause him.

While his brain told him his course was wise, his body told him that he was a damned fool. And it was becoming more and more difficult not to succumb to his hunger for Rachel.

Damn, but he wanted her as he had never wanted another woman, and he hated himself for his weakness.

Dinner with her had become pure torture as he was forced to make polite, stilted conversation in the presence of a half-dozen servants in that god-awful dining room that he had always hated, when all he wanted to do was carry her off to his bed.

Jerome ached to bury himself in Rachel's soft, passionate depths. It had been five days since he had done so, and his body acted like it had been five years. It was making him increasingly short-tempered and irritable. The way he had snapped at that poor footman at dinner tonight had been inexcusable. Jerome had never spoken that way to a servant before in his life. He had not needed Rachel to tell him he should not have and, when she did, he had snapped at her, too.

Finally, after tossing and turning for an hour in a fruitless quest for sleep, he conceded defeat. Getting up, he went to the connecting door to his wife's chamber.

And found it locked against him.

# Chapter 23

For a moment, Jerome could not believe that Rachel would have locked him out of her bedchamber. This was his house, for God's sakes! She was his wife!

He tried the door again. It was indisputably barred to him. Furious, he stormed into the hall and tried that door to her room. It opened easily. As it did, it occurred to him that perhaps the connecting door had been locked by accident.

He stepped into Rachel's room. She was sitting up in bed, reading a book by the light of the candelabra.

Jerome's breath caught as she looked up at him. Her violet eyes were wide with surprise; her lips, slightly parted. Her ebony hair, brushed to a high gloss, fell in long, shimmering waves over her breasts. She was wearing that wisp of pink silk and lace that had driven him crazy the first time he had seen her in it.

And it was doing so again.

If he had any sense, he would return to his own room, but he wanted her too much. It had been thus since he had first laid eyes on her.

Shutting the door behind him, Jerome desperately fought the wave of desire that threatened to overpower him. As he walked toward her bed, he tried to give her the benefit of the doubt. He said, "I believe the door between our rooms has been accidentally locked."

"It was not accidental." Rachel was staring at him with an odd, startled expression. "Do you often wander the halls at night like that, Your Grace?"

He glanced down. He had been so angry when he discovered the door locked against him that he had burst out of his room, forgetting that he was stark naked.

He felt hot color suffusing his face. "Only when my wife locks me out of her room. Would you mind telling me why?" It sure as hell couldn't have been because he didn't please her in bed, he thought, remembering her passionate response when he made love to her.

She shrugged. "I cannot see why you would care when you banished me from your room. I was merely locking you out of my bedchamber as you are locking me out of your life."

"Is that what you think I am doing?" he asked in surprise. In his desperate effort to curb his desire for her, he had not thought what his behavior must seem like to her. And now that he did, he felt like a scoundel. "I am sorry, my sweet," he said, his voice husky with regret and restrained passion.

He reached out to stroke her cheek comfortingly. As his fingertips touched her satin skin, longing for her blazed through him like wildfire, incinerating his doubts, his distrust, his fears. Nothing mattered except that he have her again.

He plucked the book from her hand and laid it on the table beside the candelabra. "I have something better than a book to make you sleep."

"Is it an herbal?"

Jerome laughed huskily. "No, it is better than that."

He buried his fingers in the shimmering ebony silk of her hair, and his lips claimed hers. She stiffened and tried to push him away, but he would not let her. Instead his kiss became coaxing, teasing, enticing, and after a moment, his seductive ardor overcame her resistance. She relaxed against him, her tongue mating with his. He breathed deeply of her lavender and roses scent.

His hands fell away from her hair to slip the slender straps of her nightgown off her shoulders and draw it down around her waist. She was so lost in their kiss that she did not seem to notice.

His hand cupped the fullness of her breast. His thumb lightly rubbed its peak that hardened instantly beneath his touch. He felt her body's quivering response to him, and it made him wild. He had to fight to retain his control.

He finally raised his mouth from her lips so he could join her beneath the covers. Pulling her down on the pillow beside him, he noticed a single tear trickling down her cheek.

"What is this?" He touched it gently, absorbing the moisture with his finger.

"I do not understand you; you act as though you do not want me," she said in a small, desolate voice that told him how much he had hurt her. "Then you come to me like this."

"Oh I want you, my sweet temptation. I want you too damned much. You are driving me mad." Silently, he cursed himself for what he had just given away.

Then he saw the sudden glow of relief and happiness in her remarkable violet eyes, and his anger dissipated in its warmth.

"I want you, too," she confessed shyly.

He pulled her into his strong embrace. God, but he loved the feel of her body against his own.

He wanted to make long, slow, tender love to her, but the intense need building in his body defeated him. When his fingers discovered the abundant, welcoming moisture that already bathed her, he could wait no longer.

"I am sorry, but I must have you now." His voice

was urgent and strained. He eased himself into her. A moan of pleasure escaped him as he felt the warm, tight embrace of her womanhood.

He struggled to go slowly, to stoke her pleasure before he surrendered to his own, but his body, so starved for her, spiraled out of control, and he climaxed with shuddering force.

Jerome held her tightly against him. Her earlier words echoed in his mind. *You act as though you do not want me. Then you come to me like this.*

She deserved so much better than what he had just given her, he thought in self-loathing. Determined to make their lovemaking as good for her as it had been for him, he did what he had intended to do initially, before his own need had consumed him. He lavished kisses and caresses on her as he brought her to ecstacy time and again before he once more buried himself in her velvet depths.

They moved together in the rhythm of love until she gave a muffled little shriek and her body convulsed around his, sending him over the edge with a force that left him gasping for breath.

Afterward he lay joined with her, so contented that he could not bear to break their union. He told himself that he should return to his own bed, but he did not possess the strength of will to do so.

Rachel was awakened the next morning by her husband carefully trying to extricate his limbs that were entwined with hers. She forced one eye open.

Jerome looked chagrined. "I was trying not to wake you."

"Where are you going?"

"To see a tenant," he said noncommittally as he turned away from her and dropped his legs over the edge of the bed.

"Take me with you."

"No. Go back to sleep. You did not get all that much last night."

That was the truth. He had made love to her again and again, like a man perishing of drought who had suddenly found a pure, sweet spring from which to drink and could not stop.

Yet now, after the ecstacy of the night they had spent in each other's arms, he was withdrawing from her again, just as he had that day he had her moved into this bedchamber, and that made Rachel furious. She was not going to let him do that to her again.

She pushed herself into a sitting position, forgetting that she was naked. "Like it or not, Jerome, I am your wife, and I will not be treated like a . . . a convenient!"

He turned and stared at her, clearly taken aback by her anger. "What the hell are you talking about?"

"You ignore me for days. Then you suddenly invade my bedroom in the middle of the night, make love to me, and now you are going to walk out again, refusing to let me go with you."

She flounced out of bed. "No doubt, you are intending to ignore me again for days on end!"

He gave her a wide, lascivious grin that deepened his eyes to the most glorious blue and sent heat pulsating through her. "Not if you walk around like that."

Her face flamed as she realized that she was naked. She grabbed for her rose dressing sacque. "I will not have you ignore me. I am your wife, but you make me feel like an unwanted and unwelcome intruder here. Do you think I have no feelings?"

Jerome looked abashed. "Rachel, I am not going for a pleasure ride. If I were, I would happily take you with me. I have business on the estate that requires my attention."

"Not very pleasant business from your expression," she observed.

"No," he admitted. "And that is why I cannot take you with me."

"Please, Jerome, do not shut me out of your life as

you are doing. Let me go with you. I promise I will wait well out of earshot while you conduct your business if that is what you wish, but I want to be with you."

Rachel could see from the set of his face that he still meant to refuse her. "Can you not understand, I am your wife, and I want to be part of your life. Is that too much to ask? I want you to discuss your problems and worries with me. I want to see Royal Elms through your eyes. I want to share your life with you."

He stared wonderingly at her for a long moment as though she were speaking a language he could not entirely comprehend. Then, his sudden, brilliant smile sent her heart skittering. He held out his hand to her. "Come with me."

With a surge of joy and relief, her fingers closed around his. He drew her into his arms and kissed her long and hard.

Later, as Rachel and Jerome rode past well-tended fields and tenants' cottages in excellent repair, she noticed that he was constantly vigilant, just as her late father had been at Wingate Hall, to the smallest sign of disorder or neglect.

"You should be very proud of Royal Elms. It bespeaks a dedicated owner."

"I am proud of it," he admitted.

"How did it get its name?"

"King Henry the Eighth once had a hunting box nestled in a grove of majestic elms here. Later he sold it to one of my ducal ancestors. The structure is long gone, but several of the elms are still standing."

Rachel asked Jerome about his farming techniques. After answering several of her questions, he broke into a delighted laugh. It was the first time since his return to Royal Elms that she had heard him laugh like that, and the joyous sound lifted her own spirits.

"I have never met another woman who could discuss farming so knowledgeably as you."

"You forget that I managed Wingate Hall."

"And very well from what I heard."

She sat straighter in the saddle, buoyed by his unsolicited compliment. They rode in companionable silence until they reached a tenant farm that contrasted sharply with its neighbors. The buildings were in need of paint and repair, and the fields looked neglected.

Rachel frowned. "What happened here?"

Jerome sighed. "I see you appreciate the problem. The tenant is a hard worker and a good man, which is why I have been patient with him for as long as I have. He cannot manage so that he puts aside enough money for seed and stock the following season. Even when crops were excellent, he fell into arrears on his rent. The poor harvests the past two years have compounded his problems until there is no hope for him. I should have stepped in well before now. It would have been kinder if I had."

As they rode up to the cottage, Rachel noted its deteriorating condition. A tall, stoop-shouldered man came out to greet them with fear in his eyes. His long, narrow face reminded Rachel of a mournful hound's.

Jerome said, "David, I suspect you know why I have come."

To Rachel's dismay, the sympathy and concern for the man that her husband had revealed to her moments earlier was now hidden behind his ducal reserve.

David nodded miserably. "Me hopes to catch up on me arrears this autumn if the harvest is bountiful."

"But you know that you have no hope of that. You did not plant enough, and your stock is all gone. Everything is in such a bad case that I cannot let it go on like this any longer."

Jerome spoke with a stiffness that made him sound remote and unsympathetic, although his wife knew that was not true. His tone stemmed from his distaste for what he was doing. Yet, to David, he must surely sound utterly uncaring.

Jerome said, "I must take the farm back into my own hands."

The despair in David's eyes was so intense that it made Rachel want to cry.

"What is me and me family to do, Yer Grace?" the man asked bitterly. "Where's us to go?"

The question seemed to surprise Jerome. "Why nowhere. You will stay here and take care of the farm for me. I will pay you wages for managing it for me."

Rachel wanted to hug her husband for his wisdom.

David stared at the duke in confusion. If only Jerome had been more relaxed and affable with the man, Rachel was certain he would have been terribly relieved and grateful. But her husband's manner prevented David from appreciating what a wise and generous solution he had just been given to his shortcomings.

As Rachel and Jerome rode away, he said, "If it is David's farm, it is his responsibility. If he works for me, it is mine. I will have his stock replaced and his buildings repaired and refurbished. Next spring I will see that he has plenty of seed and manure."

Rachel beamed her approval at her husband. "That was the perfect solution." She knew that behind his reserve and arrogance, he cared deeply for his people's welfare. She discerned that he did not want to be so aloof. He simply did not know how to be any other way unless he was with one of the few souls, such as Ferris, that he liked and trusted.

She intended to try to remedy this.

In his estate office, Jerome read a dull report from an export business that he owned, but his mind kept drifting back to Rachel's glowing smile of approval for his solution to David's problems. Her praise had made him feel eight feet tall.

Honest compliments had been few and far between in Jerome's life. His father had never praised him for succeeding, only criticized him for not measuring up to impossible standards. Jerome had long ago learned to discount the false compliments of the toadeaters. Better none at all than the insincere mouthings of those wanting only to better themselves in his opinion.

But Rachel's praise had been genuine. So had her interest in Royal Elms.

Most of all today, Jerome had enjoyed being with his wife, seeing her lovely face, hearing her warm honey voice. sharing the way he felt about Royal Elms with her.

He knew that he could no longer stay away from her, no longer intended even to try. Slowly, but surely, she was eroding the barriers he had built around his heart.

And it scared the hell out of him.

What did Rachel really feel for him? She had abducted him in a desperate attempt to escape marriage to Lord Felix. Jerome had been convenient. He was also rich and titled, and one of the few men to whom her aunt could not object.

Jerome could excite Rachel's passion, but had he ever touched her heart? No word of love had crossed her lips. Not once during their lovemaking had she told him that she even cared for him.

At least, she was not a liar. He supposed he should be thankful for that. He remembered with a contemptuous curl of his lip Cleo's profuse lies about loving him.

Jerome's thoughts were interrupted by Ferris's appearance at the door. Knowing that Ferris would not disturb him in his estate office except on crucial matters, Jerome asked in alarm, "What is it?"

"A stranger was at the village tavern last night, asking odd questions about your new duchess."

Cold fingers of fear clutched at Jerome. That was what had happened at Wingate Hall before the shot had been fired at Rachel.

Ferris's worried face told Jerome he was thinking the same thing. "The man wanted to know how the servants feel about their new mistress and whether there are any who do not like her."

"Are there?"

"None that I know of. I looked for him today, but there was no sign of him in the village. I will be at the tavern the next few nights in case he returns."

Jerome nodded, terribly afraid that whoever was stalking Rachel had followed her to Royal Elms. Jerome had thought to save her by marrying her and bringing her here, but danger still threatened her.

His voice was suddenly hoarse with apprehension. "Do not let her out of your sight."

"Come with me," Rachel told Jerome when he came down to dinner that night. "I have a surprise for you."

Startled, he quirked a quizzical eyebrow at her. "Before dinner?"

Nodding, she pulled him with her. Her eyes were alight with excitement, and she looked so enchanting in a pale blue overgown over a white silk petticoat that it was all Jerome could do to keep from stopping and taking her in his arms.

She led him to the small sitting room that was one of his favorites. He had sat sometimes in the evening in its oriel, playing his guitar and looking out at the woodland beauty.

As he stepped inside, Jerome stopped in astonishment. It had been transformed into a charming, intimate dining parlor with a round table in the center. What surprised him most, however, were not the two place settings laid on the table, but its chairs. They were covered in the same colorful Indian needle-work, embroidered with bright blue and rose flowers, as the room's window valances.

He turned to Rachel in surprise. "Why this must have been the room's original use."

"Did you not know that?"

"No." Jerome felt a little foolish. It had taken his wife only a few days to discover what he, who had lived here all his life, had not known.

Rachel smiled. "I have ordered dinner to be served here tonight. I hope you do not mind. I find it very daunting for just the two of us to dine in that huge dining room with all those footmen hovering over us."

So did Jerome. The thought of escaping the burdensome show delighted him.

"I have also reduced the number of footmen serving us to one and instructed him to remain in the hall except when we summon him."

Jerome was overjoyed at the prospect of dining in the privacy of this pretty, cheerful little room overlooking one of his favorite vistas at Royal Elms.

After the footman served the soup and retired into the hall, shutting the door behind him, Jerome reveled for a moment in the blessed privacy, then asked, "When was this room previously used for dining?"

"Until your father became duke. He decreed meals must be served in the state dining room."

"My father! I should have known." Jerome had never liked eating in the oppressive formality of the state dining room but his father had insisted that was the way the Dukes of Westleigh had always dined. Tradition must be upheld.

Now Jerome discovered that the tradition had begun with his father.

"I am told that until your father this was part of the suite of rooms used for informal family living. I would like to use them for that purpose again."

Jerome felt a lightening of his spirit at the prospect

of an alternative to the intimidating grandeur of the house's state rooms. "So would I."

Rachel asked Jerome about his day. He never discussed his problems with anyone, but under her skillful questioning he found himself confiding much more to her than he had ever done to anyone before, even Morgan.

His wife's interest in Royal Elms delighted him. So did the intelligence of her observations and her suggestions for handling its problems. No wonder her father had put her in charge of Wingate Hall.

By the time the dinner concluded, Jerome could not remember when he had enjoyed a meal so much at Royal Elms. He was far more relaxed and at ease in this pleasant, comfortable room.

As they rose from the table, Rachel said, "I discovered your guitar. Would you play a little for me?"

He had work waiting for him, but he remembered her plaintive plea: *Please, Jerome, do not shut me out of your life as you are doing.* He picked up his guitar and settled in the oriel seat. Rachel sat down beside him.

He started with a haunting ballad. Rachel began singing it, and he joined her, pleased by how well their voices blended together.

She knew most of the songs that he did, including one or two that raised his eyebrows. She explained that her brothers with whom she used to sing like this at Wingate Hall had taught them to her.

The time flew by. It had been a long time since Jerome had spent such a pleasant night at Royal Elms. He would have hated for it to come to an end had he not looked forward to taking Rachel to bed with him.

He smiled in anticipation. He could not ask for a more passionate and responsive wife. But his happy mood suddenly disintegrated into doubt. He could not hope that such a dazzling woman would continue to be satisfied with only her husband.

It would not be a problem at Royal Elms where

there was no one to vie for her attention, but once he took her to London, her beauty would draw every handsome rake in the city like flies to honey. She would not be able to resist their polished and persistent attentions.

Perhaps the answer was never to take her to London. She would be safe here.

At least from the rakes. Jerome's mouth tightened as he thought of the unknown person who wanted her dead. He was terribly afraid that the villain was her brother George. He was the only one with anything to gain from her death.

After Ferris had told Jerome about the man at the tavern, he had sent a messenger to Morgan in London that he urgently needed him at Royal Elms.

Jerome prayed that he, his brother, and Ferris, would be able to protect Rachel from the specter that threatened her.

# Chapter 24

"**E**mily Hextable has come to call on you," Jerome told his wife the following morning. "I will introduce you to her. She is a wonderful woman."

Rachel wondered why Emily would be calling so early in the day, but she dutifully went with her husband to the drawing room to meet the "wonderful woman" whom she had prevented him from marrying.

She was already a little weary of hearing how marvelous Emily was. Rachel's first callers at Royal Elms after her arrival had been the fat vicar of the parish church and his complacent, equally fat wife. Both of them had lauded Emily's virtues so effusively that they had set Rachel's teeth on edge.

"I do not know what the parish and its poor and sick would do without Miss Hextable," the vicar had said. "It is rare, indeed, in this day and age, to find a woman so devoted to good works."

Jerome guided Rachel into the drawing room where Emily awaited them. She was a tall, thin woman, perhaps a half-dozen years older than Rachel. Her narrow face was neither pretty nor unattractive, but nondescript with no outstanding feature to attract attention. Her gray eyes held no sparkle and her mouth was thin and unsmiling except when she caught Jerome's eye.

Emily's gaze remained on him even as she acknowledged the introduction to his wife.

Rachel said politely, "The duke tells me you are devoted to helping others."

"Yes," Emily said, her gaze still on Jerome, "I never shirk my Christian duty."

He told Rachel admiringly, "Emily is tireless in her efforts on behalf of the less fortunate."

Emily gave a small sigh tinged with weariness. "I must be tireless, for the poor things depend upon me so. They all say they do not know what they would do without me. Indeed, it is that knowledge which keeps me going."

She gave Jerome a smile that seemed to Rachel—who admittedly was prejudiced—more calculating than sincere. "Their gratitude is so touching. The sick tell me how much my coming to comfort them in their illness means to them. They say I am the only one who dares to do so. No one else will go near them."

"You are very brave," Jerome agreed.

Emily smiled proudly at his compliment. "I could not bear to be otherwise," she assured him. "But I do not neglect the hungry. Poor Mrs. Quigg tells me over and over that she and her children would starve were it not for me. It is so sad, Jerome. It makes me weep to see their plight."

She wiped delicately at her eyes, although Rachel, looking closely, could see no sign of tears.

"You must forgive me for calling at this early hour," Emily said, still looking at Jerome. "But I have so many visits to make today, several of them to your tenants. I shall be happy to take your wife with me, if she should wish to go."

Rachel suspected that only another woman would have caught the subtle nuance in Emily's tone that betrayed she was certain Jerome's new duchess would want nothing to do with such calls.

Rachel did not intend to give her that satisfaction.

"I shall be delighted to go with you," she lied. Emily's chagrined expression was worth subjecting herself to the woman's company.

Jerome said to Emily, "I hear that the eldest child of Bill Taggart over at Stanmore Acres is ill. Perhaps you could stop by to see her."

"That Godless man," Emily exclaimed, her face mirroring her revulsion. "I will pay no visit to his home. He is a shocking blasphemer and an ungrateful, lazy lout."

"A lazy lout? I am surprised," Jerome said with a frown. "When Lord Stanton owned Stanmore Acres, he used to say that he wished he had another dozen tenants like Taggart."

Emily sniffed. "No longer. You would be shocked at how neglectful that wretched man has become."

"I am very sorry to hear that," Jerome said.

Since her husband was now Taggart's landlord, Rachel thought, it was one more problem with which he must deal.

As Jerome took his leave, Emily's gaze followed him until he had left the room. He might have married another woman, but she still wanted him.

As Emily's chariot rolled across the rich, verdant hills, Rachel tried to converse with her, but she had very little to say now that Jerome was not around. Emily clearly was not happy to have his wife's company.

Rachel's thoughts turned to her husband. She was stung by his continuing appreciation for the "wonderful" Emily. Would she ever measure up in his eyes to the saintly paragon? Rachel tried to cheer herself by recalling the great success the dining parlor had been the previous night. Jerome had clearly loved it.

When they had gone upstairs after their evening of music-making, he had led her past the door to her bedchamber and taken her to his own. There he had made such tender love to her that it revived her hope that, even though he had married her only to save his brother, she might yet win his heart.

Emily told Rachel that their first visit would be to comfort a Royal Elms's family in which four of the five young children had been stricken with an ague and were very ill.

When the chariot stopped in front of a neat cottage, one of the two footmen riding behind the passenger compartment jumped down with a small basket on his arm and went to the door. Rachel would have opened the chariot door, but Emily placed a restraining hand on her arm. "We are not getting out."

"Then how can we call upon them?"

"We dare not go inside." Emily sounded appalled. "The children are sick. They might be contagious."

"I do not see how we can comfort them from the chariot." Rachel observed tartly.

"We will leave them food."

A woman, clearly exhausted and distraught, opened the door, and the footman handed her the little basket. A loud feverish wail drifted through the entranceway. The woman bobbed her head in thanks and started to close the door, but the footman prevented her from doing so.

He hissed, "You must come out and give proper thanks to Miss Hextable for her generosity, you ungrateful woman."

The wailing from inside the cottage grew louder and was joined by a second child's reedy voice. The woman cast a harried look over her shoulder as she obediently stepped outside and walked toward the chariot.

"Do not come any closer," Emily called in alarm when the woman was still eight feet away. "You may thank me from there."

Rachel shrank back into the seat in embarrassment. The woman obediently stopped and curtsied to the chariot. "Thank you, Miss Hextable," she said in a toneless voice. "You are most generous."

Emily nodded her dismissal. The woman, clearly frantic to get back to her crying children, turned and ran into the cottage.

The footman returned to his seat, and the chariot drove on.

They had gone some distance when Rachel saw a small, thin boy in coarse homespun and bare feet picking bilberries near the side of the road.

Emily saw him, too, and cried, "That dreadful child is stealing your berries!"

She called to her coachman to stop at once. As the equipage rolled to a halt, she exclaimed, "It is one of that Godless Bill Taggart's brats. Their father has no respect for anything, so what can you expect of his children?"

The boy was on Rachel's side of the chariot. Emily leaned across her and thrust her face through the open window. "Why are you picking those berries, Billy Taggart?"

The boy turned to face her. He looked to be no more than six years old. " 'Em's for me sister. Maggie's sick and craves 'em somethin' fierce."

"You cannot have them," Emily said sternly. "They do not belong to you. You are stealing."

A defiant look gripped his thin little face. "They'll only go to waste."

"Yes, they will," Rachel interjected. "You are welcome to the berries, Billy."

"You cannot reward him for stealing!" Emily cried in a scandalized tone.

"I said he could have them, so he is not stealing."

Emily flopped back against the seat, muttering darkly, and the chariot moved on.

The great number of calls that Emily had to make totaled exactly three. The final one was to what could only be called a hovel. Once again Emily and Rachel remained in the chariot while Mrs. Quigg, a haggard

woman, old before her time, came outside. She was
trailed by seven children in garments as tattered as
her own. The oldest was about nine. In her arms, she
carried a scrawny baby.

"Are these Royal Elms's tenants?" Rachel asked,
much shocked at the sight of the gaunt faces and thin
bodies before her. They looked half-starved. Knowing her husband's concern for his people, she could
not conceive that he would have permitted them to
fall into such a state.

"Now they are. This is part of Stanmore Acres."

The children's eyes fastened hungrily on the tiny
basket of food that the footman handed their mother.
Rachel was certain that it could not hold enough to
provide one decent meal for a family half the size of
this one.

The rehearsed way that Mrs. Quigg and her offspring lined up and curtsied to Emily told Rachel
that this was a frequent ritual for them.

Their voices uttered praise for Miss Hextable's
generosity, but their eyes bespoke animosity rather
than gratitude. And Rachel could not blame them. To
be required to go through that for the little dab of
food in the basket was outrageous.

Morgan's words echoed in Rachel's memory: *Emily
is very careful to conceal her real nature from Jerome, and
he has never seen her as she really is.*

After Emily returned her to Royal Elms, Rachel immediately sent word to Ferris that she wished to go
riding. Then she went upstairs to change into her
nondescript brown habit and collect her leather case
of herbal remedies.

It was already midafternoon, and Rachel would
have time for only one visit today. The children suffering from the ague were most in need of her attention.

"Where are you going?" Jerome asked the following day when he saw Rachel in her old brown riding
habit. She was carrying her leather case.

"To call on a sick tenant."

"With Emily?" he asked. Emily's concern for others had been her principal, indeed her only attraction for Jerome. He had wanted a duchess who would give generously of herself to help his people. And he was beginning to hope that he had found her in Rachel.

"I prefer to make my own calls," she said.

Jerome did not want that. He had known that Rachel would be safe the previous day with Emily because she was always accompanied by a coachman and two footmen. The more people around Rachel the less likely a possible killer would make another attempt on her life. "I prefer that you go with Emily." His fear for his wife made his voice sharper than he intended.

For a moment, Rachel's face was shadowed by some pain he did not understand, then she said quietly, "By calling separately, Emily and I can benefit twice as many people."

Jerome could not argue with the logic of that, but still he worried about his wife's safety, and that made him frown disapprovingly.

As Rachel and Ferris rode away from the stable, she was still smarting that Jerome would want her to make her calls with Emily. Rachel could think of no reason for that, except that he thought her incapable of doing it properly on her own, and that hurt her deeply.

Rachel stopped first to check on the children with the ague. Once again her fever remedy had worked. All four patients were improving to the tearful relief of their frightened mother.

Rachel's next call was on the Quiggs, where she left such a large quantity of food that their eyes bulged at the sight.

When they started to line up to give their thanks to her as they were required to do to Emily, she implored them, "I beg of you, do not. You would embarrass me."

After they left, Ferris said, "It is pitiful the way the previous owner of Stanmore Acres bled the Quiggs and his other tenants dry."

Rachel stopped beside a clump of bilberry bushes loaded with fruit. With Ferris's help, she picked a generous amount to take to Maggie Taggart.

As they remounted, Rachel reflected that Ferris seemed especially uneasy today. His eyes were constantly searching the landscape as though he expected to find something amiss there.

The Taggarts' home was a small cottage built of native stone with a shed behind it that served as a barn.

While Ferris waited with the horses, Rachel went to the door with her leather case in one hand and the bilberries in the other. Billy appeared in the doorway, his big brown eyes widening in surprise at the sight of her.

Rachel smiled at him. "I came to see how Maggie is."

"Awful sick," the boy said in a scared voice.

"I brought her some more berries." Rachel handed him the container.

"Who's here, Billy?" a hoarse voice called from beside one of the two beds inside the small cabin.

"The lady what said me could have the berries, Pa. Her brought more o' 'em for Maggie."

Rachel stepped inside the cottage and went over to the man. He was gripping the hand of a little girl in the bed. Her thin face was pinched with fever.

Taggart was a wiry man with sandy hair, a square face, and sharp nose. Rachel had seen the terrible look in his eyes before. It was that of a frantic, frightened parent watching helplessly as his child slipped away from him into death's arms.

A towheaded toddler whimpered on the floor beside him. Taggart eyed Rachel suspiciously.

If she told him she was the new Duchess of Westleigh coming to help his daughter, she doubted he would believe her, so she said simply, "My name is Rachel, and I am an herbal healer. I have an excellent remedy for fever that I think will help your daughter."

Hope flared in his exhausted gray eyes, then died. "Me got no money to pay you."

"I do not want money, only to make this pretty little girl well."

"I'd be most thankful for you to do anything you can for me poor lass."

As Rachel coaxed Maggie to swallow her medicine, an infant's wail rose from a corner of the room.

Taggart hurried to a wooden cradle that Rachel had not noticed, scooped up a baby from it, and rocked it in his arms, comforting it so tenderly that a lump rose in her throat. "Where is Mrs. Taggart?"

"Died giving this little one life," he said, a catch in his voice as he looked down at the babe in his arms. "Me's both pa and ma now."

Rachel looked around the clean, tidy little cottage in amazement. "How do you manage?"

His mouth twisted grimly. " 'Tis not easy. Maggie takes care of the younger children while me's in the fields, but with her so ill . . . " His voice trailed away. He was a man on the knife-edge of despair.

Rachel's heart went out to him. To think that Emily had dismissed him as a lazy lout!

After Rachel returned to Royal Elms, she changed out of her riding habit and was on her way to the stillroom when she heard Morgan's voice in the marble hall.

She ran to greet him in his dusty, wrinkled riding clothes. "You look as though you have been in the saddle since dawn."

Morgan nodded. "I have been. Jerome sent for me to come at once, but he did not tell me why."

Rachel frowned. "He said nothing to me about asking you to return, although I know he did not expect you to stay so long in London."

"I was giving the two of you a little time together without me around." Morgan drew her into a small anteroom off the hall. "How is married life going?"

Rachel's mouth drooped. "I am afraid that I cannot measure up to Emily Hextable in Jerome's eyes."

Morgan grimaced. "Jerome has never been able to see Saint Emily for what she is. How can he? He has only her word—actually many thousands of her words—assuring him how wonderful she is."

"I understand that I am deeply indebted to you." Rachel tried to swallow the lump that had risen in her throat.

"For what?"

"For getting Jerome to marry me by agreeing to abandon your life as a highwayman."

"Hell and damnation, surely he did not tell you that was why he married you?"

"He said that was how he got you to bury Gentleman Jack forever."

"But that is *not* why he married you. He rejected my offer, but when he decided to marry you, he held me to it. I told you before that he married you because he discovered he cared about you."

Rachel wanted so much to believe her brother-in-law, but did she dare? She studied him curiously. "Why did you become a highwayman?"

"I craved adventure; I wanted to right wrongs, and I was bored."

"Will you miss it?"

"No." Morgan grinned wryly. "I did not find getting shot particularly pleasant." He hesitated, then volunteered, "Even before that, though, I had come to the conclusion that robbing the rich to help the poor they have wronged—much as it may appeal to my sense of justice and adventure—accomplishes only a little for a limited number of people. Hell,

Jerome does more good with all the extra people he employs at Royal Elms."

"You and your brother are much alike, I think."

"Perhaps," Morgan conceded. "Jerome has argued with me since I began my criminal career that I could find far more effective ways within the law to try to aid the poor and oppressed. Being shot made me realize I would be no help to anyone dead, and it was time to try another way."

Rachel smiled. "And what will that way be?"

"I am not certain yet. Perhaps campaigning to change the Poor Law, perhaps establishing a model community that would offer people dignity and employment."

"I hope you are planning a long stay at Royal Elms while you decide."

"There is nothing for me to do here."

"Yes, there is. The steward is still ill, and Jerome is overburdened."

"But he would not think of sharing his responsibilities with me."

Although Morgan spoke lightly, Rachel detected pain, too. "Is that why you left Royal Elms? Because Jerome would not share his burden with you?"

Morgan gave her an approving smile. "How astute you are. Speaking of my brother, I had better find him and discover why he sent for me."

Jerome could not hide his relief as Morgan strode into the estate office. Jumping up from his chair, he said, "Thank God, you are here. I did not expect you before tomorrow."

"Your message said it was urgent I come at once, and I did."

"I need your help. Why are you looking at me so oddly?"

"Do you know, Jerome, this is the first time that you have ever asked for my help? What can I do?"

"Help keep Rachel safe." Jerome told his brother

about the stranger at the tavern. The mere thought of someone harming his wife made his heart constrict.

"It sounds like a repeat of what happened at Wingate Hall," Morgan said in alarm.

"Precisely. The man has not returned to the tavern nor has Ferris been able to find any trace of him, but I am afraid we have not seen the last of him. Ferris is guarding her, but I would prefer both of you with her wherever she goes."

"I will do whatever you want, but she would prefer your company to mine."

Jerome sighed. "I wish that were possible, but I cannot spare the time. Too much on the estate requires my attention."

Jerome watched Morgan's face cloud for an instant as though his answer had somehow hurt him. "And your estate is more important to you than your wife?"

Stung, Jerome snapped back, "At least I do not have to worry about my estate betraying me."

Morgan shook his head sadly. "You still cannot trust Rachel. If she eventually is unfaithful to you, you will have only yourself to blame."

"Ah, yes, because I have failed to win her love." Jerome realized how much he wanted to do that, and it rankled him that not once as he pleasured her in his arms had she so much as murmured the word. "I wish to hell I knew how to win it."

"You already have it."

Jerome's jaw dropped. "What?"

"Why do you think she wanted to marry you?"

"To escape Lord Felix." And that knowledge still festered painfully in Jerome's heart. "She has never mentioned the word love to me."

"Because I warned her before she abducted you that she must not do so. I know you, Jerome, and if she had, you would have dismissed her as a conniving liar who was professing an emotion she did not feel."

Jerome started to protest, then fell silent as he realized that Morgan was right. That was exactly what he would have thought, and he would have hated her.

"She could not win with you. She was damned if she told you and damned if she did not."

Much as he wanted to, Jerome could not deny the truth of his brother's statement.

"Why the hell did you give her the impression you married her only to get me to stop being Gentleman Jack?"

"I did not! I said—hellsfire, she misunderstood me." Jerome sighed. He seemed to have a talent for hurting his wife even when that was the last thing he intended.

When Rachel and Jerome were alone that night in his bedchamber, she said, "I think Morgan enjoyed our musical trio tonight. He sings as well as you do."

Her husband began lazily untying the four taffeta bows that fastened the bodice of her striped silk nightgown. "Perhaps the changes you have made to Royal Elms will entice him to make it his home again." The hopeful note faded from Jerome's voice. "But I doubt it. He gets too restless here."

"It is you who can entice him to stay."

Jerome's hands stilled. "How?"

"Let him help you. Turn some of your responsibilities over to him. You have too much to do anyhow."

"Estate affairs bore him. Besides, it would be most unfair of me to burden him with responsibility for what cannot be his."

"Oh, Jerome, can you not see that Morgan is bored because he has nothing to do here. That is why he does not want to stay. Would you want to remain under those circumstances?"

"No," Jerome admitted, "but—"

"At least give him the choice."

"Perhaps I will," Jerome said thoughtfully. After a moment, he cupped her face in his hands.

Alarmed by the gravity of his expression, she asked, "What is it?"

"Rachel, I did not marry you to put an end to my brother's career as a highwayman."

Relief and hope flowered within her. "Then why did you marry me?"

"I could not bear to leave you at Wingate Hall."

Her heart gave a little leap of happiness. Smiling, she confided, "And I abducted you because I could not bear to have you leave Wingate Hall without me."

He looked as though he could not quite believe her. "I thought you only wanted to escape marriage to Lord Felix?"

Rachel decided to take a chance and tell him the truth. "I did it because I had fallen in love with you."

"Do you still love me?" There was an odd urgency to his voice.

She smiled at him. "Of course."

Something flared in his eyes, deepening their color to rich, cyan brilliance. "I am glad," he murmured. His mouth came down on hers, hard and demanding.

Disappointment raked her. Rachel had hoped that he would confess he loved her, too. But at least he had accepted her love and not mocked it. That was a start.

# Chapter 25

Awaking one morning a fortnight later, Jerome
reached automatically for his wife, only to discover she was not in the bed beside him. His eyes
flew open, and he sat up in alarm.

He saw her standing by one of the windows, already dressed in a green riding habit. "Why are you
up so early?"

"It is a glorious day," she cried with an enthusiasm
that was irresistible. "It rained during the night, and
the air is as fresh as a newly washed babe. I want to
be out in it. Come riding with me, just the two of
us."

"You are mad," he grumbled, but her proposal appealed to him. Anything involving Rachel's company
did. As he got up, he ran his hand over the thick,
rough stubble on his face. "I will have to shave first."

"Please, do not take the time. You do not have to
act the duke so early in the morning. Wear the old
clothes you wore the day I met you. You will be far
more comfortable."

Yes, he would be, and he did as she bid him.

As they were leaving, she picked up her leather
case. "Why are you bringing that?"

"I want to check on a sick child on our way back."

He was instantly conscious of his unshaven face
and old clothes. "I thought no one would see us."

She smiled at him. "You can pretend to be my
groom and stay with the horses as Ferris does."

Jerome chuckled. The thought of passing himself off again as a groom also appealed to him.

As they rode across Royal Elms's park in the fresh morning air, he was happy at Rachel's suggestion.

"Do you mind if we ride to Stanmore Acres?" Jerome asked. He wanted to look over Ben Taggart's farm. Taggart had once been Stanmore Acres's best and most dependable tenant, but the estate's former steward insisted he had become a dangerous troublemaker, and Emily had complained that he was a lazy lout. Now Jerome decided to see for himself.

Rachel said, "I am happy to go wherever you want, but why do you choose it?"

He smiled at her. "Thanks to your advice that I turn some of my responsibilities at Royal Elms over to Morgan, I now have time to devote to my new acquisition." Jerome had been amazed at how eager his brother had been to help him. "If it were not for you, my sweet, I would still be laboring under the mistaken belief that Morgan had no interest in estate affairs."

Rachel's dimples flashed beguilingly. "And all the while you thought you were sparing him."

"It turns out he has an impressive aptitude for management."

He and Morgan were not the only ones happier since Rachel's arrival at Royal Elms, Jerome thought. The servants were more cheerful. Even Mrs. Needham had lost her sourness and smiled frequently, especially when Rachel was around.

What a change his wife had made in only four short weeks. Jerome looked forward now to meals in the cozy dining parlor. Even the food tasted better.

The darkest cloud on his horizon, the threat to Rachel's life, had receded. The inquisitive man had not been seen again either in the tavern or elsewhere in the vicinity. As the days passed with no sign of him, Jerome's apprehension had diminished but not disappeared entirely. The thought of losing Rachel opened a black, aching void within him.

As they passed David's farm, Rachel observed, "How much better it looks now that you have taken it over. Morgan and I talked to him yesterday, and he is so relieved to be out from under its burden that he is a different man."

Jerome smiled. "And I am relieved that he is reconciled to what I had to do."

"I heard that Emily Hextable left for London quite unexpectedly last week."

"Yes, I heard that, too." Jerome wondered what had prompted her sudden departure. He supposed that he would always feel a little guilty about Emily, but with each passing day, he grew increasingly appreciative of the wife he had.

Gradually, his fear that Rachel would betray him, and break his heart as Cleo Macklin had done, was fading. He was confident that as long as he kept his wife at Royal Elms, he had no reason to doubt her. Still he could not shake the dread that she would be unable to resist the London rakes. He told himself his worry was irrational, but he could not dispel it.

They had reached Stanmore Acres. As they rounded a curve in the road, a small boy in coarse homespun and bare feet was walking toward them. When he sighted Rachel, he broke into a run toward her, crying in a panicked voice, "Please, ma'am, help us!"

He looked to be no more than five or six. Tears were streaming down his cheeks.

"Billy!" Rachel reined her mare to a stop.

Startled that she would know the child, Jerome dismounted and helped her down. She handed her leather case to him, then opened her arms to the boy. He tumbled into them, and she held him comfortingly.

"What is it, Billy?" she asked as her hand brushed his sandy hair soothingly. "Is Maggie ill again?"

" 'Tis pa this time! Him's taken real bad, coughin' somethin' awful and fightin' for breath. You must come."

"Aye, I shall." She gave the boy a final comforting pat, then released him.

Jerome helped her remount her mare. "Who is the child?" he asked in a low voice as he helped her back into the saddle.

"Billy Taggart."

"Bill Taggart's son?" Jerome asked with a frown as he handed Rachel her leather case.

"Aye, poor man. He has had a most difficult time since he lost his wife in childbed last year."

"No one told me his wife died."

"He was left with four little ones including the newborn. He is overburdened trying to care for them and the farm, too. The eldest child, Maggie, is only seven. Although she tries, she cannot begin to do all that her mama did."

That explained Taggart's sudden "laziness." Why had Emily not told him Taggart had been left with four motherless children?

Jerome held out his hand to Billy. "Come. You can ride in front of me."

Their destination was a tiny cottage built of native stone. A shed behind it apparently served as a barn. It was a tidy property, far better kept than most tenant farms on Stanmore Acres, but Jerome's keen eye picked out signs of neglect. The garden needed weeding and the pile of chopped wood was sadly depleted.

He followed Rachel into the cottage, ducking his head beneath the low overhang of the door. The interior was clean and tidy.

A moan came from a man lying in one of the two beds crowded into the room. His breathing was loud and labored. A thin little girl stood beside him, looking helpless and terrified.

Another child, a boy who looked to be about two,

huddled in a corner, sucking his thumb. A cradle with a sleeping baby in it sat near the bed.

The toddler's eyes were big and frightened as were his older brother's. Despite little Billy's best efforts to stem his tears, they were trickling down his cheeks.

Who could blame them for being afraid? These children had already lost one parent and now might be in danger of losing the other. Jerome remembered how scared he had been when, as a child of eleven, his own mother had died.

The girl turned at the sound of their entry. Her face was exhausted and frightened and far too old for seven years. Then she saw Rachel, and her expression of relief was so intense that Jerome was startled. His wife set her leather case down and gathered the little girl into her arms.

The child began to sob. "Please don't let me pa die and go 'way like me mum."

Rachel hugged her. "I shall do everything I can for him, Maggie. Now let me look at him."

She went over to the man on the bed and felt his forehead. His eyes fluttered open at her touch. She said softly, "I am afraid your fever is very high."

"Hotter 'an a fire, he is," Maggie agreed.

The sick man was suddenly wracked by a fit of harsh, unproductive coughing that made Jerome ache to hear it. He stepped nearer the bed. Although he knew of Taggart, he had never seen him before.

He was about the same age as Jerome, with sandy hair, a square face, sharp nose, and wide mouth. Once he must have been handsome, but illness and anxiety had left their mark in the gauntness of his face and the deep lines chiseled about his eyes and mouth.

Bill blinked at the tall stranger who had suddenly appeared in his home. "Who're you?" he inquired weakly.

Jerome was acutely conscious of his unshaven face

and old stained clothes. The man would think him an impostor if he tried to tell him the truth.

"My husband," Rachel answered for him. "How long have you been ill?"

The man was coughing again, and Maggie answered, "Three days, but him didn't take to his bed 'til yesterday."

From the easy rapport his wife had with the family, Jerome was certain its members had no idea of her identity.

Rachel opened her leather case, selected a bottle filled with a dark, vile looking substance, and removed its cork.

"First, I will give you some of this. It is what worked so well on Maggie." She gave Taggart two spoonfuls of the concoction. "Now I will make a poultice for your chest to try to ease the congestion. I will need some hot water."

She looked toward the stone fireplace. The fire was all but extinguished and Jerome, seeing a way to make himself useful, quietly went out to bring in additional wood.

From the corner of her eye, Rachel saw her husband step outside. Surely he did not fear he would contract Taggart's illness if he remained in the tiny cottage.

When Jerome came back inside, she was surprised to see that he was carrying wood. He knelt beside the fireplace, and carefully coaxed the dying blaze back to life.

She went over to him. "Thank you," she said softly. "I will be here for some time. You may wish to go back."

He merely shrugged noncommittally.

Taggart was seized by another fit of coughing that was terrible to hear. The toddler who had been sucking his thumb in the corner began to cry in fright.

Rachel cast a distracted glance in his direction. "Hush now, Tommy."

Jerome went over to the corner and swept the weeping toddler up in his arms, then he held out a hand to Billy.

"We can be of no help here," he told them, "and we do not want to get in the way while my wife is trying to make your father better."

He led both boys outside. Rachel blessed Jerome for his quick, quiet discernment of what would help her most.

When she glanced outside a few minutes later, the two little boys, their worries forgotten for the moment, were in an animated discussion with Jerome, who had dropped down on one knee beside them.

An hour passed, and Bill's fever began dropping a little. The poultice Rachel had applied to his chest eased his breathing, and he dozed off.

Another half hour passed, and Bill was racked by a fit of deep, hoarse coughing, but at least this time it was productive. Seeing Maggie's frightened face, Rachel hastened to reassure her that this was actually a good sign.

Bill's dull eyes opened, and he looked about the cottage. "Where are me boys?"

"Outside with my husband."

"Me'd like 'em to come in."

Rachel went outside but did not immediately see them. She headed toward the shed, drawn by the sound of wood being chopped behind it. One of Bill's friends, hearing of his illness, must have come by to help out.

As she rounded the corner of the shed, she saw Billy and his little brother sitting on a crude bench.

They were watching a man, silhouetted by the sun, splitting firewood. He was clad only in buckskin breeches, and the light danced on his bare, tanned chest and on his golden hair, damp and curly from the sweat his exertions had raised. The muscles in his powerful arms rippled as he rhythmically swung the ax.

The sight robbed Rachel of her breath. He was the most beautiful man she had ever seen. The mythological Hercules made of earthly flesh and blood. So stunned was she by this splendid sight that it was a second before she recognized this glorious, golden creature as her husband.

She wondered what her brother Stephen, who would not know one end of an ax from the other, would say to see the duke he regarded as so haughty and condescending chopping wood for a tenant farmer. "I am going to take the boys inside."

Jerome nodded and strode over to the bench. Rachel could not take her eyes from him as he pulled his shirt on.

He looked up, catching her avid perusal, and grinned. "Still like what you see?" he inquired softly.

She did. Oh, yes, she did. She smiled at him. "Better than ever." The answering warmth in her husband's eyes made her heart skip a beat.

Reluctantly tearing her gaze from him, she held out her hand to Tommy. "Come, we must go inside."

"Me wanta stay with Jer'm," the toddler said.

"I will take you in." Jerome swung the boy, who giggled with great glee, up over his head, then settled him on his shoulders for a ride to the house.

Watching them, Rachel could not help smiling. Jerome would make a fine father, she thought with joy in her heart.

She noticed that enough wood had been chopped to provide the Taggarts with cooking fuel for at least a month.

At the door to the cottage, Jerome put Tommy down and, ducking his head, followed him through the low door.

Tommy scampered to his father's bedside. Bill took the child's hand. "Where you been, son?"

The child nodded toward Jerome. "With Jer'm."

Jer'm smiled.

So did Rachel. Although her husband wrapped

himself in his ducal consequence when it suited him, he seemed to enjoy himself more when he could shed it.

"Tell pa what Jer'm done," little Tommy urged Billy.

His older brother said, "Him chopped the wood for us, Pa."

When Taggart tried to thank Jerome, he said, "I was happy to be of some help. You look and sound much better than you did a couple of hours ago."

"Feeling better, too, thanks to yer wife. She cured me Maggie, too, when her was so sick. Me gives thanks to the Lord for sending her to us."

That did not sound like the godless man Emily Hextable had called him, Rachel thought. But then he was not a lazy lout either, only overburdened.

Bill said bitterly, "Yer wife be so much better 'an that other one."

"Other one?" Jerome inquired.

"The high and mighty Miss Hextable. Nobody hereabout can tolerate that one."

"But she devotes herself to good works," Jerome protested.

"Good works! Her'd never come inside this cottage with me or me daughter sick as yer wife done. Her'd be too afeard o' catching it."

Jerome's brow knit. "But I understood she called frequently on the sick."

"And sits in her fancy carriage outside the door. Which is just as well. That way the sick don't have to listen to her preaching that'd only make 'em sicker. The day me wife died in childbed, she showed up to tell me how it was God's will and I should get down on me knees and thank him for his blessings. It was more than me could take. Me told her me wanted nothing to do with her God or her. Called me an ingrate and a heathen, she did." Bill broke into a pleased smile. "And she ain't been back since."

Jerome looked so shocked that Rachel had to bite back a smile. At last, he was hearing about the real Emily.

Bill's lips curled in contempt. "People hate her coming with her pitiful bit o' food and expecting to be thanked as though her'd brought a feast. Hear her's gone off to London now that the duke up and married someone else. Surprised he didn't marry her. From what me hears o' him, they're two o' a kind."

Dismayed at the turn the conversation had taken, Rachel opened her mouth to tell Bill the true identity of his visitor, but Jerome gave her a quelling look.

"Ne'er met the duke meself," Bill continued, "but they say him's as arrogant and haughty as they come."

"I have often heard the same," Jerome said so pleasantly that Rachel had to smother a giggle. He pulled a wooden stool over and sat down beside Taggart's bed.

Tommy sidled up beside Jerome with a hopeful expression. As he obligingly lifted him on to his lap, the toddler chortled happily.

"Bill, you need help until you are well," Jerome said. "I know a woman, a widow, who will care for you and the children until you are up and about. I will send her over."

"Nay, I cannot pay her."

"She will ask for nothing from you," Jerome said.

"You mean to pay her yerself," Taggart guessed. " 'Tis kind o' you, but me can't let you. Me'll not be able to pay you back." Bill's voice turned bitter. "Don't know how much longer me'll have this farm. The duke's bought the land. He won't care none about crops being bad fer two years. We're afeard him'll keep raising our rents like the last owner done."

"You need not worry. That will not happen."

"You can't know that, Mr. Jerm whate'er yer name is."

"It's Parnell."

Bill's pallor became even more pronounced. "You related to the duke?"

"I am afraid it is worse than that," Jerome said apologetically. "I am he, but I hope you will not hold that against me."

Bill's eyes darted questioningly to Rachel. She gave a little confirming nod of her head. He gulped. "Why didn't you tell me afore that you're him?"

Jerome grinned at the sick man. "And ruin my reputation for hauteur and condescension? That would never do! What would people talk about?" He rubbed his thumb and forefinger over his unshaven chin. "The truth is that between this stubble and the clothes I am wearing, I did not think you would believe me."

"Yer right on that," Bill said. "Ne'er heard o' a duke choppin' wood ne'ther."

"I like chopping wood. No doubt," Jerome added wryly, "because I have the luxury of doing it only when I wish to. Now, Bill, as your landlord, I am telling you that I will send Mrs. Pierce here as well as men to help with the farm until you are back on your feet. You will repay me by getting well." He took the sick man's hand in his own and gripped it. "You are the best tenant that I have on Stanmore Acres, and I do not want to lose you."

Rachel would always remember the look of profound relief on Bill's face. She suspected that Jerome had just given him better medicine than she ever could by removing the fear that he would lose his farm.

Her love for her husband overflowed her heart, and she smiled proudly at him.

After they returned to Royal Elms, Jerome stopped in the marble hall to look through the letters the day's post had brought while Rachel went upstairs. On top was the first report from Neville Griffin, the investigator Jerome had hired to look into Stephen's disappearance. He scanned it, then hurried up the steps to his wife's bedchamber.

When he told her that he had received it, she asked eagerly whether he had learned anything new.

"Yes, but I fear it only adds to the puzzle," Jerome said with a frown. "Contrary to the letter from the captain of *The Betsy* that your uncle received, Stephen did sail from Calais to Dover on that ship. They interviewed several of the Betsy's officers and sailors who all swear that he was aboard during the voyage across the channel."

"Then why did the captain write us that letter?"

"I do not know. He is now the captain of another ship that is presently at sea. Griffin will not be able to question him until he returns, but I suspect that the captain may have had something to do with Stephen's disappearance."

"But if Stephen returned to England, what happened to him?"

"Sailors from *The Betsy* and several other ships that were docked at Dover that night report seeing a man matching Stephen's description seized and impressed aboard a British frigate, *The Sea Falcon*. It, too, is currently at sea on a voyage to the Americas."

His wife's lovely face was suddenly alight with joy. "But that means Stephen is still alive! That's wonderful!" Her voice faltered at Jerome's expression. "Why do you look so grim?"

"Not many men survive impressment." Especially not when they had led as pampered a life as Stephen had.

"But perhaps my brother was able to convince them of his real identity."

Jerome hated to have to deflate her excitement and happiness, but it would be even crueler to build her hopes in vain. He said quietly, "If that were the case,

Stephen would have been home by now. I am sorry, my sweet."

He pulled her into his arms and held her against him, offering her the comfort of his body.

"I know he is still alive," she cried. "I know it!"

Jerome had drawn exactly the opposite conclusion from the report and had expected her to do the same.

"Did the report say anything else?"

"No." Jerome did not tell her about the second investigation that he had ordered, the one into Sophia Wingate's background. Griffin had written that he had not yet been able to turn up anything about her.

"I am so grateful to you for doing this for me." Rachel arched her head back and looked up at her husband with a dazzling, dimpled smile that he found irresistible.

He bent his head to capture her mouth in a long, erotic kiss that left them both panting. Her hands began unbuttoning his shirt. It was all the invitation he needed.

Later, when she came to shuddering satisfaction in his arms, she cried in that warm, honey voice, "I love you. I love you so much."

Jerome thrilled at hearing her say it. He even believed her. So long as he could keep her at Royal Elms, away from London and its determined rakes, she would be safely his.

Although he was not such a fool that he would let himself love her in return, she had become very important to him. In fact, it scared him a little at how important. Not that he would admit that to her. He would not give such a beautiful woman that power over him.

Jerome lay on his back beside a clear blue stream that twisted and burbled through the floor of a narrow, secluded vale. The spreading, drooping branches of an alder shaded him while he watched his wife wading happily in the creek.

When he had first shown Rachel this spot, she had fallen in love with it. This afternoon, she had coaxed him into returning with her for a picnic.

He reflected that his self-discipline had gone to hell since he had married her.

And he did not care.

Jerome thought about their visit to the Taggarts' cottage that morning. It had been quite unlike any other morning he had ever spent. Although he had always been generous to those who needed help, all of his contributions in the past had been through intermediaries—his hirelings or the parish—and much of it had been anonymous donations.

His visit to the Taggarts was the first time he had helped people directly, had become involved in their lives, and he was surprised by how happy and satisfied that had made him feel.

He remembered the admiring smile that Rachel had given him as they left the Taggarts. It had warmed Jerome to the darkest corners of his soul.

Yes, he thought happily, he was as content and at peace with the world as he could ever remember being.

He turned to watch his wife splashing about in the stream. What a remarkable creature she was.

Desire for her surged through him, and he thought about making love to her here. Would it be private enough?

He propped himself on one elbow and scanned the hillside above them. Sunlight glinted on something extending from a rock outcropping at the edge of a cluster of two oaks, halfway up the hill.

As he watched, the object fluttered about. Puzzled, Jerome stared at it, trying to determine what it could be. It was long and narrow like a stick, but a stick would not glitter in the sunlight. Then he caught a glimpse of a man's head at the end of it.

And, in a heartstopping flash, he knew what it was. A musket barrel.

And it was aimed at Rachel playing in the creek.

Reacting instinctively, without conscious thought, Jerome catapulted to his feet. From the bank of the stream, he launched himself at his wife in a flying tackle. The sound of a shot shattered the idyllic quiet of the vale a split second before he and Rachel went crashing down into the shallow creek.

The ball whizzed over Jerome's head and splashed into the water a few feet beyond him, sending up a spray. Had he not knocked Rachel out of the way, it surely would have hit her.

He poked his head above the water in time to see a burly man dart from behind the rock with the musket in his hand and run without a backward glance around the shoulder of the hill.

No doubt he thought he had hit his target and decided against staying around to make certain.

Jerome pushed himself to his feet on the slippery rocks in the creek bottom and lifted Rachel out of the water.

As he did so, he heard the sound of a horse galloping beyond the hill. The attacker was making good his escape.

Rachel sputtered and choked from the water she had swallowed. When she was able to talk again, she eyed Jerome as though he were a lunatic. "What on earth did you think you were doing?"

"Saving your life."

"Really? I thought you were trying to kill me."

"Did you not hear the shot as I knocked you into the water?"

She gaped at him. "I heard a noise, but surely, you are mistaken."

"I wish to hell I was."

Jerome carried her from the stream and laid her on the cloth spread beneath the alder tree.

In that moment, he at last admitted to himself how much he had come to love her.

# Chapter 26

**"T**he bastard has vanished," Jerome said to Morgan. "He has clearly fled the neighborhood."

The two brothers were in the library at Royal Elms, discussing the man who had fired the shot at Rachel two days earlier.

"If he had not, I am certain that he would have been drawn and quartered by now," Morgan said.

That was the truth. Jerome had been surprised by the anger and outrage the attack on his wife had generated. Word had traveled like wildfire, and he had been swamped with volunteers for search parties that had beaten the bushes in vain for her attacker.

"People love Rachel," Morgan was saying.

Yes, they did. Jerome had been deeply moved by the secure spot his wife had won in the hearts of his people in the brief time she had been at Royal Elms. She had turned out to be exactly the kind, caring wife that he had wanted, and the thought of losing her to a stalking murderer terrified him.

Morgan rubbed the back of his neck. "They are incensed that anyone could mean Rachel harm."

"I wish she could believe that someone does," Jerome grumbled. "She still thinks the shot must have been a mistake even though I have pointed out to her repeatedly that it could not have been. Nor could it be accidental that two shots have been fired

285

at her in the past three months. But she cannot believe that anyone would want to kill her."

"You have not told her about the kittens?"

"No. I know I should, but she will be so distressed to learn they are dead." And the thought of causing his wife any upset was repugnant to Jerome. His mouth curved downward. "Given her reaction to the shots, I am not at all certain she would believe that it was the milk meant for her that killed them."

Morgan rose and went over to a mahogany tripod table that held a decanter of brandy. "I gather you have not told her of our suspicions about George either?"

"If she cannot believe the clear evidence that someone is trying to kill her, do you think she would accept our theory that her brother, whom she loves dearly, may be responsible?"

"No," Morgan admitted. He held up the decanter. "Do you want some brandy, too?"

Jerome nodded absently as he pondered the problem of how to get Rachel to accept the serious danger she was in.

As Morgan poured the liquor into two glasses, he said, "You need to use your influence to have George brought back to England where Griffin's men can shadow him."

Jerome frowned. "That would require me to go to London. I will not be separated from Rachel." Since the shot had been fired at her, he could hardly stand to have her out of his sight. He worried about her constantly. During the night, if she rolled out of his arms in her sleep, he would wake up and reach out to her to assure himself that she was still there.

Although he had acknowledged to himself how much he loved her, he had not been able to tell her. A nagging fear that she would eventually disillusion him when he took her to London held him back.

"Take Rachel with you." Morgan handed his

brother one of the glasses of brandy. "Why does that suggestion bring such a scowl to your face?"

"I am afraid of what will happen once she is in London. You know that every damn rake there will be after her, and they will not give up." Jerome had tried to tell himself his apprehension that Rachel would betray him was ridiculous, but he had not been able to banish it. He had seen too many sweet girls whose exposure to London society had changed them into something far less admirable. "For most of the rakes, the pursuit is the game. How long will Rachel be able to resist such a determined onslaught?"

"You underestimate your wife."

"You underestimate those reprobates' determination and charm." The thought of Rachel succumbing to their lures filled Jerome with bitter, intolerable pain.

"You are wrong about Rachel. Nor can you keep her hidden away here." Morgan took a sip of brandy. "Remember when I was a child and the horse I was riding threw me? I would not get back on him, and you insisted I must. You told me it was better to confront my fears for it was the only hope I had of defeating them."

Jerome smiled at the memory of how Morgan had gotten back up on the horse and showed him who was master.

"Well, now I am giving you that same advice, big brother. Take Rachel to London and learn the truth instead of hiding here, worrying about what *might* happen. Once you are there, stay as long as it takes to convince yourself that your worries about her are foolish and unwarranted."

Morgan was right. Better to find out the truth rather than speculating about what it might be. Jerome did not even have the excuse that he was needed at Royal Elms. The past fortnight had proven to him that he should have no qualms about leaving his brother to run it. He would take Rachel to London, and they would stay there for as long as it took to banish his apprehensions.

"You must be here for the annual feast," Morgan was saying, "but that is only two days away. You and Rachel can leave the next morning."

"Will you manage Royal Elms for me while I am gone?"

Jerome's request brought a look of pleased pride to Morgan's face that would remain in his brother's memory for a long time. Rachel had been right about what Morgan needed.

As she had been right about so many things.

Morgan said, "You will not regret your trust in me."

Jerome raised his brandy glass in salute to his brother. "Believe me, I have always trusted you, but I felt guilty about burdening you with my responsibilities."

Two days later, Jerome looked out at the preparations on the broad, green sward for the annual feast. Long tables had been set up. Soon they would be groaning beneath the weight of great platters of food. Games and contests would be held around the perimeter for both children and adults. Later there would be dancing on the large flagstone terrace overlooking the sward.

All of Royal Elms—servants, tenants, workers, and their families—were invited. That meant the number of attendees, swollen by all the extra people Jerome had hired in recent months, would be staggering.

Rachel had thrown herself into preparations for the festivities. Her enthusiasm had been contagious, and even Jerome, who had always abhorred the feast, had been a little infected by her excitement.

He did not know which of his ancestors had started the tradition of the annual feast. It dated back at least to the fifth duke, perhaps earlier. Jerome had been to his first feast while still a babe in arms.

In all those years, the ritual had never changed: The duke, dressed in his richest clothes, appeared on the terrace to welcome his guests, who then stood about stiff and respectful and uncomfortable until he disappeared back in the house. Then their fun began.

No wonder Jerome dreaded the event. He sighed and turned away from the window. It was time to dress. Peters had already laid out his most elegant and elaborate *habit à la francaise* in red burgundy velvet.

Rachel entered, clad in a simple gown of violet muslin and a gauze apron edged with bobbin lace. Jerome's breath caught at the way the gown's color accentuated the brilliance of her eyes.

"Oh pray, do not wear that!" she exclaimed when she saw the suit he was about to put on.

"Why not?"

"It is too, too—," she paused, searching for a word—"too off-putting."

"But this is the sort of thing the duke always wears," he protested.

"Not today." Rachel was already selecting from his wardrobe a pair of buff breeches and a coat of blue broadcloth. It was one of his plainer coats, its front and wide cuffs unornamented with the embroidery that was so fashionable.

She thrust the garments at him. "You will be more comfortable with these and so will your guests."

Certainly he would be. If the truth be known, he hated dressing up in those elaborate clothes to meet his tenants. His father had insisted it was what the duke must do, that the people expected it of him, but Jerome always felt like a peacock on display.

As they went down to the feast, he said, "We need stay but a few minutes, only long enough for me to give the welcoming speech."

She stopped, her face indignant. "After all the work I have done for today, I do not intend to miss the fun."

*What fun?* he wondered to himself.

They strode out upon the terrace. He stopped at its edge and welcomed his guests, inviting them to partake heartily of the food and the games that had been provided for them. When he finished, he would have turned and gone back into the house.

It was what his father had always done, and Jerome had followed his sire's example, staying only long enough to give his welcome.

But now Rachel was urging him in the opposite direction, and they stepped down on the sward. People drew back to make way for them. Jerome felt the opening of the gulf that always separated the duke from his people.

Little Tommy Taggart propelled himself across the sward toward Jerome, shouting "Jer'm, Jer'm."

The toddler was clearly so delighted to see him and had such an excited look on his face that Jerome could not resist swinging the boy high over his head. That was clearly what Tommy wanted, and he shrieked with glee.

When Jerome would have put him down, he protested and wrapped his little arm around the duke's neck, saying, "Me wants to stay as tall as you, Jer'm."

Jerome laughed and let him stay, carrying him with one arm.

Billy ran up and held out his hand. Jerome took it with his free one. "Me's gunna be in the sack race, Jer'm. Will you help me put it on?"

Jerome forgot his stiffness, forgot the chasm between him and his tenants, forgot everything but Billy's eager, trusting expression. No child had looked at him quite like that before, and Jerome grinned. "Of course I will help you." He glanced toward Rachel. She was beaming proudly at him.

As Billy led him toward the spot for the sack race, stunned faces gaped at this unlikely trio.

"Where's your father, Billy?" Jerome asked.

"O'er there."

The elder Taggart, recovered from his illness, was standing a little apart from the crowd of people, trying to comfort his squalling infant. Maggie was at his side. Jerome went over to talk to him.

Rachel, who had followed her husband, said to Bill, "Let me take the baby." She held out her arms, and he handed over the crying infant with obvious relief.

As Jerome talked to Taggart, Rachel made nonsense sounds at the baby who stopped crying and began laughing at her.

A wave of pleasure, warm and sweet, washed over Jerome at the sight of his wife with the babe. He had never thought much about children, although he had known he must beget an heir. Now, however, he discovered that he was eager for the day when she would hold their own child in her arms.

Remembering his boyhood, he made a silent vow to be a better father than his own. He smiled as he thought of all the things that he wanted to do with his son of Rachel's making.

After talking to Taggart for a few minutes, Jerome went with Billy to help him into his sack.

After the race, in which Billy finished second, Rachel took Jerome's arm and led him through the crowd. They made slow progress as she stopped constantly to talk with one or another of the guests. Jerome was amazed at how many people she called by name and how much she knew about them and their families. He found himself drawn into her conversations, and he soon forgot his awkwardness in his genuine interest in what was being said.

At least a couple of hours had gone by, and people were filling their plates with food when Jerome saw Rachel whisper to Morgan. He nodded and disappeared into the house. When he returned a few minutes later, he was carrying Jerome's guitar. He handed it to him, saying, "Time for some music while people are eating."

Jerome was taken aback. He had never played for anyone but his own family before. For an instant, he thought of refusing, but Rachel's dimples flashed in such a beguiling, expectant smile that he began strumming the instrument.

Jerome led off with a lively song. Rachel and Morgan joined their voices with his. The crowd fell silent.

When the song was finished, spontaneous applause burst from the audience. "More," someone cried, and Jerome complied.

After a few more songs, Morgan urged the crowd to join them in an impromptu musicale. As he played, Jerome realized that for the first time in his life he was thoroughly enjoying an annual feast.

He glanced over at his wife who had brought so many happy changes to his life. He loved her more than he had ever loved anyone, but still he had not told her. His bedeviling fear that she would disillusion him once she was in London had kept him silent.

But Rachel deserved to hear of his love for her, to hear how happy she made him. A hideous thought clawed at his heart. What if the killer who stalked her were to succeed, and he had never told her how much he loved her?

Tonight Jerome would remedy that.

Twilight was creeping over the lawns, still crowded with people. Rachel watched her husband moving easily among his guests, talking, joking, and laughing with them, all the stiffness and reserve that had been his father's curse having melted away.

How she loved it here. Royal Elms had become her home now. She hated to leave tomorrow for London, but Jerome had said they must go because he had urgent business there. Rachel had another reason for not wanting to go. Ever since her husband had told her about the journey, she had been plagued by a strange, disconcerting premonition that their visit to the city would end unhappily.

The lively strain of a country dance started, and Jerome led her on to the terrace to begin it.

"It is the first time we have danced together," he remarked. "It has been a day of many firsts for me, thanks to you, my love."

A thrill went through Rachel at the endearment that he had never used with her before. Did he mean it?

Soon the terrace was crowded with dancers. Rachel quickly discovered that her husband danced as well as he played the guitar.

After several vigorous dances, she begged for a rest, and Jerome led her off the floor.

A footman came up to him with a letter, saying that a messenger from London had just delivered it. Jerome opened it and scanned the contents. His smile disappeared and his face turned grave.

He took Rachel's arm and led her silently into a small anteroom that opened on the terrace.

"What is it, Jerome?" she asked in concern. "Who is the letter from?"

"Neville Griffin, the investigator that I hired to discover what happened to Stephen."

Fear gripped her. "Is it bad news about Stephen?"

"I fear so. *The Sea Falcon* has returned to England. Its captain confirms that a man matching your brother's description was impressed aboard the frigate on the night Stephen arrived in Dover from Calais. The man even claimed that he was Lord Arlington, but no one believed him. It was thought to be a lie designed to escape impressment."

"If the ship is back now, where is Stephen?"

"In a desperate attempt to escape, he dived from the ship before dawn one morning off the coast of America. In the mist, he apparently mistook the lights of a another ship for land, which was actually several miles away." Jerome paused and drew her into his arms. "I am sorry, my love. Stephen was drowned."

"No!" Rachel cried. "Was his body recovered?"

"Not that Griffin could discover."

Rachel clung to that slender thread of hope. "Then, I do not believe he is dead! Stephen was an excellent swimmer."

"I am sorry, my sweet, but he could not possibly have made it to shore. It was too far."

Tears spilled down Rachel's cheeks. "I cannot believe it."

Jerome held her to him for a long time, comforting her with soothing murmurs, gentle caresses, and the warmth of his body.

Memories of Stephen, of the bright, laughing boy, of the sometimes maddening, sometimes tender, big brother tormented Rachel's mind. "He cannot be dead. He was my family."

"You have another family now," Jerome gently reminded her. "Me."

Her chin quavered. "But Stephen loved me."

Jerome's lips lowered toward hers. When they were only an inch away, they hesitated, and he whispered, "And so do I. God, help me, so do I love you, and so very much." His mouth came down in a kiss that was simultaneously demanding, arousing, and comforting.

Happy as Rachel was to hear his confession, she had not missed its undertone of reluctance. She had won his love, but not his trust.

Without that, how long would his love survive?

# Chapter 27

The women's voices swirled around Rachel in the elegant London drawing room with its damask-covered settees and chairs, delicate French marquetry tables trimmed with ormolu, and ornate plasterwork on walls and ceiling.

To her left, three aristocratic ladies were discussing, as though it were one of the year's most momentous topics, who had *not* been invited to the Duke of Devonshire's ball that night.

To her right, four others, led by the malicious Lady Oldfield, were speculating with the venom of vipers on suspected love affairs between lords of the realm and ladies not their wives.

Both conversations bored Rachel, and she begrudged the wasted hours she had spent since her arrival in London nearly four weeks ago on these required social calls upon ladies who had nothing to occupy them but the latest fashions, their cherished social status, and spiteful gossip.

The nights were as bad, as she went from one soiree or ball to another. The beautifully appointed rooms were generally hot, stuffy, and crowded. She was inevitably surrounded by rakes all eager to be the first to engage the beautiful new duchess in an illicit liaison. Rachel felt like a doe being stalked by hunters, and she loathed it.

Most of all, she hated not having Jerome at her side. Although she had learned since her arrival in

London that society considered it bad form at evening entertainments for a husband to dance attendance on his own wife instead of someone else's, she did not understand why this should be so.

Rachel longed to go back to Royal Elms. She had been so much happier there. She would gladly trade all the entertainments London had to offer for the quiet nights she had spent with Jerome at his country estate. Yet he showed no inclination to leave the city.

He was so busy with his extensive financial affairs that she saw less of him than she would have liked. She had taken to leaving him notes, telling him how much she loved him.

Rachel no longer had any worry that he reciprocated it. She had to smile when she thought of how protective he was of her. Ever since that shot had been fired while she was wading in the stream, Jerome worried constantly about her. She was still convinced it was accidental for no one had any reason to kill her, but her husband would let her go nowhere in London without Ferris and four armed riders surrounding her equipage.

"Even the king is not so well-guarded," she grumbled to her husband.

Her happiest moments came in the early hours of the morning after their social rounds had ended. Then her husband would take her to bed and make passionate, ecstatic love to her. In his arms, Rachel forgot her persistent, disturbing premonition that this London visit would end unhappily.

Now, sitting in the ornate drawing room only half hearing the women's chatter around her, Rachel wondered how her brother Stephen could have loved London so much. And she longed to go home to Royal Elms, where her life had purpose.

Rachel smothered a yawn. She was so sleepy lately. It was totally unlike her. Usually she was full of energy. And the past two or three mornings, her stomach had been unsettled. She was beginning to suspect that she might be pregnant. The thought filled her with joy, but she wanted to be more certain of her suspicions before she confided them to Jerome.

One of the women said, "I hear Emily Hextable leaves London in three days for Bedfordshire to prepare for her wedding to Sir Henry Lockman."

Emily's surprise betrothal to Sir Henry had been announced two days after Rachel and Jerome had arrived in London.

Lady Oldfield said cattily, "What a comedown for poor Emily to have to marry a mere baronet when she thought she would be a duchess. Once she lost her duke though, she wasted no time in accepting another offer." She snickered unpleasantly. "But then at her age she had no time to waste."

Rachel might not like Emily, but she liked Lady Oldfield and her rancorous tongue even less.

The ladyship turned to Rachel with a nasty glint in her eye. "Your Grace, that charming Anthony Denton has been paying you such close attention. Everyone is remarking upon it."

Yes, he had been. Far too close, and nothing Rachel said discouraged him. If Tony was lavishing her with his unwanted attention to inflame Jerome, he was succeeding.

"Tony is such a handsome devil," Lady Oldfield was saying with an insinuating smirk, "and such an accomplished lover."

Rachel was incensed by this slanderous innuendo from a woman reputed to have once been Denton's lover herself, and she could not resist giving the vicious-tongued harpy a taste of her own medicine. Raising her eyebrows skeptically, Rachel asked, "Is he *really*? You obviously know and appreciate his accomplishments much better than I."

Lady Oldfield gasped, and her face turned a dull red. Several of the other women hid their smiles behind their bejeweled hands. For once, her ladyship's tongue failed her, but the furious glint in her eye told Rachel that she had made a dangerous enemy.

Jerome looked around the Duke of Devonshire's ballroom, packed with the cream of English society. He would have no trouble finding his wife in it, he thought sardonically. He had only to look for the largest throng of men, and he would be certain to find her in the center of it.

During the nearly four weeks they had been in London now, it had been thus at every entertainment she had attended. Rachel's incomparable beauty and charm had made her the belle of London. Every man in the city seemed dazzled by her.

She clearly did not return their interest but, as Jerome had feared, that only caused the more determined of the rakes to redouble their efforts to conquer her. Jerome still was not entirely certain that they would fail. He and Rachel would stay in London for however long it took to convince himself that his wife would not betray him. He had to acknowledge that the fault lay not with Rachel, but with himself and his memories of Cleo and of other wanton beauties.

At last, Jerome located Rachel in the crowded ballroom. She was, as he had expected, surrounded by eager admirers including Anthony Denton. It enraged Jerome the way Tony hung around her.

Clenching his jaw, Jerome fiercely told himself that Rachel would not succumb to Tony's lures as the faithless Cleo had. Rachel loved her husband. He smiled at the thought of the notes that she had taken to writing him since they had been in London. She would tuck them in odd places for him to discover, and it delighted him to find these loving missives.

As Jerome pushed his way through the crowd, he saw Sir Henry Lockman, Emily Hextable's stolid betrothed, ahead of him. Jerome had been startled by how quickly Emily had accepted an offer of marriage, but then he was hardly in a position to cast stones.

Watching Lockman, Jerome realized how much he envied the man. Not because he was marrying Emily, but because he would never have to worry about her being unfaithful to him.

A man who looked a little like Neville Griffin brushed past Jerome, reminding him that he must tell Rachel about the investigator's latest finding. The former captain of *The Betsy* had returned to England and had confirmed what his men had said. Stephen had sailed from Calais to Dover on that vessel. The captain emphatically denied writing the letter that the Wingates received.

Jerome had asked Griffin, "Do you think he was involved in Stephen's disappearance and is lying now to protect himself?"

"Your Grace," the investigator had replied, "I do not know what to think."

The orchestra resumed playing, and Lord Rufus Oldfield sidled up to Jerome. Rufus had only one rival for the title of London's most malicious gossip, and that was his own wife. What a disgusting pair they made, Jerome thought contemptuously.

"Has Your Grace heard about Lord Birkhall's latest wager?"

Birkhall was both an incorrigible gambler and a rich reprobate who delighted in robbing young innocents of their virtue. He was always eager to bet vast sums on anything that amused him. Generally what amused him was cruel or salacious.

"No, I have not," Jerome answered. Nor did he care, but he knew that Oldfield would insist upon telling him.

"Birkhall has wagered Anthony Denton twenty thousand pounds that he cannot seduce a certain lady of quality."

"What lady?" Jerome asked before he could stop himself.

"Ah, that is the rub." Oldfield gave him a mocking smile. "Neither Birkhall nor Denton will tell who she is, but given the attention Tony has been paying your duchess, there is considerable speculation that the mysterious lady is your wife."

Jerome longed to smash his fist into Oldfield's smirking face.

"I own I am surprised you had not heard about it," Oldfield said, his smirk widening. "Every man in London is talking about it."

Now Jerome understood why, when he had approached groups of men the past two days, they had suddenly stopped talking. They had been discussing the wager—and his wife.

"Denton needs the blunt," Oldfield said. "When Birkhall proposed the wager, Tony is reputed to have said he would seduce Medusa and each snake upon her head for that sum. Oh, there is Marlborough. I must speak to him." Oldfield hastened away, no doubt to spread his poison farther.

In the dim light cast by the carriage lamp, Rachel stared at the hard set of her husband's profile, wishing she understood why he was so upset. He had marched up to her as she was talking to Tony Denton and announced in a voice that brooked no opposition that they were leaving Devonshire's ball.

She had dutifully gone with him, hoping he would tell her why he wanted to leave so hastily. But now that they were alone inside their carriage as it sped toward Westleigh House, he still had not seen fit to enlighten her.

Finally, she asked, "What is wrong?"

"Rachel, I must insist you stay away from Anthony Denton. People are beginning to talk about you and him."

"Surely, you do not believe them!"

"It does not matter whether I do or not."

"It does matter. It is all that matters to me! Do you think that I would—"

He cut her off. "Rachel, I will not have my wife the scandal of London."

Jerome had evaded answering whether he thought she would betray him. Clearly, he still did not entirely trust her. This realization hurt Rachel as much as if he had slapped her across the face.

"I have done nothing wrong, Jerome." In her distress, her voice rose. "You say you love me, but if you truly did you would trust me. Love is trust. Your inability to trust me will eventually undermine our marriage."

Her husband's eyes narrowed. "If you want to earn my trust, then refuse to acknowledge Denton. Give him the cut direct."

Rachel's hurt and dismay turned to anger. She did not deserve Jerome's distrust of her with Denton or any other man. Her chin rose defiantly. "No, I will not do that."

A muscle in Jerome's cheek twitched. "So Denton means that much to you?"

"He means nothing to me! But he will only be the beginning. Next week it will be some other rake you want me to cut. Oh, Jerome, why can you not have more faith in me? I love you. I am not Cleo Macklin. I beg of you, do not treat me as though I were."

"Listen to me, Rachel. Tony has more at stake in this than you understand." Jerome told her about the wager between Birkhall and Tony, and the latter's desperate financial condition.

Rachel felt only contempt for two men who would make such a wager. She pointed out, "They have not identified me as the woman."

"No, but everyone knows it is you."

"If it is, Tony will lose!"

"For God's sake, Rachel, why will you not listen to me? Tony is desperate. That is why you must avoid him. He is not above using trickery—perhaps even force to win."

Jerome sat brooding at his massive walnut desk in the library of Westleigh House, paying no attention to the ledger in front of him. In the two days since Oldfield had told him of Birkhall's wager with Denton, Jerome had not been able to force it from his mind.

And Rachel's refusal to cut Denton had done nothing to ease her husband's fears.

Jerome did not truly believe that Rachel would willingly cuckold him with Denton, but he was convinced that Tony was capable of almost anything to win the lucrative wager. Rachel had not believed Jerome when he had told her that, just as she had not believed someone was trying to kill her.

With a sigh, he opened the ledger and found a note tucked in it from Rachel to him. He unfolded it and read:

*"My dearest husband, I love you more than words can tell. Please, seal our love with your trust. I will never betray it.*

*Rachel.*

He stared down at the note. Her handwriting was as unique, beautiful, and graceful as she was. He had never seen an R rendered as artistically as the one in her signature.

His butler appeared at the door to tell him that he had a caller, a man who would say only that he had something that Jerome would want very much to see.

His curiosity piqued, Jerome agreed to see him. Anything to take his mind off his worries about his wife and Denton.

The caller was a strapping young man with reddish hair. He was quite handsome at initial glance until one noticed his shifty gray eyes. He looked vaguely familiar, something about the shape of his face and nose, yet Jerome could not recall having seen him before. "My name is Leonard Tarbock. I am Anthony Denton's footman."

A cold foreboding assailed Jerome. "Why are you here?"

"I have letters that Your Grace would find most interesting, and I will sell them to you for a price."

"Whose letters?"

"Your wife's to my master. They are yours for five hundred pounds."

Jerome fought against the aching anguish that threatened to overwhelm him. "I do not believe you have any such thing."

"But I do. I have 'em right here." Tarbock pulled two folded documents from his coat pocket and pointed at the handwriting on the top one, directing it to Anthony Denton at his Mount Street address.

It was written in Rachel's distinctive, graceful hand. There was no mistaking it.

The explosion of rage within Jerome was so intense that the world turned red before his eyes. Before he even realized what he was doing, he slammed his fist into Tarbock's face, sending him staggering back.

As he fell against a green velvet settee and went crashing down, he tried to catch himself with his hands and the letters fell to the floor. Jerome seized them before the man could recover.

The door flew open and the butler and two footmen, drawn by the noise, ran in.

"Throw this man out," Jerome said icily.

A sullen Tarbock let them lead him from the library. Not that he had much choice. Still Jerome was a little surprised that the man had not made more of an effort to collect something for the letters.

As soon as he was alone again, Jerome unfolded the letters and read their contents.

Phrases and sentences branded themselves searingly in his mind:

> *I live only for the moments that you and I can be together, my beloved Tony ... Jerome suspects nothing ... Nor does Ferris, Jerome's watchdog ... When Jerome touches me, I pretend it is you. Otherwise I could not bear his hands upon me.*

Both letters were signed with his wife's name in her own hand.

Jerome sank down in the chair at his desk, clutching the damning letters. He remembered Cleo's betrayal of him, but the pain he had felt then was nothing compared to the agony and devastation he felt now.

Cleo had been his first love, but what he felt for her had been a pale shadow of what he felt for his wife. Rachel had become his life.

How could he have been such a fool as to let this happen to him a second time? He had known better than to trust such a beautiful woman, but he had let his insatiable desire for Rachel overrule his good sense. He felt as though he had just died—certainly his heart had—and gone to hell.

Jerome laid the two letters beside her note that had been hidden in the ledger. Only a blind man could doubt that they had all been written by the same person.

He stared with rising hatred at her artistic R that he had found so pleasing only a minute earlier.

*Please, seal our love with your trust. I will never betray it.*

The damn, lying bitch!

Jerome nearly choked on the bile rising in his throat. He felt his love for her disintegrating and its fragments coalescing into a loathing stronger than he had ever felt in his life.

He was not certain he could trust himself to set eyes on the wanton, deceiving jade again. He feared the sight of that exquisite face and the sound of her honeyed *lying* voice would drive him to violence.

In his current rage, if she tried to deny she had written those letters, he might well throttle her. He had to regain control over his fury before he could chance confronting her with the full evidence of her perfidy against him.


As Rachel returned from another hated round of social calls, she contemplated how she should tell her husband of her increasing certainty that she was with child. She decided that tonight, when they were in bed and she lay in the warmth and protection of his arms, would be best.

And then she would beg him to take her back to Royal Elms. Everyone knew that pregnant wives must be indulged.

As her chariot pulled up in front of Westleigh House, she was startled to see her husband's traveling coach in front of the door, and two footmen carrying baggage to it.

Hope rose within her. He had already decided that they would return to Royal Elms. She would wait until they were there to tell him about the baby. Knowing how Jerome worried over her, he might cancel the journey, thinking it too hard for her, and she would be stuck in London.

Delighted at the prospect of returning to the country, she ran to the library, which was the most likely place to find her husband at this time of day, and burst in without bothering to knock.

Jerome was standing at the window looking out at the garden behind the house. His back was to her.

She cried, "Are we going home to Royal Elms?"

He stiffened but did not turn from the window to

greet her. Instead he said in a voice she hardly recognized as his, "Shut the door."

Always before when she had come in like this, he had moved instantly to take her in his arms and welcome her with a kiss. Apprehension bubbled in her as she closed the door.

Only then did he turn to her, and her heart blanched at the sight of his face. He made no move to come to her.

"*You* are going to Royal Elms," he said in that awful voice. "You will leave in a quarter hour. I am remaining in London."

Rachel gasped in shock. "Why are you sending me to Royal Elms alone?"

"You are not as clever a deceiver as you thought." The look he gave her was such a corrosive mixture of hatred and disillusionment that she knew it would be etched in her memory forever. "I know the truth, Rachel."

She felt as though she was caught in some hideous nightmare. Swallowing hard, she started toward him. "What—"

"Do not dare come a step closer to me," he rasped. "Or I may do violence to you."

Shocked and dismayed, she stopped abruptly. "Darling, what on earth is wrong?"

The fury in his eyes seemed to scorch her with its heat. "Damn you, do not ever call me that again. I am not your darling, and you damn well know it, you lying jade. Now get the hell out of here before I throttle you."

The fury in his eyes and his voice frightened her, but she gamely stood her ground.

"I will not go anywhere until you tell me what this is about."

"You know what it is about! We will discuss it when I can trust myself not to strangle you. Now, you have two choices, you faithless witch. You may walk out of this room now and go to Royal Elms, or I will have you forcibly removed there."

She gasped. "You would not dare!"

"Try me."

The icy hatred radiating from Jerome paralyzed Rachel. Her loving husband had vanished, replaced by this hard, intractable stranger who, she knew, would do exactly as he threatened. Better to go to Royal Elms voluntarily rather than suffer the humiliation of being taken there like a prisoner in chains.

Defeated, she turned and left the library.

Jerome stood at the window of the small anteroom off the entrance of Westleigh House, watching his traveling coach as it waited for his duchess to come down so that it could depart for Bedfordshire.

He was torn between an eagerness to be rid of her and an irrational desire to cancel this journey he had ordered for her. She had looked so innocent and vulnerable when he had confronted her in the library. Idiot that he was, it had been all he could do to keep from taking her in his arms and kissing her.

If it had not been for her letters to Denton, written in her own damning hand, he would never have been able to believe she had been unfaithful to him.

He marveled at what a magnificent actress she was, looking at him with those wide, seemingly guileless violet eyes and pretending to have no idea what he was talking about.

Then she made the mistake of calling him darling in that caressing voice of hers. It ignited his temper like a torch tossed into dry straw, and he knew that he had to get her out of his sight before he did something he would regret. He was too angry even to confront her with her letters.

Ferris appeared at the door. "You wished to see me."

Jerome turned. He stifled an urge to lash out at Ferris and demand to know why he had failed him by letting his wife rendezvous with her lover. But he knew that was unfair. Ferris's charge had been to protect her and to deliver her safely to the destinations she specified. Once she was inside, he had no way of knowing whom she might meet there.

Jerome held out a sealed letter. "Deliver this to Morgan."

As Ferris took the document, he said with a troubled frown, "I don't understand why you are ordering her grace to Royal Elms. Do you not think it is more dangerous there for her?"

Unfortunately, Jerome did. At least in London, there had been no attempt to harm her. He saw again in his mind the musket barrel pointed at her and the bodies of the poisoned kittens.

The thought of her lying dead sent a cold shudder through him. And in that moment he knew that, despite everything, she still meant far more to him than she ought. He cursed himself for his weakness and stupidity. But that did not stop him from saying, "Guard her well, Ferris. I would not have anything happen to her."

# Chapter 28

~ ⟋⟍ ~

**R**achel, dressed for riding in a green habit, came down the broad marble staircase at Royal Elms. She had arrived from London late last night so exhausted that she had slept until nearly noon today.

Depressed and confused over her husband's inexplicable fury toward her, she had lingered listlessly over the breakfast tray that had been brought to her room. How right her premonition had been that her trip to London would end unhappily.

She tried to tell herself that, under the circumstances, she was better off at Royal Elms than in London where she would have had to attend endless, vacuous social affairs while pretending nothing was wrong between herself and her husband.

Rachel had never been one to pine when she was unhappy, and she was determined not to do so now. The antidote to grief and depression was to keep herself too busy with worthwhile tasks to mope. She would begin by calling on the tenants to see how they were faring. At least at Royal Elms, she would have useful work that would keep her mind off the state of her marriage.

As she finished her toilet, she glanced out the window and saw Ferris gallop up to Morgan, who was walking toward the house from the stables. Ferris was clearly agitated, and whatever he told her brother-in-law disturbed him for he slammed his fist angrily into his open hand.

When she had arrived at Royal Elms last night, Morgan had greeted her with surprise and affection, but then he read the letter that Jerome had sent with Ferris, and his demeanor toward her changed from warmth to cool politeness.

Rachel left her bedchamber and went down the broad marble staircase. As she reached the bottom, Morgan came into the hall.

"I am going riding," she told him.

He frowned. "I am sorry, Rachel, but I must insist that you remain in the house."

"What?" she asked in disbelief. "I am going to visit the Taggarts."

His lifted his eyebrow quizzically, as though he were skeptical that was her destination. "Are you now? I am afraid you will have to postpone it."

She could scarcely believe her ears. "Why?"

"I suspect you know why."

It was too much. Rachel's temper kindled. "Well, I do not know why! Nor do I know why Jerome bundled me off here. Will you please explain to me why he is so angry at me? And explain, too, why I cannot leave the house. Why am I a prisoner?"

"Your lover arrived at the Crown Inn a half hour ago. Ferris saw him."

Rachel gaped at Morgan. *My lover?* Sweet heaven, I have no lover. The only man I have ever lain with is my husband. Who on earth are you talking about?"

Morgan looked puzzled. "Anthony Denton."

"You must be joking." But she saw from Morgan's troubled expression that he was not joking. "I despise the man." And that was true. As far as she was concerned, any man who would make such a wager as he had with Birkhall was beyond contempt.

"Jerome says he has proof of your infidelity with Denton."

For a moment, Rachel was so stunned she could

not speak. Then she cried furiously, "He cannot have proof of something that never happened."

"Then explain to me why Denton, who has never before come to this neighborhood, should suddenly arrive here today, one day after you?"

"I have no idea why he is here. You will have to ask him that." Silently she cursed Denton for showing up at such an inopportune moment. She could not deny that it looked highly suspicious for him to do so.

Given Jerome's recent actions, Rachel unhappily concluded that she had made a terrible mistake by not giving in to his demand that she cut Denton. She had done so because she wanted to force Jerome to trust her. She wondered miserably whether she had lost him instead.

What possible proof could he think he had of her infidelity? She considered the rumors surrounding Tony's dreadful wager with Lord Birkhall. Was she the object of it as everyone believed? His arrival here on her heels argued strongly that she was.

An even more painful thought occurred to her. A man who would make such a wager as Tony had would not hesitate to do other despicable things. Could it be that in his eagerness to win the wager, he had falsely claimed she had slept with him? Would Jerome unequvocally accept his word for proof? The thought made her sick to her stomach.

In that instant, she hated Tony Denton more than she had ever hated anyone in her life.

The door knocker sounded, and the butler glided silently to answer it.

Rachel stared in shock at Denton standing there.

He said, "I wish to see the duchess."

All Rachel's pent up pain and anger and frustration exploded. "Well, I do not wish to see you, Anthony Denton, you unprincipled scoundrel, not now, not ever! What lies have you told my husband?"

Denton's jaw dropped in shock, and he seemed to have been robbed of his voice.

Rachel, taking his silence as a sign of guilt, cried furiously, "I hate you. I hate the sight of you!"

He looked so stricken that for an instant Rachel almost felt sorry for him. Then she reminded herself that he was undoubtedly thinking of the wager she was costing him.

She turned on her heel and left the hall without a backward glance at him.

Morgan caught up with her by the door to the still-room. "I doubt that was the reception Tony expected."

She raised her tear-filled eyes to Morgan. His gaze was confused and troubled. "I think that Tony must have lied about me in an attempt to win that awful wager." She told her brother-in-law about Birkhall's bet, and her husband's order that she cut Tony. "I refused because I wanted Jerome to learn to trust me."

"I warned you once that it was very difficult for my brother to trust a beautiful woman. I am afraid that you expected too much of him."

"But trust is the foundation of love. Without it . . ." Rachel's choked voice faded into despairing silence.

It had been a week since Jerome had learned of Rachel's perfidy, and it still hurt as much as it had the moment he had discovered it. Since he had exiled his wife to Royal Elms, Jerome had grown to hate his London house in general and his bedchamber in particular. It held too many memories of Rachel.

Especially the bed. Her lingering scent of lavender and roses had tormented him. Nor could he look at the bed without thinking of Rachel smiling up at him as though he were the only man in the world, of Rachel kissing him passionately, of Rachel writhing beneath him in uninhibited ecstasy.

He found himself staying out later and later each night, then drinking himself into oblivion in the library before he could face another night alone in the bed where he had once lain entwined in such joyous pleasure with his wife.

Tonight he was at his club, watching the faro table with unseeing eyes as he wondered what Rachel was doing at this moment at Royal Elms.

Lord Rufus Oldfield came up to him. "I hear your duchess has gone home to Royal Elms." Oldfield's sly smile widened. "And that Anthony Denton unexpectedly departed for Bedfordshire the day after she did."

The unwelcome news that Denton had followed Rachel to Royal Elms caught Jerome by surprise.

Malice glinted in Oldfield's gray eyes. "Such an odd coincidence, would you not agree?" With a little chuckle, he turned and strode away through the crowd.

Jerome swore viciously to himself, then turned, and left the club.

Jerome was in the saddle early the next morning. He would not allow his brazen, wanton wife to entertain her lover in his own home. He rode hard, and by evening he was approaching the Crown Inn at the junction of the main north-south and east-west roads, a mile south of Royal Elms.

If Denton were in the neighborhood, he must be putting up at the Crown. It was the only inn worth staying at. Jerome decided to stop there and inquire. If Denton were there, maybe Jerome would call the bastard out now and get their inevitable confrontation over with.

The inn's fat proprietor, almost as broad as he was tall, frowned when he was asked whether Denton was there.

"He has taken a room here, Your Grace, but I can't rightly say that he's staying here. He's not here now, and his bed's not been slept in since he's come."

Jerome's jaw clenched so hard at this news that

pain radiated up his cheek. In a suddenly hoarse voice, he asked, "Do you know where he is spending his nights?"

The man frowned. "Can't rightly say. He rides off each night down that path." He pointed toward a narrow, winding track that meandered northwest through a beech wood.

Jerome could think of nothing in that direction but Royal Elms Dower House. It had been built by the seventh Duke of Westleigh for his mother with whom he had feuded most of his adult life. He had located it as far away from the main house as he could in an isolated section of the park that bordered on the Hextable property.

Since both the tenth and eleventh dukes' wives had preceded their husbands to the grave, the Dower House had been empty since the death of Jerome's great-grandmother, the ninth duke's widow. It had been locked up and neglected until the past year when, in an attempt to keep some of the additional servants he had hired busy, Jerome had begun having it cleaned once a week.

Isolated and hidden, it was the perfect place for a tryst. Was his faithless wife meeting her lover there?

Rachel awoke that evening from a long nap. With each passing day, she had becoming increasingly certain of what she had suspected when she had left London. She was pregnant.

That would explain why she was so sleepy, as well as her nausea in the mornings.

It might even help explain why she tended to be so weepy. But the lion's share of the blame for that could not be laid upon her pregnancy, but upon her unborn child's father.

She missed Jerome dreadfully. Not the hard-eyed stranger who had banished her to Royal Elms. She did not know that man. No, she missed the tender, loving husband who had shared her bed. Rachel wanted to lay in his arms and discuss the child that was growing within her.

She had thought that Jerome would not be able to remain away, that after a day or two his temper would have cooled, and he would come to her.

But eight days had passed now, and he had not come.

Rachel was convinced that Tony had to have been the source of her husband's supposed "proof" of her infidelity, that he must have lied to Jerome about her. Any man who would accept the disgusting wager that he had from Lord Birkhall could not be trusted.

Mrs. Needham came in, carrying a tray of food beneath a white linen napkin.

"I am not hungry," Rachel protested.

"No matter, you must eat for two."

Rachel colored. "You guessed."

"Aye, and I will not allow you to starve the next master of Royal Elms."

After the housekeeper left, Rachel forced herself to eat for her child's sake. It should not suffer, as she was suffering for sins she had not committed.

Rachel had just finished her dinner and put the tray aside when her door flew open and Jerome strode in, looking dusty and travel-worn but still unbearably handsome in his brown riding coat and buff breeches that accentuated his strong, muscled body.

At last he had come to her!

She was so overjoyed to see him that she threw herself at him and wrapped her arms around him. As she did, she saw the fire leap in his eyes and knew that he was as delighted to see her as she was to see him. He had missed her as she had him. She pressed herself against him, feeling the hard evidence of his desire for her.

"Thank God, you have come!" Rachel tried to kiss him, but he evaded her mouth and moved back a step, his arms at his sides instead of returning her embrace.

"What do you think brought me?"

His voice was cool, and she could feel him slipping away from her again. She could not let that happen. Surely if he knew about their baby, he would soften toward her. "I have the most wonderful news for you."

She felt him stiffen a little. "What is that?"

"You are going to be a father."

"Am I?" The words came out like the growl of a savage beast. He thrust her away from him, glaring down at her. "Pardon me, madame, but I doubt that very much."

She stared at him blankly. "What do you mean? Sweet heaven, are you saying you do not believe I am going to have a baby?"

"Oh, no, I am quite willing to believe that you are pregnant." He looked at her as though she were a repulsive, loathsome creature that had just climbed up from the depths of the earth. "What I doubt very much is that I am your child's father."

It was more than she could bear. She heard an anguished cry of someone in terrible pain and realized that the sound had come from her own throat. Her legs turned to mush, and her knees buckled. Had she not grabbed the carved walnut bedpost and clung to it, she would have collapsed.

Jerome stepped forward to catch her. His hands grabbed her arms and steadied her. Then he drew back as though she burned him.

"How can you say that to me? I have never been with any man but you. I swear it."

His eyes hardened into blue-gray flints. "You liar," he growled. "Explain why Anthony Denton has suddenly seen fit to visit this neighborhood where he has never come before?"

"I do not know why Tony is here."

Her husband's face did not soften. "Are you telling me that he has not come here to see you?"

"He came, and I sent him away." She could tell

from Jerome's expression that he did not believe her. "Ask Morgan if you do not believe me. He was here when Tony came."

Jerome sneered. "So you gave one of your magnificent performances for my brother."

Her husband was determined to think the worst of her. Rachel exclaimed in frustration, "Why will you not believe that I love only you? Why are you doing this to me?"

"This is why." He pulled two letters from his pocket, unfolded them, and thrust them at her.

She glanced at the paper, started, then looked more closely. Sweet heaven, if she had not known better, she would have sworn that they were in her handwriting.

Her gaze jumped to the signature at the bottom. "With all my love, Rachel."

She could not believe her own eyes.

Rachel began reading them. Terrible phrases leaped up at her:

> *I live only for the moments that you and I can be together, my beloved Tony ... Jerome suspects nothing ... Nor does Ferris, Jerome's watchdog over me. . . . When Jerome touches me, I pretend it is you.*

She looked up at her glowering husband with horrified eyes, so stunned and sickened that she was unable to speak.

"I do not blame you for looking shocked, my dear," he ground out, misinterpreting the reason for her stricken silence. "You never dreamed that your letters would fall into my hands, did you?"

"These are not my letters! I never saw them before; I did not write them. I swear I did not."

A muscle in Jerome's cheek twitched, betraying how angry he was. "How can you deny them? They are written in your very distinctive, indeed unique, hand."

"I could not tell the handwriting from my own," she admitted, "but I swear to God that I did not write these letters." Rachel could think of no way to prove that to her husband. He would have to trust her, and she already knew that he did not. "I told you I have never seen them before."

"And, of course, you also deny that you have been meeting Tony in the Dower House since your return here from London."

"Yes, I deny it! How can you think I would be unfaithful to you? I hated my grandfather for what he did to my grandmother, and it is more despicable for a woman to betray her husband. Even if I did not love you as much as I do, Jerome, I would never be unfaithful to you. I would never humiliate you that way. Surely you know me better than that."

Jerome ran his hand over his eyes. He looked tired and unhappy.

Rachel held her breath. Their future and that of their unborn child lay in the balance.

His lip curled contemptuously. "I doubt that I ever knew *you* at all. But I do know that you and Tony have continued your affair since you returned here."

"I could not continue what never happened." Desperate, she snatched up the Bible from the bedside table and laid her hand upon it. "I give you my oath upon this sacred book that I have been faithful to you."

"Are you willing to court eternal damnation to try to make me believe that lie?"

"It is not a lie! Dear God, what can I do to make you believe me?"

"Nothing! Nor will I ever believe the child you are carrying is mine. Damn you, could you not at least have waited to cuckold me until you had given me an heir?"

He turned and stalked into his bedroom, slamming the door hard behind her.

Rachel sank to her knees in despair, utterly shattered that Jerome could believe she had written those terrible letters and that she would betray him like that. The worst blow of all was his refusal to accept their child as his own.

Her pride would not permit her to let him hear her crying, and she buried her head in the bedclothes to drown the noise of the wracking sobs that shook her.

# Chapter 29

Jerome stared moodily through the library window at the meandering hills of Royal Elms park, thinking of Rachel's sick, stricken face when he told her he would never believe the child she carried was his.

He should not have said that, but he had been consumed by rage. Reason told him that he must be the father. For her to know for certain she was pregnant, the child must have been conceived during the early days of their marriage while they were at Royal Elms. He knew that she had been faithful to him here. Even if reason had not told him he was the father, Rachel's face had.

No matter how much provocation she had given him, he should not have denied their child. Jerome turned away from the window just as Morgan came into the room. It was the first time he had seen his brother since his return to Royal Elms an hour earlier.

Before Jerome could speak, Morgan demanded, "Will you kindly tell me what the hell is going on?"

"I told you in my letter. Rachel is cuckolding me with Anthony Denton." It amazed Jerome how much it hurt to say the words aloud, even to his brother.

"I do not believe that!" Morgan shook his head negatively. "She cannot help it if that jackass Birkhall decided to wager Denton. Rachel would not betray you."

320

"I did not think so either until I read her letters to Denton." Jerome's voice was laced with bitterness. "I will show them to you. They will give you an entirely different view of her character."

He pulled them from his pocket and handed them to Morgan. As his brother read them, Jerome extracted several other papers from another pocket and spread them out on a mahogany table by the window.

Morgan looked up from the letters, clearly as stunned as Jerome had been when he first saw them. "I cannot believe that Rachel wrote these. She loves you too much. They must be forgeries."

Jerome took the letters from him and laid them beside the sheets he had already spread on the table. "These are notes that Rachel wrote me in London." As Morgan studied them, Jerome said, "You can see that her handwriting is very distinctive, indeed unique."

After Morgan had compared the letters with Rachel's notes to Jerome, he said in dismay, "I have to agree that it is her hand. How does she explain the letters to Denton?"

"I thought, when presented with the evidence, she would at least be honest." Disillusionment permeated Jerome's voice. "But, no, she lied and denied that she had written them. As if there could be any doubt!"

Morgan shook his head. "I cannot believe it. I would have wagered my life that Rachel would never betray you."

"And because you could not believe she would, you have let her continue to do so since I sent her here. Damn it, Morgan, I trusted you to watch her for me, and you failed me. You allowed her to spend her nights with Denton in the Dower House."

Morgan gaped at him. "What the hell are you talking about? That is impossible! Much as I hated to do it, I followed your instructions that she was not to be permitted to leave the house."

"Did you know that Denton arrived here the day after she did?"

"Yes, he called here, and she told him in no uncertain terms that she hated him and never wanted to set eyes on him again. She told me that she believed Denton was responsible for your thinking she was having an affair with him."

"She is a remarkable actress, is she not?"

Morgan's face scrunched in perplexity. "Jerome, I cannot believe she faked that scene. No one could be that good an actress."

"There is none better than she." Jerome's mouth twisted in a sneer as he remembered how completely she had deluded him into thinking she loved him. "Why else would Denton be here, other than to bed my wife and win his wager with Lord Birkhall?"

"He may have come here for that reason, but I am convinced he has not been sleeping with your wife."

Jerome would give anything to believe that, but the evidence to the contrary was overwhelming. "Of course he has been. With whom else would he be spending his nights at the Dower House?"

"Instead of our arguing about this, let us find out the truth," Morgan suggested. "We will pay a visit to the Dower House."

Rachel, her storm of tears spent, had come to a decision. She would not, could not continue to live with a man who doubted he was the father of the child she was carrying.

During her short sojourn in London, she had learned the grim fate of a child born to a titled lady whose husband did not believe himself the sire. The innocent babe was banished from its mother, often farmed out to an impoverished couple to raise in squalor until its early death. The babe's only hope was a natural father who would make some other arrangement for it.

But in Rachel's case, what hope did her unborn babe have when its father would not believe he had sired it?

She would not subject the innocent child she was carrying to such a fate. Rachel would never give up a baby of her flesh. Nor would she continue to subject herself to her husband's anger and hatred.

Maxi sidled up to Rachel. She picked the terrier up in her arms and lay her cheek against his silver coat. No, she could not stay beneath Jerome's roof when he believed what he did about her.

But what could she do? She realized with a sinking heart that there was only one place where she could go.

Wingate Hall.

Rachel hated the thought of doing so. It was no longer her home. It had not really been that since Aunt Sophia had seized control, but Rachel had no other choice.

Sophia would not be happy to see her niece at Wingate Hall, but Rachel hoped to persuade Uncle Alfred to take her back or at least to give her money so that she might seek shelter elsewhere. There was not much chance of the latter, though, because Sophia was sure to object.

Hearing the sound of horses through her open window, Rachel raised her head from Maxi's fur and looked out. Jerome, Morgan, and Ferris were riding away from the stables. She wondered dully whether Jerome had shown those awful letters to his brother. If he had, Morgan would hate her as much as her husband did.

And could she blame either of them? Those notes to Tony looked so much like her handwriting that she could scarcely believe herself that she had not written them.

The daily stage to the north would be leaving the

Crown Inn in an hour. If Rachel hurried, she could be aboard it. To forestall the possibility that her unpredictable husband might come after the stage and drag her back, she wanted to postpone anyone realizing that she had fled from Royal Elms for as long as she could.

Rachel would have to dress so that she would not be recognized. She thought of the old black cloak and veiled hat that she had found in the attic while she was looking for the dining parlor furnishings. They would be perfect for concealing her identity.

Her heart sank at the realization she did not dare take Maxi along for he would call attention to her. Instead she would have to leave him at Royal Elms, at least for the time being. Jerome was very fond of the terrier, and Rachel told herself that he would take care of him.

Mrs. Needham came in to retrieve the tray she had brought earlier. How fortunate that Rachel had eaten it before Jerome's arrival for now she felt as though she never wanted to eat again.

The housekeeper's shrewd glance took in Rachel's red, swollen eyes. "Are you all right, Your Grace?" Her voice was laced with concern.

Rachel, determined that her plan to leave Royal Elms be a success, seized the opportunity Mrs. Needham unwittingly presented her. "No, I am feeling most unwell." Which was true. "I am going to bed immediately." Which was not true. "I do not want to be disturbed by anyone *for any reason* until morning."

"Poor child, you look exhausted. Sleep will be the best thing for you."

Mrs. Needham looked so worried that Rachel felt terribly guilty about misleading her as she was, but it was necessary to her plan. If she were lucky, her departure would not be discovered until morning.

As the housekeeper left, Rachel thrust her terrier toward her. "Please take Maxi with you so that he

will not awaken me during the night. Perhaps Cook
could find a bone for him in the kitchen."

"Aye, Your Grace." Mrs. Needham complied, bal-
ancing the tray in one hand and taking the dog
under her other arm. "I'll take care of him."

After the housekeeper and Maxi were gone, Rachel
went to the connecting door to Jerome's room and
turned the key in the lock, then slipped it into her
pocket.

She wrote Jerome a note that she left on her pillow.
Then she put on a pair of sensible shoes for her walk
to the Crown Inn and donned the black cloak and the
veiled hat.

Once she escaped Bedfordshire undetected, she
would leave the stagecoach and hire a post chaise to
take her the rest of the way to Wingate Hall.

Rachel took one last look around her bedchamber.
She dreaded going back to Wingate Hall and facing
the uncertain reception she would receive from Aunt
Sophia.

Tears of sorrow and regret welled in Rachel's eyes
at the thought of leaving Royal Elms. She had been
so happy here. She loved the estate, loved its people
and, most of all, loved its master. But she could not
stay with a man who could not believe their child
was his.

Much as she hated to go, Jerome had left her with
no other choice.

It took Jerome, Morgan, and Ferris a good half
hour to reach the Dower House, a substantial brick
structure surrounded by trees in the remotest corner
of Royal Elms.

"Our ancestor was certainly determined to keep
his mama as far away from him as he could," Morgan observed.

Recent hoofprints on the path leading to the
Dower house indicated it had been visited very recently, but it appeared silent and deserted now.

The three men dismounted. As they went up to the door, Ferris pointed out two pair of footprints leading away from the house that had been made while the ground was still wet after the last rain.

Jerome's face hardened as he studied them. One set was clearly a man's, while the other outlined a lady's delicate foot. "When did it last rain here?"

"Early this morning," Ferris answered.

"So they used the house last night."

"I cannot believe it could have been Rachel with him," Morgan protested. "I am certain that she was in her room all night."

"Who else could it have been?" Jerome demanded.

"Why speculate?" Morgan asked. "Let us see what we find inside." He knocked, but there was no answer. Finally, he pushed open the unlocked door.

In the dowager's bedroom, they found several intimate items of women's apparel in delicate silk and lace. The thought of Denton seeing his wife's gorgeous body in them and then removing them from her sent a bolt of fury through Jerome.

"Since no one is here now," Morgan said, "we might as well have dinner and come back later to wait for your uninvited guests to show up. We can dine at the Crown Inn. It is half the distance from here that Royal Elms is."

"Excellent suggestion," Jerome agreed. "After all the riding I have done today, I have no desire to do any more than I must tonight." Nor did he wish to be forced to dine with his errant wife. And especially not in that charming dining parlor she had created in which they had spent so many happy hours together.

So they went to the Crown Inn. As they rode up, the stage for the north was pulling away. Jerome caught a glimpse through its window of a woman, apparently in deep mourning, who was so heavily veiled that he could see nothing of her face.

During dinner, Jerome picked at his food. Rachel's betrayal had robbed him of any appetite. He listened idly to the two men at the next table. "Wonder who that woman in black was," one of them mused. "The one who left on the northbound stage."

His companion, a beefy man with a cast to his left eye, said, "The way she was wrapped up, she could have been me own sister, and me would not have known her."

After dinner, Morgan and Ferris lingered over their tankards of ale. Jerome drank brandy. He tried to banish from his mind the haunting memory of Rachel's devastated face when he told her he would never believe the child she carried was his. He regretted saying it, but he had been so damned furious.

Nobody had ever provoked his temper as Rachel did. Why is that, he asked himself. *Because you have never loved anyone as much as you do her, not your mother, not Cleo, not even Morgan, and you know it.* Yes, God help him, in the darkest recesses of his heart and mind, he did know it.

When Rachel had greeted him so joyously today, all he had wanted to do was take her to bed, bury himself in her sweet, passionate depths, and forget all else including her betrayal and perfidy. And he had hated himself for his weakness. Jerome's hands tightened around the brandy glass.

Morgan and Ferris were certain that Rachel could not have been spending the past few nights with Denton, but Jerome did not see how he could be wrong. He drained his glass. He would soon know the truth.

It was nearly midnight when they returned to the Dower House. They tied their horses some distance down the path so as not to alert anyone who might be inside of their arrival.

The night was brightly lit by stars and a lopsided, nearly full moon. They made their way easily toward the house. As they approached, two horses near the front door, one bearing a lady's sidesaddle, were clearly visible in the moonlight.

Candlelight shone through the sheer curtains that covered the partially opened windows in the dowager's bedchamber.

The three men crept closer. The sounds of a man and woman in the throes of passion wafted through the opened windows.

Fury ripped through Jerome. Hardly knowing what he was doing, he stalked into the house and slammed into the dowager's bedroom with Morgan and Ferris close behind him.

The noise belatedly penetrated the lovers' passion, and Jerome heard Anthony Denton exclaim, "What the hell!"

Denton rolled off the woman beneath him, and Jerome stared down at her lying naked on the bed.

He could not believe his eyes.

# Chapter 30

**M**organ's amused voice penetrated Jerome's shock. "My, my, Saint Emily, what devilish company you do keep."

"Get out of here. How dare you burst in upon us like this," Emily screeched, sounding like a Billingsgate fishmonger. "I will have you whipped for daring to do so."

"Not us," Morgan retorted. "It is you and your lover who are trespassing on Royal Elms's property. You know the penalty for trespass."

That shut her up.

Denton, naked as the day he was born, scrambled out of the bed and yanked on his breeches.

Jerome turned away in disgust from the sight of Emily on the bed and started down the hall. He thought pityingly of her betrothed. Poor Sir Henry. Not even wed yet, and already he had been betrayed by his intended.

If Jerome had not seen Emily with his own eyes, he doubted he would have believed she was capable of such dishonorable behavior. Of all the women he had ever met, he had thought the pious Emily the one most certain to be faithful.

Was there no woman who could be trusted, he wondered in bitter disillusionment.

As he made his way down the hall, it occurred to him that Bill Taggart and the other people of the neighborhood had been far more astute at seeing Emily for what she really was than he had ever been.

Jerome had reached the front door when Denton, still fastening his breeches, caught up with him.

"Before I left London," Jerome told him, "I had a visit from one of your footmen, Leonard Tarbock."

Denton looked puzzled. "I have no footman by that name. For that matter, I have no servants at all. They all left weeks ago because I was so far behind in paying their wages. I am one step away from debtors' prison."

Jerome's anger gave way to the smallest glimmering of hope. Could it be Rachel was telling the truth? He remembered her agonized face. *I swear to God that I did not write these letters. I have never set eyes on them before.*

The glimmer grew stronger as he recalled that the former captain of *The Betsy* also denied writing the letter that had misled everyone into thinking that Stephen had disappeared in France instead of England. Could there be a connection?

Denton's mouth twisted in bitter self-contempt. "Believe me, I would not be here if I were not desperate."

"So Emily was the woman who was the object of Birkhall's wager?"

Denton nodded in confirmation. "Do you think I enjoyed seducing that unpleasant shrew? I agreed to the wager only because it was my last hope of pulling myself from the River Tick."

"And now you have three witnesses to confirm you won it," Jerome remarked.

"Would . . . would it be too much to ask you not to tell your wife about this incident?"

"Why would you care?"

"I hate to have her think worse of me than she already does. Rachel is the only woman I ever loved." Denton's voice took on a self-mocking edge. "And the one woman who has never had any interest in me."

Jerome stared at him.

"Did you know that I offered for her several months ago, but her damned aunt would not hear of it. If only Stephen had not disappeared. I am certain I could have gotten him to agree to my marrying her."

Lucky for Rachel that Stephen had vanished. But was it? What had marriage to Jerome brought her? Pain and misery, thanks to his inability to trust her. The terrible look on his wife's face when he had denied their child's paternity tormented him.

He asked Denton, "Why did you pick my Dower House?"

"It was Emily's idea. She said it was never used, and no one would know."

"She was wrong." And so had Jerome been to think Rachel had betrayed him. She had not done so.

But he had betrayed her. His refusal to believe her, to trust her had been every bit as much a betrayal as if he had been physically unfaithful. Hellsfire, but he was guilty of so much.

Jerome went outside to his horse. All he wanted was to get home to his wife and beg her forgiveness for ever having doubted her.

As he and his two companions rode away from the Dower House, Morgan said dryly, "Well, Jerome, you might have married Emily and been bored, miserable, *and* cuckolded."

Yes, he would have been, fool that he was, had Rachel not abducted him and saved him from his own stupidity. *Rachel is as beautiful within as she is without. Hell and damnation, why can you not see that?*

Jerome hated himself for his blindness and distrust, but most of all for how terribly he had hurt his wife. He did not know who had written those letters, but it had not been Rachel, no matter how much the writing looked like hers.

They were a quarter mile from Royal Elms when a man on horseback came up behind them at a gallop. As he reached them, he slowed his lathered horse to their pace.

The bright moonlight illuminated his face, and Jerome saw that he was a young, dark-haired man, lean and handsome.

"Where are you headed?" Jerome asked.

"Royal Elms."

"What business have you there?"

"I am chasing the Duke of Westleigh. Talk about wretched luck, I arrived at his London house today, three hours after he had left for his country seat."

"Who are you, and why are you so anxious to see me?"

The man's face tightened. "So you are Westleigh. I am George Wingate."

Jerome was so startled that he could only stare at the stranger for a moment. The last person he expected to show himself at Royal Elms was the man he feared was behind the attempts on Rachel's life. "What the hell are you doing here?"

"I have come for an explanation of why you wrote me that hectoring letter full of nonsense about my brother being missing and—"

"What do you mean nonsense?" Jerome interrupted. "Stephen has been missing for more than a year now."

"Are you mad? I have had regular letters from him. Why, in the very mail that brought me your letter I had one from Stephen."

"Written when and from where?" Jerome asked.

"From Wingate Hall and written only the day before yours. Stephen assured me that he was coming to enjoy Yorkshire and life in the country. I own I would not have believed him had I not also had a letter from Rachel, telling me how happy she was that he had come home and settled down at last."

Suddenly all that had been happening made terrible sense to Jerome. "We had better stop here for a few minutes."

When they had done so, he said, "Stephen has not been near Wingate Hall in more than a year and a half."

"But that is impossible." George's voice rose in indignant protest. "He has written me from there, and Rachel, in her letters, has talked about all that he is doing."

Jerome said, "The only letters Rachel wrote you of late begged you to come home and take charge of Wingate Hall before Sophia destroyed it. Rachel could not have written you the letters you received. Neither could Stephen."

George looked utterly bewildered. "But I tell you I know my own brother's and sister's handwriting."

Just as Jerome had thought he had known Rachel's.

"Have you noticed, Jerome," Morgan interjected, "all the letters floating around from Rachel that she did not write."

"Aye." Jerome remembered with a grim curl of his lips how insistent Sophia Wingate had been that she alone handle all the mail going in and out of Wingate Hall.

"Rachel's hand is very distinctive," George was saying.

"Yes, I know," Jerome said. *I could not tell it from my own.* No wonder Rachel had looked so confused and stricken when he had shown her the letters he had gotten from the bogus footman. "Your brother was seized and sold to a press gang when he returned to England from the Continent more than a year ago."

George reeled back in his saddle. "My God, I cannot believe it! Where is he now?"

"He tried to escape by jumping from the ship when it was several miles off the coast of America.

Apparently, he mistook the lights of a passing ship for land."

"Did he ... " George's voice, no more than croak, failed him entirely.

"I am afraid not," Jerome said gently. "I am sorry."

In the moonlight, tears glistened on George's cheeks.

"Any letters you received from him must have been forged."

George looked grief-stricken and bewildered. "Who would go to all that trouble and why?"

"Someone who wanted to keep you from returning to England to claim Wingate Hall after Stephen disappeared," Jerome said.

"But who?"

"Sophia Wingate." Jerome was certain of this now. "Your brother purportedly left a document placing your Uncle Alfred in charge of his estate should anything happen to him and—"

"Stephen would never have done that!" George interrupted. "He thought my uncle a hopeless fool."

"After what you have told us, I am certain that document is a forgery, too," Jerome said. "The letters you received were undoubtedly designed to keep you from suspecting anything was wrong. Did you bring them with you?"

George tapped his coat. "Yes, I have them here."

"Good, I would like to compare them to two letters that I have at Royal Elms."

Jerome urged Lightning to a gallop, and the other riders fell in behind him. Within a few minutes, they were striding into Royal Elms's great marble hall.

They were met by the housekeeper, glaring at Jerome with more disfavor than he could ever remember, but he had too much on his mind to pay any heed to her moods.

"Mrs. Needham, tell my wife I wish to see her in the drawing room at once."

The housekeeper's look grew even darker. "Nay, I

shall not," she said defiantly. "She was ill tonight and went to bed early. She is asleep now, poor dear, and I'll not wake her."

Alarmed, Jerome started for the steps to go to Rachel.

Mrs. Needham, her voice as sharp as broken glass, said, "Sleep is the best thing for the poor thing in her condition. If you have any consideration for her, Your Grace, you will not disturb her before she wakes."

That stopped him dead. *In her condition*—pregnant with his child that he had cruelly told her could not be his. He felt like the world's greatest scoundrel.

He remembered how exhausted—and devastated—Rachel had looked. Mrs. Needham was right. Rachel needed sleep. Much as he longed to go to her immediately to try to repair the damage he had done to their marriage, better for her to rest undisturbed and wake naturally. For her sake, he would curb his impatience.

Jerome would do anything for Rachel.

He turned away from the stairs and went into the drawing room. "Your sister will be delighted to see you," he said to George who had followed him.

"Not as delighted as I shall be to see her. The irony of all this is that if Stephen is dead, Wingate Hall is Rachel's, not mine, although she does not know that."

Jerome and Morgan exchanged a meaningful look. "How is that?" Jerome asked casually.

"I promised my father that if anything happened to Stephen, I would either resign my commission, which I have no intention of doing, or Wingate Hall would go to Rachel. She will be a far better steward of it than either Stephen or I."

Morgan looked at George with narrowed, suspicious eyes. "Then why were you so angry when your father insisted you sign that agreement?"

Clearly stunned, George blurted, "How do you know about that?"

"I have sources," Morgan said vaguely. "Are you going to answer my question?"

"I was furious—and insulted—that my father would not accept my word I would do as I promised but thought it necessary to draw up a formal agreement. My word is my bond, and I would not have gone back on it."

Jerome eyed George with approval. "In light of the other letters you had received, you must have been astonished to get mine."

"To tell you the truth, I was already uneasy, although I could not tell you precisely why. I think it must have been Stephen's letters. They sounded so unlike him. As soon as I got yours, I asked for immediate leave and sailed for home."

A horrified look crossed George's face. "My God, do you think that Sophia or whoever forged the letters could have been responsible for Stephen's disappearance?"

"I think it is extremely likely," Jerome said. "There were also two unsuccessful attempts on your sister's life before she left Wingate Hall."

The color retreated from George's face, leaving it ashen. "Before she left Wingate Hall? Where the devil is she now? Is she safe?"

"Very safe. She is upstairs asleep. I would awaken her, but as you heard my housekeeper say she needs her sleep. It is early days yet, but we are in the process of making you an uncle."

George sank down into a chair. "She is your wife?" Jerome nodded.

"If you have any more surprises for me, pray wait until morning. I do not think I can take them."

When Jerome went up to bed that night, he crossed his chamber to the connecting door to his wife's room. He gently turned the knob, only to find that it was locked against him.

Jerome's heart sank, and his pain was all the

greater because he knew that he deserved to have her bar her door to him.

Pulling on his robe, he went into the hall and tried that entry to Rachel's room, but it, too, was locked. With his ear pressed to the door, he knocked softly and called her name. He heard no stirring from her.

Remembering his housekeeper's warnings and Rachel's exhaustion, he hated to wake her. If he told her all that he had to tell her, she would get no more sleep tonight. After all he had put her through, the least he could do was let her get a decent night's sleep.

He went back to his room and climbed into his own lonely bed, reminding himself it would only be for tonight.

Secure in the knowledge that his wife was faithful to him and that she was lying in the next room, safe from the evil of Wingate Hall, he fell into the first good sleep he had had in days.

# Chapter 31

**I**t was nearly noon when Jerome awoke the next day. He jumped out of bed and went immediately to the connecting door to his wife's chamber.

The door was still locked against him. He swallowed hard in disappointment, then knocked hard and called loudly to Rachel, but there was no answer. Pressing his ear to the door, he could hear nothing.

She had probably been up for hours, he thought with chagrin as he rang for his valet. He would have missed her happy reunion with George.

When Peters came in, he said, "A Mr. Griffin arrived from London a few minutes ago. He said it is most urgent that he see you immediately, Your Grace."

Jerome knew that it must be very urgent indeed for Griffin himself to have come all the way from London. Jerome could think of only one thing that it could be. Stephen Wingate must have been found alive. If he could give Rachel that news . . . He anticipated his wife's joy. "Send him up to me."

When Griffin appeared, Jerome said, "You must have news on Lord Arlington."

Griffin looked surprised. "Yes, I do, although that is not why I came. A sailor who saw him jump from *The Sea Falcon* confided to one of my investigators that he is certain the ship Lord Arlington mistook for land fished him out of the water and took him aboard. The sailor said nothing earlier because he feared the authorities would try to run the escapee down as a deserter. He thought it was better if *The Sea Falcon*'s officers thought the man dead."

"Then Arlington may well be alive!"

"Aye, but unfortunately the sailor could not tell us what ship picked him up, only that it flew a British flag."

"Not much help," Jerome observed. "So if that was not the news that you brought here, what was?"

"I have finally discovered Sophia Wingate's history. It is so shocking that I had to tell you in person at once. I rode most of the night to get here. As you suspected, she is no lady. Her real name was Sophia Tarbock."

"Hellsfire, does she have a brother named Leonard?" Now Jerome knew why the ersatz footman had looked familiar.

"Yes, how did you know? They are the illegitimate offspring of a baronet and a chambermaid. Sophia's father secured her a position as a lady's maid when she was still in her teen years. She was eventually dismissed without a character for stealing from her employer, but by that time she had learned to act the part of a lady."

"And decided to pass herself off as one?"

"Not immediately. There was an interim step. She became the mistress of a master forger, who taught her the trade. She apparently was even more talented at it than he. She was said to be the best in the business."

Another piece of the puzzle clicked into place for Jerome. "I can testify to that." He thought ruefully of the havoc Sophia's handiwork had wrought in his and his wife's lives.

"What comes next is even more shocking. Alfred Wingate is not her second husband, but her fourth. Shortly after marrying her, each of the first two, both well-to-do merchants, one in Gravesend and the other in Bristol, died of the same mysterious symptoms that claimed her third spouse, Sir John Creswell. It is my strong suspicion, Your Grace, that all three were poisoned. I believe that Alfred Wingate is in great danger."

No doubt he was. And if Jerome had not dragged Rachel from Wingate Hall, she would almost certainly be dead. Thank God, he had carried her away, and she was safe now at Royal Elms.

Jerome longed to take her in his arms and hold her. He ached to comfort and reassure her and beg her forgiveness for having doubted her.

As Griffin started out the door, Mrs. Needham brushed past him into Jerome's room. "I am very worried about her grace. She has not left her room, and she does not answer my knock."

Fear clutched at Jerome's heart. He was across the room to the connecting door in an instant, pounding on it and yelling at Rachel to open it.

Only silence answered him.

With all his strength, he threw himself against the door. It groaned beneath his onslaught, but did not give way. He tried again, and this time, amid the sound of splintering wood, it did.

He ran into the room. There was no sign of his wife, only a note lying on the pillow, addressed to him.

Hastily, he opened it:

*Jerome,*
*I have left Royal Elms. I shall never subject you to my unwelcome presence again. I ask only one thing of you: Do not attempt to find me for I shall never return to you.*
*I would rather be dead than to live again with a husband who could not believe he is the father of our child. Our baby deserves better than that, and so do I.*

*Rachel*

* * *

Yes, by God, she did deserve better. Jerome felt as though a knife had pierced his heart, and the wound was all the more painful because he knew he had brought it on himself by his own blindness, his own lack of trust. *Love is trust*, Rachel had said, and she was right.

Where had she gone and when? She must have left early this morning. How much of a head start would she have on him? Five, maybe seven hours. He remembered the dead kittens and felt sick.

Turning, he cried to Mrs. Needham. "Send someone down to the stable. I want to know when and how my wife left and where she said she was going. Question all the servants to see if they know anything."

He went into his own chamber where he scrambled into riding clothes, then headed downstairs.

Ferris was coming in the door, his face worried. "No one has seen your wife at the stables since she came back from London. No horse or tack is missing, and she requested no help of anyone. She must be on foot. She could not have gone far."

Relief flooded Jerome. His greatest fear was that Rachel might try to go back to Wingate Hall. But if she had walked away, she must mean to stay in the area—perhaps in the hope that he would come to his senses.

He ordered, "Dispatch men along every road and path to look for her. Tell them to ask everyone they come across whether they have seen her."

He hurried down to the stables and ordered Lightning saddled for him. As he waited, he considered where Rachel might go to seek shelter. A few minutes later, he was galloping at breakneck speed toward Bill Taggart's farm.

But the Taggarts had not seen her.

Ferris met Jerome as he returned to the house. "All

but one or two of the men are back. No one has seen your wife."

How could Rachel have seemingly disappeared off the face of the earth? Thoroughly worried by now, Jerome ran into the house where he was met by the housekeeper. "What do the servants say?"

"Jane, the scullery maid, thinks she may have seen her grace leaving yesterday evening on foot."

"What do you mean she thinks?" Jerome's fear sharpened his exasperation. "For God's sake she knows what her mistress looks like."

"Except," the housekeeper said tartly, "when she is wearing a voluminous black cloak and a hat so heavily veiled that her face could not be seen."

Jerome's stomach knotted, twisting with dread, as he remembered the woman he had seen on the northbound stage the previous evening. Hellsfire, could that have been Rachel?

He closed his eyes as fear engulfed him. She was going to Wingate Hall.

Jerome had to stop his wife before she reached it, or she would be a dead woman. He headed for the door, yelling for Morgan, George, and Ferris to come with him. They came running.

As the four men pounded northward, Jerome prayed for his wife's safety as he had never prayed before in his life. He would happily trade his dukedom, fortune, and everything else he owned to have his wife back safely in his arms.

Two awful images haunted his mind. The first was of the dead kittens. The second, and even more painful, was of his wife's shattered expression when he had told her he did not believe the child she carried was his.

If anything happened to her, if he were not granted the time to erase that awful look and see her happy and laughing again, he did not think he could live with himself.

Certainly he would never be able to forgive himself.

Jerome tried to calculate the speed of the stage versus the many hours head start it had. He concluded that they ought to catch up with it before it reached the White Swan Inn where she would disembark for Wingate Hall. But it would be a near thing. And even if he managed to save Rachel from Sophia, he knew that it would be no guarantee that his wife would ever forgive him for his unjustified distrust of her and for his repudiation of the child that he knew could only be his.

*I would rather be dead than ever again live with a husband who could believe he is not the father of my child. Our child deserves better than that, and so do I.*

If only she would let him, Jerome would spend the rest of their lives trying to make up to her for what he had done.

*If she would let him.* She could be as stubborn as he. His heart ached as he remembered her standing so proudly when they had returned to Wingate Hall after she had abducted him.

Would she ever again look at him with love and happiness in her eyes? Would he ever again see her glowing with passion and pleasure as he made love to her?

His heart bled for what his foolish distrust and jealousy had cost them both.

Rachel started toward the Wingate Hall stable to find out how the two motherless kittens she had entrusted to Benjy's care were faring.

When Rachel had arrived at her old home in the post chaise that she had hired after leaving the stage at Leicester, her reception had been far warmer than she had expected. The Wingate Hall servants had all been delighted to see her, which had not surprised her, but even Aunt Sophia had seemed pleased.

That was as fortunate as it was surprising because

Uncle Alfred was in bed, suffering from a mysterious malady that had been plaguing him for several days, and he was too ill to be bothered about anything.

Astonishingly Sophia, who loved to haggle over every groat, had paid off the postboys' charges without so much as a quibble.

Once Sophia had heard Rachel's story, she further astounded her niece with the sympathy she showed for her plight. "You cannot go back to such a man. It is an outrage that Westleigh could think such a thing of you."

Then Sophia honed in on what had been the deciding factor in Rachel's decision to flee her husband. "Only think of your poor unborn babe. Believing what he does, Westleigh is certain to tear the child from your arms and send him away. I shudder to think of what the poor infant's fate would be. You cannot let that happen, dear girl. No, you must stay here at Wingate Hall."

This was so unlike the Aunt Sophia Rachel knew that she could only give thanks that at last someone understood her fears and believed her to be telling the truth.

Perversely, Rachel also felt compelled to defend her husband. "I cannot entirely blame him after I saw the letters he has. You would not believe it, Aunt Sophia, but I could not tell the handwriting from my own."

Sophia's eyes narrowed. "Do you have any idea who could be responsible for them?"

"I have given it a great deal of thought on the journey here. I can only think of one possibility, and even that seems so highly unlikely I can hardly bring myself to mention it, but Lady Oldfield has taken a great dislike to me."

"I have heard unpleasant things about that woman," Sophia said. "Does your husband know where you have gone?"

"No, I did not tell him I was coming here, and I

begged him in the note I left him not to try to find me." Rachel's voice cracked with emotion. "Not that he is likely to bother. He hates me so that I am quite certain he will be happy to be rid of me."

Now, as Rachel reached the stables, her thoughts turned back to the two kittens that she had hidden in the maze. She hoped Benjy had taken good care of them.

When the young stable hand saw her, he came running up, a wide grin splitting his freckled face. "M'lady, m'lady, you come back! Me missed you. Everyone has." His smile faded. "Sorry me am about them poor kittens in the maze. Me knows how you loved them."

"What happened to them?" Rachel demanded in alarm.

The youth looked surprised. "Me would o' thought his grace or his brother would o' told you."

"Told me what?"

"They's dead, poisoned they was."

"What!" Rachel gasped, an unhappy shadow falling across her return to Wingate Hall. "Where?"

"In the maze. Me found them lying all stiff aside their dish and an empty pitcher o' milk."

"But no one except you knew I had hidden them in the maze. When did you find them?"

"Why the day you left with his grace. Was him what found 'em first. That's what led me to 'em. Me seen him come out o' that maze. Ne'er afore seen such a look on a man's face as him had. Then him marched into the house and carried you off. Did him not tell you about them being dead?"

"No, surely he could not have known."

"Oh, him did," Billy assured her. "When his brother come, him asked me whether me had buried the poisoned kittens and me told him me had."

Rachel remembered the shadow that had crossed Morgan's face when she had asked him about the kittens. Why had neither he nor her husband told her the truth?

Slowly she turned and made her way back to the house.

Jerome and his companions finally caught up with the northbound stage on a desolate, windswept moor. The driver was reluctant to stop at Jerome's command, being under the mistaken impression the four riders were a gang of highwaymen attempting to rob him.

Finally, after much shouting back and forth, he was persuaded to stop.

As Jerome dismounted, he explained to the still wary coachman, "I am seeking my runaway wife, who is your passenger."

"That be yer wife?" The coachman looked incredulous.

Wild to see Rachel again, Jerome threw open the coach door to be met by the glare of the only female occupant, an enormously fat, middle-aged woman. He cursed under his breath and slammed the door shut.

"Did you not pick up a woman at the Crown Inn in Bedfordshire wearing a black cloak and veiled black hat?" Jerome demanded of the coachman.

"Aye, but she left at Leicester. Hired a post chaise there, she did, to carry her the rest o' the way to Yorkshire. 'Twas near a full moon last night, and she intended to make use o' its light to continue her journey. Must o' beat us by many hours."

"Oh, God, no!" Jerome exclaimed in despair as the one hope he had clung to during the long ride north was demolished. It had not occurred to him that Rachel might leave the stage and travel through the night in a faster equipage.

Behind him, he heard his companions cursing softly. He vaulted into the saddle, and urged his tired mount on toward Wingate Hall. Terror for his wife's safety constricted his chest, and bile rose in his throat at the thought of losing her.

Would they be in time?

Rachel sat on the terrace of Wingate Hall, staring up at the stars brightening the night sky. She was trying to sort through her confusion over all that had happened to her.

Sophia stepped out on the terrace. "You should go to bed. You need your rest."

"Yes," Rachel agreed, but she made no move to rise. "I think, though, I will stay out here for a little while. It is such a pleasant night, and I do not think I would be able to sleep if I went to bed."

Too many memories to haunt her; too much pain to rip at her heart. Her marriage was over. Even if Jerome came after her, and she doubted that he would, she would never again be his wife. When he had repudiated their child, something within her had died. And she would never, ever allow anyone to separate her from her baby when the child was born.

Even if he did not try to do so, even if he eventually accepted that he was the father, she would not be able to forgive him.

Her aunt went back inside, leaving Rachel alone on the terrace again.

But within ten minutes, Sophia was back again, carrying a glass in her hand. "What you need, dear girl, is this warm milk to help you relax and sleep."

"Why, thank you." Rachel had never particularly liked warm milk, but she was touched by Sophia's thoughtfulness, and she would drink it to please her.

"I have some letters to write tonight for the morning post," Sophia said. "If you want anything I will be in my office." She turned and went into the house.

Her aunt was being so nice that Rachel could scarcely believe it. The change in her was nothing short of miraculous. Perhaps that was why it made Rachel a little uneasy.

She glanced up at the stars again and yawned. Her exhaustion was catching up with her. She might as well drink down the milk and go to bed. Perhaps, as Sophia said, it would help her sleep.

Rachel, an odd, undefinable unease nagging at her, reached for the glass.

When Jerome and his companions reached Wingate Hall, he did not bother to knock but threw open the great front door and dashed inside.

Kerlan came running. "Your Grace!" he gasped.

"Where is my wife? In her old room?"

"Nay, out on the terrace."

Jerome sagged in relief. Thank God, he was in time.

Sophia Wingate hurried into the hall from the room she used as her private office.

"Your Grace, what a pleasure to see you." From Sophia's dismayed expression, however, it was anything but. "What brings you to Wingate Hall? Surely, not your unfaithful wife. She told me that you had somehow gotten hold of her letters to Anthony Denton, and then guessed the truth—that the babe she carries is his."

"You mean the letters you forged and had your brother, Leonard Tarbock, try to sell to me."

Sophia gasped, and the color faded from her face. Then she visibly rallied, saying unconvincingly, "I do not know what you are talking about. I will not allow you to make such slanderous statements about me. I order you out of this house."

"You have no authority at Wingate Hall."

"Lord Arlington left my husband—"

Jerome interrupted her. "No, he did not. The document *you forged* left your husband in charge of the estate until George Wingate returned from America."

"And I am here now." George came up to stand beside Jerome.

Sophia's composure deserted her. "No, you cannot be back!"

"But he is, and I am having the bodies of your *three* former husbands exhumed for traces of the poison with which you killed them. You will hang for their murders."

Sophia turned and darted back into the room from which she emerged. Jerome followed in time to see her open the drawer of a pretty French writing table. She yanked out a small dagger and ran toward him, her eyes glittering with madness.

She ran at Jerome, slashing viciously at him with the dagger. "I will kill you, too!" she shrieked.

The blade narrowly missed his face as Jerome grabbed for her wrist but could not catch it.

They danced about each other as she lashed at him with the dagger and he dodged its lethal blade.

At last he managed to capture her wrist. Her eyes gleamed with a crazed light as she struggled to break his grip.

He tried to force her to drop the weapon, but she was possessed of a devil's strength. Hellsfire, he had fought men twice her size who had less, but he had heard madness often gave its victims superhuman might.

Over and over as he struggled with her, she slashed at him with the tip of the dagger.

Once she came within a hairsbreadth of his cheek.

Then she sliced at his chin.

Odd, Jerome thought, the way she was wielding the dagger. If she wanted to kill him, why did she seem more intent on scratching him with its tip than plunging it into him?

Morgan finally succeeded in grabbing her arms from behind. Between the two brothers, they managed to subdue her frenzied strength.

Slowly Jerome forced her wrist back to make her drop the dagger that she was clutching so tenaciously. For an instant, her resistance flagged, and the tip of the blade snaked up, scratching her chin.

A blood-curdling scream escaped her lips. The craziness in her eyes gave way to terror, and she went limp. Morgan caught her and lowered her to the floor. With mounting horror, Jerome understood why Sophia had been trying so hard to use the point of the dagger.

"The tip is poisoned, is it not?" His voice was so hoarse he hardly recognized it.

"Aye, and there is no antidote," she whimpered. Then her eyes grew bright with hatred. "Just as there is none for the poison in the milk I gave your wife tonight."

"What?" Jerome whirled on Kerlan, who was standing frozen in the doorway.

"You told me my wife was on the terrace."

"She is."

Jerome's throat was suddenly so dry and constricted that he could scarcely get the words past his lips. "Did Sophia bring her a glass of milk there?"

Kerlan nodded. "To help her sleep."

The words were like a knife carving Jerome's heart into mincemeat. The milk would have brought Rachel eternal sleep.

He sprinted past Kerlan, running toward the terrace and calling himself every kind of fool for not having told Rachel about the dead kittens and the poisoned milk. Jerome had wanted to protect her from the pain and sorrow it would cause her.

What he had meant as a kindness might have unwittingly caused his wife's death—and that of her unborn child.

His child.

"Rachel," he called, frantic now.

Only silence answered him, and he knew that he was too late after all. Jerome ran onto the terrace, illuminated by two flambeaux on either side of the door.

It was empty.

Kerlan followed him. "She was sitting there." The butler gestured at a vacant chair.

On a low table beside it sat an empty glass. Jerome picked it up and examined it.

Only a few drops of milk remained in the bottom.

# Chapter 32

**I**n his rage and grief, Jerome picked up the empty glass. With a violent curse, he flung it down on the stone terrace, smashing it into fragments.

Then he turned and ran back into Wingate Hall. He heard footsteps pounding behind his own as he bounded up the broad staircase to the room from which he had carried Rachel the day he had married her. He threw open the door, frightened and uncertain of what he would find there.

He found nothing. The room was empty.

Wherever Rachel had gone, it was not there. He turned back to the door. George, Morgan, and Ferris stood there with faces as bleak as his own heart.

"Search the house from top to bottom," he ordered. "We must find her."

But the search turned up nothing. Jerome met George and Ferris at the foot of the main staircase. Tears of grief streaked George's cheeks. He said in a choked voice, "Kerlan is certain that Rachel did not come back inside from the terrace."

"Comb the grounds." Jerome looked around for his brother. "Where the hell is Morgan?"

His brother's voice called urgently from Sophia's office, "Jerome, come here. You must see this."

He ran into the room. Sophia's body, covered with a blanket, was still lying on the floor. His brother stood by her French writing table.

"Look." Morgan pointed to a sheet of paper par-

352

tially written upon. A pen lay beside it. "It is what Sophia must have been doing when our arrival interrupted her."

Jerome picked up the note that mimicked his wife's handwriting to perfection. As his eyes skimmed the words, he saw that Sophia had been composing a "suicide" note, to which she had undoubtedly planned to sign Rachel's name. The forged note blamed Jerome's treatment of his wife and his repudiation of their child for driving her to take her own life.

He sank down in the chair beside the table, fighting back the waves of nausea that washed over him. Sophia had been diabolical. Had Griffin not discovered the truth about her, Jerome might well have believed this terrible note.

He glanced with loathing at the covered body on the floor.

"The poison works very quickly," Morgan observed grimly. "Sophia was dead within minutes."

"If she were not, I would kill her now with my bare hands," Jerome said fervently, giving voice to the helpless fury and grief that consumed him.

Morgan shuddered. "It was damn near you instead of her. If she had managed to scratch you with that dagger . . . "

He thrust a small leatherbound book toward Jerome. It was open to a page filled with spidery handwriting. "You must read this. It is Sophia's diary, and this entry is particularly illuminating. She was truly insane."

Jerome read with growing horror. Sophia, in her worsening madness, had intended him to be her next husband—as if he would ever have had anything to do with her. But she believed that once she had done away with Rachel and Alfred, she would have him and become a duchess. To achieve this end, she was slowly poisoning her husband.

Morgan said, "Alfred is exceedingly lucky that we came when we did."

If only Rachel had been so lucky.

Morgan showed Jerome other pages of the diary. Much earlier entries recorded Sophia's hatred for Stephen because he had tried to stop his uncle from marrying her.

Determined on vengeance, she hit upon hiring ruffians to seize Stephen in Dover. They were instructed to turn him over to a press gang, telling it that Stephen was a petty thief pretending to be Lord Arlington to hoodwink shopkeepers, eager for an earl's custom, into giving him credit. That was why the press gang did not believe Stephen's protestations of his real identity.

Sophia knew that Stephen would have virtually no hope of surviving impressment and returning to England alive. She knew, too, that he would suffer hideously from the brutal treatment he would receive, before he eventually died. That was what the wicked female wanted.

Another entry revealed that she had been violently jealous of Rachel's beauty and popularity. When Sophia belatedly discovered that if Stephen were dead, his sister, not George, might own Wingate Hall, she had her brother hire a killer to dispose of Rachel. He had been instructed first to visit the local tavern to try to plant the impression that he was working for George.

The very day the assassin's shot had missed Rachel, Lord Felix had contacted Alfred about marrying his niece. The greedy Sophia, seeing a way to turn a handsome profit, postponed her murderous plans for Rachel until after she could collect the bounty Felix would pay her for arranging the marriage he wanted.

But Rachel ruined her aunt's scheme by marrying Jerome, the man for whom Sophia lusted. Enraged, she tried to poison Rachel with the milk that killed the kittens. When that failed, she ordered her brother to hire another killer, this one a better marksman. He was sent to Royal Elms with instructions to make it appear again that George was the one trying to slay Rachel.

When Jerome foiled the assassin and the Westleighs went off to London, Sophia produced the forged letters to Denton and had her brother offer to sell them to Jerome. She was certain that the duke would be so angered by them that he would send Rachel away. Sophia reasoned that her niece would have nowhere to go but Wingate Hall. Once Rachel arrived, Sophia would dispose of her as she had her husbands, leaving the forged suicide note.

Who would question that the distraught young duchess, repudiated by her husband and supposedly pregnant with another man's child, would take her own life?

Shuddering, Jerome dropped the small volume on the writing table and hurried out on the terrace where Rachel had last been seen. He snatched a flambeaux from its holder by the door, rushing from the terrace, and began a frantic, frenzied search of Wingate Hall's darkened grounds for his wife.

He shouted her name over and over, but only silence answered him. If she were dead, he did not think that he could bear to go on living, knowing it was he who had unwittingly driven her to her death.

He was dimly aware that others—George, Morgan, Ferris, and servants weeping for Rachel—had joined the search, too.

There was no sign of her, but their efforts were hampered by the blackness of the night.

Jerome did not know how many hours he had been looking when Morgan approached him. In the light of the torch he carried, he saw that his brother's eyes glistened, and he knew that Morgan believed Rachel was dead.

"It is futile, Jerome, to continue the search in the

darkness. You have to face the fact that the best we can hope for now is to find Rachel's body."

But Jerome, reeling with misery and guilt, would not face it. He stubbornly refused to admit that his wife was truly dead until they found her body and he could deny it no longer. As a drowning man clings to a rope that can pull him to shore, he clung to the faint, foolish hope that by some miracle of miracles she was still alive.

"I cannot give up." His voice was raw with grief. "I will not, until I find her."

The others gave up the search, knowing it to be hopeless, but he continued. After more hours of futile looking—the night had become an eternity in which time had no meaning—he knew despair deeper and blacker than ever before in his life.

He went to the stable where he quietly saddled a mount and rode into the night toward the lodge her grandfather had built. When Jerome reached the dark, silent structure, a lump the size of an ostrich's egg rose in his throat as he remembered how Rachel had "abducted" him there. How furious he had been when he had awakened to find himself bound to the bed.

Now he would give everything he owned to be in that position again.

Hellsfire, what a fool he had been. Too late, he appreciated the precious treasure he had let slip through his fingers. His heart felt as though it had been ground into dust.

The lodge door was not locked, and he stepped inside, groping for the candlestick on the table in the entry. Finding it, he pulled out his flint to light the candle.

By its light, he strode to the bedroom where he had made Rachel his own. As he approached the bed, he thought of that ecstatic night he had spent with Rachel and of awaking the next morning to see her lovely, sleeping face upon the pillow.

He looked down and nearly dropped the candle at the sight of her face in that very spot, her shining ebony hair fanning out about her in luxurious waves. For an instant, he thought it was a trick of his imagination.

But it was not. It was truly Rachel in the flesh.

And miraculously, she was breathing in the deep, even rhythm of sleep.

For a moment, he could only stare at her in joyous incredulity. Then he set the candlestick on the table and swept her into his arms. He uttered a prayer of fervent thanks as he crushed her living warmth against him and breathed deeply of her lavender and roses scent.

Her lovely eyes fluttered open, and he drank in their beauty as she looked at him with sleepy blankness.

Jerome knew the instant she came fully awake—and remembered all that had passed between them. Her eyes frosted. She stiffened in his arms and tried to pull away from him, but he would not release her.

"Let me go," she cried, fighting him with such determination that he reluctantly relinquished his grasp on her. Holding her against her will was hardly the way to win her forgiveness.

His heart constricted at the look she gave him as she scooted across the bed to get as far away from him as she could.

She pulled the covers up about her neck. "I will have nothing to do with a man who repudiates his own child!"

Jerome reached a placating hand out to her. "Please—"

"Do not touch me!" Her voice was as cold as winter snow.

It sent icy shivers of dismay through Jerome. He saw the angry disillusionment in her eyes, and a black hole of terrible loss engulfed him.

The tables had been turned. Now he knew what it

had been like for her, what she had felt, the pain she had suffered when he had rejected her.

"Listen to me," he pleaded. "We were both the victims of Sophia's diabolical plot to drive us apart. Do not let her succeed."

"Sophia?" Rachel blurted in shock.

"She forged the letters to Denton in her insane determination to destroy you and our marriage. Sophia was behind it all: the attempts on your life, Stephen's disappearance, the forged document that gave your uncle control of Wingate Hall."

Jerome told Rachel about Sophia's past and her skill as a forger.

His wife shuddered. "What an awful talent she had. I could not tell the handwriting from my own."

"Nor, obviously, could I, but I should have known better." Jerome reached out and tried to take Rachel's hand in his, but she yanked it away. "I was an incredible fool to doubt you."

"Yes, you were," she said coldly.

"Thank God you did not drink the glass of poisoned milk that Sophia gave you."

Rachel's eyes widened. So her awful suspicion had been right. She shivered. "I was afraid it might be."

"What made you suspect?"

She frowned, trying to give voice to the nebulous misgivings that had swirled in her mind. "Aunt Sophia was being so nice to me—and so sympathetic. When I arrived, she did not seem surprised to see me. I cannot explain it, but it was as though she expected me. She was so unlike herself, especially bringing me a glass of warm milk with her own hand instead of having a servant do so."

"So you decided against drinking it?"

"I came within a hairsbreadth of obliging her." Rachel shuddered at how close to her lips she had brought the glass before the prickling, nagging unease over what Benjy had said to her about the kittens had halted her hand. She had not truly believed the milk was poisoned, but after the inexplicable things that had been happening to her—the shots, the fake letters in her handwriting—she had decided to err for once on the side of caution.

"A stable hand told me about the dead kittens and the empty milk pitcher beside them." Rachel looked at Jerome sharply. "Why did you not tell me they were poisoned?"

Her husband ran his hand through his already disheveled golden hair. Rachel had told herself that she would never forgive him for denying their child was his, yet he looked so distressed that she had to fight down a subversive urge to smooth the wayward locks from his forehead.

"You do not know how many times I have cursed myself the past day for failing to tell you, but I knew how much you cared for those kittens. I was trying to spare you the pain of knowing that they were dead and why." Jerome looked at Rachel with loving concern. "I was afraid you might blame yourself for giving them the milk."

She did. Her husband understood her better than she thought. In that moment, Rachel finally divined why Jerome had acted the way he had that day he had taken her from Wingate Hall. "You found the dead kittens. That is why you burst into my room and carried me off."

"Yes. I loved you then, but I could not admit it even to myself. I only knew that I had to get you away from that house before whoever was trying to kill you succeeded." He swallowed hard and reached out to touch her.

Rachel recoiled from him. He had hurt her too much when he had rejected paternity of their child.

He flinched at her silent rejection. "What—what did you do with the milk that Sophia gave you tonight?"

"I poured it on the ground by the edge of the terrace. I was afraid that if I left it and it were poisoned, someone else might accidentally drink it." Rachel looked down at the quilt covering her. "Then I came here to hide until I could think of somewhere else I could go."

"Sophia will never trouble us again. She is dead."

Rachel's head snapped up. "What! How?"

"She attacked me with a dagger that she had dipped in poison. In the struggle, she scratched herself with the point. It killed her."

"Sweet heaven," Rachel exclaimed faintly. She had been certain that she had closed her heart against her husband for disavowing their child, but the way it constricted at learning Sophia might have killed him told her that she had not entirely succeeded.

"Do not look so sad, the world is better off without her," Jerome said, clearly misinterpreting the reason for Rachel's stricken expression. "I do have some good news for you about Stephen. You may be right about his still being alive."

Rachel gave a gasp of joy at learning that her prayers for her brother's safety might actually have been answered.

When Jerome told her what the sailor had said about the passing ship plucking Stephen from the ocean, she exclaimed exuberantly, "I know he is alive. I know it."

"Do not get your hopes too high, my love. If he was indeed rescued and is still alive, he should have come home by now." Jerome tried again to take Rachel's hand, but she pushed it away. "Unfortunately, we know nothing about the ship that picked him up, other than it flew a British flag."

"I know he is still alive!"

"If he is, my love, we will find him. We will not give up the search for him, I promise." Jerome smiled at her. "I have another piece of good news for you. George has returned. Those puzzling letters you thought he wrote you were actually Sophia's handiwork."

Rachel, her face jubilant, jumped up. "Why did you not tell me before? I cannot wait to see him."

When Jerome and Rachel reached Wingate Hall, she ran up the steps, threw open the big door with a bang, and dashed inside. The dimly lit hall was empty, but her noisy arrival brought George from the library. He stopped abruptly when he saw Rachel and stared at her as though she were an apparition.

She flung herself exuberantly at him. For a moment, her brother stood frozen, then he returned her embrace fiercely, as though he feared she might vanish if he did not hang on to her tightly.

George, his voice choked, said, "Dear God, Rachel, we thought you were dead."

Her husband silently watched the reunion. It was clear that George loved his sister every bit as much as she did him.

Jerome could not help but be a little envious of the way Rachel clung to her brother. She had not let her husband touch her since he had discovered her at the lodge.

For the next half hour brother and sister, sitting side by side on a settee, talked as though they were the only two in the room. Even when Jerome spoke, Rachel did not look at him.

When Rachel hid a yawn behind her hand, George said, "You must go to bed. It has been a terrible day for us all, and for you especially. You need your rest." He grinned at her. "Your husband tells me that you and he are making me an uncle."

At the mention of their baby, she cast Jerome a seething glance that sent his heart plummeting. He had hoped that after Rachel learned of Sophia's treachery, she would pardon him for having doubted her. But now he knew himself to be unforgiven.

After that look, Jerome did not try to accompany his wife upstairs. She and George left the drawing room, and Jerome waited twenty more endless minutes. Then, when he was certain that she was in bed, he picked up a silver candlestick and, with a heart as heavy as a granite boulder, went up to her chamber.

When he opened the door, the room was dark. He stepped inside and gently closed the door behind him. As he crossed to her bed by the light of the candle he carried, his wife sat up and glared at him. "Get out of here."

"It pains me to deny you anything you want, my love, but in this instance I must." He sat down on the bed beside her, fear clutching at his heart. Had he wounded her too deeply for her to forgive him? Had he lost her forever? What would he do if he could not win her back? He could not even stand to consider that possibility. His life without her love was unthinkable.

Somehow Jerome had to persuade her that he was worthy of it, that her heart was safe with him, that he would treasure and cherish it all the rest of his days. He would move heaven and earth to have her back, soft and yielding, in his arms.

He held them out to her. "Please, my darling love, let me hold you."

She jerked back from him. The anger in her violet eyes scorched him with its heat and shriveled his hope.

"Do not ever call me that!" Her voice was as hard as his demeanor had been to her that day in London when he had sent her away. "I am neither your darling nor your love, and you well know it."

Jerome flinched at having the cruel words he had uttered in London flung back at him, but he would not accept defeat. "Yes, you are, and I intend to spend the rest of our lives proving it to you."

"Eternity would not be long enough for you to succeed!"

She might be right, he thought in despair, given the implacable way she was glaring at him.

"I told you in my note that I would never live with you again, and I meant it."

The cold resolve in her voice flayed his heart. If he could not persuade her to forgive him, his own life would not be worth living.

Jerome reached out, but Rachel avoided the contact once again. After all, this was the man who had repudiated their child! She could not forgive him that. "Do not touch me. I do not ever want you to touch me again!" Perhaps if she said it often enough, even *she* might believe it.

"Rachel," he pleaded, "you are my wife. I love you more than I have ever loved anyone or anything. I did not think I could love as much as I love you."

She regarded him with suspicion, unable to reconcile the furious, hating man who had banished her from London with this penitent, loving one.

Did she dare trust this change in him? Or would he be transformed again into the hateful stranger who denied their child was his? Since the moment he had done that, Rachel had been haunted by the terrible fear that when their babe was born, her husband might take it from her and give it to strangers. The possibility made her voice shrill. "I will never let you tear my child from my arms."

"*Our* child," he corrected.

She eyed him with suspicion. "You said you would never believe the child I am carrying is yours."

Jerome looked agonized. "Oh, God, I did not mean that, my love. Even when I said it, I did not mean it!"

Could Rachel chance believing him? Their child's fate was at stake. She said defiantly, "I will not let you give my baby to strangers to raise."

He was clearly appalled. "I would never do that. I would not deny my child its mother."

There was such shattered sadness in Jerome's eyes that Rachel was certain he must be remembering all the times as a child that his own mother had deserted him.

"What a bastard you think I am." His jutting jaw quavered. "And perhaps I deserve it. What I said to you in my jealous fury was beyond the pale, but I was too consumed by my own pain to think rationally."

Jerome's searing self-loathing for his conduct slowly began to thaw Rachel's frozen emotions. He ran his fingertips caressingly along her cheek, sending a little shiver of pleasure through her. She had never expected him to touch her so tenderly again.

"Believe me, my love, I intended to beg your forgiveness for questioning our babe's paternity as soon as I saw you again." His eyes were filled with empathy and remorse. "Do you think I do not know how much hurt I have caused you? I would give anything to be able to erase it."

Before she realized what he was about, he pulled her into his arms. She tried to push him away, but he would not let her.

"No, I need to touch you. I need to reassure myself that you are alive. You cannot know, my love, how frightened and devastated I was when I found you gone and that empty milk glass on the terrace. I was so afraid that you were"—his voice cracked—"dead."

The agony in Jerome's face told her how much he loved her, but the wound he had inflicted on her own heart was still raw.

"Please," he begged, "you must believe that I love you."

She believed it, but could she trust his love? He had loved her before, too. Yet he had been willing to believe that she had written those terrible letters and, in his fury, to disavow their child. That memory reignited her anger at him, and she shoved him away. "I told you trust was the basis of love, and I no longer trust you."

"I deserve that." His voice was hoarse with self-disgust. "No one knows better than I what it is like to have one's love and trust destroyed. You see now how hard it is to trust again once you have been terribly hurt."

Yes, Rachel did, but that did not make it any easier for her to overcome her wariness of him.

"I thought I paid an awful price when I discovered Cleo's infidelity, but the price will be infinitely higher than I thought if, by crippling my ability to trust, it has cost me you."

Jerome looked so shattered and penitent that Rachel again had to stifle an urge to reach out to comfort him.

"Listen to me, my love. What we have together is very special. Very rare. What I felt for Cleo was nothing compared to what I feel for you. And that is what made me so vulnerable to you. Please, forgive me."

Did she dare?

Suddenly, he captured her mouth in a kiss full of tenderness and hunger. Rachel tried to push him away, but she failed.

"No-o-o-o." What began as her protest faded into a reluctant, elongated syllable of pleasure as his hand caressed her breast with erotic finesse. Fiery longing exploded within her.

His mouth wooed hers with a heated intensity that melted her resistance.

He broke their kiss, his beautifully sculpted face tormented by regret. "I am so sorry, my love, that I doubted you. I swear I never will again."

"How can I believe that?" Sadness tinged her voice. "You have disappointed me so often."

"I know, my love, but never again. Word of a Parnell."

But Rachel was not convinced. "What if Kerlan tells you that I have taken a lover here, one of the footmen?"

"I would not believe him. I may be a stupid idiot at times, but I am also a man who learns from his mistakes. Forgive me, my sweet."

His lips recaptured hers, his tongue courting her.

He unbuttoned her chemise and pushed it from her shoulders. It fell about her hips.

Desire exploded within her as his skillful hands caressed her body, but still she wrenched her mouth from his and said, "What if I tell you that Tony Denton is arriving tomorrow to take me to London?"

Instead of the scowl she expected, her husband grinned at her. "But you would not tell me that because it would be a lie, and you would not lie to me, would you?"

Jerome had her there. "What if Denton follows me here as he did to Royal Elms?"

"I know you would have nothing to do with him. My guess, however, is that Denton, having won his wager with Birkhall, is undoubtedly on his way to London to collect his winnings."

Rachel stiffened. "But he did not win. I never—"

Jerome placed his hand gently over her mouth. "Contrary to what all London thought, you were not the object of the wager."

"Who was?"

"Emily Hextable. She was the woman with whom Denton was spending his nights in my dower house."

Rachel began to laugh. She could not help herself.

"Amusing, is it not?" From Jerome's sarcastic tone, it was clear that he did not find it so. "As Morgan so kindly pointed out to me, I might have married her and been bored, miserable, *and* cuckolded. Thank God, you saved me from that awful fate by abducting me, my sweet temptation. Please, my love, come home to Royal Elms with me."

"No! Now that Sophia is dead, I must remain at Wingate Hall to undo the damage she has done. I have so much to do here before Stephen returns. After all, he *trusted* me, and I will not disappoint that trust."

Jerome sighed in defeat. "Very well, then I will stay here and help you."

"I do not want you here! Only think how much you dislike the North."

"I *love* any place you are." His jaw set stubbornly. "I will not leave Wingate Hall until you come with me. I do not care how many months it takes."

Knowing how much Jerome loved Royal Elms, Rachel was astonished that he would forsake it to remain with her at Wingate Hall. It told her as much about his love for her as his words did.

He pushed her gently onto her back and gazed down at her, his cyan eyes brilliant with appreciation and adoration. "You are the most breathtaking, wonderful, exciting creature I have ever seen. Say you will forgive me."

"No-o-o-o-o."

Her refusal faded into a moan as his mouth spread kisses over her face and neck. As his hands moved lovingly over her body, he murmured, "Please, forgive me."

She did not answer him. His head dipped and his mouth closed over the crest of her breast. She arched beneath him in pleasure.

He placed both hands gently on her still flat belly and, lowering his mouth to it, bathed it with kisses.

"What are you doing?"

"Telling our child how much his father loves and wants him," he said in a voice as soft and caressing as midnight velvet.

Rachel's heart thudded with joy and love and excitement.

Jerome raised his head, and his gaze met hers. "I cannot wait, my love, until I can hold this babe we have made in my arms. Do not deny our child his father. Forgive me my moment of jealous insanity."

"No!" She moaned as his mouth and his hands resumed persuading her.

"Forgive me," he murmured, as he turned his attention back to her breast. His mouth suckled it as his hand again explored her body, sending waves of heat and desire through her.

"Forgive me," he begged.

Actually Rachel already had, but she was in no rush to tell Jerome so. She was enjoying too much his method of seeking her forgiveness.

He laid seductive kisses down her body that sent quivers of pleasure through her.

"Forgive me," he pleaded as his tongue teased her, and his fingers skillfully exploited her most sensitive spots, building within her an aching need for him.

She was writhing, desperate for his body to free her from the hunger that gnawed at her. But he showed no inclination to do so.

Instead he was using everything in his erotic repertoire to bring her to the brink of fulfillment, then retreating. It was like a carefully orchestrated dance, and he was driving her out of her mind.

"Please," she begged when she could stand it no longer.

"Forgive me." He lifted his head, and she saw the love and humble entreaty in his eyes. "Forgive me for ever doubting you. I swear I never will again."

And she knew that he would not.

"Forgive me, my one and only love."

She could bear his sweet torment of her no longer. "Yes-s-s."

His eyes were suddenly misty with unshed tears of relief. As his mouth closed over hers again, he murmured, "You will never regret it, my love."

Turn the page for an exciting
advance peek at
MIDNIGHT LORD,
Marlene Suson's thrilling,
sensual sequel to *Midnight Bride,*
coming soon from
Avon Books.

*Virginia, 1741*

**R**un. Damn you, *run!* he ordered his blistered, recalcitrant feet that felt as though they had been plunged into boiling pitch. He had to keep going.

He had to escape his pursuers. He would not be taken alive.

He would not be sent back to that living hell into which his unknown enemy had cast him. No man deserved to be treated as he had been, torn from everything he held dear and treated as though he were something less than human, some brute beast born only to toil for a cruel master.

He did not deserve such a fate. No man did, especially one who was guilty of no wrong.

And, as God was his witness, he was innocent.

He plunged on, picking his way through the dark forest. The night was bright, but not here among the dense trees and brush in this godforsaken American wilderness. The canopy of foliage overhead—thick as a newly thatched English roof—blocked the moonlight.

In the darkness, he lost the narrow path he had been following through the woods, and could not find it again. Pushing dizzily ahead, he made his own route through the undergrowth, stumbling over protruding roots and debris. He wore only ragged breeches torn off above his knees and a homespun shirt with the sleeves missing. The thorny brush tore at his bare legs, arms, and face.

His head whirled like a dervish. He was so hot with fever that he felt as if he was being consumed by it. His every muscle and joint ached agonizingly. His back tormented him as though it were one giant open sore.

Perhaps it was.

He vowed woozily that not only would he escape his pursuers, but some day he would find a way to return to England. He would ferret out who had done this to him, and he would make the villian pay.

No matter who he was.

The sweet promise of vengeance kept him moving, but he soon reached the limits of his endurance. He stumbled and nearly fell before managing to catch and steady himself on the thin trunk of a sapling.

How tempting it was to sink to the earth. His fevered brain urged him to do so. He was too weak and sick to go on. Why not let his tortured body lie down and die and end his suffering?

Raucous sound suddenly pounded at his head like the bark of muskets. Or was it the bark of dogs? The noise came from behind him.

Close behind him.

He thought he lost those vicious, howling, man-chewing hounds from hell two days ago, but apparently he was wrong.

That possibility gave his sick, exhausted body a final spurt of energy. Those snarling beasts were not going to rip his flesh from his bones.

Something was wrong. That was Meg Drake's first thought as she awoke in the darkness. Apprehension swept away the sluggish haze of sleep from her mind as a driving rain washed the air.

She was neither timid nor easily frightened. No young woman living in a frontier cabin surrounded by wilderness with only her fifteen-year-old brother for company and her wits for protection could be.

Meg listened intently to the sounds of the night, analyzing what had triggered her subconscious alarm. It came to her quickly. The neighing of the horses, the hoot of the barn owl, and the howl of the wolves had taken on an uncustomary urgency.

Someone or something alien was out there.

"Meg?" Her brother Josh's voice drifted to her from his narrow bed. It was no more than a frightened whisper. "I—I fear we have a caller."

"Yes," his sister agreed. She knew that she had not been asleep very long, and she guessed that it was about midnight. No visitor who meant them well would be skulking about outside their cabin at this hour.

Choking down her fear, Meg got out of bed, her voluminous white shirt billowing about her, and grabbed one of the muskets that she kept nearby, loaded and ready.

She went to the window by the door and moved a corner of the greased paper covering it, so that she could peer out.

Brilliant moonlight illuminated the clearing in front of the cabin. She searched it, and the trees beyond, but could detect no sign of life.

The eerie howls of the wolves were very close now. They had never come so near the clearing before. The hair on the back of Meg's neck rose.

Then a movement to the side near the giant oak tree caught her eye. She clutched her musket and went to the door.

He could go no farther. His tortured, abused body no longer obeyed his brain. If only he could fall down and die and get it over with.

But his pursuers would find him, and they would keep him alive.

Not out of kindness, though. No one had been

kind to him in the endless months since he was abducted from his luxurious, pampered former life and consigned to perdition on earth. No, they would keep him alive because he was more valuable to them living than dead.

At that moment, he stumbled out of the forest into a small clearing. In the center of it, like a welcoming beacon, stood a small cabin. He wondered dizzily whether it was a mirage in the moonlight.

Real or not, he staggered toward the cabin, but he could not make it. His legs buckled beneath him and he collapsed on his knees three feet from the door.

It opened, and an ethereal figure in a flowing white gown appeared there. An angel! His fevered mind, on the edge of delirium, decided he must be already dead. The angel before him had come to lead him to the gates of paradise.

Then he saw the ugly musket in her hands, pointed at his chest.

The angel of retribution!

He looked into the barrel of the musket without fear. Better to die cleanly from a ball through the heart than to suffer more agony.

"Kill me," he croaked defiantly. "Kill me and be done with it. Put me out of my misery!"

Then blackness claimed him, and he keeled over face-first on the hard ground.

# *Avon Romantic Treasures*

Unforgettable, enthralling love stories,
sparkling with passion and adventure
from Romance's bestselling authors